PRAISE FO
TERROR'S SW...

Terror's Sword "definitely satisfies as the pace never falters, the cutting-edge timely plot never stumbles, and the ending delivers. A romp of a read." —Steve Berry, *New York Times* and International #1 Bestselling Author

Terror's Sword is a counterterrorism espionage thriller that goes into the deep state, politics at its absolute worst, and the heroism of those trying to do what's right inside government. Kuhens knocks it out of the park with this one." —Grant Stinchfield, Emmy Award-winning investigative reporter, radio and television personality, and national podcaster

"A fast-paced, spellbinding plot that takes readers on suspense-filled missions to save the world. Readers will love this breathtaking action-packed thriller and won't be able to put it down!" —Foluso Falaye, *San Francisco Book Review*

"A powerful saga that blends high-octane action, psychological interplays, and acts of political desperation that probe presidential actions, traps, moves and countermoves, and special ops processes." —Diane Donovan, *Midwest Book Review*

"Kuhens' writing is reminiscent of the great thriller authors Frederick Forsyth and Robert Ludlum. With a heroic character on the scale of a Jason Bourne, *Terror's Sword* is a top-flight, fast-paced story guaranteed to satisfy readers across genres." —Rex Allen, *Readers' Favorite*

"The author's prose is captivating. The action scenes are edge-of-your-seat brilliant. You may find yourself gripping the reader or the book so tight, that your knuckles may bleed." —*N. N. Light's Book Heaven*

"Mesmerizing! Kuhens' action descriptions were so realistic they put me in the scenes alongside the characters! Great plot and never-ending misdirection. Colorful, well-developed characters including a very powerful female lead." —P. Atencio, *Goodreads*

"*Terror's Sword* is a superb combination of suspense and intrigue that will keep readers on the hook until the very end. A highly distinctive work with memorable characters and a fast-paced storyline." —*BookLife*

"The author has given us a well-researched, well-plotted, well-paced, and very realistic fictional book that mirrors non-fiction in many ways. We have a new hero in the vein of James Bond, Jason Bourne, Jack Ryan, and Jack Reacher." —James L. Thompson, Jr., Supervisory Special Agent (retired)

"Unlike many thrillers about terrorist threats, Kuhens injects inner bureaucratic workings and political processes which serve to work against themselves and each other as desperate men and entities struggle against an impossible weapon and timeline." —D. Donovan, Editor, *Donovan's Literary Services*

"Spectacular Debut Novel! A lean, mean thriller where characters are quickly and convincingly rendered and the plotting immersive and compelling. I recommend this book highly for any fan of the political action/thriller genre." —S. P. Johnson, *Goodreads*

"Kuhens brings you as close to real world as it gets, real locations, real scenarios, genuine religious complaints. Revenge is a powerful motivating factor and Kuhens milks this for every penny. These military scenes were as close to actual as you can get." —G. Coker, *U.S. Air Force* Pilot

"An incredible read for high-action junkies! The author's rich descriptions literally painted mental images putting me in the scenes. The action was so riveting and intense I could feel my heart pounding. Great, authentic characters." —B. Detra, *Amazon*

"Action packed. Adrenaline filled. Rich characters. You won't be able to put the book down. A work of fiction that could become reality." —LTC M. J. Vowell, *US Army*

"Every page overflows with explosive action. If you only have time to read one action-packed novel this year, this page-turner is it!" —*Beach Reads*

TERROR'S SWORD

A KYLE MCEWAN NOVEL

KEVIN KUHENS

www.kevinkuhens.com

Library of Congress Cataloging-in-Publication Data
Kuhens, Kevin.
Terror's sword / Kevin Kuhens.
Library of Congress Control Number: 2022901325

ISBN 979-8-9854473-0-9 (Paperback)
ISBN 979-8-9854473-1-6 (eBook)

Printed in the United States of America

Cover & Interior Design: Creative Publishing Book Design

(Appendix of Abbreviations & Acronyms at the end of the book)

Islam says: "Kill all the unbelievers just as they would kill you all! Kill them, put them to the sword and scatter them. Whatever good there is exists thanks to the sword. The Sword is the key to Paradise, which can be opened only for the Holy Warriors!"

— Ayatollah Ruhollah Khomeini

Islam Is Not a Religion of Pacifists (1942)

CHAPTER ONE

SHIELDED BY DARKNESS, Ahmed Mansour stole into the American University of Beirut Medical Center. Arriving at his office, he entered and threw the deadbolt, locking himself inside. Despite offering no real protection, the paper-thin walls might buy him time to achieve a single goal: living long enough to expose the conspiracy.

Mansour's hypervigilant ears detected squeaky leather soles creeping to a stop outside his office. A loud rap on the door's opaque glass window sent him burrowing beneath his desk. Stifling cries, he curled into a ball, waiting, seconds ticking away. He stole fleeting glances at his watch as a minute elapsed, then two. *Nothing.* Inhaling deeply, Mansour swallowed and peeked around the desk.

A misshapen face, pressed tightly against the frosted window, cast a roving whale's eye toward Mansour's hidey-hole.

The doorknob creaked slowly, turned partway, then stopped. Panic raced through his veins—every nerve in Mansour's body fired simultaneously, waves of nausea roiling over him. The door rattled violently in its frame, squeezing the air out of Mansour's lungs and gripping his heart. Trapped inside his stockade, death seemed seconds off.

The anonymous assailant, thwarted by the engaged deadbolt, muttered a curse and kicked the door vigorously. Slamming a fist into a wall, the stalker abandoned his mission.

Mansour remained stock-still after the footsteps vanished, the only sound in his ears the pounding of his heart. He controlled his breathing;

his lungs filled, returning his heart rate to normal. *They are here looking for me!*

Mansour weighed the odds his hunter would revisit his office against the dangers of executing his plan in public. He concluded he would find safety among the old men munching pistachio nuts and playing backgammon down at the Beirut waterfront. Wiping perspiration beads from his upper lip, Mansour tiptoed to the door and placed an ear against the window. *Silence.* Grasping the knob and turning it, he pulled the door open a crack and glanced at the ceiling security mirror. *Corridor empty.*

He squeezed through the narrow gap into the hallway. Clicking the door shut softly, he locked it with a deft flick of his wrist then pocketed the keys. Tiptoeing to a stairwell, he hurried down the steps to the bottom landing. Dropping to a knee, he feigned tying a shoelace, a ploy to smoke out tails. *None.*

Mansour straightened up and crossed the medical center lobby in four long strides, leaning so hard into the exit door it banged loudly against the outer wall. No one seemed to notice. Moving swiftly past an ancient banyan tree and a guard shack, he hustled up to Abdel Aziz Street. Balancing on the curb, he looked to his left and right, then scooted over to the sidewalk. Turning toward the main campus, he melted in with students arriving for classes.

The bespectacled Mansour caught himself continuously twisting his head and darting his eyes. Slowing his pace, he lifted his eyeglasses and dabbed the trickling rivers of sweat from his face and neck with a handkerchief. Scouring the cars parked two- and three-deep on Bliss Street, a movement in the bright early sunlight caught his eye. *Young man on cell phone—cutting and weaving through cars. Sunglasses—cannot read his eyes. Heading toward me!*

Mansour turned abruptly through the main campus stone entrance as the college hall tower bell tolled the hour: seven o'clock. A sharp glance over his shoulder revealed the young man entering the university grounds several paces behind. Alarm bells clanging, Mansour stopped to study the terraced green slopes and jasmine trees highlighted by rays of sunshine.

The man, chatting animatedly on his cell phone, walked by without a glimmer of interest.

Mansour resumed his expedition to the Mediterranean waterfront. Passing through the Avenue de Paris pedestrian gate, safely bolstered by other commuters, he relaxed. Retrieving a prepaid disposable cell phone from his pocket, he dialed a memorized number; the call connected after a short delay. Several agonizingly long rings later, a mechanical voice answered, "Leave a message after the tone."

Concentrating on leaving his message, Mansour did not see the looming threat until it was too late. Barreling toward him was his imagined young stalker from before, now sans sunglasses, his eyes burning with malevolent intensity. Mansour was paralyzed, his sixth sense screaming, "Flee!" but his feet remained glued to the asphalt, causing him to miss the second threat—a delivery van skidding to a stop. Escape route blocked, he was easy prey for two hooded men leaping out of the side door. Strong hands seized Mansour's flailing arms, dragging him to the van. A shoulder launched into his back, driving him through the door opening. The cell phone flew from his hand, skittering across the steel floorboard. Multiple fists pummeled his face, crumpling orbital bones. Innumerable punches savaged his stomach, kidneys, and liver.

Ahmed Mansour's world disintegrated into a mass of searing pain and blackness.

CHAPTER TWO

KYLE MCEWAN FOUND THE hard tarmac of Naval Air Station Sigonella, Sicily, a welcome relief after tossing his cookies aboard the US Marine Corps helicopter over the Mediterranean. However, the noticeable lack of activity and absence of any large transport aircraft was troubling—he had no connecting flight.

Marching over to the passenger terminal building, he flung open the door. Naval personnel milling about the lounge gave the civilian a wide berth as he stormed up to the counter. McEwan slapped down his travel orders and ID card identifying him by one of his covert identities. "Didn't the helo pilot radio in our ETA?"

The peach-fuzzed seaman scanned McEwan's priority travel orders. "Yes, sir. Bad weather over the Med dictated an earlier-than-anticipated departure for your aircraft."

"Bullshit." McEwan knew a well-rehearsed script when he heard it.

The perplexed sailor gave McEwan a straight-from-boot-camp glazed look.

A well-fed senior chief petty officer shook his head. With a "Gimme those papers, doofus," he waddled up to McEwan.

"Base Ops released your flight because some DV had a higher priority mission than you. A royal pain in the ass who bitched the whole time he was here. It's probably not any consolation, but I'm glad the asshole's gone."

McEwan sympathized, having seen so-called distinguished visitors in action before, but the explanation didn't solve his problem. "My options?"

"I've priority-manifested you on the next flight to Rota, Spain, in four hours. You'll connect there with a military charter to Philly, then into Dulles on a commercial flight."

McEwan held back a sigh. Accepting he had no other alternatives, he grabbed his gear and looked for a place to park. He chose a row of seats overlooking the flight line. Plopping down his kit then his butt, he unzipped his briefcase and extracted a bottle. Breaking the seal, McEwan upended and drained it in three large gulps. Screwing the cap back on, he hurled the empty vessel into a trash bin. He hoped the extra strength Maalox would quell the full-gale storm churning in his stomach.

A short time later, McEwan glimpsed a familiar face walking across the tarmac. The man, a CIA pilot, flew executive jets leased by one of the agency's covert front companies. His gaze shifted to a Gulfstream jet parked on the apron. McEwan jumped to his feet and hustled between the rows of seats. "Well, if it isn't the Freakin' Deacon!"

The tall, slender man shot McEwan an irritated look and spoke with a slow Texas drawl. "You gonna bust my stones or show some gratitude?"

"What?"

"Radio traffic said you were delayed at Sig. Some jackass in the Global Ops Center declared you persona non grata on agency aircraft, said you had to wait on military transport. I disagreed—heard something weird in the engine. Happens all the time. Jokes aside, get your freakin' shit aboard. Let's get in the air before somebody figures out what I'm up to."

Fifteen minutes later, an upbeat McEwan was DC bound. Once they leveled off at cruising altitude, he went forward to the cockpit. After introducing himself to the co-pilot, McEwan engaged the Texan. "It seems you've developed the habit of putting your rear end on the line a lot for me lately. It's a rare commodity in short supply these days. But appreciated."

"Sooner or later, I'll cash in all your chits," Hank Deacon grinned. "Guaran-damn-teed."

"And guaran-damn-teed I'm good for them," McEwan chuckled.

Returning to the cabin, he pulled out his encrypted satellite telephone from his briefcase, set it on a seat, and grabbed a pillow. Settling into the plush leather, substantially more accommodating than the Navy standard-issue imitation leather chairs at Sig, he reclined. A dinging sound drew the American counterterrorism case officer's eyes to his flashing and vibrating phone. Tapping the touch screen, he opened a message: "Perfect storm brewing. Ring London Weather Centre straight away."

McEwan bolted upright in his seat. The late-night message including the ciphered phrase meant there were major problems with his United Kingdom operation. He typed "Expect phonecon ASAP" and punched Send. Dialing a number, he waited for his call to connect and go secure.

Forty-eight hours ago, McEwan's seventeen-month-long operation with the Brits was running smoothly. He'd recruited Jamil El-Harith, the informant, several years earlier in Beirut. The source earned his bona fides by informing on a Gaza City Islamic radical claiming to be brokering a cease-fire between warring Muslim factions, which was technically true. But the peace accord between the two rival groups was for the purpose of joining forces to conduct attacks and suicide bombings against the Israelis following Ramadan. McEwan filtered the information about this dangerous new alliance to the Mossad, Israel's national intelligence service. In the weeks leading up to the sacred Muslim holiday, McEwan planted crumbs implicating the radical as the informer instead of El-Harith. During a secret raid on the group's hideout, Israeli commandos assassinated the organization's chief of operations but narrowly missed capturing the group's leader. El-Harith fed the leader a bogus tip that the radical was seen meeting with the Israelis and the man was promptly executed. Using a credible pretext, McEwan relocated El-Harith to the UK.

McEwan's source landed in Beeston, a slum in metropolitan Leeds, three hours north of London. The man connected with a distant relative believed to be networked with suspected terrorists in the West Yorkshire city. After McEwan's briefing, Her Majesty's intelligence services eagerly embraced the opportunity to infiltrate a cell in the second largest business and financial center in the UK. Long a hotbed of radicalism, Leeds had spread its terror tentacles throughout Great Britain, counting among its native sons three of the four London subway and bus bombers, plus the London Bridge attackers. Understandably, British officials expected police supervisors in the Leeds regional counterterrorism unit to control the operation.

For McEwan, this was a no-go. During El-Harith's first conversation with his relative after moving to Leeds, the relative bragged about owning an unidentified member of the regional police unit. McEwan had his source tell the relative he preferred to live in London and wanted an introduction into the local community. The relative agreed, as did senior intelligence and police officials. The operation initiated in London was controlled by the Metropolitan Police Service Counterterrorism Command and directed by SO15 commander Nigel Hurst.

With El-Harith's credentials firmly established by the Beirut network and vouched for by his relative, he forged bonds quickly with a handful of London-based, Leeds-reared radicals. Operating out of an East London halal sandwich shop and cybercafé, the terrorists were unaware the popular spot was a wholly-owned SO15 storefront staffed entirely by undercover police officers. Wired 24-7/365 for surveillance and internet monitoring, the operation produced an abundance of intelligence, spawning a dozen antiterror investigations. Authorities thwarted plots to detonate bombs in a Glasgow nightclub and aboard the *Flying Scotsman*, the daily express passenger train service between London and Edinburgh.

The SO15 commander's message made McEwan nervous. For months, both men feared the source was living on borrowed time. Finally, his call to Detective Chief Inspector Hurst went secure.

"You take rapid response to new heights, Yank. Where are you?"

"In the friendly skies above Sardinia and Corsica. Problems? Tell me anything but our op is going south."

"I'm afraid so. One of my detectives overheard a conversation at the cybercafé. They have tagged your man as an informer. Word is, they're luring him to their lair with the promise of including him in an important mission."

McEwan understood the subtext. They planned to interrogate El-Harith and finish him off. "Do we know when?"

"Sometime in the early morning. We do not know where the source is; he's not answering his mobile."

"Have you told your bosses?"

"Oh, hell no. Better to keep them in the dark until after we take it down—that way they can't bonk it up. They won't care as long as I provide them juicy tidbits for their press conferences."

"Keep calling him. Sit on the hideout. And get me clearance into Northolt." RAF Northolt was the airport closest to central London used by military and business aircraft.

"Done. I'm planning a hard hit on the house before daybreak. I'll have the particulars for you when you land."

Terminating the call with one hand and unbuckling his seat belt with the other, McEwan went forward and rapped on the cockpit door.

Deacon stuck his head out. "What's up?"

"We need to divert to London. I've got an op that's unraveling and an asset who's going to be killed if I can't extract him."

"No freakin' way. Making an unscheduled stop for engine problems is one thing. If I change my flight plan—"

"Just get me into London. I'll take it from there."

"Come on, bro," Deacon pleaded. "I'm gonna get my freakin' ass kicked for even letting you aboard. I was warned, divert again without authorization or back you up on another one of your off-the-reservation ventures and they'll shitcan me." Deacon glanced over at his co-pilot for support.

"Don't look at me, Captain. You assigned me one mission on this trip—humping your bags."

McEwan ignored their banter and Deacon's plea for a reprieve. "Once I deplane, contact Global Ops. Tell them I approached you in Sig and said I'd obtained supervisory approval for the ride. Same thing for the flight-plan change. That way, whatever rolls downhill lands on me."

While the case officer's word was golden, the pilot doubted his explanations would fly at Langley. Luckily for McEwan, Hank Deacon valued his moral obligations much more highly than any blowback or ass-chewing. Reaching for the door, he gave his answer.

"You're running my tab for the rest of your freakin' life, you got that, bro?"

CHAPTER THREE

IN A CITY WHERE residents are oblivious to ubiquitous flashing red, white and blue emergency lights and wailing sirens, the three-vehicle motorcade whisked largely unnoticed through the rain-soaked streets of Washington, DC. A heavily armored Chevrolet Suburban, sandwiched between two equally menacing black SUVs, plowed through one rain puddle after another, blasting jets of water on everything in its path. Pointed in the direction of the White House, the motorcade continued with a singleness of purpose, as if having a mind and schedule of its own.

Behind the dark-tinted, bulletproof windows of the bracketed vehicle, time had new meaning for the solitary woman seated in the second row: hours wasted equaled lives lost. Director of National Intelligence Daniela Sanchez doubted the average American fully understood the real threats each of them faced. It was the job of the DNI—*her* job—to battle those threats every day, in secret, for her fellow citizens.

Daniela Sanchez was no stranger to the White House. Formerly a senior official of the CIA, she'd conducted numerous briefings for two different presidents, their vice presidents, cabinet officers, members of Congress, and national advisers for terrorism and intelligence. However, this was the first time she'd been summoned this late to meet alone with the president.

The caravan reached the West Executive Avenue gate. Secret Service Uniformed Division officers waved them through the checkpoint, and the lead SUV's driver punched the accelerator without stopping. Tires squealing under heavy weight, the high-performance engines slingshot the

SUVs up the asphalt driveway. The protectee's vehicle stopped smoothly before the West Wing lower-level entrance.

A trim female Secret Service agent in a brown pantsuit stepped from beneath the entrance canopy and discreetly opened the door for the DNI. "Hello, Director."

"Nice to see you again." Sanchez stepped onto the driveway and straightened her gray Brooks Brothers skirt. Wrapping her raincoat tightly, she tied it at the waist to ward off the drizzle. Grabbing her satchel off the back seat, she fell in step with the agent. The two women entered the West Wing and once through the magnetometers, proceeded through the lobby. Sanchez exchanged greetings with several Secret Service Uniformed Division officers standing post. She followed her escort down the main corridor and was drawn in by the power of the Oval Office.

Deposited inside the Roosevelt Room, waiting to be summoned into the Oval, the raven-haired and elegant Daniela Isabella Sanchez recalled fondly how one month earlier, she'd been sworn in as DNI by America's new chief executive. In their brief personal moments before the ceremony, the president told her his upbringing on a farm was not altogether different from her own as the only child of Mexican immigrants working the citrus groves of Florida. She knew she'd never reach the pinnacle he had but remained amazed at how far she had come.

The door opened, and the shift leader for the Secret Service Presidential Protection Division detail announced, "Director, the president will see you now."

Sanchez followed the agent inside the Oval Office, her eyes landing on the president of the United States sitting behind the Resolute desk. French-blue shirtsleeves rolled up, Nelson J. Englewood studied the President's Daily Brief, the summary of critical national security intelligence she'd presented him earlier in the day. Sanchez waited silently on the alternating walnut and cherry planking.

Sanchez was proud to serve under this president. A Louisville native billionaire businessman and racehorse owner, Englewood was persuaded to jump into the political arena by his boyhood friend, the then-sitting senior US senator from the Bluegrass State, who, diagnosed with an extremely aggressive and terminal form of cancer, was stepping down. Englewood agreed to serve out the remaining fourteen months of the term. When no one came forward to claim the mantle, he won a full six years. He'd planned to return to private life at the end of his Senate term, but party elders had other plans—they handed him the reins to run for higher office.

Englewood was a rare commodity among politicians, bluntly honest. This quality and his likeability, along with a Reaganesque style of humor, wit, and folksy delivery, charmed the citizenry, media, and pundits alike. Dropping their usual colloquialisms, they played up his Kentucky roots, using phrases such as "Cutting to the chase as fast as a thoroughbred on Derby Day" and "Foes who misjudge his talents find themselves on the short end of a whippin' crop". Originally a dark horse candidate, talking heads predicted a photo finish on Election Day. Instead, he swept into office aboard a backlash against his opponent, whose dalliances with a young staffer were exposed in the home stretch of the campaign. His poll numbers were off the charts, at levels unprecedented in the annals of American politics.

The grandfather clock chimed midnight, prompting Englewood to close the PDB folder. The tanned and fit man in his mid-sixties, blessed with a thick silver mane and warm gray eyes, smiled at Sanchez. Pushing back from his desk, he rose and crossed the circular sunburst-patterned carpet woven with the presidential seal. Ever the gentleman, he gently clasped her hand, his rich voice exuding Southern hospitality. "Thanks for coming in at this hour, Danni. Hope you didn't mind."

"Of course not, Mr. President."

Leading her to the seating area in front of the white marble fireplace, Englewood pointed toward a cream-patterned sofa. Sitting, Sanchez placed her heavy satchel at her feet.

The president slid into a satiny light-blue-and-gold-striped chair and tossed the folder onto the inlaid wood coffee table. "Today's PDB contains a sentence that has bothered me ever since I read it this morning: 'CIA is following up on information suggesting a new attack on Western interests may be forthcoming'. I was clear to both you and Carl Stefan—do not finesse me."

"For some reason, the agency insisted on wordsmithing it until sensitive sources can refine it. I couldn't see papering them and setting off a squabble. I accept full responsibility. I should have demanded a more detailed explanation of the threat before agreeing to that approach."

Englewood looked over at Sanchez and saw a glint of anger in her eyes. The first time they met, he sensed he'd found the right person to keep the CIA director in check. The president's instincts were confirmed when Stefan went on the offensive—unsolicited—trying to dissuade him from promoting Sanchez. The president considered Stefan a prototypical "swamp monster" who spent more energy burnishing credentials for a post-government career than protecting his country. To the CIA chief's chagrin, his former subordinate was now the top gun of the US intelligence community, standing between him and the president. Englewood considered Sanchez one of his finest picks, and he had bigger designs for her when the time was right.

"Sir, my job is to cull, sift, and analyze raw data and present unambiguous and meaningful intelligence assessments. I won't let Stefan or anyone stand in the way of that. I failed here."

"Give it to me, however unrefined."

Sanchez delivered the details. "Over the last two weeks, we've seen a significant spike in chatter among terror group leaders of both Islamic sects. NSA intercepted two dozen nearly identical communiqués stating, quote, 'Terror's Sword will make eleven September pale in comparison' end quote. The persons being monitored referred to him variously as 'the Sword' and 'Terror's Sword' but clearly they're describing the same man. The common thread in their comments is the September eleventh boast; it's universal. They suddenly went silent on the subject, for reasons we can only speculate." Exasperation colored her words.

Government officials remained infuriated over the legacy media's exposé of several highly classified global electronic surveillance programs under the prior administration. Inside the Capital Beltway, a unique consensus emerged: the disclosures damaged America's national security immensely. While the news organizations hotly disputed the premise, claiming they only reported intelligence abuses, its effect was dramatic. The world learned that America's intelligence agencies intercepted billions of worldwide electronic communications—specifically voice and message traffic, internet chat rooms, financial transactions, and data transmissions. Predictably, the unveiling resulted in the world's terrorists modifying their methods and disappearing. Though the intelligence community scrambled to fill the void, to date, they'd not succeeded. Hamstrung by civil libertarians, the government operated under stricter controls than commercial credit card companies and banks.

"We haven't been able to verify the identity of the 'Sword'. Our data mining projects found a single reference to a man named Ali bin al-Dosari and the 'Terror's Sword' pseudonym. Analysts assess the probability of him being the person discussed at 1 percent—meaning not at all."

Englewood understood the process. America's intelligence, law enforcement, and military agencies combined and analyzed data from their respective human sources and communications and information systems to identify terrorists and plots. He waved her to proceed.

"We have nothing about the impending attack other than this Sword individual is the alleged mastermind. On al-Dosari, Western intelligence services are drawing a blank. We have so little on him we can't even do a threat profile. In my view, our prospect of learning anything more using current means is virtually zero."

"With our resources, how is that possible?" Although Sanchez wasn't one of them, the president loathed the "No" and "We can't" pessimists entrenched in the executive branch.

"The agency has adept case officers running source networks and operations. Presumably, they're collecting the intel we need. There's a disconnect somewhere between them and here. My general sense is there's a Chinese wall in place on certain issues. In those instances where we do receive information, it's watered down. I'm having difficulty getting my arms around why. An excellent case in point is how the Terror's Sword threat was glossed over in today's PDB."

"I want your opinion. How do we address a threat like this with so little to go on?"

"I'd hand it off to our best counterterrorism case officer with orders to run the threat to ground and eliminate it."

"And who might that be?"

"You know him as Saber."

Mention of the operative's classified code name elevated Englewood's blood pressure. During his initial briefing prior to inauguration, CIA Director Carl Stefan insinuated Saber was a highly classified clearinghouse for the agency's counterterror intelligence. Later, the president was dumbfounded to learn that Saber was actually a single case officer developing that vast amount of intelligence. This deception made Englewood question the validity of all of Stefan's assertions from that point forward.

"Okay, Danni, let's have it."

Sanchez chose her words carefully. America's chief executives needed shielding or "wiggle room"—official deniability—there were some things no president wanted or needed to know. "In the event diplomacy fails, and conventional military and intelligence methods cannot eliminate national security threats, we have an off-the-books remedy: liquidation of the threat and retaliatory measures against the responsible parties."

Although Sanchez had stopped short of revealing specifics, Englewood deduced that the deep cover operative was the solution. Contemplating the consequences of learning the details about Saber, his eyes landed on a photo. In it, he held the fabled Patton Cavalry Saber at the George S. Patton, Jr. Museum at Fort Knox. *Hollywood couldn't write a better script—the president of the United States sending America's best, Saber, head-to-head against this Terror's Sword, whoever he is.* Englewood locked his eyes onto the DNI. His intense gaze left no doubt: he wanted more.

Taking a deep breath, Sanchez plunged in. "His name is McEwan. Kyle McEwan."

CHAPTER FOUR

DANIELA SANCHEZ GAVE A concise summary of Kyle McEwan's story to the president. "In college, McEwan's mastery of foreign languages with near-perfect pronunciation and dialects came to the attention of a CIA talent spotter. When they approached McEwan, he took minimal convincing. During training, he exhibited many of the innate characteristics senior case officers spend years acquiring. He was the sole trainee in his basic ops course tagged as a NOC." Sanchez checked whether she needed to elaborate.

Englewood's slight nod indicated he understood that covert case officers who operated without benefit of diplomatic immunity were called nonofficial cover, or NOCs. Their use provided the government deniability if covert intelligence operations went awry.

"After specialized training, he was posted to Beirut. McEwan quickly demonstrated an extraordinary ability for recruiting assets and developing productive covert ops. For the last few years, he's been the agency's bedrock on Middle Eastern and Southwest Asian terrorism, specifically al-Qaeda and ISIS. Recently, he's produced intel on Islamic terror start-up groups in Europe that is typical McEwan: twenty-four-carat." Sanchez sipped from a glass of water before continuing.

"McEwan's led source extractions and snatch-and-grabs of high-value targets. His paramilitary skills rival tier one operators in DOD and the CIA's Special Operations Group, Special Activities Division. McEwan's baptism by fire was his single-handed elimination of a five-man hit squad after they killed one of his assets. Since then, when diplomacy and all conventional efforts have failed, McEwan's been the method we've used to neutralize our enemies. Rest assured, while he's taken lethal actions, McEwan's no rogue operator—all were sanctioned by your predecessors."

Despite a presidential executive order prohibiting assassinations of foreign heads of state, targeted executions remained the best method to eliminate terrorists and their benefactors. Englewood believed in using "wet work" as the need arose.

"If ever a person was born to serve as a clandestine case officer, it's McEwan. He has the ability to place himself into his adversary's mind and see the world through their eyes. Intel he provides allows us to disrupt plots proactively. He is *prescient.* Whatever the source of McEwan's gift, it's a shame we can't bottle it."

"Remarkable. How come he isn't already on this?" Englewood quizzed.

"Only Carl Stefan can answer that question. McEwan is CIA. It should have been turned over to him but hasn't."

Englewood wasn't surprised. Knowledge equaled power in government and politics. Except for the FBI, no agency was as adept at information-hoarding as the CIA, no single player more practiced in the art than Carl Stefan. "Why not give it to him?"

"In short, personal vendettas that eclipse national security. McEwan is headstrong and polarizing because he's completely intolerant of political demagoguery, bureaucracy, and lack of candor. Small petty people perceive him as arrogant, bordering on insubordinate, resist his efforts, and are envious of his achievements. Smart managers ignore the downside and ride the coattails of his successes. Many field agents strive to emulate him but don't possess his gifts. He's admired for his honesty and courage in standing up to Stefan, who's renowned for ending the careers of outspoken officers."

"We could use more people who stand on principle."

"Yes, sir. McEwan is a man of integrity and conviction. His Achilles' heel is that the mission is paramount, political ramifications be damned.

Myopic policy wonks and politicos at Foggy Bottom and Langley don't share that philosophy and allow ruffled feathers to color their judgment. They dismiss Saber intel as radioactive despite the fact that all agency counterterrorism chiefs, including their own, agree that his intel is the gold standard."

The final statement convinced Englewood. Differences of opinion between these chiefs being the norm, on the rare occasions they achieved consensus, one ignored it at his or her peril.

"Sir, no one's given more and asked less in return. Hands down, McEwan *is* our best covert weapon. If he worked for anyone other than Stefan, he'd have more than one Intelligence Star and single Distinguished Intelligence Medal."

Englewood's low whistle signaled recognition of the CIA's highest honors, often awarded posthumously to agents whose actions involved grave risk and exceptional service. "Who outside the intel and law enforcement communities knows about Saber's operations?"

"The Senate and House leadership, intelligence committee heads, plus a handful of cabinet members due to their roles in the presidential succession plan."

"What's Stefan's involvement?"

"He personally approved most of the operations. Grapevine buzz has it that Stefan secretly looks forward to the day he can chisel McEwan's star in the marble."

"What in the hell for?" Englewood sat up in his chair, well aware of the memorial wall honoring agency employees fallen in service to their country.

"Stefan harbors great animus toward McEwan, who's been less than circumspect in voicing his beliefs that the director needlessly risks lives and undermines covert operations. The rumor mill claims McEwan has proof Stefan withholds critical information impacting major counterterror ops that he then mismanages, causing unnecessary deaths. True or false, with McEwan's sources, anything's possible. If true, the constant threat of disclosure must haunt Stefan, but if McEwan dies on assignment, his problems disappear." Sanchez's finger-snap emphasized her point.

Englewood sighed. "It sounds like McEwan's the man for the job, but before I agree to a plan of action, see what else you can get me on this threat."

CHAPTER FIVE

CONCEALED BY DENSE FOLIAGE hanging over a tiled walkway, Kyle McEwan and his detective escort walked toward the rear of the terrace house on the quiet London street. Buzzed in through the locked rear door, they tromped up a staircase to the second floor.

Entering the surveillance post, the stench of cigarette smoke engulfed them. A cluster of heavily armed plainclothes officers in body armor huddled around a bank of monitors, focused intently on an imposing Victorian residence across the street. Glancing toward the computer screens, McEwan observed four different angles of a peaceful, predawn setting on the north side of the River Thames. However, looks were deceiving—the impressive house hid a nasty secret.

Through the hanging haze, he glimpsed Detective Chief Inspector Nigel Hurst across the room, cigarette clenched tightly between his teeth.

The lanky, wafer-thin SO15 commander stubbed out his cigarette in an ashtray and waved over his American colleague. Instead of the usual handshake, Hurst slapped a bulletproof vest into McEwan's chest. His tongue-in-cheek greeting was coated with the effects of smoking and a thick Cockney accent. "Welcome to the bash, Yank."

"Not my idea of a party." McEwan parried while donning the vest.

"I suppose it depends on your frame of reference."

"Without a doubt. Thanks for the call, Nigel."

Hurst brought McEwan up to speed. "I know nothing of your informer. The technical chaps say we cannot track him because the radicals tinkered with his mobile. We surmise he believes it's safe to come here. Bad luck, they plan to torture the truth out of him then do him in."

"That's not going to happen."

"Spot-on. He understood the risks and could have backed out to save his neck."

McEwan agreed but shot Hurst a troubled look. "What's the activity so far?"

"Eavesdropping equipment confirms two men obviously waiting for the others. Only chitchat thus far." Hurst pointed toward a 9 mm SIG Sauer semiautomatic pistol resting on a table. "An all-out assault may be unavoidable if they want to play rough. The ROE? Non-negotiable. British soil, our show. Your man, you remove him. The firearm is only a last resort for your safety."

McEwan's nod signaled he understood and accepted the rules of engagement. Strapping on a tactical belt and holster and securing it to his right thigh, he worked the pistol's action smoothly. He inserted a fully loaded magazine and chambering a round, decocked the pistol. Extracting the magazine, he topped it off with another round and reinserted it. Before deplaning at Northolt, he'd secured his CIA-issued Glock in the small of his back. He tucked a radio in a vest compartment and affixed a tactical headset with earpiece and mic.

The Englishman shook another smoke from a Benson & Hedges box. He tamped the cigarette on the box, lit it, and blew a smoke ring. "I plan to put the whole lot in shackles and transport them to Paddington Green, our high-security station. They'll remain there as guests of Her Majesty long enough for me to extract what we want. Even if I must draw and quarter the smarmy bastards."

A knot formed in the pit of McEwan's stomach. While Scotland Yard's team was topflight, experience told him all too often overconfidence spelled disaster. "Let's not screw around with this, Nigel. Just execute a hard hit and get him out."

Hurst sensed McEwan's apprehension. "Most assuredly, I want him out as much as you."

"We have a visual on the informer," an officer interrupted, pointing to a laptop screen. "The Jaguar, sir, turning onto the street now."

McEwan squinted at the scene playing out on the live video feed. The Jaguar pulled up to the curb and stopped. The driver—McEwan's source—stepped out and shuffled through the front door, opened by an unseen person. It closed immediately.

"The fox is in the henhouse," Hurst transmitted tersely to the Specialist Firearms Team, Scotland Yard's equivalent of SWAT. "All teams stand by to move into position."

"Sir, two other guests are joining the party."

The monitor showed a delivery van careening around the corner and screeching to a stop. It double-parked beside the Jaguar, blocking it in.

Instinctively tensing like a panther ready to pounce, McEwan watched two men in matching uniforms spring from the van and disappear through the magically opening front door.

Hurst radioed for the assault teams to remain in position, then turned to McEwan. "Our little enterprise is going tits up quickly. He's your man—make the call."

McEwan's answer was an unspoken but unmistakable nod.

"Let's get on with it then." Hurst transmitted through his tactical throat microphone: "Prepare to execute."

Hurst and McEwan scrambled down the staircase and outside, where the early morning darkness and tall hedgerows obscured their movements. Trotting past plainclothes detectives coiled in idling cars, the two men crossed invisibly to the Victorian. Darting past a tactical team in a rear garden, they joined another stack of officers at the back door.

A masked set of ice-cold blue eyes stared at McEwan; he recognized them as belonging to Winston Murdoch, co-handler of his source. McEwan gave the thumbs-up, and Hurst's execute order hissed in his earpiece.

An officer responded by taking the door off its hinges with a spring-operated battering ram then stepped aside.

Murdoch charged through the kitchen doorway—Hurst and McEwan branched off in the opposite direction amid shouts of "Armed police! Armed police!"

Gunfire answered the police warnings.

The SO15 commander let loose a sharp cry when rounds found him. Hurst managed to rip off a burst with his Heckler & Koch MP5 before falling in a clump.

With officers dashing for cover, McEwan snatched Hurst by an arm and hauled him to safety behind a refrigerator.

Suddenly, silence. Neither side moved nor uttered a sound.

McEwan detected muffled voices in Arabic, then three separate sets of footsteps bounding up to the second floor. *They're making too much noise—trap!* To confirm his hunch, McEwan used the wall as cover and fired his handgun once down the hallway.

Pistol rounds punched into the wall and doorframe near McEwan's head, sending shards of plaster and splinters biting into his lips. He hand-signaled Murdoch: *Two shooters waiting to ambush us.* McEwan holstered the SIG Sauer and grabbed Hurst's MP5.

Murdoch unhooked a flash-bang grenade from his tactical vest and lobbed it to McEwan.

The American pulled the pin and rolled the device down the hallway.

A searing white flash and concussive wave blew wood, plaster, and smoke back through the kitchen. After a split-second delay, McEwan stuck the submachine gun around the corner and hosed down the hallway.

Screams pierced the air.

McEwan pivoted into the hallway and advanced with three-round bursts.

One man in a delivery uniform staggered as bullets thudded into flesh and bone and he dropped. The other man jerked wildly when rounds ripping into his torso drove him backward into a corner.

McEwan snagged a fully loaded magazine tossed to him by Murdoch. He performed a quick exchange and covered the staircase.

Officers cleared the dining room and parlor and then positioned themselves on McEwan's six.

Sounds of scuffling came from the second floor.

Controlling his breathing, McEwan inched slowly up the creaky staircase.

A short volley sailed harmlessly overhead, dotting the ceiling and shattering a light fixture.

McEwan responded by raking the second-floor landing with the MP5.

A resounding click echoed down the staircase.

It was all the prompting McEwan needed. Bolting up the remaining stairs two at a time, he found the second deliveryman at the top of the staircase struggling with a jammed AK-47. McEwan double-tapped the man's chest, then put one in his head for good measure.

The terrorist collapsed like an empty oat sack. *Three down.*

As McEwan moved guardedly around the dead man into the loft, glass and spent bullet casings crunched beneath his feet, betraying his presence in the hallway.

From inside the room, a loud smack accompanied a deep voice that commanded with a snarl, "Come any closer and I will kill the dog!"

McEwan sneaked a quick peek around the doorframe. The first rays of light flickering through a window outlined a man holding a knife to the throat of McEwan's source while using him as a human shield. The terrorist's contemptuous sneer telegraphed Jamil El-Harith's fate.

In a single fluid movement, McEwan spun into the room. The instant the reflex red-dot sight acquired the terrorist's forehead he pressed the trigger—the MP5 coughed once.

In a millisecond, a hole replaced the terrorist's smirk and a pink-mist cloud sprayed the window behind his head. After a momentary pause, blood spurted down the bridge of his nose—the terrorist, El-Harith, and the knife clanged to the floor.

McEwan's shot was too late.

Ripping off his tactical headset and rushing forward, McEwan fell to his knees and applied pressure to the source's gaping neck wound. He couldn't staunch the blood loss. El-Harith's life was spurting through his fingers in gushes.

"Jamil, tell me what you know."

"He ... an attack ... the Sword ..."

"The Sword?" McEwan fired off questions rapidly. "Who is he? Where will he attack? With what?"

El-Harith gurgled, "America ... millions will die ..."

McEwan cried out, "I need details!"

No answer. Jamil El-Harith was dead.

Standing, blood dripping onto the carpet, McEwan turned to Murdoch. "Did you hear that?"

"Yes." He placed his hand on McEwan's shoulder. "It was unavoidable, you know."

Fuming, McEwan ignored him. "Where's Nigel?"

"In the kitchen."

McEwan crossed the loft. Angrily stepping over the dead terrorist, he stomped down the staircase. Bullet casings cascaded down to the first floor, sticking in the congealing blood. In the entryway, the early morning sunlight revealed McEwan's handiwork. The deliveryman was sprawled on his back, half his skull blown away. The other man was missing his nose entirely, his left eye an empty socket.

Continuing into the kitchen, McEwan spotted a Kevlar vest flung on a table, studded with four zigzagged bullet holes. The color drained from his face, Hurst winced as a medic prodded four corresponding red welts on the SO15 commander's exposed chest.

"You okay, Nigel?"

"Pissed more than anything. The reception we received? They were expecting trouble—I need to figure out why."

"Agreed."

"I don't need the aggravation of accounting for your presence here. I'll have quite the time explaining this balls-up mess as it is."

"For sure. Does the alias 'the Sword' mean anything to you?"

"Never heard it before. You'd best run off before the chaps from the security service turn up and we have a row. I'll tidy up here."

Plunking the MP5 submachine gun on the table, McEwan walked to the sink. Turning on the faucet, he rinsed off El-Harith's blood, then doused his hands with bleach. Next, he washed with soap, rinsed, dried his hands on paper towels, and removed the rest of his gear. Glancing at Hurst, he found a hand extended toward him.

"Her Majesty's government may not see fit to formally express its appreciation for what you did here, but my men and I thank you. You have a marker to cash anytime. Now be off, or my illustrious commissioner and that tyrant you work for will turn this into an excuse to dash what little careers we have left."

Nodding at the possibility, McEwan proceeded swiftly out the back door. He trotted around to the street and hustled toward the open rear door of a BMW sedan and jumped in. The driver gunned the engine, pinning McEwan firmly against the seat. Speeding off, the car passed bobbies in high visibility reflective jackets securing the street with barricades. Curious curler-headed, bathrobe-clad onlookers began emerging from nearby homes.

McEwan was angry and disappointed. He always exercised extreme caution handling assets because, as just demonstrated, mistakes got them killed.

A vibration on his hip interrupted McEwan's self-flagellation: *Voice mail.* The screen displayed a message from an unknown caller, which hit his box about the time they raided the house. Entering his security code, McEwan played the message. The familiar voice coming through the speaker surprised him. He listened intently.

His face turned ashen at the sound of bloodcurdling screams and screeching tires.

CHAPTER SIX

DETERMINED TO CHASE DOWN the undefined threat to his country, McEwan wasted no time returning to the US. Complicating matters was the need to crack Ahmed Mansour's cryptic voice mail message: "I need your help urgently. Someone is killing all my colleagues with similar backgrounds. I am afraid I will be next—" followed by screams and sounds of a struggle. Unable to reach Mansour, McEwan learned from American University of Beirut officials that the microbiologist had "vanished". As that call concluded, atmospheric conditions over the Atlantic disrupted all satellite communications, preventing McEwan from accessing agency databases for the duration of the flight. Needing those resources to define the threat and unravel Mansour's predicament, the highly-agitated McEwan headed straight to Langley after landing at a private airfield in Leesburg, Virginia. Holing up in his office, he existed solely on tepid coffee and stale cafeteria sandwiches for the next forty-eight hours.

Between brief naps, McEwan ran parallel investigations: one to decipher Jamil El-Harith's cryptic warning, the other to determine Ahmed Mansour's whereabouts and who had kidnapped him. Combing through hundreds of dossiers and reports, running scores of database searches, and reaching out to dozens of contacts and assets yielded nothing about an attack, a terrorist known as the Sword, or anything on Mansour. Anxiously awaiting responses to data mining inquiries, McEwan recalled the improbable beginning of his relationship with Ahmed Mansour.

A couple of months into his first posting as a covert CIA case officer in Beirut, McEwan went to meet an asset at a local shop. Hearing gunshots, he found the source, his wife and infant son shot execution-style, five assassins laughing and standing over their bodies, guns smoking. In the ensuing gun battle, McEwan dispatched the killers, then discovered the infant clinging to life. Despite a bullet lodged in a bicep, McEwan scooped up the child and raced to an agency safe house where staff summoned Mansour. The physician saved the toddler's life, patched up McEwan, and Mansour adopted and raised the boy. Over the years, the two men became friends. They saw each other whenever Mansour came to the US or McEwan traveled to Beirut. During one of the visits, McEwan gave him a number to call if he ever needed help. It remained unused until now.

Trying to untangle the microbiologist's message, McEwan generated a threat profile on Mansour. An internet search produced an in-depth article that precisely encapsulated Mansour's value to a terror organization. For years, Mansour worked in obscurity in the field of infectious diseases, primarily smallpox. His anonymity ended when he assembled a multidisciplinary research team of microbiologists, epidemiologists, and virologists from around the world to study the application of poxvirus eradication measures to other diseases. Under his leadership, the team achieved phenomenal breakthroughs in eradicating both natural and man-made infective agents.

Heralded as the pioneer behind these scientific discoveries led to his earning the Lasker Award for Medical Research, making Mansour a hot commodity overnight. His consult was sought by the world's finest medical research entities: the Centers for Disease Control and Prevention in Atlanta, the National Institutes of Health in Bethesda, the World Health Organization in Geneva, and the Paris-based Pasteur Institute. Though not mentioned in the article, McEwan knew another customer had knocked on Mansour's door: the US Department of Defense. Mansour invented medical solutions for virulently contagious, genetically engineered viruses under highly classified DOD contracts.

Acting on a hunch, McEwan ran searches on other members of Mansour's team. He stumbled across a news article about a CDC epidemiologist killed during a carjacking in Atlanta. Pursuing that nugget allowed him to connect the dots. Over the previous three years, nearly a hundred medical scientists worldwide, including thirteen Americans, died from other than natural causes. Disinclined to believe in coincidences, he analyzed the circumstances surrounding each death. Ninety percent of them fell into one of three categories: freak incidents like explosions, laboratory mishaps, and hit-and-run accidents; random crimes such as robbery, burglary, and carjacking; and professional-style hits. Even more unsettling, most of the dead scientists were collaborators with Mansour on his project. Mansour's phone message closed the loop: someone was killing off the world's top infectious disease experts, and Mansour feared he was heading toward the same fate.

A few hours after persuading the CIA Beirut station chief to find and relocate Mansour's family to a safe house, McEwan's access to agency databases and files was terminated, crippling his investigation. McEwan's pleas to his superiors revealed the revocation came from the top: Director Carl Stefan personally issued the order. Undeterred, McEwan headed down the corridor to the director's seventh-floor office and stepped inside.

The resident battle-ax spoke without being addressed. "I can't believe you're still seeking a meeting. His answer is no, Mr. McEwan."

"Please, all I need is two minutes. Can't you squeeze me in?"

"It's not what I can do. He's made it clear he's not seeing you anytime, for any reason." She detested the gatekeeper aspect of her job. While she respected and liked McEwan personally, her marching orders came from Stefan himself. She wasn't about to make waves for anyone, not with her retirement just months away. "I suggest you work your supervisory chain."

McEwan persisted, using every trick in his book: cajoling, flattery, and sweet-talk. The cumulative effect of his buttering-up softened her demeanor. Appealing to the silver-haired guardian's sense of fairness broke up the ice jam.

"Okay, Prince Charming. I'll mention it on his next break and get back to you. Until then, vamoose."

"No can do. I'm leaving town and can't depart until he sees me."

Exasperated, she reached for the telephone and buzzed the conference room. "I need to speak with him." Then seconds later, "Sorry to disturb you, sir. Mr. McEwan is here, respectfully requesting that you reconsider meeting with him."

She paused, listening to Stefan's response, her face flushing red. "Yes, sir. I will." As she hung up, her hesitation confirmed she was sugarcoating her boss's comments. "He'll give you two minutes after he's finished reviewing the input for the PDB. Have a seat and cool your jets."

"I prefer to wait in the hallway."

"Suit yourself." She turned back to her computer screen.

Pivoting one hundred eighty degrees, McEwan exited the office. He wandered over to thick, green-tinted windows overlooking the agency's campus. He suspected his request to relocate Mansour's family had triggered the suspension of his access. This was the first time McEwan couldn't maneuver through the bureaucratic minefields or dodge his nemesis Stefan.

A half hour passed, then forty-five minutes. Sticking his head into the office got an abrupt "Not yet." Another half hour ticked by, reminding McEwan why his relationship with Stefan was so rancorous.

Stefan represented the worst of senior executives running the civil service, and in particular, the intelligence hierarchy. A former legislative staffer who pulled political strings to gain his initial appointment, Stefan, on his best day a subpar performer, soon found his career dissipation light blinking. Banished to a cubicle at Langley, career salvation came in the form of rigid administrative procedures he used to ruin operations and burn assets. Exceedingly successful at the art of bureaucratic bullshit and red tape, Stefan used congressional chits called in by his benefactors to grease his meteoric rise to the top rung. Ruling with Machiavellian gusto, safely protected behind wind-up soldiers marching lockstep to his drumbeat, the petty and cruel Stefan wrecked careers purely for blood sport.

McEwan realized the CIA director despised him because he was everything Stefan was not: an apolitical, balls-to-the-wall, dedicated, "can do" case officer who always put his country, fellow agents, and assets above political concerns. Despite Stefan's attempt to keep a tight leash on him, McEwan's elimination of scores of threats saved untold lives, garnering the deep respect of colleagues within CIA and out. Out of pure jealousy, Stefan kept McEwan's accomplishments cloaked in secrecy, even from America's chief executives. McEwan had given his all to his country, and the physical toll included countless injuries, wounds, and scars. McEwan believed he was a normal person forced by extraordinary circumstances to do reprehensible things, allowing him to escape the psychological damage that plagued other agents.

McEwan glanced at his watch. *Two hours? Long enough.* He knew Stefan was trying to provoke him to justify terminating his security clearance—the career kiss of death. Stomping back into the office, he nearly ran over the assistant.

Surprised to see him, she sputtered, "I was coming for you."

McEwan strode straight into the conference room.

Stefan, tall and thin, white hair lacquered in place by layers of hair spray, sat king-like at the end of a shiny wood conference table. Chatsworth Godfrey, director of the National Clandestine Service and McEwan's senior manager, sat next to Stefan. Godfrey was the "consummate politician"—bureaucratic euphemism for being adept at kissing asses in multiple directions, often at the same time and place. Flanking the two executives were special assistants Jake Crowley and Bert Flannery. Universally despised throughout agency ranks, the inept desk jockeys acquired their positions by supergluing their lips to the backsides of Langley's ruling blue bloods.

"Sit." Godfrey sneered contemptuously.

Seething at the hostile reception, McEwan bit his tongue, taking a seat near Crowley.

"All right, let's have it," Godfrey smirked. "What's so important you went around me and demanded a meeting with the director?"

McEwan didn't take the bait. "I appreciate the opportunity to explain why it's critical my access be restored immediately."

"How stupid do you think I am?" Stefan jumped in, scoffing. "You expect me to approve your misuse of government resources?"

McEwan remained respectful. "If I may, sir, it *is* official business—"

"Bullshit. You've violated a host of regulations squandering agency resources on a personal wild-goose chase. Precious resources you diverted from our search to uncover who is about to attack us."

McEwan's fists clenched involuntarily beneath the table. "I admit Mansour and I have a personal relationship. That doesn't change the fact that he's one of our bioweapon experts and the current threat—"

Stefan's reply dripped sarcasm. "I don't give a crap about him or your so-called intel. You're through. I'm burying you so deep inside a file room you'll never come up for air!"

McEwan's dam broke. "You really don't get it, you sanctimonious, self-serving son of a bitch! What I'm working on *is* vital to national security, which in my world trumps everything."

The dim-witted Crowley, misinterpreting the phrase "carpe diem", validated rumors that his IQ barely topped room temperature. Intent on manhandling McEwan out of the meeting, he launched. McEwan's lightning-quick reflexes left Crowley upside down, dazed, moaning.

McEwan laughed disdainfully. "You shouldn't tolerate violence in the workplace, *Carl*."

Stunned by the speed and ferocity of McEwan's reaction, Stefan struggled to maintain his composure. Unaware his bulging eyes and neck veins betrayed him, he refused to retreat. Stefan drew upon the same poor skill set he'd used in the field—misjudging his adversary.

"That's your problem, McEwan, your hair-trigger temper. I know all about London. If you were less quick on the draw and more concerned with the safety of your UK asset, we'd know more about this Sword and his attack. No, once again, Kyle McEwan goes in guns blazing, leaving a wide swath of destruction in his wake!"

Recognizing the brick wall, McEwan spoke with finality, his words cold. "This country's national security infrastructure is rotting because of assholes like you. You and your lackeys are a disgrace. The American people and the dedicated men and women of this agency who risk their lives every day deserve better. My mission in life will be to expose each of you for what you are. I'll only stop when you're behind bars. Until then, I'm done with you and all of this." McEwan turned and departed, leaving his stunned audience speechless.

Much to his surprise, the rest of the day passed without incident as he signed personnel forms, turned in his assigned equipment, and packed up personal items. Heading out for the final time, he surrendered his ID at the security checkpoint.

The guard spoke quietly. "Good luck, sir. It's been an honor."

Obviously the grapevine is operating at warp speed. McEwan walked through the parking garage of the Old Headquarters Building and over to his Jeep Warrior. He tossed in three boxes of personal items and slammed the tailgate. Hearing his name called, he turned to face a group of fellow case officers crossing the garage. One by one, they wished him the best, each disappearing as quickly as he or she had arrived. After the last handshake, McEwan climbed behind the wheel, fired up the engine, and proceeded to the exit. He blew past the guards with a two-finger salute, leaving the CIA behind forever.

Freed from his jailers, McEwan felt liberated. A small smile spread across his face, then vanished as he replayed Mansour's ominous words for the thousandth time. Each time he recalled his friend's screams, shudders ran up and down his spine.

McEwan resolved to stop at nothing until he found Mansour.

CHAPTER SEVEN

AHMED MANSOUR, MD, PhD, shifted position to prevent the plastic cable ties securing his wrists from cutting off circulation. Blindfolded, he fell into the wall, scraping his face. Vague images floated into his consciousness, his battered brain processing them as best as possible: a van screeching to a halt, two masked men jumping out and seizing him, hauling him into the basement of a building in Beirut's Hezbollah-controlled suburbs, beatings until unconsciousness, awakenings by buckets of cold water, the beatings resuming. He promised to tell them whatever they wanted if they stopped. It was no use; the vicious cycle repeated endlessly, but no interrogations. Mansour knew of people softened up for weeks back during the Syrian occupation. After waking up in new surroundings, one of his torturers pummeled him relentlessly as punishment for forcing them to travel to the Bekaa Valley.

Prior to his abduction, Mansour spent days mentally probing and dissecting his life. Each analysis yielded the same result: his murder was imminent, and although he knew why, he was powerless to prevent it. While Mansour could not unravel who issued his death warrant, its genesis had to be his work. His hard-earned credentials had been a source of pride until his research discovered a distressing reality. One by one, every single colleague with comparable expertise was dead, many dying under suspicious circumstances. Accepting that a bull's eye had been painted on his chest by persons unknown, instincts screamed at him to flee Beirut, saving himself, his wife, and his children. Ignoring that message, Mansour had separated from his loved ones, hiding them in Tyre, fifty miles south. *I will give them what they want so my family will be spared. But they—whoever they are—must tell me what they want! Then they can end this.*

Mansour was distressed that he had not alerted Kyle McEwan to the scheme he had discovered: he was the last scientist alive capable of defeating certain bioweapons. He hoped, he prayed that McEwan would learn the truth by some means and stop the killers. Petrified by what faced him, he prayed for strength but grudgingly accepted his situation was hopeless. He and many others would die because he failed to warn McEwan. Mansour wept silently, the tight blindfold subduing his tears.

Voices entered his ears; two sets of powerful arms jerked him up and ripped off the blindfold. Several hands pushed him through a doorframe into a room reeking with the acrid smell of burning hashish. Dazed from physical abuse and blinding light, he blinked rapidly, trying to focus. A group of coarse, hostile men spit mucus in his face. The largest one kicked him in the groin, doubling him over. A boot to the abdomen released a warm stream that flooded his lower extremities.

"Look, the worm pissed himself!"

One burning sensation after another stung Mansour's neck. He turned toward a man in military fatigues clenching a cigarette, holding the burning embers tauntingly close to Mansour's eyes. He spoke through nicotine-stained teeth. "Are you going to tell us what we want to know, you son of a camel humper?"

Choking on bile and tears, Mansour gasped. "What do you want?"

His captors stepped aside, turning deferentially toward a well-groomed man in Western attire.

Acknowledging the others with a curt nod, the man addressed Mansour. "Who else knows about my plan?"

"Plan?" the confused doctor croaked. "I do not understand."

"Stubbornness will only make matters worse," Mansour's interrogator growled. Reaching for his captive's testicles, he squeezed. "I want names."

Mansour howled, pleading, "I know of no plan. I know no one who does!"

"Are the Americans capable of stopping my plan?"

"I beg you, please stop. What plan are you speaking—"

Snatched by his hair, slaps stung his face, and a loud crack rang out. Blood sprayed from his nose as the blow knocked him to his knees. Jerked to his feet, Mansour swayed in a circle. A hard punch to the stomach sent him back to the floor. A stomping boot crunched down on his right hand. Other boots mashed an ankle and kicked him in the abdomen and back, voiding his bowels.

A voice mocked, "Camel dung!" and the others laughed.

The interrogator leaned down into Mansour's face, his green eyes searing the doctor's soul. "I must know! Are the Americans capable of stopping me?"

Seeing stars and tasting blood, the microbiologist was incapable of answering.

"Do not force me to hand over your jezebel wife and daughters to the Army jackals for amusement. Give me what I want, or the desert rats will feast on your son's penis."

Mansour's field of vision narrowed.

"Do not pass out on me!"

Mansour blacked out.

"Strip him of his clothes. No light or covers. Wet him down and leave him. Soften him up some more. I want him talking next time. Understood?"

The two men nodded fearfully as their leader strode from the building.

CHAPTER EIGHT

ENGROSSED IN HIS PLAN to find Ahmed Mansour, McEwan nearly blew through a red light at Wisconsin and Massachusetts Avenues in northwest Washington. When the signal turned green, he crossed the intersection, made an abrupt turn, and headed toward a high-rise building nestled in the shadows of the National Cathedral. Punching a remote control button, the security gate rose, allowing him to enter the parking garage beneath the pre–World War II structure. Turning a corner, his tires squealed on the concrete floor as he wheeled into his reserved slot and parked. A quick elevator ride to the top floor took McEwan to his condo.

Inside, McEwan scooped up the mail off the floor and dumped it in a heap on the dining room table. Slipping into a familiar routine, he executed tasks with military precision. Walking into a closet, he grabbed a large, prepacked duffel bag and set it on the bed. After showering and dressing, he rolled the gear bag to the elevator and returned to the garage. Ensconced again in his Jeep, he promptly became mired in DC's evening rush-hour traffic. He made good use of the time en route to his destination in the Shenandoah Valley's Blue Ridge mountains.

Three hours and some forty-plus phone calls later, he'd recontacted most his of Middle Eastern sources, seeking updates. Each came up dry—Ahmed Mansour had vanished. The Israelis were his last shot at finding his friend, and they were out working their sources. McEwan would have no cell service at his destination, so it would be morning before he had their response.

Exiting Interstate 81, McEwan traveled several miles on a county highway until he reached a sharp bend. Slowing, he turned onto an almost-invisible gravel side road and shifted into four-wheel drive. The Jeep climbed steadily up a steep grade on a switchback road. Bouncing and zigzagging, it finally crested a mountaintop. McEwan brought the Warrior to a bone-jarring stop, its headlights silhouetting a small cabin.

Climbing the steps onto a covered porch, McEwan removed a padlock from the door and pushed it open. A quick check with his flashlight satisfied him the place was untouched since his last visit. Firing up two kerosene lanterns illuminated a double bed, Buck Stove, kitchen table and chairs, and small cooking stove. The rustic cabin was everything his condo wasn't, full of warmth and character, reflecting the real Kyle McEwan, unsullied by his ugly profession. A side all too rarely seen by others or the man himself.

McEwan collected his gear from the Jeep and tossed it on the table. Tiredness setting in, he decided to wait until morning to climb into the crawl space beneath the cabin to access a safe secreted inside a false foundation piling. He'd extract several thousand dollars in cash and IDs in an alias known only to him. On his return to DC, McEwan would rendezvous with a source, a Lebanese government official, for pertinent visas and travel documents. If nothing new surfaced, he'd head to Beirut. McEwan faced a daunting task—he might fall short in his most important mission ever, particularly without access to US government resources. Latching the door, he darkened the cabin. Exhausted and consumed with conflicting emotions, he fell into the bed.

Tonight's sleep would not be restful.

CHAPTER NINE

A FORMALLY ATTIRED NELSON J. ENGLEWOOD shifted his gaze from Daniela Sanchez to the CIA director, a deep furrow creasing his forehead. "Carl, it appears you know nothing about this threat. Why aren't your people producing intel?"

"It's not as easy as you think. These things take time to develop," Stefan lectured condescendingly. "The best we can do is continue intercepting communications and work our human intelligence assets. Maybe we'll turn up something useful, maybe not."

"It seems time is the one thing we don't have," observed Englewood.

"She doesn't have any solid intelligence an attack is imminent. It's pure speculation—"

Englewood cut off Stefan's Washington two-step by raising his voice, his irritation obvious. "I characterize that PDB blurb as pure bull crap. What are you holding back from me and why?"

"I'm doing no such thing!" Stefan shot back indignantly. "History shows she's prone to hitting the panic button and, I might add, needlessly. No reason to raise unwarranted red flags."

"What does Saber say about this attack?"

Stefan's jaw slackened, then he recovered. "He hasn't produced a damn thing lately. But I'll have my people check with him and get back with you."

The president glanced toward Sanchez, focused intently on her encrypted phone. Her dark-brown eyes widened, then narrowed to tiny slits. She passed Englewood the device.

The president read the message: "Saber confronted DCI over missing asset, then quit employment immediately. Repeat, Q-U-I-T. Confirmed. Attempts to locate him unproductive."

Englewood returned the phone to Sanchez and glanced at his white-and-yellow-gold Breitling chronograph watch, a gift from the Navy Blue Angels. He addressed Stefan, his beet-red face contrasting sharply with his crisply starched white wing-collared shirt, satin bow tie, and vest.

"Carl, in your inestimable wisdom, it seems you've overlooked a few things. I can smell horseshit a mile away, and you aren't very adept at shoveling it. Try managing me again and you'll find out how badly it stinks when it lands on you."

Several hours later, Daniela Sanchez sat in the same chair, facing the now casually-attired president. The DNI shared what she'd uncovered about the CIA director's shenanigans.

"A couple of days ago, the Brits had an antiterror op go awry in London. By all accounts, it was a total disaster. While I was generally aware of it, Stefan neglected to mention it was a joint op with CIA and McEwan was present because he'd recruited the source. His asset's identity was compromised somehow, and things turned ugly when Scotland Yard rolled it up. One of theirs was shot, and our source was killed. The Brits admitted—unofficially—that McEwan took out the four-man cell but couldn't save his asset. Before dying, the man warned about an attack on America by an individual calling himself the Sword. Until I speak with McEwan, I can't confirm that, though the source's mention of the Sword dovetails with the information gleaned from the NSA intercepts. Fortunately, our involvement remains unpublicized."

"That's a relief. Is this why McEwan quit?"

"Tangentially, yes. My contacts tell me McEwan used agency resources to search for a friend who's disappeared from Beirut, microbiologist Dr. Ahmed Mansour. Stefan cut off his access to classified databases and files and McEwan confronted him. They argued, McEwan walked. Stefan's boys are uncharacteristically tight-lipped. Nobody's talking. I'm not sure about the origin of the McEwan-Mansour relationship. What I dug up is part fact and part speculation."

The president waved her on.

"If McEwan was using government resources to locate Mansour, it was for legitimate reasons. Mansour isn't your garden-variety microbiologist—he's under contract to DOD to invent, quote, 'medical solutions to defeat highly contagious genetically engineered viruses' end quote. McEwan must be onto something, and if it potentially involves a link between Mansour and the Sword, it's beyond troublesome—he's a world-renowned expert in infectious diseases."

Englewood grasped the connection. "Mansour, who just happens to be an infectious disease scientist, and who develops US countermeasures against engineered viruses, has disappeared. And this so-called Sword character is probably going to hit us with a bioweapon. Correct?"

"My take exactly. We'll know for sure if we find Mansour. I put out feelers to Mossad. Their sources reported back that he was kidnapped by a man named Ali bin al-Dosari and is being stashed in the Bekaa Valley. His is the name that minimally popped up on our data mining project."

"Did the Israelis confirm he's Terror's Sword?"

"No. They have nothing on al-Dosari or any terrorist using that alias. They believe it's a wannabe jihadi trying to make a name for himself by causing us to expend resources on a hoax. Not sure I agree, but we don't have anything else. Back to McEwan. My agency contacts say he's so furious with Stefan there's no way he'll go back. I propose we tell McEwan that we think a terrorist named al-Dosari, who *might* be going by the nom de guerre Terror's Sword, is likely responsible for Mansour's disappearance and is planning to attack us. We want Mansour back for obvious reasons, and if McEwan will lead the effort to rescue him, we'll assign him military assets. I'll take the point on the op. With Stefan out of the picture, he'll do it. If al-Dosari is this Terror's Sword, our attack problem disappears."

"What makes you so certain McEwan will deal with you?"

"When I ran the Counterterrorism Center, we created an alliance to deter Stefan's meddling. Trust grew out of that over time. McEwan knows I won't betray him."

Englewood leaned back in his chair and took a moment to reflect on what he knew about the rift between his DNI and Stefan. Sanchez's first assignment post-covert operations officer training was to the CIA's Madrid station as a Commerce Department trade representative. Her talent for recruiting valuable intelligence assets surfaced immediately. Resenting her success, a poorly performing spy colleague blew Sanchez's cover. Blaming his loose lips on one too many cocktails at an embassy social affair, the coworker—a longtime associate of the CIA director—received a light reprimand. Sanchez lost her blossoming clandestine career forever. Reassigned to the CTC at Langley, she made the best of her banishment, toiling in a unit tracking the world's Islamic terrorists. Repeated operational successes attributed to her steady hand caused her star to rise both within and out of Langley, eventually coming to Englewood's attention. When the CTC chief was canned for leaking the existence of a highly classified program to several network and cable news outlets, he ordered Stefan to name Sanchez to the post. Stefan adroitly sidestepped the directive by naming her interim chief, thereby keeping her under his thumb. When briefed on Stefan's bureaucratic machinations, Englewood checkmated the CIA director by appointing Sanchez DNI when that vacancy occurred.

The president leaned forward. "If I go with McEwan, he'd damn well better pull it off."

"He's accomplished the impossible before," she asserted. "When no other intelligence agency in the world could track down certain threats, he did and eliminated them.

"Sir, I cannot express a greater sense of urgency. All signs point to an imminent attack. In my judgment, Kyle McEwan is the only one who can identify and eliminate this threat. Knowing him, I can assure you he's trying to find Mansour on his own. He's an expert at becoming invisible;

once he goes deep black, we'll only find him when he wants to be found. I'm told he's still in the DC area, but I can't guarantee for how long. I think I know where he's holed up—at least for now."

"Get McEwan back, no matter the cost." Englewood locked onto Sanchez's eyes like a laser beam finding its target. "I want that attack stopped overseas."

"Yes, sir. I'll prepare the presidential finding myself. He'll need Pentagon resources to get it done."

"Wilkinson!" Englewood hollered for his chief of staff.

CHAPTER TEN

THE NEXT MORNING, MCEWAN rose, shuffled across the cabin, and fired up the stove. Opening a bottle of water, he took a swig, then poured the remainder into a stovetop percolator. Next stop, the outbuilding. Several minutes later, necessaries out of the way, he poured a steaming cup of coffee. Snatching a lawn chair and his mug, he went behind the cabin and settled in on a flat plateau. Having tossed and turned all night long, he stared out into the early morning mist. Shrouded physically and mentally, he zoned out, never noticing the fog burn off.

An hour later, still caught up in his reverie, McEwan's hyperalert ears detected the sound of helicopter rotors beating off in the distance. Becoming fully alert, he closed his eyes, fine-tuning his senses. *They're definitely drawing closer. Nobody I know makes a social call in a helo!*

Bolting to his feet, McEwan grabbed the chair and sprinted back to the cabin. Snaring his FN Five-Seven semiautomatic pistol and two twenty-round magazines, he ran back outside and positioned himself behind a large boulder obscured from the air by a stand of trees and bushes. A black helicopter approached the ridgetop.

"Kyle McEwan!" A voice pierced his ears. "This is Danni Sanchez. I'm setting down!"

What the hell? Shielding his eyes from flying debris, McEwan stuffed his pistol in the rear waistband of his pants and sized up the situation. Only hours off the agency's payroll, Sanchez had pulled out all stops to find him. Either she had bad news, or Stefan was in another jam and she'd come hat in hand to get McEwan to bail him out.

Daniela Sanchez hopped down out of the hovering helicopter, turning to grab the accordion-style folder and radio a hand passed out to her. Lifting, the helo banked sharply away from the plateau and disappeared.

McEwan stepped into view. His eyes hardened, an icy look spreading across his face. "Did Stefan send you? I'd do anything in the world for you, but I'm not bailing out that corrupt bastard!"

Sanchez had anticipated McEwan's reaction but wasn't sure how far she could push him—he was a very dangerous man. She chose her words carefully because if she leaned too hard, he'd go gunning for Stefan. "We've both got big problems. I'll help you with yours, but you've got to help me with mine."

"Whatever you're selling, I'm not buying." Jaw set sternly, he didn't budge.

"Kyle, I'm not here for pleasantries or BS. Either you listen, or I'm gone. But if I leave, you'll never forgive yourself for not hearing me out."

McEwan glared, then assented with a nod.

Sanchez shared the latest NSA intercepts on the threatened attack by a terrorist known variously as both Terror's Sword and the Sword. She disclosed the one name linked to the two aliases: Ali bin al-Dosari. "It's thin, Kyle, very thin. But it's all we have."

The name al-Dosari rang no bells with McEwan, but combined with what he had discovered, along with Jamil El-Harith's warning, the intel was sizing up quickly as a legitimate threat. He studied the DNI with unblinking intensity. "What aren't you telling me?"

Sanchez delivered her bombshell. "Mossad says this man al-Dosari kidnapped Ahmed Mansour and is holding him in the Bekaa Valley."

McEwan read Sanchez as being truthful. "I know why," McEwan said coldly.

He related Mansour's message that someone was killing off the world's top medical scientists and Mansour suspected he was next. McEwan explained what his research uncovered about the murders and described Jamil El-Harith's warning. "The fact they haven't executed Ahmed yet is a testament of his value to them and us. I just don't know the endgame. I tried to brief Stefan and crew but they blew me off. So I quit."

"This is beyond our worst scenario, Kyle. We all know what Stefan is capable of, but this is much bigger. He didn't even relay El-Harith's warning; we learned about it from the Brits. He'll be lucky if he doesn't wind up in Gitmo. The president orders you to hunt down al-Dosari, and if he's this Sword, eliminate him. And get Dr. Mansour out before it's too late. The Pentagon will provide all the support you need. I'm running this operation under direct authority of the president. Stefan and his people are out."

McEwan's eyes bored into Sanchez's. "I'll do it for Ahmed and for the millions of Americans who deserve more than Stefan gives them. Then I'm done. And when it's over, I'm taking Stefan down for all the case officers he's ever shit on. Until then, keep him and his merry band of assholes out of my way!"

Ignoring McEwan's tirade, Sanchez pressed on. "Our friends in the Mossad are of the opinion that al-Dosari and Terror's Sword are not the same person. However, your source's information and Mansour's warning suggest there is some connection between the two. You need to resolve this on the ground.

"I'll inform the president that you're on board with the plan. A helicopter will arrive in an hour to collect you for the hop over to Andrews and drop someone to drive your Jeep back to DC. You'll be manifested aboard a military transport and briefed in transit to the op staging area."

Sanchez handed him the accordion folder. "Your access to all classified networks has been restored. You'll also need these."

Releasing the elastic band, McEwan removed a satellite telephone. He'd be able to communicate securely from anywhere in the world with Sanchez and others via encrypted voice, data transmission, e-mail, high-speed web browsing, and video streaming.

Tearing open a sealed envelope marked "EYES ONLY", he found fictitious IDs in the name of one of his long-established but unused agency aliases. The passport contained all necessary stamps, courtesy of the CIA Science and Technology Division. He thumbed through several bundles of cash. His eyes widened as he examined a single sheet of letterhead.

A subtle grin crinkling the corners of her mouth, Sanchez keyed her radio. "I'm ready."

The helicopter came around the bend and descended. Climbing aboard, Sanchez buckled in. As it rose from the crest, she looked out the window at the case officer. The DNI found the look on his face reassuring—she'd seen it before.

America's top counterterrorism case officer was fully engaged.

CHAPTER ELEVEN

NELSON J. ENGLEWOOD MOTIONED Daniela Sanchez to sit, then sat facing her. Crossing his legs, he tucked his hands behind his head. "I've been on the phone with SecDef. I understand McEwan will be linking up with a special ops unit and heading to Lebanon." Englewood sounded upbeat, referring to Defense Secretary Samuel K. Wilson.

Sanchez related McEwan's newly provided intel. "He found independent corroboration we're going to be hit with a bioweapon."

Her words were a gut punch that took Englewood's breath away.

Sanchez mapped out McEwan's discovery of the plot to kill the world's infectious disease scientists. "Mossad's assessment notwithstanding, it's looking more likely that al-Dosari is Terror's Sword. Mansour is important because he may be the only expert left alive who can tell us which bioagent is involved and how to defeat it. Putting McEwan on the ground is our only chance of getting the answers we need."

Englewood growled, "We have thousands of intel analysts whose jobs are to ferret this stuff out. Why didn't we have this Sword business?"

Sanchez shook her head, signaling her inability to justify the intelligence community's failure to surface the killings and connect them to a conspiracy. "I'm confident McEwan will unravel it."

Englewood put it more succinctly. "Unravel, hell. If McEwan kills him, game over."

The Air Force Special Operations Pave Hawk plucked McEwan from the mountaintop with the speed and efficiency of a recovery mission for a downed aviator, providing him the first aerial view of his holdings. He spotted his jeep bouncing down the dicey switchback road as the helicopter banked away.

The MH-60G helicopter covered the distance to Joint Base Andrews in slightly over an hour. In southern Maryland bordering Washington, DC, the air base supported the offices of the president and vice president of the United States. From time to time, Capitol Hill dignitaries and visiting heads of state used the base, along with special mission aircraft such as the Pave Hawk.

The voice of the crew chief came over McEwan's headphones. "Two minutes."

Pulling his bag closer to his feet, McEwan looked down at a row of gleaming F-16 fighter jets parked on the tarmac, ready to scramble at a moment's notice to protect the skies over the nation's capital. The Pave Hawk set down near the Eighty-Ninth Airlift Wing hangar housing Air Force One. When the bay door opened, McEwan grabbed his bag and jumped down onto the hardstand. An Air Force lieutenant in crisply starched digital utilities, aviator sunglasses, and beret marched toward him. Hot on his heels trailed a security forces airman cradling an M4.

"You Burns?"

"Yes," McEwan responded to his alias.

"Orders!" the officer snorted, officiously holding out his hand.

McEwan presented his official travel orders, government ID card, and passport, all in his fictitious name.

The officer snapped open the document and read it, moving his head from side to side. Most of the standard language he was accustomed to seeing, including the purpose of the travel, accounting classification and other pertinent codes, was missing from the document. Removing his sunglasses, he pulled the orders closer, scrutinizing every word:

OPERATIONAL IMMEDIATE - SECRET

From: Director of National Intelligence
To: All DOD Commands, US Government Agencies and Personnel
Subject: Burns Neil (NMN) Civilian

Subject Burns ODNI is conducting presidentially-directed mission under authority of the undersigned. Burns has Priority 1A1 access to all military and/or commercial air, sea, rail, or road transportation to any CONUS or OCONUS location he deems necessary in furtherance of his mission.

Subject Burns has TS/SCI security clearance and unrestricted access to all US government facilities, transportation, equipment, records, and personnel. Addressees will provide Burns complete, unconditional support without exception on an operational immediate basis as deemed solely by him.

Direct questions to the undersigned, Secretary of Defense, Chairman Joint Chiefs of Staff, or Attorney General of the United States.

BY ORDER OF THE NATIONAL COMMAND AUTHORITY:

D.I. Sanchez
Director of National Intelligence

The officer's demeanor changed seeing the ordering authority. In DOD-speak, National Command Authority was the president of the United States. While he'd routinely handled travel documents for the most senior government officials, he'd never seen presidentially-directed travel documents like these. All personnel, of every US military command and government agency, were to provide the man standing in front of him unchallenged, unlimited, and unrestricted access to everything and everybody, on an urgent basis. Whatever the man's mission, it was unquestionably above his and most everyone else's pay grade. Refolding them awkwardly, he thrust them back toward McEwan as if they singed his fingers.

"I'd say these orders are in order. I mean, fine, er—ah, crap. Follow me."

Regaining some semblance of official bearing and now a paragon of cooperation, the officer marched McEwan over to a large "load-out" deployment bag and soft-side rifle carrying case. "These are yours. Wherever you're going, whatever the hell you're doing, good luck."

"Any idea what time my aircraft is arriving?"

"Within the hour. We'll advise when we get an ETA." The officer gestured toward a nearby hangar, then strutted away.

Escorted by the armed security forces airman, McEwan hoisted his load-out bag onto his shoulders like a pack. Grabbing his duffel and rifle case, he took the proffered path and entered the large bay. The airman pointed to an empty room and stood guard outside. Inside, McEwan placed his bag and rifle case on tables and rested the duffel alongside.

Unzipping the rifle case, he inspected a Daniel Defense MK18 short-barreled rifle with 10.3-inch barrel and collapsible buttstock. He noted the serial number, confirming it was his agency-issued select-fire rifle. He verified that it was unloaded, and swiftly performed a series of function checks to ensure it operated properly. Next, he checked both the weapon-mounted red dot optic and infrared and white light for functionality, then turned his attention to the accessories in the case side pocket. They included spare batteries, a small parts kit, six fully loaded Magpul thirty-round magazines, a SureFire SOCOM 556-SB Fast-Attach suppressor, and Blue Force Vickers sling. Satisfied, he returned everything to its case and zipped it shut.

McEwan opened a hard-shell pistol case and extracted a 9 mm Glock 19 semiautomatic pistol; it was the government-issued handgun he'd surrendered upon resignation. He performed function checks, returned the pistol to its case and set it aside. Rummaging through the bag, McEwan found loaded pistol magazines, a handheld flashlight, HSGI quick-reaction chest rig, and battle belt with drop leg pistol holster.

Footsteps on his flank signaled the security airman's presence. "Sir, your aircraft is on final approach. Allow me to escort you in one of our premier limousines."

McEwan followed the airman to a waiting Humvee. Heaving all of his gear into the back, he climbed aboard. The hot tarmac elicited screeches from the Humvee's tires, and shortly they pulled up to a mammoth C-17 Globemaster.

An aviator in a Nomex flight suit strode down the ramp. "You Burns?"

McEwan responded, "Yes, Major." McEwan surrendered his pseudonym ID and travel orders.

The aviator scanned and returned them without comment. He stuck out his hand. "Welcome aboard. Marc Yager."

"Thanks. Nice to meet you," McEwan replied.

"Need help with your gear?"

"Negative."

"Wheels up in ten." Yager turned smartly and disappeared inside the cavernous aircraft.

McEwan stood by as a forklift entered the plane's massive cargo bay, set down a pallet of equipment, and returned to the tarmac. Treading up the ramp, McEwan handed off his gear bags to the loadmaster and was directed to a seat. In minutes, they were airborne.

Aside from his goal of rescuing Ahmed Mansour, McEwan was confident he'd complete another mission. Al-Dosari would pay for kidnapping Mansour—and if he was Terror's Sword, the threat to America would be terminated.

CHAPTER TWELVE

A CLICK REVERBERATED AS THE scanner read Daniela Sanchez's ID badge. She slipped unnoticed into the White House Situation Room amid the din of sidebar conversations and low chuckles. She took stock of her colleagues around the table; though few in number, they exuded palpable power.

Flanking the president were SecDef Samuel K. Wilson and Attorney General James William Davidson. Across from them sat Carl Stefan of the CIA, FBI Director J. Philip Olsen, Homeland Security Secretary Donald Hyde Moss, and Health and Human Services Secretary Patricia Longstreet, MD. The heads of the military services, collectively known as the Big Four, sat alongside Joint Chiefs of Staff chairman General Cameron T. Fuller, US Marine Corps. Occupying the backbench seats were the presidential advisers for National Security, Homeland Security, and Counterterrorism. All present comprised the crisis team for the now named Operation Steel Trap.

The president cleared his throat. "Give it to us straight, Danni."

"We are in possession of highly actionable intelligence that indicates we will be attacked with a bioweapon. If successful, the death and destruction could be incalculable. If we fail to act decisively, the American way of life as we now know it could cease to exist."

Shock registered on the face of everyone but Stefan. Angry no one shared his skepticism, the CIA director glared at the DNI.

Sanchez ignored him; focusing instead on the others, she continued.

"NSA was monitoring chat rooms frequented by known Sunni and Shi'a terrorist groups when a flurry of messages appeared about a pending attack by an individual known as Terror's Sword that will be even worse than September eleventh. What's disturbing is that religious leaders of both sects speak of this man with great reverence as if he is the second coming of Muhammed. Without warning, the monitored chat rooms shut down and there have been no further relevant intercepts. Then we developed similar intel from Islamists in Indonesia and Chechnya. The coup de grâce, however, is information developed from an op in London that an individual known as the Sword is going to attack us. While we do not know the timetable, the intel was obtained by Saber."

That piece added an extreme degree of credibility to the threat to all present, save one.

Stefan was about to interrupt Sanchez but was preempted by the attorney general who turned to his FBI director. "Damn it to hell! Did you know about this?"

"Absolutely not! CIA is supposed to share everything with my people at the National Counterterrorism Center." The normally unflappable Olsen blew a gasket in Stefan's direction. "You're supposed to help me protect this country!"

"Now, wait just a minute!" Stefan shot back. "I wasn't briefed on this!"

"Enough!" Englewood slammed a folder on the tabletop. "Close the loop, Danni."

"A man named Ali bin al-Dosari and the terrorist they call Terror's Sword are apparently the same person." Sanchez described al-Dosari's recent abduction of Dr. Ahmed Mansour, developer of vital biowarfare countermeasures and biomedical solutions for DOD, and the murders of the world's experts possessing similar backgrounds. Sanchez delivered the final blow: al-Dosari likely engineered the murders in preparation for his attack on America with an unknown bioweapon. "Piecing together the facts as we know them, Mansour is the only person left who can identify the bioagent and help us defeat it."

Again, heated accusations flew.

Unruffled by the angry outbursts, Sanchez yelled, "Stop!"

The room quieted immediately.

She disclosed the Saber-led military operation currently underway to rescue Mansour in the Bekaa Valley.

"You didn't clear that with me!" Stefan exploded. "*I* run all overseas ops, and *I* own Kyle McEwan—"

"Carl!" Sanchez snapped. "You've outed a covert operative by name!"

All present knew that connecting a person's identity to a code name or classified operation was in direct violation of laws governing sensitive sources, methods, and operations.

The attorney general turned his ire on Stefan. "Mr. President, how long are you going to tolerate this prick playing games with our national security? Give me the word and Philip will frog-march his ass out of here in handcuffs!"

Stefan rolled his eyes. He took aim at the president, his demeanor disrespectful, his words scornful. "You must scrub this operation immediately. The blowback McEwan causes isn't worth the take. I demand to know who authorized her to use that morally depraved—"

"I did." Englewood held his temper in check. "It will relieve you to know it's not your responsibility. You've demonstrated you're incapable of objectively running Saber operations. Danni's taking the point with DOD, and you're out of it. Am I clear?"

Stunned, Stefan's face flushed purple with rage. Stuttering to find the right words, he finally choked, "DNI is not lawfully authorized to run counterterror ops, but I suppose you've decided she can. It's your show, Mr. President."

"Thank you for acknowledging that fact." Englewood's frosty glare matched the minus-twenty-degrees Fahrenheit temperature of his words. "As of now, Saber reports to DNI and no one else. Be sure you and your professional plotters keep your hands off, or I'll wield the ax myself." Unfolding his legs, Englewood stood and left the room.

Brief moments ticked by before the remainder of the crisis team, save Sanchez and Stefan, gathered their belongings and scampered out.

The CIA director's fiery eyes bored holes into Daniela Sanchez.

The alpha female stared back unflinchingly, her eyes ice cold.

Forced to break eye contact, the browbeaten Stefan swept up his papers and shoved them into his briefcase. Slamming the lid, he snatched it off the table and departed, tail tucked.

Alone in the Situation Room, Sanchez could feel her cheeks burning. After accusing her of a backroom power grab, Stefan would come after her with a vengeance, pulling out all stops to take her down. It was his way, the Washington way.

Fortunately, her ace in the hole was Kyle McEwan.

As the plane leveled off at cruising altitude over the Atlantic Ocean, McEwan spotted the loadmaster pointing toward the flight deck.

Unbuckling, McEwan made his way forward. Yager gestured toward a headset. He placed it over his ears, and the voice coming over the airwaves announced his presence.

"This is Colonel Thomas O'Brien, JSOC. National Command Authority has green-lighted Operation Steel Trap. The target objective is Rayak, a former French air base in the Bekaa Valley. We've recommended a plan linking you with the Unit at Incirlik Air Base. You'll be briefed on the details when you land in Turkey. We're busy spinning up ops elsewhere, so that's it for now."

Signing off, McEwan returned to his seat. The operation would be a collaborative effort between the ultimate paradigm in joint service warfighting, the JCS Special Operations Division in the Pentagon and the US Special Operations Command in Tampa. USSOCOM's elite counterterrorism command at Fort Bragg, the Joint Special Operations Command, would direct the mission. JSOC was hammering out the assault plan and logistics, and all necessary pieces were moving into place on the board. McEwan was pleased to work again with the US Army's

1st Special Forces Operational Detachment-Delta, the elite USSOCOM special missions unit more commonly known as Delta Force or the Unit.

Mind racing, sleep impossible, McEwan sank deep into thought. In his business, success and longevity lulled even the best case officers into complacency, laxity, and mistakes. One had to stay on top of his game—a single error could put a case officer six feet under. His life always on the line, McEwan necessarily trusted virtually no one and nothing, living by his platinum rule: Do unto enemies first what they have done or will do unto others. McEwan didn't care that his principles offended the narrow-minded; he served a higher moral calling. Some of his superiors misconstrued his desire to undertake the most dangerous missions as proof of a death wish. McEwan knew better; he and like-minded colleagues were the only ones standing between freedom and tyranny. He'd long ago grown weary of the bureaucrats who inflicted "death by a thousand cuts" on so many fine case officers, but Stefan's response to Mansour's kidnapping was his Rubicon. One final op and out.

After seeming like minutes but in reality several hours later, the loadmaster handed McEwan a flash precedence message and again pointed toward the flight deck. He went forward and placed the headset back over his ears.

"This is O'Brien again. I've got the deployment order, but your special missions unit has been diverted. We're going with MARSOC; they are already in theater. You're rerouted to Akrotiri."

McEwan recognized the Royal Air Force air base on Cyprus.

"You have a fan or two in JCS. You're authorized to go in with the trigger pullers. Just sit back and enjoy the ride and leave the heavy lifting to MARSOC. They'll conduct the hostage rescue and seize your high-value target, then turn both over to you."

The link with Fort Bragg terminated, McEwan removed the headset. Taking in the star-filled night over Yager's shoulder, he contemplated the looming events. Due to increased demand for military special missions units to support counterterrorism efforts, the US Marine Forces Special

Operations Command had begun backing CIA operations. Like the US Navy SEALs and Army Delta Force, the elite MARSOC Raiders specialized in direct action. The Raiders launched their deep-penetration reconnaissance missions from naval vessels, eliminating the need for in-country logistic networks.

McEwan surmised the MARSOC component was from the Camp Lejeune-based Second Raider Battalion, and deployed with a Marine Expeditionary Unit as part of an overseas contingency operation. Knowing he'd have these answers soon enough, McEwan returned to his seat. He cleared his cognitive functions, closed his eyes, and shut out the lights.

Operation Steel Trap was a go.

CHAPTER THIRTEEN

AS ONE HEADS EAST out of the seaside capital of Lebanon, a road winds its way through hills and small villages to a sparsely populated agricultural area resting between two mountain ranges. Free from the hustle and bustle of Beirut, the lushly fertile valley produces most of Lebanon's vegetables and fruits. The seeds of its most famous crop, however, usually take root elsewhere and come here to ripen. The Bekaa Valley is the biggest producer of the world's most insidious crop: terrorists. Every season yields a new harvest of murderers, torture masters, and bomb makers. For decades, countries espousing radical anti-Western philosophies have sent their budding plants to flourish in the valley's inviting and hospitable lands.

The small village of Rayak is situated forty-eight kilometers east of Beirut near the Syrian border, and thirty-two kilometers south of the Roman temple ruins at Baalbek. Decades ago, France built, then abandoned, a military airfield there. Over the years, corrupt Lebanese military officers transformed it into a safe haven transit point for black marketeers. Most recently, one enterprising officer found a more lucrative use for the airfield's buildings: leasing them to a new international terror organization at a monthly rate of fifteen million LBPs, or $10,000 US.

The roar of a car's engine in the distance racing toward the airfield startled a snoozing guard. Jolting awake, the sentry squinted—a set of headlights turned onto the dirt road leading to the airfield. Bolting to his feet, he warned, "Wake up! He is back!"

A panicked acknowledgment came from inside.

Not wanting to be discovered sleeping on the job, the guard vigorously rubbed the sand from his eyes. Their leader was not a man to anger.

A swirling cloud of dust trailed a white Mercedes as it veered around several old oil barrels. The sedan climbed onto the landing strip, and the driver gunned its engine, sending the rear end fishtailing and spitting gravel bullets. It screeched to a stop just inside the compound.

Dressed neatly in pressed tan fatigues, a red and white checkered headscarf secured in place with black headband encircling his head, a green-eyed man stepped from the rear seat.

The two sentries snapped to attention.

"Good evening, brother warriors," Ali bin al-Dosari said in a gentle voice. "All is well, I trust?" Not a kind man, he understood the importance of appearing interested in those serving him.

"Yes!" the taller of the two guards replied, stepping aside, allowing al-Dosari to pass.

As he turned to the purpose of his visit, al-Dosari's thoughts hardened. He would attempt to extract information from the stubborn goat one final time. Striding purposefully into the windowless building, he nearly gagged on the stifling air polluted by putrid water, urine, blood, and human excrement. Al-Dosari walked over and kicked the human clump on the floor.

"I see things have gone well for you."

Groaning, Ahmed Mansour peered up through swollen, nearly closed eyes. *My interrogator is back!*

"Are you ready for our promised chat?" Al-Dosari motioned to the two guards.

Before the small man replied, they beset him, kicking him savagely. A boot to the mouth shattered his few remaining teeth, which he swallowed. He vomited the pieces back up.

"That should give you something to chew on. I forgot," al-Dosari sneered, "you lack teeth." The man turned to the guards. "Leave us!"

The two sentries bolted out the door.

The interrogation lasted close to an hour. The diminutive man gave no information because he had none. It no longer mattered. Al-Dosari told the condemned microbiologist the awful truth, explaining his plan in detail to Mansour.

The spray of hot urine on Mansour's face barely registered as he blacked out.

Al-Dosari walked outside and scraped excrement off his shoes. "When he comes to, tell him my men are having their way with his family, especially his children. Then beat him to death. Make it painful."

"Yes, as you command!" the heavyset guard bowed reverently. Ali bin al-Dosari climbed into the back seat.

The driver threw the Mercedes in gear and hit the gas. Exiting the compound, he turned onto the airstrip. Accelerating, the sedan evaporated into the darkness.

CHAPTER FOURTEEN

THE C-17'S APPROACH INTO Cyprus evoked memories of McEwan's last visit to the small island nation. While assigned to Beirut, McEwan made regular roundtrips to the village of Larnaca and on his final trip, a Hezbollah-fired RPG—fortunately a dud—struck his helicopter near Beirut International Airport. Sometime during the pilot's evasive jinking and hard landing, McEwan damaged two lower back disks that still hurt far too frequently. Pushing aside the unpleasant memory, he went forward and looked out through the cockpit windshield. Taxiing off the main runway, the C-17 trailed an RAF jeep with a brightly lit "Follow Me" sign like an elephant lumbering behind its keeper. When the engines stopped, McEwan returned to the cargo area to collect his gear. A booming voice caught his attention.

"Well, now, look who the Air Force has dragged in! *You're* 'Neil Burns'?" Grinning from ear to ear, an extremely large, heavily muscled US Marine tromped up the ramp. Meeting halfway, the Marine gripped McEwan's right hand tightly with his massive mitts, and the two men shook hands. "How long's it been, bro?"

"I can't say for sure, Jason, but definitely too long." McEwan took the arrival of Major Jason "No Middle Name" Cartwright, US Marine Corps, as a good omen. When he'd learned the MARSOC Raiders were involved, he hoped it would be Cartwright's unit. Though they had been friends for several years, this was their first joint op together.

The African American Cartwright descended from the Gullahs who inhabited the coastal islands of South Carolina. After four years as a defensive tackle for the USC Gamecocks, Cartwright passed up the high dollars of the NFL for a career in the Marines. It was a perfect match. In addition to a master's degree in organizational leadership, he possessed in abundance the attributes of the finest Marine Corps officers: resolute, fearless, decisive, and when required, ruthlessly efficient. Cartwright's rich-caramel patina allowed him to pass as a Middle Easterner, except for his perfectly shaved dome and enormous frame. An Arab headdress could disguise the former, but little could be done about the latter—he stood out in every crowd.

On the personal side, Cartwright's spirited nature matched his oversized physique. A syrupy Southern drawl laced with politeness and charm effectively countered his menacing appearance, enchanting the fairer sex. Though able to turn off the accent at will, his Southern roots invariably reemerged after "knocking back a few". His tough-as-nails facade aside, his love of America, the US Marine Corps, and his friends ran deep, and he counted McEwan in the friend column.

Turning to the man standing behind him, Cartwright grinned. "This is Captain Juan Humberto Lopez. I call him Don Juan, but he prefers Hubie."

McEwan extended his hand to the recruiting poster Marine—lean, muscular, and hardy in an All-American way. Obviously, the handsome Lopez was a ladies' man. "Good to meet you."

Lopez's grip was strong. "I'm accustomed to abuse from my CO, so call me what you wish."

Cartwright good-humoredly rolled his eyes and bowed with an exaggerated sweep.

McEwan grabbed his rifle case, and the Marines carried the rest of his equipment. The three men stomped down the ramp and turned to business.

"Jason, how'd you get tapped for this?"

"We were the closest SOCOM unit that could do the op. We just finished a joint deal with the Brits and got the orders when we landed at Akrotiri. Once we're done with your thing, it'll be a C-17 back to Lejeune."

Conversation and laughter greeted the men as they entered the hangar, ceasing abruptly upon Cartwright's appearance. He led McEwan to a group of tables where Marines analyzed integrated intelligence, surveillance, and reconnaissance data supporting the operation. The ISR platform included satellites, unmanned aircraft systems—drones, and pre-positioned reconnaissance teams. In the background, radio traffic provided the soundtrack. The developers and approvers of Steel Trap, along with Theater Special Operations and Central Command-Forward headquarters in Qatar, were monitoring the same platform.

Cartwright conferred briefly with his officers and senior NCOs, then faced his Marines. "Men, this is the individual I briefed you about earlier. He'll bring us up to speed on the in-extremis hostage rescue and our high-value target."

McEwan hit the high points. Dr. Ahmed Mansour, a US bioweapons expert, had been abducted by a terrorist named al-Dosari, who was holding Mansour in the Bekaa Valley. He explained they had little intel on al-Dosari and they were operating in the blind with no photos. He provided minimal information about the threatened attack on America. McEwan returned the baton to Cartwright, who handed the briefing over to Lopez.

"H-hour is set for 04:00 tomorrow. We inserted two scout sniper teams a few hours ago. Sierra 1 has the compound overwatch and Sierra 2 is positioned overlooking the north end of the airfield. They hoofed it in to five hundred meters then leopard-crawled the rest of the way—"

McEwan pictured the teams' stealthy approach, first on foot, then belly-crawling and slithering inch by inch to their positions. Compromise was always a concern whenever deep-penetration operations occurred in enemy territory. Despite precision-guided ordnance, close proximity to the target area increased the risk of a friendly fire incident.

"Satcom links are up and running, and there's no indication they're onto us. Weather is clear and slightly hazy."

They all feared blinding dust storms, which could scrub or doom their mission, as occurred in Iran decades earlier during the attempted rescue of the US Embassy hostages.

"When's your next situation report?"

Lopez glanced at his watch. "Next sitrep is nine minutes. The target objective consists of three concrete structures clustered inside a walled compound on the southern tip of the airfield. The largest of the three—target building 1—is a two-story structure billeting at least thirty guards equipped with small arms. The barracks almost totally blocks access to building 2, which we believe is the HVT's headquarters. Your hostage is in building 3, a single-room structure.

"Foot patrols suggest booby traps ring the perimeter walls, except for the rear of the compound, which backs up to an oil pit. This leaves frontal assault our only option. We'll launch a backpack drone to provide updated intel prior to our arrival. After overwatch sanitizes the area, we'll do a hard hit on the barracks then kick in the doors on the other two. Burns, once we own the ground, Master Sergeant Duke Jess will lead you in—stick to his back pocket. When the objective is secured, the command-and-control bird will set the major here." His pointer landed on an X on the photo.

"What about al-Dosari?" McEwan voiced the question on everyone's mind.

"We don't know. At 19:00 local, Sierra 1 reported the arrival at the compound of a white Mercedes sedan. The back seat occupant, not further identified, entered the hostage building and exited fifty-five minutes later. The guards bowed reverently at the man, who climbed into the rear seat of the sedan. It sped off and hasn't been seen since. JSOC assesses with high probability it was al-Dosari, due to the reverence shown to him by the others present."

McEwan shot Cartwright a glance and received one in return, each with the same thought: *If al-Dosari has come and gone, will he return? If not, where is he?*

"ISR shows two sentries at the compound entrance with the rest of the guards racked out for the night. There's currently no activity in the HVT's quarters. Moving to the north end of the airfield, a company-size force is housed in a barracks next to the control tower." Lopez's laser again landed on the photo.

"Initial intel was Lebanese Army. Sierra 2 has since advised all are military-age, jihadi-type males. JSOC has designated them as heavily armed enemy combatants who pose an imminent threat. They must have had some type of celebration in town. Three hours ago, they returned to the airfield in troop trucks amid a lot of laughter and stumbling about. ISR opines they're all shit-faced—'scuse me, intoxicated. As of the last sitrep, everybody's crashed up north."

"Not surprising," McEwan said. "A lot of these guys are cowards who hide behind religious robes. Some of them can outdrink just about anybody on liberty."

Cartwright interjected, "Maybe my Bible-thumpers, but not ole Duke. He'd leave a slew of can carcasses on his way to another beer run."

Beaming broadly, Master Sergeant Jess relished the ribbing, and the ensuing laughter lightened the mood considerably.

Lopez went on. "Estimated flying time to target is seventy minutes. The package we're laying on has us going in with seven aircraft, including the command-and-control UH-1Y Venom Super Huey. Two AH-1Z Viper Super Cobra attack helicopters will fly close air support, and three MV-22 Ospreys will off-load teams near the front of the compound. A fourth Osprey will have a blocking force, evacuate any casualties, and exfil both of our prepositioned teams. An EA-18G Growler from the *Abraham Lincoln* will implement electronic countermeasures. Two of its F-18Es have a surprise for anybody else who shows up; one of them will give the combatants on the north end a free ride to paradise. Once we have boots on the ground, we plan no more than fifteen minutes on target. We'll haul ass to Tel Aviv, gas up on the military side of Ben Gurion, and return to Akrotiri. Except for the two sentries, the objective is buttoned up for the night. We're confident we've covered all bases."

McEwan silently agreed. There was no fly-by-the-seat-of-the-pants angle to this extraordinarily well-choreographed plan, consistent with USSOCOM's penchant for thoroughness.

Lopez pointed his thumb over his shoulder at the Marines working the computers. "We've hacked into the power grid controlling a twenty-mile radius around Baalbek, which includes Rayak. They'll shut it down at H-hour."

McEwan looked up. "After we rescue Mansour and snatch the HVT, I want the men to conduct sensitive site exploitation—search and seize all computers, flash drives, cell phones, and documents about the threat or anything mentioning al-Dosari or the Sword aliases."

Cartwright nodded and ordered the SSE.

McEwan added, "I have to get my hands on al-Dosari. The most recent intel indicates he's not there, so we wait. When he returns, we snatch him and anybody with him. If he's a no-show, it's a hostage rescue—I must return with Mansour."

Cartwright announced, "Both Sierra units report they've been watching a set of headlights for about two clicks and it's just turned onto the airfield road. They'll let us know if it's the same car."

Four minutes later, Cartwright read his computer tablet again. "It's the same white Mercedes."

McEwan responded instantly. "Is al-Dosari in it?"

"Three men got out of the sedan; two stayed with the car. They didn't get a look at the third man but believe he's your guy because he went inside the building we believe is his quarters. Should we give it a go?"

"Hell, yes!" McEwan growled.

Cartwright turned to his communicators. "Advise JSOC that I'm issuing the 'go' order immediately based on local intel."

To the rest of his Raiders, Cartwright spoke with fire in his eyes. "Now let's go whack those sonsabitches!"

CHAPTER FIFTEEN

FIFTY MINUTES INTO OPERATION Steel Trap, the tight formation of seven aircraft skimmed the surface of the Mediterranean Sea. Twenty-five nautical miles west of the Lebanese coastline, the heliborne assault force banked north in unison, invisible to both the naked eye and enemy radar installations. Loitering above, the EA-18G Growler jammed the air defense systems of the Iranian, Russian, Lebanese, and Syrian armed forces and anyone else snooping at that hour.

Escorting the flight were the two Viper attack helicopters, lethal killing machines slung with three-barrel rotating 20 mm cannons, missiles, and rockets. Three Osprey tilt-rotor aircraft ferried McEwan, Lopez, and the Marine Raiders along with their US Navy Special Amphibious Reconnaissance corpsmen. Following in the moonlit night were the exfil Osprey and Cartwright's command-and-control Venom. Undetected, the aircraft banked sharply east inland over the sparsely populated insertion corridor.

McEwan glanced around at the equipment-laden Marines strapped into troop seats. Faces darkened with camouflage paint, each wore USSOCOM's latest-generation helmet and full battle dress with state-of-the-art weaponry and equipment. All carried sidearms, and most had short-barreled close-quarter combat carbines similar to McEwan's. A handful carried light machine guns or semiautomatic shotguns loaded with high-explosive slugs. Certainly intimidating, McEwan knew the Marines were even more lethal than they appeared.

McEwan watched Captain Hubie Lopez toggle between screens on his computer tablet displaying tactical data, satellite and thermal images, and video feeds. One screen showed GPS overlays atop a picture of the airfield. Another streamed close-range video from the tiny drone circling above the target area. He knew the military chain of command at various locations, along with the president and senior leaders in DC, were watching the attack. Real-time audio and video of the raid would be transmitted by the operators' helmet cameras. McEwan spied a flashing message on the screen but couldn't read its contents.

McEwan mentally narrated the thermal images on Lopez's tablet. *Two roving sentries at south end compound ... numerous sleeping men building 1 ... one person building 2 ... the dead man al-Dosari ... single stationary form building 3 ... if Ahmed were dead there'd be no heat signature.*

Cartwright's voice entered McEwan's ears, communicating with Sierra 1, the overwatch team positioned at the south end. "You've got two movers no more than two hundred meters to your ten o'clock. You'll acquire them in four ... three ... two ... *now.*"

The sniper team whispered in reply, "Roger, we've got 'em on scope."

Cartwright ordered Sierra 2 to light up its target on the north end.

Acknowledging the command, the second scout sniper team lit up the airstrip's northern barracks using a Special Operations Forces Laser Acquisition Marker.

McEwan's ears hissed as the Raider commander issued the execute order. The Ospreys went to full power, streaking inbound toward their target. The Vipers broke off to cover the assault force.

McEwan watched Lopez tap another quick key sequence. Lopez thrust the "V" sign in the air. "Two minutes!" crackled over the internal radio net.

H-hour.

CHAPTER SIXTEEN

THE PALE GLOW OF a dangling cigarette illuminated the guard's face. Turning toward the odd gurgling sound, he stiffened in shock watching his fellow sentry's knees buckle, blood gushing from an all but severed neck. The man fell forward, dead. The startled guard did not foresee his own demise in the split second between recognizing the threat and his final breath. A second projectile fired by the Marine sniper replaced his cigarette, caving in the guard's face and decorating the building with a mixture of blood and brain chunks.

"Both hostiles down" filled the airwaves. "Target is clean. You have a green LZ."

"Roger," Cartwright shot back, "eyes on target. One minute."

The thundering arrival of the assault force was the last sound ever heard by the terrorists on the north end of the airfield. McEwan snapped his eyes shut to avoid the searing yellow-and-red explosion. He opened them as the dust cloud disappeared, revealing a huge hole of smoldering rubble. In seconds, a one-thousand-pound Mk 83 bomb from an F-18E had erased the control tower, barracks, and all occupants on the north end of the landing strip.

McEwan's ears crackled with radio transmissions of "Go! Go! Go!" as the assault force landed on the southern edge of the airfield.

Pouring onto the runway from Osprey ramps, the Marines broke into assault, defensive, and security teams. The two Vipers blew by above the deck at a hundred knots. The methodical advance of the main assault element resembled a fast-moving tidal wave about to crash into the compound.

AK-47 chatter erupted as McEwan hit the ground.

The Raiders responded with extreme violence—a furious hailstorm of gunfire that raked the barracks and eliminated the shooter.

Grenade launchers thumped and the white Mercedes sedan exploded. Two half-dressed guards hurtled in the air. Their burning bodies rained down, followed by flaming debris.

Lopez dispatched orders for Master Sergeant Jess, Gunnery Sergeant Griffin, and Staff Sergeants Fox, Elbaum, and Lundblad. "There's about twenty left in the barracks. I'm sending a rocket through the front door. Once the dust clears, move out."

In seconds, a Viper-launched rocket slammed into the structure. The building's face collapsed, exposing its rooms and occupants. Through dust and debris, McEwan saw several insurgents trying to regain their feet. The helo pilot opened up with his 20 mm minigun, cutting them down midrise. The deadly *bbrraaaap* sounded again, eviscerating another band of scrambling militants. The attack helicopter hovered menacingly, seeking additional targets. Finding none, it pivoted and broke contact.

With the skin of the building peeled back like a sardine can, McEwan watched the entire show, ably managed by the Raiders' NCOs. Elbaum's team trained their weapons on the front of the barracks, unleashing a torrent of suppressive fire.

Lundblad's team bolted single file, taking up an ambush position behind the barracks. Two Marines provided rear security for the team, aiming their rifles at the al-Dosari headquarters building next door, waiting for its lone occupant to appear.

Storming the barracks from the front, Fox's team blazed its way inside. Breaking down doors, tossing grenades, and firing well-aimed shots, they eliminated resistance room by room. About a dozen remaining guards fled out the rear of the barracks. Trapped in a kill box between Lundblad and Fox's teams, they met their fate.

A trigger-puller himself, McEwan wasn't easily impressed, having participated in numerous ops with other tier one operators. However, the high degree of speed, shot placement, and target elimination demonstrated by the Raiders was noteworthy.

McEwan's peripheral vision caught movement: *Straggler … escaping through first-floor window.* Raising his MK18, McEwan fired a single round. The guard's head exploded and he crumbled to the ground.

"I forgot to mention," Master Sergeant Jess said approvingly, "feel free to use that thing anytime."

Following Gunny Griffin's lead, Lundblad's team breached al-Dosari's headquarters. Barely a minute later, Griffin transmitted, "Building two secure. We've got a live one—the HVT."

"Objective is secure!" Lopez broadcast. "Hang on to him, Gunny. I'm on the way."

As quickly as it began, the overwhelming assault was over. The Raiders owned the ground.

The all-clear sign propelled McEwan to action, sprinting full steam toward Ahmed Mansour's prison. As he approached the second building, Gunny Griffin emerged dragging a bloodied, kicking, and screaming man by the scruff of his neck: *al-Dosari*. McEwan bolted past, intent on rescuing Ahmed. The next transmissions almost stopped him in his tracks.

"The live one is not our jackpot."

"Say again your last?" Cartwright responded.

"Repeat, he doesn't appear to be the high-value target."

"Do a quick check of the KIAs. I'm setting down. Where's Burns?"

McEwan kicked his legs into overdrive. Reaching Mansour's building, he launched in the air and the force of his full weight dislodged the door, knocking it off its frame. Rolling inside and springing upright, McEwan scanned left and right. His weapon-mounted white light locked on a feral clump in the corner of the room, lying naked in a pool of blood, urine, and feces.

Blinking back at Kyle McEwan were hollow, expressionless eyes, barely distinguishable from the mass of welts, bruises, and cuts. *Oh my God! These savages beat you to a pulp!* Slinging his rifle around his back, McEwan fell to his knees and picked up Mansour, cradling the frail man gently and carrying him outside.

A Navy SARC corpsman raced up, and together the two men laid him down gingerly.

The corpsman began working furiously out of his medical pack. In seconds, he had two IV lines running, one into Mansour's neck and the other into an arm. Checking Mansour's heartbeat with a stethoscope, the corpsman dropped it and rhythmically began compressing the doctor's chest to reinflate his lungs. As he looked over his shoulder at McEwan, the corpsman's small shake of his head from side to side said it all: *He's dying.*

"Okay, Doc, give me some room." McEwan waved the corpsman away. Ripping off his headgear, McEwan leaned over his friend. "Ahmed, I'm here!"

"Oh, Kyle? Can it be you?" Mansour looked in disbelief at McEwan through swollen eyes. "Look what they have done to me!"

"Who did this, Ahmed? Who?" McEwan propped up the battered and ravaged body.

"Come closer … your ears only …" Ahmed looked pointedly above McEwan's head.

Following Ahmed's gaze, McEwan found Cartwright standing over his shoulder. He jerked his head and the commander retreated.

"A man named al-Dosari!" he uttered, spraying foamy blood.

"Ali bin al-Dosari?"

"Yes … calls himself Saifulislam!"

McEwan cringed, recognizing the Arabic phrase for the Sword of Islam. "Is he here?"

"Gone."

"Why did he do this to you?"

Mansour spasmed, coughing up more foamy blood. "Night and day … always the same … 'Who knows of my plan?'"

"What plan?" McEwan puzzled.

"Asked if … Americans capable … stopping his plan …" Ahmed coughed. "Help me … lungs filling …"

McEwan compassionately repositioned his friend against the wall. "Take it easy, Ahmed. I need to know about his plan."

"Hunting my team of microbiologists … virologists …" Mansour halted, coughing violently. "Epidemiologists …"

"Is his target America?"

Mansour gave a wave of his hand. "Yes … Sword murdered Pasteur scientist … stole virus … my team could stop him … Davies CDC … carjacking … all dead … I am last …"

McEwan's neck hairs tingled as Mansour verified his research and Jamil El-Harith's warning. "Is it Ebola?"

Shaking his head no, Mansour struggled for air. "Smallpox …"

"He has *smallpox*?" Cold fear contracted McEwan's chest.

"Yes, much worse …" Mansour could not stop coughing. Bloody foam reappeared, his breaths growing shallower, his respirations wet and audible.

McEwan bit his lip. *The death rattle. Every word might be his last.* He readjusted Mansour, trying to improve his breathing, but the end was near. "Ahmed, I need more."

Mansour pushed himself. "He has weaponized it!"

"Are you certain? Is it resistant to our vaccine and antibiotics?"

"Yes … he has vaccine for Muslims only …" Convulsions wracked Mansour.

"Where is it, Ahmed?"

"Africa … Hala'ib Triangle."

"What does he look like, Ahmed?"

Mansour pushed with finality. "Very handsome … flawless skin … dark like Spaniard … evil green eyes … a killer … come closer …"

McEwan listened intently as Ahmed spoke into his ear, his words barely decipherable, but clear enough to paint a complete picture. The need to end Ahmed's suffering far outweighed McEwan's need for more information. "Thank you for your help, my friend."

"Please, Kyle ..." Ahmed gurgled. "My family ..."

"I have them, they are safe. I will care for them as if they are my own."

"My ... brother ... thank you."

"Now go in peace to God."

The light flickered from Ahmed Mansour's eyes as he expelled his last breath.

You have not died in vain, Ahmed. I will avenge you. He handed Mansour's body to the corpsman. McEwan stood, his face morphing from sad to rage-filled in a fraction of a second. Storming around the building, he found Ahmed's torturer at the feet of Cartwright, Jess, and Griffin.

The terrorist read the murderous look in McEwan's eyes: he was a dead man.

"Leave us," McEwan growled.

Master Sergeant Jess and Gunny Griffin froze for a split second, long enough to draw a blistering tirade from Cartwright. Both Marines left the area.

Grabbing the torturer by his hair, McEwan hauled him out of sight behind the building. The man screeched, his words incomprehensible but his message clear. He was begging for his life.

"I'm pulling the plug on this op," Cartwright's voice snapped in McEwan's earpiece. "Where the hell are my Marines?"

"Loading up" was the instant response.

"Get this show on the road!" The Raider commander ordered. He approached McEwan from the rear. "Don't do him here. Let's take the asshole alive and get everything he knows."

"I'll get what I need now. Just makes sure Ahmed's on your helo and wait for me."

The man staring pointedly at Cartwright wasn't Kyle McEwan but an alter ego. "Call when you're ready." The Marine trotted toward the front of the compound.

McEwan leaned over the terrorist. "You're going to die. It can be peaceful or painful. Your choice. But you will tell me what I want to know."

Unable to decipher the words, the man's eyes registered fear from the inflection.

Powerful rotors thundered, filling the air. "So you don't speak English? I'll help you understand." He drew his Glock; it spit once, turning the terrorist's left knee into a mishmash of bloody tissue and bone fragments.

The man rocked back and forth, screaming and cursing.

McEwan's linguistically attuned ear detected an urban Damascus dialect—*Syrian*. Holstering his pistol, McEwan addressed the terrorist in his native tongue.

"Now, you'll answer. Where is the Sword?"

Astonished by his nemesis speaking his language, the man whimpered.

McEwan stamped his boot down on the man's knee, evoking another wail. "I said, where is the Sword?"

Ahmed's torturer replied instantly in a high-pitched voice. "He has already departed!"

McEwan's earpiece crackled—the Marines were withdrawing. He applied more pressure to the mangled knee. "Is he going to attack America?"

The terrorist shrieked but managed to nod yes.

"Is he carrying a virus?"

Receiving no response, McEwan ground the terrorist's knee with the heel of his boot until it nearly severed. "Unless you want this to happen to your other leg, you'll answer me. What is he using to carry out the attack?"

"I do not know," the terrorist moaned, "but it is deadly."

McEwan reached down and yanked the terrorist up by his throat and squeezed his windpipe until it almost crushed. Dropping him, McEwan kicked the man in the testicles.

The howling terrorist grabbed his scrotum and wailed, "Stop! I will tell you all I know."

Several questions later, he had all the remaining details the torturer possessed. McEwan was finished with the killer.

"This is for my friend!" He ground one last time on the knee, detaching the lower leg from the thigh.

Al-Dosari's disciple screamed defiantly. "The Sword of Islam will succeed in Allah's name!"

"No, by my God, he will fail," came McEwan's deadly whisper.

Hatred oozing from every pore, McEwan drew his pistol and pointed it at the middle of the terrorist's forehead. Their eyes locked. All jihadist bravado vanished—the man no longer wanted to die a martyr. He begged McEwan to spare him.

"There are no seventy-two virgins where you're going, you piece of shit. You'll burn in hell right beside the Sword."

McEwan pressed the trigger.

CHAPTER SEVENTEEN

IT WAS LATE WHEN Ali bin al-Dosari departed the Bekaa Valley, even later when he left his Damascus safe house for the flight to Saudi Arabia. Traveling now by vehicle through a sparsely populated area south of Riyadh, he was flooded with a host of emotions. Sinking back in the seat of the Land Cruiser, memories of the terrible night rekindled his hatred.

Al-Dosari never told anyone about the recurring nightmares that tormented him, reliving the horror of his parents' obliteration by bombs from US Navy warplanes and the massive guns of the USS *New Jersey*. While he survived unscathed, his younger brother Yousef was severely wounded. Ali remained by his brother's side day and night until Yousef was well enough to leave the makeshift hospital in the Bekaa Valley. Although barely school-age, the brothers vowed to avenge the deaths of their martyred parents.

Surviving those first weeks was an ordeal. The two rag-clad boys shuffled between refugee camps, scavenging food from garbage dumps. One blessed day a religious leader, Sheikh Zaid Abdel-Fattah, took pity on the young brothers. Taking them under his wing, he became their spiritual compass, teaching them the Sharia, the religious law of Islam. The sheikh was the first to realize Ali's unique talents—encouraging his development, he set Ali on his course with destiny.

Ali recalled the sheikh's declarations: "Allah has chosen you to strike terror in his name. If the apostates seduced by the infidels' filth and immoral behavior do not submit to him, pierce the hearts of all disbelievers with the Sword of Allah. There is a caveat, Ali. To deceive the infidels' intelligence agencies and shield you from detection, you will do your duty only as 'Terror's Sword'. One day your humility and self-restraint will be rewarded when all come to know that Ali bin al-Dosari is Allah's messenger of vengeance. The son of Aamir bin al-Dosari the Sunni and Aisyah, daughter of Ali Reza Shihab the Shi'a, will be celebrated as Islam's greatest warrior."

Ali undertook his responsibilities with zeal, finding he liked the power, respect, and affinity others attached to his mystical nom de guerre. In Islamic circles, the reputation of Terror's Sword grew in direct proportion to the number of his righteous killings of the blasphemers and the infidels who massacred innocent Muslim men, women, and children. Buoyed by his growing moral authority, al-Dosari eloquently and persuasively recruited others to kill for him. And they did, willingly and without remorse, allowing him to remain masked while taking credit for their deeds.

On the sheikh's deathbed, his mentor reinforced Ali's role: "Allah will enlighten you when you have fulfilled your obligations to him as Terror's Sword. You will become the Almighty's Sword of Islam in the eyes of the world. You are blessed—he will be your guide to paradise."

While fully embracing the sheikh's final words, mere proselytizing did not vanquish his deep fires of revenge. Many killings and years of preparation had brought him to this moment. His commitments to Allah as Terror's Sword now satisfied, al-Dosari no longer needed the security afforded by anonymity. The infidels' day of atonement had arrived. His brilliant plan would inflict retribution, reaping him both the glory and recognition he so richly deserved as the Almighty's Sword of Islam.

Breaking his reverie, al-Dosari glanced at his driver. When he got into the vehicle at the airport, he had commanded silence. Now he addressed the man. "Are they prepared for me?"

"Yes, Saifulislam!"

Sohaib Abassi held the highly sought position of chief mechanic for a priceless collection of automobiles owned by the powerful governor of Riyadh, Prince Sultan Safaa bin Al Saud, nephew of the ironfisted ruling monarch of Saudi Arabia.

Taking his responsibilities seriously, Abassi often tested the prince's armored vehicles on this remote stretch of road in the Saudi desert south of Riyadh. He put each car through a series of demanding evasive maneuvers and tests, knowing someday it might have to outrun assassins. The blistering sun in the hotter months pushed desert temperatures to unbearable levels during the day, forcing Abassi to test the cars after sundown, when it was substantially cooler, like tonight. Then there was the powdery sand—it got into everything, affecting performance.

Abassi's pulse quickened at the unexpected glint of headlights in his rearview mirror. In over nine years, he had never seen another automobile on this stretch of road at night. Abassi realized the vehicle was traveling extremely fast, creeping closer each time he checked his mirrors. Only twenty miles of flat road from the safety of Prince Sultan Air Base, he was unconcerned. The specially constructed Bentley Continental Flying Spur was capable of sustaining a top speed of 314 kilometers, or 195 miles per hour. The mechanic confidently pushed the Flying Spur over 200 kilometers, 125 miles per hour. Confusingly, the gap did not widen—it continued narrowing.

In the distance ahead, Abassi saw a set of flashing headlights—actually, two sets of headlights. He eased off the accelerator. *Two cars blocking the road. An accident? Military vehicles?* He slowed the car rapidly, then remembered the one behind him, suddenly positioned on his bumper, lights flashing. *I am trapped! Penned in!* Abassi braked forcefully, sliding the Bentley to a stop. Several men came up from behind the cars, pointing guns; one of them commanded him to exit. Petrified, he watched a man in a flowing white robe approach in his side-view mirror.

The man tapped nonchalantly on the window using a ring on the middle finger of his left hand. "You will not be harmed, Sohaib. We wish only to talk."

He knows my name! Bandits! They want money! Seeing no choice, Abassi stepped out. Instantly grabbed by two men and marched over to a car, they slammed him down on its hood. Flopped over, Abassi was spread-eagle, his arms held firmly. The man in the white robe punched him in the solar plexus and assaulted his stomach and kidneys with blows.

Released, Abassi plopped to the ground. Immobilized by a foot planted squarely in the middle of his back, he was pinned face down. A hand reached in between his legs and the mechanic's world exploded in pain. His testicles in a vise grip, Abassi heard a low, menacing voice.

"Sohaib, I have a proposition for you."

Abassi struggled mightily to focus. "W-what is it you want from me?"

Grinning evilly, the Sword of Islam told him.

CHAPTER EIGHTEEN

HAVING WATCHED THE BEKAA Valley raid live, those present in the White House situation room—including the president—held out hope that McEwan had prevented the threat from reaching America's shores. After consulting JSOC at Ft. Bragg, SecDef Samuel K. Wilson, and JCS chairman General Cameron T. Fuller, US Marine Corps, along with DNI Daniela Sanchez, officially conveyed the outcome. The man referred to by the various Sword soubriquets was positively identified as Ali bin al-Dosari, but McEwan and MARSOC missed capturing him in Lebanon. Whereabouts unknown, he remained free to attack America.

Englewood finally understood what it was like to be a prizefighter being pummeled against the ropes. Rubbing his temples did nothing to relieve the stress hammering his brain. "Frankly, I don't see how matters can get any worse."

"Unfortunately, sir, it has. Dr. Mansour revealed the bioweapon is a virulent form of vaccine-resistant smallpox, manufactured at a pharmaceutical facility under al-Dosari's control in Africa. Mansour believed al-Dosari is there now preparing his attack."

Englewood blew his stack, looking pointedly at his defense secretary. "Sam, I can't imagine we have a plan on the shelf to level this Hala'ib Triangle place, so get one made quickly. I want it cleaned out and destroyed."

"Yes, sir, Mr. President."

"Dust off plans for Khartoum. If those bastards get in our way, I'll bomb 'em back to the Stone Age. If I need the military on the home front, I want Northern Command prepared to ramp up an exercise for a domestic bioweapon attack. I'm saying this only once: Danni calls the shots. No Pentagon tap-dancing. You provide the muscle—we do this together."

"Aye, aye, Mr. President!" The powerfully built, barrel-chested Marine snapped.

"Danni, have DHS and HHS put the wheels in motion to roll out a simulated national disaster exercise."

"Yes, sir, right away."

The president pushed his chair back and stood, causing the others to spring to their feet. Nelson J. Englewood was no longer the courtly Southern gentleman but a leader obsessed with protecting his country. "That man threw down the gauntlet when he targeted us with a WMD. I will destroy him and any country supporting him."

Face flushed with rage, Englewood stormed from the Situation Room.

A professional warrior, Jason Cartwright had long accepted the worst but unavoidable aspect of military command: in combat, good men and women under your command die. Watching a defenseless friend die from torture was quantitatively different. McEwan's drawn face, stooped shoulders, and low-hanging head telegraphed that what he was feeling was personal. The MARSOC commander knew McEwan's ability to purge himself of guilt would determine whether Mansour's death became an unfortunate memory or a destructive event haunting him. The Marine let him work through his grief alone.

McEwan remained withdrawn throughout the flight to Lod military air base in Tel Aviv. The Venom's landing jolted McEwan back to the present.

"Jason, I'd like to speak with your Marines."

The purging begins. Cartwright read a message handed to him. "Okay, we've gotta make a call first. Follow me."

McEwan and Cartwright entered an Israeli Air Force hangar and crossed to a makeshift communications unit placed atop a crate.

Cartwright grabbed the handset and announced their presence over the encrypted link.

"Stand by one," came the reply.

Seconds later, both men recognized the booming voice. "O'Brien, here. Is Burns with you?"

"Yes, sir."

"National Command Authority has ordered MARSOC to capture the HVT at his Hala'ib Triangle lab. You will conduct SSE to seize evidence and any bioagents and vaccine you find."

Looking at the map spread out before them, McEwan and Cartwright spotted the area in the northeast corner of Sudan on the Egyptian border.

"You're cleared to overfly Egyptian airspace; you'll skirt along the Gulf of Aqaba and rendezvous with the Twenty-Sixth MEU in the Red Sea. After we hammer out the assault plan, we'll send it to you aboard the *Bataan*. Questions?"

"Negative, sir," the Marine commander replied.

The link terminated with JSOC at Fort Bragg.

Cartwright turned to McEwan. "I'll do a quick muster and advise my men about round 2. Address them during the briefing on the ship."

Aboard the amphibious assault ship USS *Bataan*, all hands received their first hot chow since Cyprus. Fed and hydrated, the Marines cleaned weapons and refreshed gear.

Having been briefed on the deployment order and final details by JSOC, Cartwright moved to the front of the bay. "Listen up. We're conducting another mission to capture al-Dosari and seize critical materials. The objective is an abandoned tanning factory on the outskirts of Hala'ib, a port city here." He circled an area of East Africa on the Sudan-Egypt border.

"A SEAL sniper team from Camp Lemonnier in Djibouti was inserted an hour ago. They're providing intel from an airstrip adjacent to the target area. Within the hour, we'll drop one of our scout sniper teams to link up with them. At H-hour, these prepositioned units will sanitize and secure the facility perimeter and landing strip. We'll set down on the runway and move on foot approximately one hundred yards to assault the facility. Unlike Rayak, this is his pharmaceutical laboratory. We expect it to be hot with bioagents. SSE should produce incriminating documents and other forms of evidence. A C-130 from Djibouti will land and deposit cargo vehicles to transport whatever we seize back to the aircraft. After clearing the objective, a Navy sub off the coast of Somalia will destroy the facility. It's the same basic package we laid on for Rayak, except we will hit it in full MOPP protection gear and use biosensors to search the facility. Hubie will lead the main assault element consisting of Fox and Lundblad's teams."

A Marine raised his hand. "Is the HVT expected to be at this facility?"

"We're operating under the assumption he is." Seeing no more questions, Cartwright turned the show over to McEwan.

McEwan described the documents he expected to find, then voiced a concern. "It pains me to say, but it is imperative that I get my hands on a living and breathing al-Dosari. I must verify we've eliminated all bioagents, his ability to deliver them, and seize all infectious diseases and vaccines."

McEwan paused and inhaled deeply.

"I can't thank you enough for trying to save Dr. Mansour. He was a hero who gave his life not for his country but for ours. It wasn't in the cards for him to live, but thanks to you, he tasted freedom before going to his reward. It is my honor to go to battle with you men. God bless you all. America is fortunate to have you on her side."

Walking over to his friend, Cartwright clasped McEwan's hand in his and pulled him in for a bear hug, whispering, "Now, let's go put this asshole down and be done with it."

CHAPTER NINETEEN

McEWAN EXPERIENCED DÉJÀ VU, heading into his second kinetic military operation within a twenty-four-hour period. He hoped that it would be the last of this adventure.

Next to him, Cartwright watched a live drone feed on his computer tablet showing the landing strip and pharmaceutical factory.

The voice of the SEAL sniper responsible for sanitizing the airstrip came through McEwan's headset. "Four greeters are down. Your LZ is green; repeat green."

The prepositioned Raider scout sniper team at the pharmaceutical factory accomplished the same task and reported it. "Target is clean."

Receiving the second transmission, Cartwright ordered the assault. The formation descended rapidly and landed. Still airborne, McEwan watched dozens of Marines disgorge, the assault reminiscent of the earlier one at Rayak.

The Raider scout sniper team provided an update. "We've eliminated two more that exited. They must have heard you inbound."

McEwan watched scores of Marines in MOPP suits closing in on the factory. Lopez's voice crackled in his ear. "Entry door blown!" Gunfire punctuated subsequent transmissions. McEwan's and Cartwright's Venom streaked overhead as the ground attack continued.

It ended quickly.

"Objective is secure," Lopez transmitted.

"Roger, we're setting down."

Once the command-and-control helo landed, McEwan and Cartwright trotted over to a fence line where Master Sergeant Jess was speaking with two Navy SEALs.

Cartwright greeted the familiar Navy operators with a nod.

The older of the two SEALs spoke. "So far, it's been a walk in the park. We did four sentries here, and your boys took out six next door. You're good to go."

Cartwright gave a thumbs up and the two SEALs tromped off.

"Kyle, let's put a move on it, or they're liable to smoke your boy before we get there."

Sprinting to the factory, McEwan glanced periodically at the gargantuan Marine Raider, who, despite grunts, kept pace. Rounding a fence, they found Gunny Griffin, rifle slung over his shoulder, standing in front of a gaping hole that had replaced the building's entrance.

Cartwright spoke. "Casualties?"

"Two. I've got one with a broken ankle. Another's got a nick from an AK round on his thigh. Doc says they're okay."

"Resistance?"

"We caught 'em with their pants down. The snipers took out a handful, then capped two who moseyed outside. Two more were inside the lobby, but there wasn't much left of them once the 'boom-boom' blew the door. The rest of the sleeping beauties racked out in the back didn't put up much of a fight. No survivors."

McEwan interrupted. "What about al-Dosari?"

"Not yet."

"Have you found the virus?" McEwan's voice was strained.

"Hubie's men are still searching."

The SEAL from the airstrip radioed Cartwright. "Your C-130 is on the ground, and the transport vehicles are heading your way."

Lopez transmitted next. "We're not detecting smallpox anywhere in the building."

"Keep screening all floors. Have you seen anything unusual?"

"There's an odd room downstairs and a lab on the first floor."

"Okay. We're on our way in. Keep searching for the HVT."

Lopez called again. "I've found a shipping container in a room directly below the lobby."

"They were about to move it," McEwan speculated. "Our timing is good."

Cartwright whistled under his breath. "I must be livin' right for a change."

They sidestepped a line of Marines ferrying boxes. Lopez met them in the hall, hooded MOPP headgear in hand.

"What have you got, Hubie?" Cartwright asked.

"I think I've found the smallpox; it's secured in a room behind an old single-combo bank vault door."

The men turned the corner, passing two Marines standing post over a couple dozen dead bodies lined up along one side of the hallway.

McEwan noted none of them possessed the features described by Ahmed Mansour. "These guards look in good health and well-nourished by Sudanese standards. They've obviously been inoculated; otherwise, they'd be showing symptoms of infection. We'll take a couple of bodies with us to autopsy."

Cartwright called for Master Sergeant Jess. "Get two body bags down here on the double."

After descending a flight of stairs, they found Lopez standing in front of a steel door.

McEwan asked, "Can we crack this thing?"

"Negative." Lopez shook his head. "The door's at least four inches thick. We need to wire up the hinges and dial."

"Okay, do it," Cartwright added, "but don't blow our asses to kingdom come."

Lopez keyed his mic. "Kopp, front and center!"

A wiry Marine hustled up. Lopez explained the plan and Kopp set his breaching charges.

Cartwright growled, "Fall back!" Retreating down the hallway with McEwan, they took cover inside a stairwell. Satisfied everyone was shielded from the coming blast, he nodded.

Kopp responded, "Fire in the hole! Fire in the hole!"

Three synchronized explosions rocked the area, producing a shock wave along the entire length of the corridor that filled the air with debris. When the dust settled, McEwan peeked around the corner. Hinges and dial gone, the doorframe was twisted yet the door remained in place.

"What the hell?" Cartwright expressed his puzzlement aloud, adding over his shoulder to McEwan, "Go check it out."

As McEwan made for the vault, an odd sensation washed over him: he thought he detected the door move a fraction. Stepping forward, he squinted, focusing on the hinge holes. Eyes glued to the panel, it quivered slightly outward. McEwan instantly processed what was happening. *Somebody is pushing it from inside!* Before he could utter a warning, the door crashed to the floor. Two armed guards tumbled out.

Shouting "Gun!" McEwan swiveled and ripped off a burst with his MK18.

Each man's head exploded, splattering red mist and gray matter over the debris. A round discharged by a guard's rifle ricocheted off the wall.

With McEwan squarely in their field of fire, Cartwright and the other Raiders couldn't see the threat or react to McEwan's urgent warning.

Stepping over the bodies, McEwan entered the vault. "It's clear, Jason."

"I don't believe this!" Using his right index finger, the Marine applied pressure to a flesh wound in the meaty section of his left forearm. "And here I thought I was livin' right for a change!"

The stray AK-47 round found the largest target, grazing the Raider commander's rock-solid arm. "At least you gave these assholes a little instant payback!" Annoyed, Cartwright stepped into the vault. Glancing at McEwan, he said, "What's wrong?"

"This isn't good, Jason. Look."

Following McEwan's outstretched arm, Cartwright saw they were standing in a miniature biocontainment lab. Dead ahead was a cement-encased safe secured with a state-of-the-art dual-dial combo lock. Above the lock was a thick glass viewing port. Peering inside, Cartwright uttered, "It's his smallpox. Should we hit it with C-4?"

"Too risky. It'll go airborne; none of us are inoculated against it."

The F-18E pilot interrupted them with a call over the radio. "Looks like you've stirred up a hornet's nest. We count four troop trucks and two technicals loading up at a garrison about thirty miles west of your location. ETA unknown."

"Copied," Cartwright replied. Loading up technicals, or improvised fighting vehicles with heavy weapons, meant responding forces were more than curious—they expected a firefight on arrival. "Shadow the convoy. We'll hammer 'em if they get too close."

"Roger."

Cartwright spoke the obvious. "We're out of time and can't crack this safe or blow it. Hubie, send the coordinates to the Navy. Tell 'em to get ready to pulverize this place."

Lopez nodded and stepped aside to communicate with the Navy.

Sensing McEwan's irritation, he transmitted, "Duke, update us on the HVT search."

McEwan listened intently while Jess contacted each team leader. Thirty-nine KIAs, none of them al-Dosari, no one left for interrogation.

"Somewhere inside this facility is the key to deciphering al-Dosari's plan. We've got to find it. We can't leave until we do," McEwan told Cartwright.

As if on cue, Lopez transmitted, "You need to see what we've found upstairs."

Climbing the staircase two steps at a time, McEwan and Cartwright met Lopez and followed him down a hallway. They hustled past a line of Marines wheeling file cabinets and computers out of an office. Lopez bellowed, "Gunny, everything out front in five minutes!"

"You heard him, Marines!" Gunny Griffin snarled. "Get your asses in gear!"

Edging past the supply chain, they stopped at the doorway of a laboratory. Two MOPP-clad Marines were videotaping and digitally photographing the room.

McEwan's face blanched.

Cartwright caught the change. "Now what?"

"That's a freeze-drying device." McEwan pointed to an appliance sitting atop a lab table amid Petri dishes and microscopes. Another piece of equipment caught his eye. "Holy mother of god! An aerosol dispenser!" Suddenly, everything registered. "The bastard's going to spray it!"

Both men stood tongue-tied for a moment processing the scene. Cartwright spoke first. "You and I will head down to Djibouti with everything on the C-130. I'll have the MEU send over Mansour's remains."

"Thanks." For a brief time during the frenzy of the operation, his friend had slipped from McEwan's consciousness.

Within minutes, the vehicles loaded with the shipping container of vaccine, the freeze-drying and spraying instruments in a sealed Pelican case, along with computers, file cabinets, and two bodies, were airborne in the C-130. F-18Es covered the assault force withdrawal over the Red Sea.

Cartwright nudged McEwan, pointing. "Navy's doing its thing."

McEwan peered at the grainy picture on the computer tablet. "Tomahawk."

The submarine-launched cruise missile nose camera provided real-time video as it closed on target. The camera ceased transmission when the missile slammed into its target. Another view came on screen from a second Tomahawk as it closed in and plastered the remaining rubble. Switching to a satellite image showed the smoke clearing, leaving a crater several stories deep.

"It's done," Cartwright noted with satisfaction. Then his computer showed several troop trucks pulling up to the crater. "Aw, shit. There's no way of knowing if they got there before the fireworks or after. If before, the cat's outta the bag."

"I suspect we'll know before long."

CHAPTER TWENTY

RAMSEY ABD AL SHAMMARI, chief justice of the Egyptian Supreme Constitutional Court, strummed his fountain pen on the recent lower court decision. Despite binding precedents to the contrary, the judge in the case misapplied the law, triggering the appeal to Egypt's highest court. Well aware the Cairo legal community eagerly awaited his decision, al Shammari pushed the stack of papers across his mahogany partners desk. It would take longer to pen the opinion than he had now—it would have to wait until he returned from holiday.

Three minutes later, al Shammari strode through the ornate columns of the Supreme Constitutional Court building. Still spry, the chief jurist descended the long set of steps and emerged past wrought iron gates. Moving through the trendy Cairo Maadi neighborhood, he courteously hailed friends and colleagues with handshakes, hugs, and kisses. Those he greeted were unaware that behind al-Shammari's congenial demeanor resided a very lonely man. As he left the adoring crowds behind, his normal dark mood returned, causing him to lose track of his surroundings and walk past the café on Corniche el Nil. Only the spirited call of his name jolted the jurist from his melancholy. Resuming his outwardly buoyant persona, al Shammari retraced his steps toward the café owner, who seated him promptly.

Knowing the patron well, a server hastily produced a small pitcher of anise tea and piping hot plate of pita bread coated with coarse ground wheat. Slathering it with garlicky baba ghanoush, al Shammari devoured the bread along with a tabbouleh salad shrouded in lettuce. After he chewed the last bite, the stout aroma of charbroiled marinated lamb, roasted tomatoes, onions, and bell peppers floated out under his nose. The jurist attacked the food with zest, his thoughts turning to his imminent trip to Sharm el-Sheikh. His last.

Years earlier, on their first anniversary, al Shammari took his bride to the quaint fishing village on the sparkling waters of Naama Bay. Besotted with the shimmering jewel, the successful budding lawyer bought a tiny flat in the Old Market bazaar area. The young couple spent their final night in their new apartment conceiving a child. The family of three returned there every year until their son, Saad, became engrossed in university, then medical school studies.

Saad married during medical school, and his parents envisioned a future of grandchildren-filled holidays at the resort. After five years without offspring, Saad decided to pursue further studies far away from Cairo. Too late, the senior al Shammari realized his son relocated to escape the parental pressures of infertility. Within the year, al Shammari's beloved wife died, leaving Ramsey with no one and no life other than the court to sustain him.

He came to despise Sharm el-Sheikh, now transformed into a miniature Las Vegas. At every turn, crowded restaurants, shopping malls, discotheques, and Western floor shows competed for attention. For years, al Shammari could not part with the flat, the final remnant of a happier time with his wife and son. His son's distant life and his own disinterest in the resort property forced al Shammari to accept the inevitable: time to sell.

Appetite sated, al Shammari wiped the grease from his hands and mouth with a napkin, then patted his ample stomach. The food, among Cairo's best, always came with a heavy price: the garlic and spice-laden belch rolling up his esophagus stung his nostrils, throat, and eyes. Attempting to douse the flames, he swished tea around in his mouth, then gulped it down. Al Shammari scribbled his name on the check and popped a couple of complimentary mints into his mouth. Knowing they did little to disguise his ghastly breath, he studiously avoided breathing on other patrons while exiting the tiny restaurant.

Stepping into the hot sun and stifling heat, al Shammari turned toward his low-rise apartment building overlooking the Nile River. Halfway to his flat, he experienced a sudden wave of nauseousness and dizziness. It took all his willpower and strength to stumble over to a nearby bench and sit. Hanging his head between his knees, he tried ridding himself of the wooziness. Teetering on the brink of unconsciousness, al Shammari felt a hand descend on his shoulder. A voice seemingly coming from a great distance entered his ears: "Allow us to assist you, Ramsey."

Al Shammari's eyes rolled back into his head and he toppled forward.

Two men in nondescript dark-blue clothing moved with lightning speed, catching al Shammari before he hit the sidewalk. Half-dragging the portly unconscious jurist over to a red and white van, the men used his belt and arms to hoist him through open rear doors. Piling in, they slammed the doors behind them.

Drawing nary a look from a single bystander or motorist, the ambulance ferrying the Egyptian Supreme Constitutional Court chief justice vanished into the bustling Cairo traffic.

CHAPTER TWENTY-ONE

MILITARY BRASS AND CIVILIAN officials watched Marine One hover then land on the parade ground of Fort Detrick, an hour northwest of Washington on the eastern edge of the Appalachian Mountains. In Frederick, Maryland, the installation's major tenant—the US Army Medical Research and Development Command—oversees the military's biowarfare capabilities and biodefense countermeasures and the Army's Medical Research Institute of Infectious Diseases. USAMRIID conducts research to detect and defeat highly infectious diseases used in biowarfare and bioterrorism at DOD's only biosafety level 4 medical research laboratory.

Publicly, the chief executive's schedule reflected his inaugural tour of the billion-dollar facility. In truth, Englewood was being briefed on the devastating effects if al-Dosari's attack succeeded. The president's entourage entered the administration building and walked to the main conference room. After the doors were secured, Major General Nicholas Pisarczyk, US Army, commenced the briefing without delay.

"Mr. President, thank you for coming. Today, we'll address the biological agent believed involved; strategies and responses to contain it from spreading beyond where it is released, referred to as ground zero or the hot zone; treatment of those exposed; and remediation or sanitization of anything contaminated. In Army parlance, how we cut it off and kill it, repair the damage, and mop up afterward."

The president nodded, best poker face firmly affixed.

"If the intelligence is correct, we will be attacked with smallpox. God willing, we'll prevent it. If not, America's best medical scientists are working around the clock to minimize its damage."

"General, before we get too far down the pike, something's bothering me. Why smallpox? Why not Ebola?"

"Many variables dictate a virus's suitability as a bioweapon. A person can spread Ebola only when symptoms are present. Ebola is not suitable for airborne transmission—direct contact must occur with infected skin or body fluids. It can be transferred from dead body tissue, fluids, and contaminated objects, though it's questionable how long the virus can survive on the latter. You can't vaccinate for Ebola—a person is always susceptible to infection. Conversely, smallpox is a highly desirable bioweapon. A vaccinated person can handle and transport smallpox safely. It can be dispersed in the air, transmitted by infected people not showing symptoms, and transferred from the deceased and contaminated objects. Nearly all of the world's population is unvaccinated against smallpox, virtually ensuring a pandemic. That's the short of it. We can get more detailed about Ebola if you wish, but we're prepared to cover the smallpox problem quite extensively."

"That won't be necessary, General. Forge ahead."

"CDC is the lead agency for medical response under the Federal Response Plan. Dr. Rachel Lynne of CDC co-chairs the multiagency medical task force formed to address this crisis. She'll pick up the briefing from here."

A petite woman in a seafoam-green suit strode to the podium, her shoulder-length strawberry blond hair swishing in a ponytail. "Good morning, Mr. President. I'm chief of CDC's Poxvirus Section. I assumed this position following the unexpected death of Dr. Robert Davies."

Englewood doubted Dr. Lynne knew the real circumstances behind her predecessor's death—murder by al-Dosari's henchmen.

"Smallpox is mankind's greatest disease, an explosively communicable virus with the potential for massive epidemics and substantial casualties. Much of the world's population lacks immunity as smallpox was eradicated almost fifty years ago, ending the need for immunization programs. This virus has two forms: the rarely fatal variola minor and variola major, which can kill 30 to 50 percent of those not vaccinated. Human-to-human transmission is generally the cause. If an unvaccinated person touches a skin lesion, he or she will become infected. Infection can occur from smallpox-laden breaths, coughs, or sneezes. Microparticles are well-suited for airborne transmission and dissipate quickly outdoors. Inside they can stay active for days, recirculating through ventilation systems while exposing people and tainting surfaces."

The president sought clarification. "Is it possible for a contaminated object to start the chain?"

"Yes. Until recently, it was debatable whether transfer to inanimate objects posed a significant risk. The virus was considered too fragile to remain on items for an extended period of time. However, current research indicates both airborne and human-to-human transfer to and from objects poses a longer-lasting risk than we thought."

Dr. Lynne clicked through photos on the screen. "The incubation period is seven to fourteen days, although flu-like symptoms can appear any time after day 7 and include high-grade fever, chills, headache, backache, diarrhea, and vomiting. As the disease progresses, painful lesions materialize in the nasal passages, mouth, and throat, followed by a skin rash. The rash hemorrhages beneath the skin and through mucous membranes lining body cavities, causing bleeding from the eyes and the gastric, respiratory, and urogenital systems. Patients begin to die off."

Pictures graphically illustrating smallpox damage flashed onscreen as Dr. Lynne continued.

"The scope of any outbreak is contingent upon how fast we discover its origin, the number of people initially infected, and their rate of dispersion. The more mobile these victims, the wider the disease will spread. Smallpox progresses swiftly—we could be into a full-blown epidemic before our first clue surfaces. With stepped-up surveillance, law enforcement may prevent the discharge. If a release is detected in the early stages, we'll issue an alert immediately and initiate response plans to keep it from getting a foothold. The CDC pandemic response system should function well, provided we rapidly ascertain its introduction and contain it."

"Dr. Lynne, what happens if some time elapses before we can pinpoint patient zero?"

"Our disease tracking simulation model uses a twenty-times multiplier, projecting each contagious person will infect another twenty people. Hypothetical worst-case with a large-scale release? Suppose the terrorist infects a thousand people in a contained venue, many dispersing widely. Then there's a week's delay before we detect our first illness. By the time we diagnose that first case, twenty thousand people are contagious and spreading the disease to four hundred thousand people. Worst-case involving a single, limited release? Assume two to five people are infected, each passing it on to another twenty people. Incorporate movement and delay, still a dangerously high number. In either scenario, if we have multiple discharges in a single geographic region or individual releases in several areas—immeasurable. The epidemic is raging out of control, causing an overwhelming crush on public health facilities. Medical intervention at this point is too late for up to half of those infected—they will likely die. That's just in the US."

Etched on Englewood's face was the grim reality facing America if al-Dosari succeeded. "If immunization before exposure stops smallpox from emerging, why not inoculate everyone?"

"Even the use of a thoroughly investigated and approved vaccine during pandemics can trigger new strains rendering the vaccine ineffective. Mass vaccination can be unsafe for infants, the elderly, persons with comorbidities or underlying medical conditions, the immunocompromised, or those already immune from infection. For every thousand people vaccinated, 70 percent will experience mild to moderate adverse events; 1 percent develop serious reactions; fifty suffer neurological disorders or life-threatening organ damage; two will die from complications. The remainder will recover and develop antibodies against reinfection."

Englewood, for his part, believed there were both empirical and political justifications why his fellow citizens would resist mass immunization, and he voiced them.

"In our rush to immunize the whole country against other diseases, the vaccines damaged more people than the viruses. Forgive me for being blunt—anything the CDC recommends will be met with a high degree of skepticism because of those fiascoes and due to its history of promulgating misleading information, lack of transparency, and bowing to political pressure. I accept public distrust does nothing to resolve our crisis and complicates it. But we need a strategy to assure the public this isn't a political stunt or CDC overreaction to a nothingburger."

"I agree with you on all points. However, if the attack involves a genetically manipulated or untreatable mutant strain, we may have no alternative but to impose an investigational vaccine."

Ever since an attack with an unknown bioweapon was deemed likely, Englewood grappled with the possibility of confronting an apocalyptic scenario where he and other world leaders would be unable to control a global pandemic ravaging the world's population. Well-versed on the Nuremberg Code's bioethical prohibitions on human medical experiments, he had his own moral and ethical concerns about investigational vaccines that could kill or maim millions. He'd already decided that nothing short of Armageddon could force him to mandate them.

"Understood, Dr. Lynne. Please continue."

"Our strategy surrounds hot areas with vaccinated people, leaving the smallpox nowhere to travel—in other words, we starve it to death. Pandemic protocols call for vaccinating three million people a day, starting with emergency personnel and front-line health care workers, or persons in contact with confirmed cases."

During the flight to Fort Detrick, the HHS secretary advised Englewood he'd be briefed about a top-secret program on arrival. "Explain Libertas—a non-scientific overview please."

"Libertas eliminates vaccination concerns. It is a non-vaccine, orally administered antiviral drug with zero side effects. It stimulates the immune response to produce natural antibodies that shut down the infection once it invades the body, and it stops the virus from mutating into a more contagious and deadlier variant. Reinfection is unlikely as antibodies redevelop if needed. Libertas is a remarkable drug, but loses its ability to neutralize infection if an infectibility boosting variant has been created." Dr. Lynne paused, a dark shadow crossing over her face.

"Gain-of-function research can be a game-changer if a virus has been altered to enhance transmissibility or increase its lethality. If we're dealing with an unknown strain, it will also have multiple mutations since viruses change as they propagate. Until we eradicate the disease, people will become factories for manufacturing new variants, and these will continue evolving as threats. Only a madman would engineer such a strain and release it outside a laboratory environment."

Englewood agreed, though for an entirely different reason. *Or a mad man who controls a vaccine and is supported by diehard followers on martyrdom missions.*

"If Libertas is a viable solution, can we get it on the street fast enough to avoid massive loss of life?"

"Yes, but its efficacy will be hampered by those persons and groups who object to any government-mandated medical solution. The top US pharmaceutical manufacturers are being tasked to secretly crash-produce three hundred million doses, which we're stockpiling. At first verification of confirmed cases, CDC will release the stocks and share the classified formula with drug makers in the UK, France, Germany, Switzerland, Russia, and China."

Englewood knew those present had yet to be briefed on McEwan's seizure of what was believed to be al-Dosari's vaccine.

"If we discover the terrorist's vaccine, can it be evaluated and if effective, mass-produced?"

"In theory, yes. Realistically, no. There won't be sufficient time to conduct adequate analysis to ensure its safety. It should only be used as a desperate last measure when all else has failed."

"Put yourself in the terrorist's shoes. How would you deliver it?"

"I'd transport a freeze-dried, highly virulent variant manipulated by gain-of-function research and release it surreptitiously in the air. This framework came from Russian biowarfare scientists, who perfected a freeze-drying process that maintains the lethality of respiratory pathogens while enabling them to hang suspended in the air like a gas. This process permits airborne nanoparticles to establish themselves in the respiratory system, penetrate the skin, or both. The disease takes hold when a person inhales a single particle or droplet or touches a contaminated object or person. The Russians monetized the technology by selling it to the Iranians, who thoughtfully passed it on to terror groups free of charge. Very dangerous knowledge in the wrong hands."

"What type of dispenser would you use to inflict maximum casualties?"

"I'd use a device capable of delivering a condensed or sustained spray into the ventilation systems of large, enclosed venues like indoor sports arenas or places of worship. It becomes a super-spreader event as people disperse."

Englewood did not mention the two instruments recovered by McEwan in Sudan, but both validated Lynne's hypothesis.

"If intelligence reveals the location prior to release, we can detect it using instruments developed in the labs at Sandia, Los Alamos, and Lawrence Livermore. We have handheld, vehicle-deployed, and briefcase units. All detect smallpox, anthrax, ricin, and sarin effectively."

"Dr. Lynne, before I permit the US to be the epicenter of a pandemic, I'll go public. But whatever we do, we cannot panic our citizens. They must have complete confidence in this administration and its ability to eliminate the threat and manage the situation."

"Absolutely, Mr. President. We've war-gamed the bioterrorism response scenario many times. We're initiating a series of unscheduled exercises shortly in major population centers. Medical and emergency services personnel nationwide will focus on disease surveillance, investigation, and containment to ensure treatment protocols are in place and functioning. If an attack occurs, personnel will be freshly trained to execute the actual plan, Operation Crimson Tempest. Swift implementation will reassure the public that we're managing the crisis."

"What are the mechanics of responding to a domestic biological attack?"

"They are large-scale and contained in great detail in the National Response Plan, sir."

"Let me rephrase. Give me the *Reader's Digest* version from a medical perspective."

"If law enforcement interdicts this attack, we stand down. If an attack succeeds, the most immediate obstacles will be identifying the release locations and isolating points of origin. Governors of impacted states will declare a public health emergency and order quarantine of those exposed, both actual and suspected, and issue stay-at-home orders. We'll inform the public of the symptoms, testing, treatment, and other actions that will keep the disease from spreading."

"Summarize the concurrent measures I should implement," Englewood asked.

"Society's mobile nature makes it unlikely we will contain it at its origin. You'll issue a presidential emergency declaration to accomplish actions simultaneously or in rapid succession. Execute Crimson Tempest. Release Libertas. Close the interstate highway system. Shut down rail systems. Direct FAA to ground all flights. Instruct DHS to implement contingency plans to prevent disruption of vital public services and food supplies. Contemporaneously, we'll confirm the type of virus through laboratory analysis and actual case observations. If we do not have a medical solution, you must lock down the entire country until we isolate it and determine how to treat it.

"Let me be very clear, Mr. President—it's impossible for anyone to provide a definitive timetable for containing and subduing a new, virulently transmissible variant. Models project we could exceed a hundred million cases worldwide in months if we don't attack it aggressively. We have advance knowledge it's coming, which allows us to increase our level of preparedness behind the scenes. Will life be uncomfortable for many people? Yes. Will we lose some people? Regrettably, that answer, too, is yes, perhaps far more than we can imagine."

Clinical as Dr. Lynne's words were, they were gut-wrenching for Nelson J. Englewood. For the first time since this threat began, he accepted that catastrophic numbers of casualties would occur if al-Dosari succeeded. The president stood and faced the group.

"Ladies and gentlemen, we are approaching a defining moment in our history. Many people are working to prevent this attack, and others are preparing to act if he succeeds. You, however, are the ones who will defeat him. If our citizens could be told about your achievements here, they would be immensely proud. Since they cannot, on their behalf, I want to thank you for doing humanity a great service. You are all heroes."

As his entourage made its way back to the parade ground and Marine One, a sobering thought entered Englewood's mind. The fate of the nation, and perhaps the entire world, now rested in the hands of one man.

Kyle McEwan.

CHAPTER TWENTY-TWO

EN ROUTE TO CAMP Lemonnier, Djibouti, the former French Foreign Legion military base on the Horn of Africa, McEwan mentally rewound the tape and dissected his pursuit of al-Dosari. Tallying the score, in the plus column they'd destroyed his virus and manufacturing capability, had deciphered his delivery techniques, and seized his vaccine. It could possibly be reverse-engineered and reproduced. In the negative, the terrorist remained free, invisible, and capable of launching his attack. Only McEwan's single-minded determination to find and kill al-Dosari before he struck tipped the balance in America's favor.

McEwan knew the president would be dissatisfied by his failure to eliminate al-Dosari. Despite a myriad of risks, the commander in chief had authorized two extraterritorial military operations. No matter the justification, forays and missile strikes on foreign soil wreaked havoc with international relations and could lead to armed conflict.

After landing, McEwan conducted a short briefing in the Bob Hope Dining Facility. Armed with their marching orders and under Cartwright's watchful eye, the Marines commenced inventorying, sorting, and reviewing hundreds of documents seized during the two raids. McEwan took time to grab a tray of hot chow and wolf it down, then spoke with Sanchez via sat phone. It was not pleasant.

Cartwright tracked him down. "The processing teams identified what appear to be laboratory documents and correspondence and culled them down to two legal-size file boxes. Challenging considering most aren't in English. They've scanned and copied them onto a flash drive and are transmitting them electronically to analysts in DC as we speak. We've palletized seventeen file cabinets. They're already on board the C-17 with the instruments, vaccine, and two guards' bodies. And of course, Dr. Mansour's remains."

"What about the computers?" McEwan queried.

"Onboard too. We went 'geek to geek'. Our guys here backed them up onto an encrypted DOD server and the geeks on the other end are downloading them," Cartwright explained as he escorted McEwan to the tarmac.

"Thanks for everything, Jason, especially what you did for Ahmed."

"I only wish we could have saved him. No doubt in my mind, you'll get al-Dosari. When you do, give him a thumpin' from me and my Marines."

"Count on it."

"Kyle, it's a helluva long flight—catch some shut-eye. Arrivederci, auf Wiedersehen, sayonara, and all that other happy horseshit." The MARSOC commander turned and walked away.

McEwan boarded the aircraft. He sidestepped the metal transfer cases containing the remains of Mansour and the two Sudanese guards. He passed numerous shrink-wrapped cabinets and the backup flight crew sitting in a fifteen-passenger-seat pallet section. He settled in the front row with his laptop and file boxes. Grateful he wouldn't have to spend the long flight in sidewall troop seats, he tossed his phone next to the laptop and buckled in. Wheels up, destination: Joint Base Andrews.

Within minutes, McEwan's phone began flashing and vibrating; he tried tuning out. Despite his best efforts, the constant interruptions drove him batshit. Already in an exceedingly foul mood over Mansour's demise and al-Dosari's escape, he threw the phone against the bulkhead in front of him. Predictably, the cover and battery parted ways, sailing off in different directions. Inserting a set of foam earplugs brought golden silence.

McEwan's outburst had its intended effect on the others, who left the exhausted stranger alone. He fell into a deep sleep almost right away.

Sometime later, he woke to a strange voice, "Sir!"

McEwan opened one eye. "Yes?"

"Your chain of command has attempted to reach you repeatedly on your phone. The Pentagon has tried patching through calls to you from the White House Communications Agency. You need to get them off our ass."

"Yeah, sorry. I'll contact them ASAP."

McEwan retrieved his satellite phone components, magically resting atop his laptop. After rebuilding the device, it powered up instantly, flashing brightly, indicating multiple voice mails and text messages. The first one from Sanchez set the tone: "Call me ASAP!" Scrolling through the next several messages, all were from the DNI, ordering him to call "immediately". McEwan noted a six-hour gap before Sanchez blew up his phone with a series of ten increasingly sharp messages. From their previous conversation, McEwan knew Sanchez watched the Lebanon raid in the Situation Room and the Sudan raid in the Pentagon's National Military Command Center. *I already briefed her from Djibouti, so what does she want?* Steeling himself for her anger, he punched Sanchez's number.

The DNI answered on the first ring.

"Sorry, Danni, I crashed."

Sanchez let his excuse ride, having spoken to Cartwright, who advised McEwan was "in the throes of adrenaline crash and exhaustion" and "having trouble handling his friend's death". After all, McEwan wasn't a cyborg, although she couldn't ever recall him showing a human side.

"Consider your ass chewed." Without missing a beat, her voice softened. "I'm sorry about Dr. Mansour."

"He's behind me in a metal transfer case," McEwan growled.

"Air Force mortuary personnel will take custody of his remains until you decide what to do."

Sanchez shared the preliminary results of the analysis coming in from DC experts, which was largely muddled due to language translation difficulties. She explained her persistent calls. "POTUS wants to meet with you personally. Secret Service will bring you in. Be forewarned, you're walking into a real shit storm back here. Prepare yourself." She signed off.

McEwan stared at the bulkhead. In less than a week, he'd participated in three kinetic operations and tried to quit his all-consuming career. The adrenaline highs and lows brought on by al-Dosari's threat and Mansour's crushing death reclaimed him. Surrendering, McEwan slipped back into unconsciousness.

McEwan slept undisturbed for hours, including through airborne refueling and a raucous card game behind him. Finally waking, he made a head call. Returning, he found a box lunch in his seat. McEwan devoured an apple, tuna salad sandwich, and bag of Doritos and drained a bottle of water. Firing up the laptop, he inserted the flash drive. He spent the next several hours analyzing the seized files, which his language abilities allowed him to translate. The documents were both incriminating and revealing, leaving no doubt al-Dosari was gunning for America.

McEwan peered out a porthole and recognized the familiar outline of Virginia Beach and the Chesapeake Bay Bridge Tunnel. He suppressed a flashback to his time at the Farm and focused on his next mission: orchestrating and executing the very painful demise of one Ali bin al-Dosari.

CHAPTER TWENTY-THREE

RAMSEY ABD AL SHAMMARI startled awake. Blinking rapidly, the chief justice of Egypt's Supreme Constitutional Court tried to clear the fog from his head. Focusing, he discovered he lay spread-eagle, arms and legs securely strapped to bedposts. Unable to move, al Shammari tried remembering how he arrived here. The only explanation: he was drugged. *But by whom? Why? When?* His memory held one vague image—two men helping him into an ambulance. *Why do I think I was asked about Saad?* Cringing, he tried vainly to dredge up more. The sound of a turning doorknob triggered instinctive fear.

A handsome man attired in casual Western clothing entered the room accompanied by two men. The visitor's intense green eyes burned holes into al Shammari's soul.

"Good day, honorable judge! Why, you are fit to be tied!" Amused by his clever double entendre, the man glanced at his escorts, who laughed nervously.

The visitor continued conversationally. "Ramsey, we must chat about your son. I need you to encourage Saad to assist me with a project."

Frozen with fear, the muddled al Shammari remained silent.

Not receiving an immediate response, the man in the Western attire snapped his finger and thumb. One of his captors produced a syringe and roughly injected its contents into al Shammari's arm with a single push of the plunger.

Within seconds, al Shammari could not control his thoughts and actions. His spirit and body bifurcated; disembodied, questions floated cloud-like below him. His mouth moved, providing answers about Saad. As if watching a movie, al Shammari saw his captors rip off his clothes, prop him up in various poses, and blind him with a series of searing white flashes. Al Shammari willed his mind to reunite with his body, but nothing happened.

The leader spoke disdainfully. "Saifulislam deeply appreciates your cooperation."

The Sword of Islam? was al Shammari's final thought before retreating to the comfort of unconsciousness.

Due to the late hour, no one noticed when the lights extinguished in the house located directly beneath the Damascus International Airport flight path. Ali bin al-Dosari parked the car he'd collected minutes before in the airport's parking lot.

Having spent his last days traveling, al-Dosari was tired. Because time was short, he had taken only the occasional nap. Yawning, he turned off the engine and stepped from the car, an arriving jet obscuring the sound of his car door closing. Soon his travels would span continents, not countries, with a very important purpose: his revenge, carried out in Allah's name.

Al-Dosari's catlike green eyes detected movement in the darkness: a side door opening, an almost-invisible figure gesturing to him. Striding briskly a few short paces to the doorway, he stepped inside and was guided deeper into the house. The lights came on, and four men gazed reverently at the Sword of Islam.

Taking a step forward, al-Dosari was met halfway by one of the men. The two brothers hugged exuberantly. Older by two years, Ali pulled back and spoke first. "Yousef, I missed you."

"Yes, and I as well."

Yousef excitedly introduced the Almighty's Sword of Islam to the three followers. All bowed with great reverence, each firmly believing this man was Allah's great warrior.

Though Ali thrived on the worship, he needed updates. "Anything from Rayak?"

"The power failed again in Baalbek, but be assured, Mansour was handled per your orders. I sent instructions to dispose of his family, then transmitted the Egyptian's information to our brothers in America. Your seeds in the infidel's soil have sprouted, ready to bloom upon your arrival." Yousef beamed proudly.

"Excellent. I want to record my message to the world. Where is the smartphone?"

"Here, here," a man cried, pointing at the tripod-mounted iPhone.

The Sword of Islam sat facing the cell phone. "Proceed."

Ali rose to his feet following completion of his videotaped message. "Pray with me before I embark on holy jihad."

Moving as one, the three adherents knelt, then prostrated themselves on prayer rugs.

Standing tall before them, Ali bin al-Dosari began in earnest. "Almighty, it is my solemn duty to answer your call to jihad. America is tyranny. For their crimes and sins and declaration of war on Islam, you have called me to annihilate the crusaders. I will not fail."

Al-Dosari scanned the men. Each prayed raptly without looking at him.

"The punishment I will deliver is just. *I am your Sword of Islam!* Praise be to Allah!"

During their refrains of "Allahu Akbar!" Yousef stepped behind the three men and dispatched each with a single gunshot to the back of the head, eliminating the loose ends. "May the warriors in North America be as brave and loyal as you."

The al-Dosari brothers laughed together.

Proclaiming, "I am ready!" the Sword of Islam swept triumphantly out the door, followed closely by his brother, Yousef.

CHAPTER TWENTY-FOUR

FINGERS WOVEN TOGETHER, HANDS clasped behind his head, Nelson J. Englewood recalled the day he entered public service. Wincing, he had naively believed he could remain untouched by the repugnant aspects of politics. Too late, he discovered that ethical principles and best efforts couldn't keep one's hands clean because they got washed in dirty water. Englewood knew he'd have to wade even deeper into the muck to destroy al-Dosari. If that was what it took, then so be it.

America couldn't withstand any more prolonged probes, like the congressional investigations of recent years involving a former president who abused the intelligence community and investigative assets of the US government to target his political enemies and solidify power. The lengthy inquiries fractured the country along political lines, wasted millions of taxpayer dollars, and most significantly, left the Constitution in tatters. Then there was the bureaucracy.

On a normal day, the executive branch's ability to bog down in its own morass presented difficult challenges. Complicating matters were non-elected political zealots masquerading as impartial policymakers. Firmly in control, deep state operatives often ignored presidential directives and federal law, using bureaucratic maneuvers to implement their agendas. The Justice Department, embedded with feckless decision-makers fixated on partisan prosecutions, pledged allegiance to political ideologies instead of the Constitution. Their collaborators running the FBI transformed it from an objective fact-finding agency into one heavily infected with political bias, leaving its independence seriously in doubt. The CIA with Carl Stefan in command was polluted. The Pentagon's senior leadership, civilian and military, was a tangled mix of characters but generally more responsive. The current system was fundamentally broken.

Despite these obstacles, on his watch, terrorists who attacked America would be dealt swift and merciless sentences by whatever means necessary. For Englewood, anything short of dead was unacceptable when dealing with killers of innocents. The difficulty was implementing such methods without attracting the attention of the legacy media's attack dogs and their masters in the opposing political party. His administration would implode if his actions were exposed, the revelations destroying the remaining shreds of the American spirit, which he solemnly had vowed to restore.

Pushing back from his desk, Englewood swiveled his chair and rose to his feet. Stepping over to the thick, bulletproof window, he gazed wistfully outside. Judicial activists, government bureaucracies, and the political establishment had championed draconian rules and regulations that rendered America's justice system incapable of eliminating the peril posed by al-Dosari. Only one approach guaranteed an acceptable result: extrajudicial elimination of the threat. It was irrelevant that Englewood's actions were heading down the slippery slope toward violating the Constitution and due process of law. He knew other presidents had circumvented the Constitution in order to uphold it. He, too, would protect America at all costs, consequences be damned.

Rolling down his sleeves and inserting cuff links enameled with the presidential seal, Englewood made his decision.

The C-17 Globemaster ferrying McEwan touched down at Joint Base Andrews, turned onto a taxiway, and rolled over to a hangar. After the engines shut down, McEwan retrieved his bags and rifle case and headed toward the ramp. Peering out, he spotted a uniformed Air Force lieutenant with two men in suits he made as Secret Service agents. As McEwan hit the tarmac, the taller agent took two of his three bags. McEwan handed off his rifle case to the other agent.

"Anything else?" the agent asked.

"You got 'em all. Pistol's in the load-out bag." He turned to address the officer but was cut off by the man.

"Everything's already arranged, sir." The officer gestured toward two Air Force personnel standing beside a black Chevy cargo van. "Just call me when you're ready to make final arrangements." He handed McEwan a card containing the mortuary affairs contact numbers.

"Thank you." McEwan spoke to the two agents. "Everything else goes by helicopter forthwith to Fort Detrick. Including the other two bodies."

Satisfied that teams of personnel were off-loading the remaining cargo and shuttling it to an Air Force helicopter, McEwan headed to the hangar locker room, where he found the suit bag last seen in his Jeep Warrior hanging on a hook. Undressing, he took a hot shower, melting away some of his knots and pains. Thirty minutes later, he emerged wearing gray slacks, white button-down shirt, a navy-blue blazer, and Italian loafers. As if heralding his appearance, lightning streaked across the sky followed by a thunderclap. Spotting one of the agents standing next to the open trunk of a black sedan, McEwan jogged over and tossed in his bag.

The agent pointed skyward. "We're taking the Suitland Parkway in."

McEwan slid through an open door into the back seat. The agent jumped in and they took off. Huge raindrops appeared and the intensity of the downpour made conversation difficult, so McEwan used the time to review his proposal to the president. Personally comfortable with his plan, the question remained whether Englewood had the stomach for what needed to be done.

A half hour later, the car's bouncing motion snapped McEwan back to the present. After halting briefly at the West Executive Avenue checkpoint, the sedan lurched forward and stopped in front of the lower-level entrance canopy. An agent moved toward the vehicle, hand to his mouth, announcing McEwan's arrival into the tiny microphone dangling from his wrist.

The president of the United States was preoccupied with the implications of his decision when a soft knock interrupted his thoughts.

The Secret Service detail shift leader stuck his head in. "Mr. President, they've arrived."

"Show them in."

Daniela Sanchez entered, shadowed by a muscular man of average height in his mid-thirties.

Englewood contemplated the rugged, handsome man moving toward him. McEwan's chiseled, all-American features and gold-streaked sandy hair contrasted sharply with his illustrious exploits, which took place in parts of the world where the man should stick out like a sore thumb. McEwan's innate lethality and underlying predatory nature were undeniable.

Noting his Secret Service bodyguard's uneasiness, the chief executive waved him off. The agent turned reluctantly and let himself out.

Sanchez performed the introduction. "Mr. President, Kyle McEwan."

"McEwan." Extending his hand, Englewood locked onto the case officer's eyes. *Unusual shade of amber encircled by teal with a black outer ring. They emote nothing—almost soulless.*

"Mr. President." McEwan took the proffered hand.

"I anticipated thanking you for stopping al-Dosari overseas. It didn't happen, though I'm well aware it wasn't your fault."

McEwan telegraphed neither agreement nor disagreement.

Englewood ushered his guests to a sofa, then settled into a nearby chair. "I want your assessments of the situation."

Sanchez took the cue. "Here's what we've pieced together. Al-Dosari and the Sword of Islam are one and the same. Whatever his motive, he intends to attack us with smallpox. For years we heard rumors that sometime in the late nineties, a virologist from the Russian State Center for Research traveled to Baghdad and sold smallpox to Saddam. Actual verification never happened because the virologist disappeared shortly thereafter. Conventional wisdom posited that if Saddam ever really possessed the Vector virus, his researchers destroyed it during the First Gulf War. However, we now know that theory was wrong. Before dying, Dr. Mansour told Kyle that in the weeks preceding our 2003 invasion, a Pasteur Institute virologist flew to Baghdad and took possession of the virus from a colleague. He mapped its genetic code and DNA tests proved it was the Vector strain. Based on what al-Dosari told Mansour, he stole the virus and murdered the Pasteur scientist. Worse, al-Dosari boasted he weaponized the smallpox."

McEwan stepped in. "Seized documents show that al-Dosari bribed another Vector scientist to develop technology to allow a virus to live longer on inanimate objects. Discounting the possibility they succeeded would be reckless because we know he pursued other technology that apparently works—freeze-drying and aerosol techniques. But we have a much larger concern."

Englewood felt acid burning a hole in his stomach.

"Al-Dosari boasted to Mansour that he's engineered a new variant from the Vector strain, but none of the Sudan files confirmed it. He's a devious bastard. If I had to guess, I'd say he has genetically altered it and only he has the vaccine formula."

"Any chance that the vaccine you seized will blunt or destroy this variant?"

Sanchez weighed back in. "Until we conduct autopsies on the two Sudanese guards and compare it to the seized vaccine, we can't render an opinion."

Englewood wondered aloud, "If their tissue samples show they were inoculated with a vaccine different than the one Kyle seized, can't we just reverse-engineer our own?"

"Only USAMRIID and CDC can answer that question. However, the whole process may be overcome by events because time is not on our side."

Englewood exhaled deeply, then engaged McEwan. "How do you rate the chance he'll actually attack?"

"Al-Dosari will go through with it as long as he thinks he controls the vaccine. If he discovers we're onto him, it's even odds he'll hit us anyway or abort the attack and go underground, resurfacing and striking us at a later date."

"So what are we facing, then?"

"We believe he's unaware we destroyed his facility. That information should be released only when it suits us or if developments force it. We've found no evidence of any smallpox outside Sudan, with one exception. Al-Dosari ordered an unknown quantity of smallpox delivered to him two weeks ago at an unspecified address in Damascus. It's a safe bet it's long gone from Syria."

"Not what I wanted to hear."

"Understood, sir. He's undoubtedly transporting freeze-dried smallpox. I'm told it's extremely difficult, perhaps even impossible, to detect at our ports of entry using current technology. FBI has added al-Dosari to the terrorist watch list, but we have no biometrics or photos of him. He's far too cunning to gamble slipping undetected through that juggernaut. So how will he enter? He'll bypass our ports entirely. If Mansour's torturer was correct, he's arriving through a tunnel under the California border."

Despite billions of dollars in physical security enhancements and thousands of new agents, both the southern and northern borders remained porous. Englewood dreaded his next question, "When?"

"Sometime during the next two weeks."

Englewood's stomach churned. The short timetable substantially complicated their chances of intercepting and eliminating al-Dosari. "How certain is the time frame?"

"I promise you Mansour's sentry told me everything he knew, but his information was strictly anecdotal. Regardless, we have no other intel."

Englewood accepted the certainty of the case officer's assertion. "What was in those files?"

"We recovered assassination dossiers on a hundred of the world's top infectious disease experts, most of whom collaborated with Dr. Mansour, including Dr. Robert Davies of CDC. Killing these scientists increases the odds the smallpox will inflict significant damage before we detect it and halt its spread. Finally, we found files on you and your fellow G-7 leaders."

"No surprise there," the president observed dryly, then shifted topics. "Danni, where are we on possible targets?"

"Secret Service Protective Intelligence is working with the FBI and NCTC to compile a list. It's well-documented that a bioterrorism attack that overwhelms our healthcare system is our greatest threat outside a nuclear attack or EMP event."

"What else?"

"NSA is examining all traffic remotely related to this threat. The FBI is standing up a nationwide multiagency task force at NCTC, code word Ameripox. Joint Terrorism Task Forces are on high alert, probing confidential informants and stepping up surveillance on known cells. CIA's doing the same with its global stations. San Diego JTTF is preparing to cast a net over the Mexico border. The bureau is implementing an investigative plan similar to that used in the prior Fort Detrick anthrax case."

"Which, as I recall, wasn't exactly a model of success," the president remarked sourly, recalling the 7-year debacle marred by FBI missteps.

Sanchez nodded, continuing, "Kyle requests authorization to operate on US soil. I support this, but it will cause significant problems with the FBI. I suggest a different code name for the operation. Ameripox is a dead giveaway."

The FBI enjoyed primary jurisdiction over terrorism on American soil, and every other federal agency supported the bureau. It was impossible to remove the bureau from the equation, but Englewood believed it could be marginalized and relegated to a supporting role. He needed to move quickly before things snowballed out of control.

"Name it what you want. Until this threat is destroyed, Danni, you're in command of the entire US law enforcement and intelligence apparatus. McEwan, you're her point man. It'll be in writing so there's no misunderstanding."

Sanchez paused to digest the president's decision. Notwithstanding her significant counterterrorism credentials, she had no domestic law enforcement experience and DNI wasn't an operational entity. Surely Englewood wouldn't ignite a monumental turf war in the midst of battling a credible terror threat. Sanchez silently hoped he'd reconsider.

The president didn't. "I know what you're thinking, Danni, but I have my reasons. I'm fully aware of the repercussions of my actions. As president of the United States, I swore to protect America to the best of my ability, and that's precisely what I'm doing."

Sanchez ruefully accepted she was now squarely in the gun sights of both FBI and CIA—perhaps the operation's new name should be Crosshairs.

McEwan was pleased to have the full resources of the world's most powerful nation at his disposal to help track al-Dosari. Once in hand, he'd spirit the terrorist out of the country and deliver his own form of justice.

Englewood wanted the case officer's unvarnished evaluation of the plan. "Danni, I'd like a minute with McEwan."

Still absorbing the ramifications of the last few minutes, Sanchez grabbed her satchel and left the Oval Office.

As soon as the door clicked shut, Englewood spoke carefully. "As president, I cannot permit al-Dosari to make a mockery of our criminal justice system or become a cause célèbre—"

Two moves ahead of the cautious Englewood, McEwan did the unthinkable, interrupting the president. "The FBI might be able to intercept al-Dosari and build a criminal case. However, neither a public spectacle nor an extended stay at Club Fed are in America's best interests. And we cannot afford a tortuous investigation. Am I correct?"

Watching McEwan intently, the chief executive guardedly acknowledged the statement.

"So al-Dosari must never enter the system."

"Precisely." Satisfied McEwan understood clearly, Englewood revealed another controversial decision. "In my classified executive order, I'm also authorizing you to use enhanced interrogation techniques. We don't have time to screw around pacifying the ACLU and international rights groups, hoping to get what we need."

Pleasantly surprised, McEwan nodded in agreement. One of Englewood's predecessors had banned using the techniques, a cowardly move that cost American lives.

The president could not afford any confusion. "The FBI isn't equipped to handle this the way I want to see it—"

"Well, I am." For the second time in as many minutes, McEwan cut off the president. "Your decisions are sound and will make things easier in both the short and long run. Your finding concerning elimination of this national security threat is my mandate. I will execute al-Dosari's sentence in accordance with its precepts. But I certainly appreciate your support."

Fully aware McEwan had artfully waltzed him, Englewood wasn't about to look his gift horse in the mouth. God had answered his prayers in the form of Kyle McEwan.

"One other thing, Mr. President. I require get-out-of-jail-free passes for myself and every person who helps me eliminate al-Dosari. That includes DNI Sanchez. This point is non-negotiable, or I'm not your man."

"An order granting them unconditionally will be in your hands before you depart DC."

With a slight nod, McEwan turned and exited the Oval Office.

The president of the United States was confident that once McEwan got his hands on Ali bin al-Dosari, the case officer would administer the "Englewood Doctrine" personally, using every weapon in his arsenal.

CHAPTER TWENTY-FIVE

THREE HOURS LATER, aboard a DHS jet taking off from Ronald Reagan Washington National Airport, McEwan watched Fox News Channel carrying a live satellite feed from London affiliate Sky News.

"Thanks, Monique." The correspondent took his handoff. "As you mentioned, I am live in East Africa where Sudanese government officials have confirmed an unknown number of explosions rocked a pharmaceutical laboratory in the Hala'ib Triangle region, in the far northeast corner bordering Egypt. The explosions and subsequent fire destroyed the facility, which was slated to become the largest manufacturer of antibiotics and vaccines in the third world."

Bullshit.

"During a press conference ended minutes ago, Sudanese officials concluded a laboratory mishap most likely caused the blast. Privately, however, some of my highly placed Sudanese sources question whether Egypt is behind this."

"Why is that Pembroke?" the anchor cut in from London.

"The Hala'ib Triangle is disputed territory claimed by both countries for hundreds of years. To this day, while Sudan exercises authority over it, the sovereignty of the area remains unresolved. It is truly a no-man's-land where laws are enforced loosely, if at all. One official has even suggested America may be involved—"

"Pembroke," Monique interrupted, "are you saying that officials believe US forces destroyed the facility?"

Say no, McEwan urged silently.

"No. Virtually all of my government sources discount that theory. You may recall in 1998, al-Qaeda bombed US embassies in Nairobi, Kenya, and Dar-es-Salaam, Tanzania, killing 258 people and injuring more than 5,000. In retaliation, then US president William Clinton ordered a similar facility destroyed in Khartoum, claiming al-Qaeda used it to manufacture weapons of mass destruction. Because the world community widely condemned America for destroying a legitimate pharmaceutical facility, my sources say it is extremely unlikely the US would want a repeat of that wrath. Egypt, on the other hand—"

McEwan ended the livestream and set his phone aside. His smile vanished as he realized al-Dosari probably saw the same report. Despite the disclaimer, the terrorist might suspect that the US destroyed the facility. There would be no answer until al-Dosari emerged from hiding.

Under a clean alias, al-Dosari boarded an Air France flight in Damascus and flew to Charles de Gaulle International Airport in Paris. Landing on time, he deplaned and headed over to French Customs. He passed the inspection of his travel documents and carry-on items then checked in for his connecting flight. Sitting in the waiting area surveying his fellow travelers, his eyes landed on an overhead television broadcasting LCI, France's version of CNN. Something about the scene seemed familiar. The hair on his arms stood up. *A fire destroyed the Hala'ib Triangle factory?*

Al-Dosari sat mesmerized until the segment ended. Wiping tiny beads of sweat from his forehead and upper lip, he processed what he'd heard. Relief washed over him as the truth settled in. The over-exuberant disciple Abdullah Hurayrah must have forgotten to remove oxygen and gas tanks, causing an explosion and torching the entire laboratory instead of creating a diversionary fire. Al-Dosari longed to order the idiot's immediate death, but those involved in the execution of all phases of the plan were prohibited from contacting others until holy jihad was ignited. Only complete compartmentalization would prevent the infidel's spy agencies from intercepting communications. He would lead by example. The plan would remain unaltered.

Hearing his flight called, al-Dosari stood, reached down and snapped up the collapsible handle of his rolling case. When the first-class passengers were summoned, he waited with the other travelers. Strolling with them down the Jetway, they boarded the aircraft, and he settled in his seat.

Once the cabin door closed, his deep green eyes narrowed. His smile morphed into an evil mask, distorting his otherwise handsome features.

CHAPTER TWENTY-SIX

HHS SECRETARY PATRICIA LONGSTREET, MD, spoke hesitantly. "Mr. President, I need to update you on the autopsies and toxicology tests of the two Sudanese guards."

Nelson J. Englewood's forehead was etched with concern. "Give us some good news, Patty."

"I have none, sir. Toxicology and tissue sampling determined conclusively that we're dealing with a new smallpox variant. Genetic sequencing thus far has not deciphered the vaccine's DNA code. If his attack succeeds in the near term, a medical solution is improbable."

All eyes in the Situation Room zoomed back to the president leaning forward in his chair, staring at the floor. He looked up at each person sitting around the conference table; his eyes landed on the CIA director.

Misinterpreting the look as an invitation to speak, Carl Stefan seized the opportunity to re-establish an alliance with the FBI. "We should be grateful the Marines destroyed that smallpox and his ability to make more. Perhaps now you should let the bureau do its job."

The commander in chief ignored Stefan's biting comments. "Danni, what's the latest?"

"HUMINT and SIGINT aren't producing anything relevant. We don't have a bead on al-Dosari, but think he's heading to Mexico to cross into California. We're focusing our efforts there. Kyle McEwan is en route—"

The counterterrorism case officer's name, now indelibly imprinted into everyone's minds courtesy of Carl Stefan's prior unauthorized disclosure, ignited heated exchanges. Attorney General James William Davidson's voice boomed above the commotion.

"Mr. President! It's one thing to look the other way when an operative like McEwan resolves a problem extraterritorially. But turning him loose on US soil? Out of the question. We are a nation of laws, and his methods violate scores of statutes. I can assure you there will be serious legal ramifications. Plus, the media will crucify you and the rest of us."

Englewood rapped on the table with his knuckles, silencing everyone. "James, you've known me a long time. You know I don't give a damn about the media. Do you think al-Dosari worries about how his acts will be perceived? Of course not. Negative press only boosts his image. I will not permit him to mass-murder our citizens. I will destroy him first, no matter the cost to me personally—or to you."

The HHS secretary's dire news validated the need for Englewood's next decision. Opening a dark-blue folder and uncapping his fountain pen, the president elegantly inscribed his name on the document. He recapped the pen, set it aside, and handed the folder to his chief of staff. Englewood paraphrased the classified presidential finding he'd just signed.

"The al-Dosari threat presents a clear and present danger to the United States of America. The short timetable does not permit use of established mechanisms to eliminate this danger. To preserve the lives of our citizens, I direct that the full intelligence, law enforcement, military, and civilian capabilities of the United States be marshaled and used to disrupt and prevent the attack. The Director of National Intelligence will command all government assets, personnel, and activities throughout the duration of this investigation and full resolution of the threat. All agency heads *will* report directly to the DNI, who reports to me. Effective immediately, Kyle McEwan is reassigned permanently to the ODNI. He *is* authorized to operate on US soil, something he could not do in the employ of the CIA."

Englewood's sweeping action was unprecedented.

Finally, the attorney general spoke in a low, pleading voice. "Mr. President, please, you must reconsider. DNI's charter does not allow it to execute operational matters, and your decision vis-à-vis McEwan has implications far beyond the al-Dosari matter."

Englewood became preternaturally quiet. "James, have you forgotten who you work for? You work for me. The last time I checked, I run the executive branch. *All of it.*"

Davidson wouldn't drop it. "Mr. President, ah, Congress will have—"

"Congress can kiss my ever-loving Scottish-American ass!" Englewood cut off his attorney general midsentence.

The attorney general's brain froze up, locking his tongue in place.

"All of your objections and recommendations are noted and overruled. End of discussion. DNI will supervise this investigation. McEwan will command all operational activities of the combined agencies under the auspices of the DNI. The FBI and the entire US government will support McEwan. Understood?"

"Yes, Mr. President." Davidson's head bobbed up and down. "You'll have the full support of Justice and the FBI."

Englewood swiveled in his chair, leveling his wrath on the CIA director. "Carl, I'm warning you for the last time. You'd better cooperate and start sharing all unfiltered raw intelligence immediately, or I'll install someone who can."

Unable to withstand the president's heat, the ashen-faced Stefan stared blankly at his notepad.

"Director Sanchez was drafted by me for this assignment—she did not seek it. She is serving her country, as will all of you. If any of you cannot live with my decision, fine. Resign now and I will harbor no resentment."

None of Englewood's advisers took him up on his offer.

It was a defining moment. Despite their well-founded objections, Englewood knew his decision to install McEwan over all stateside operations was the only play he had. The case officer brought special skills to the table that no other US government agent possessed. If any one individual had the intellect, courage, and balls to go toe-to-toe with the CIA, FBI, and al-Dosari, it was McEwan. The president accepted that the operation would result in one of two things for America: it would either become a blueprint for future antiterror operations or signal the end of Englewood's presidency.

"If the existence of this operation is leaked to the media or the jackals on the Hill, those responsible will be arrested and charged with providing material support to a terrorist organization." Pointedly making eye contact with each person, Englewood's voice rose significantly in volume. "Whoever does *will* spend their remaining years as a permanent resident of Guantánamo Bay. Am I clear?"

Silence reigned throughout the room.

Englewood turned back to his DNI. "Danni, brief us on our strategy for thwarting this attack."

Finishing an hour later, the meeting broke up and Sanchez left the White House. No Pollyanna, she'd experienced her share of political infighting and turf battles. She knew nothing had prepared her for the coming one. The post-9/11 creation of the DNI had stripped the CIA and FBI of many of their foreign and domestic intelligence responsibilities. Publicly, Langley and the Hoover Building embraced the changes. Privately, they tried everything imaginable to torpedo the new agency. Englewood's decision effectively neutered the agencies for the duration of the al-Dosari matter. Their respective leadership would work Washington's dark, smoky backrooms to pressure Englewood into revoking what they saw as an extremely imprudent and illegal decision. Their real fear was that if McEwan succeeded, it would permanently alter how America combatted terrorism. A tectonic shift of this magnitude was unacceptable to the careerists. Englewood's warnings notwithstanding, they'd do everything within their power to keep that from occurring, including underhandedly throwing up obstacles and even countermanding the president's orders.

Sanchez knew Stefan would attempt to regain control by having a lackey oh-so-casually let slip some juicy morsel while lapping the Washington cocktail circuit. Or he'd be the "unnamed senior administration official" who leaked items to *The Washington Post* to kill McEwan's operation before it got off the ground. She hoped the threat of a Gitmo residency would hold off Stefan and his minions. Sanchez expected the FBI director to get over his initial anger and accept the al-Dosari situation as a unique circumstance warranting extraordinary measures and jump aboard the McEwan train. Although the chief executive had issued the order, she harbored no illusions she would shoulder the blame if things went south. Sanchez accepted that her new role provided a rare opportunity for consensus between the CIA and FBI.

Perched squarely atop both agencies' hit lists, she had displaced every terrorist in the world.

CHAPTER TWENTY-SEVEN

THE PAST SEVERAL DAYS had taken their physical toll on McEwan. It seemed weeks since he'd been to his mountaintop retreat, the Bekaa Valley, and Sudan. His dustup with Carl Stefan and his trip to London felt even more distant. Suddenly unable to keep his eyes open, McEwan dozed off. Sometime later, the squeak of the cockpit door hinge woke him. He looked up.

"We're on final approach. Wheels down in ten." The pilot pulled the door closed.

McEwan looked out at the pristine skyline, rolling hills, and mesas of San Diego. By the time the jet hit the runway, he was fully alert. When the stairs deployed, McEwan stepped out into the warm sunshine and found two agents waiting on the tarmac of Montgomery-Gibbs Executive Airport.

Clambering down the stairs, he approached the two men.

One agent offered, "If you're Kyle McEwan, I'm Ron Franks. This is Tony Maldanado. FBI."

"I'm McEwan," he acknowledged, shaking hands with both men.

McEwan followed the agents over to a Chevrolet sedan. Franks took the shotgun seat. McEwan slid in behind Maldanado, who steered them down the tarmac lanes past a guard shack and out of the airport.

McEwan broke the ice. "Who's represented in the San Diego JTTF?"

Franks turned to face him. "Just about every 'alphabet' Federal agency along with assorted local PDs. Aside from us, we have several from DHS and DOD. From DHS, there's Customs and Border Protection, which includes Border Patrol Agents and CBP Inspectors. DHS Immigration and Customs Enforcement does exactly what its name suggests. We work most closely with Homeland Security Investigations, the primary criminal investigative arm of ICE. Major DOD players are the Defense Criminal Investigative Service, along with counterparts Navy NCIS, Air Force OSI, and Army CID. And ATF, DEA, plus the Postal Inspectors."

"Sounds challenging keeping the different missions focused; difficult to ensure a smooth operation, I imagine. Who runs the task force?" McEwan queried.

Maldanado shifted uncomfortably in his seat and shot Franks a nervous glance. "You need to take that up with the bosses."

"No problem." McEwan realized he'd struck a raw nerve.

Relieved at not being pressed to elaborate, Franks announced, "We're here."

Maldanado let Franks and McEwan out in front of an impressive concrete-and-glass building off Interstate 805 in Sorrento Valley. Franks ushered McEwan into the office of F. Vincent Hanratty, special agent in charge of the San Diego FBI Counterterrorism Division. The SAC was dark, stocky, and in his mid-forties. The bushy-eyebrowed Hanratty appeared of Italian ancestry despite his Irish surname.

"McEwan, Vince Hanratty." His icy greeting and combative stance telegraphed disapproval of the case officer's presence. "The rest of the JTTF agency heads are waiting down the hall, so I'll get to the point. I don't like my orders from Washington, not one bit. But like any good soldier, I'll follow them. Until told otherwise."

"Vince, you lost me somewhere between 'Hello' and 'I'm pissed off you're here'." A sour taste flooded McEwan's mouth.

Incredulous, Hanratty ran his hand through thinning hair and stared at McEwan. "You're telling me you didn't ask to run this op?"

Hanratty's attempt at bullying McEwan backfired. "Let me explain something, *Vince*. The president of the United States gave me my orders personally. I'm here to bag a terrorist hell-bent on destroying our country, and every law enforcement agency is supporting me. Either you got the wrong marching orders or a bug up your ass. Doesn't matter. I don't have time for this."

Like two bulls in a ring, they glared at each other for several seconds.

Used to unquestioning obedience, Hanratty stiffened. He blinked, stepping back. "I didn't say the FBI wouldn't cooperate. My Irish side had to blow off some steam. We're all in this together."

McEwan's bullshit meter instantly pegged red. He suspected Hanratty wasn't finished trying to wrest away some control, however slight. "Your sense of duty is admirable, Vince."

Backed against the wall, literally and figuratively, Hanratty began tap-dancing. "You can appreciate my perspective on this thing. I've been running JTTF ops here for eighteen months; suddenly, I'm not good enough—"

"Quit trying to blow sunshine up my ass. Don't you get it? This isn't about you or me. We've got one job, stopping this bastard. Are you part of the problem or part of the solution?"

Warned that McEwan had a direct pipeline to the Oval Office, Hanratty folded. "We're in. But none of us locally have any intel on anybody named al-Dosari or the Sword of Islam."

"Okay, Vince. Let's just forget this little tête-à-tête. Introduce me to the rest of the folks."

CHAPTER TWENTY-EIGHT

WITH ONLY ONE OTHER passenger seated in first class, the beautiful flight attendant paid inordinate attention to al-Dosari throughout the trip. Flying Air France was a blessing in the form of lovely Carmelita, and he found the outline of her derriere in the tight skirt intoxicating. The handsome terrorist averted his eyes as she turned and headed toward him.

"We land in thirty minutes, Señor Ramirez." Carmelita addressed him by his alias de jure. "Perhaps you would care to freshen up a bit." The raven-haired beauty batted her long eyelashes as she handed over a hot washcloth, her fingers lingering several seconds longer than necessary.

"I feel fortunate to have had the attention of such an enchanting and lovely woman. Carmelita, you would honor me by calling me Cristos." He flashed his perfect white teeth.

"Of course. Will you be in Mexico a few days?"

"Indeed. I will be here this week and next. This is my first visit to your country. I plan to see several cities between business meetings. If I can find my way around, that is."

Throughout the flight, she had provided opportunities for Ramirez to express interest in her. Now that he had, Carmelita opened the door all the way. Looking over her shoulder hesitantly, she lowered her voice to a whisper. "I share a small apartment in Mexico City with other flight attendants. After this flight, I am going to my home in Mexicali for a seven-day holiday. If you wish, I could remain in the city and be your guide."

Al-Dosari flashed another smile. "Please do not change your plans. I fly to Tijuana when we land but will visit Mexicali for the remainder of my business. I will be coming to you!"

Carmelita hastily scribbled numbers on a cocktail napkin and slid it across the tray. Leaning over, she let her silky jet-black hair brush across his cheek. "I am available for you, Cristos. This is my number in Mexicali. Do not worry about calling late. Since you have accepted my invitation, it will be my obligation to see you have a most memorable visit." She subtly telegraphed her intentions. "Mexicali is a passionate city."

The terrorist let his fingers glide lightly across her palm. He took the napkin, folding and placing it in his shirt pocket. His mesmerizing green eyes bore into her as he moved to seal the deal. "Come closer. I wish to tell you something."

As the flight attendant bent down, al-Dosari took hold of her arm. His firm but gentle touch sent a shiver up the length of her spine. Sensing his effect, al-Dosari pulled her closer and purred with hot breath, "It is not what you can do for me, but what I can do for you, my beautiful Carmelita." He flicked his tongue softly against her ear.

As he released her, Carmelita's knees buckled. Steadying herself on the seat, she regained her composure, her voice husky. "Perhaps you are correct, but do not underestimate what Carmelita will do for Cristos." She stroked her long, sinewy fingers along his cheek.

The raw sexuality of the exchange was electrifying.

Turning, Carmelita strolled back toward the cockpit.

A half hour later, after repeated seductive looks but no further conversation, the plane landed at Aeropuerto Internacionale Benito Juárez, Mexico City. Several minutes of taxiing brought the airliner to a stop in front of a gate. Unleashing her most dazzling smile, Carmelita unbuckled herself from the jump seat and stood, holding his eyes with her sultriest gaze. She did not break contact while opening the hatch.

Retrieving his carry-on items, al-Dosari walked to the front of the cabin and stopped at the cockpit door. "A most relaxing flight. I cannot remember a better one."

"Perhaps we will fly together again, Señor." She moved her lips silently. "Call me." Radiant, Carmelita's black eyes glistened like pools of oil.

Al-Dosari indicated with a nod he would. As he strolled up the Jetway, elation washed over him. Securing a hideout in Mexicali was fortuitous if he needed one. But it was not what fueled his excitement.

He had landed in North America.

CHAPTER TWENTY-NINE

McEWAN SCANNED THE CROWD, all attired like the "suits" or supervisory personnel they were, except one man lounging next to the coffee urn at the back of the room. He appeared to be fresh off a golf course.

Striding forward, F. Vincent Hanratty addressed the group. "I know you folks wonder why we called this urgent meeting. Last night, I received a call from my director and the attorney general. The president has marshaled all US law enforcement, and specifically this JTTF, to conduct a manhunt to intercept a terrorist named Ali bin al-Dosari. Also known by the alias the Sword of Islam, he's allegedly smuggling a bioweapon across the border into California sometime during the next fourteen days. We will investigate this threat, but we've been ordered to pursue it in a manner inconsistent with how we normally conduct business." Holding everyone's rapt attention, Hanratty let that sink in, then continued.

"By order of the president, this operation is under the exclusive command of Kyle McEwan, a DNI counterterrorism agent. As of now, we all report to McEwan." Hanratty took a sip of water, allowing the expected eruption.

Starting as a murmur, the noise grew to a buzz, then a hubbub as the group digested the news. Their disbelief and reactions were understandable. Told only to expect a CIA briefing, now they were being told that a DNI counterterrorism agent would run their investigation. This was clearly unprecedented. The final twist was the president's order: all were under McEwan's command.

McEwan used Hanratty's thinly veiled attempt to incite mutiny as an opportunity to survey the reactions. His eyes landed on the fit man in the golf shirt parked next to the coffee urn; he remained aloof, above the fray. Tuning back into the noise, McEwan pounded a thick case file on a table. The chaos dissolved into a tense, uneasy silence.

Pleased and convinced he'd achieved his goal, Hanratty finished up forcefully. "My bosses were crystal clear: the very existence of this operation is classified. It's time to introduce ourselves, starting with you, Denny."

A man in a blue suit said, "Dennis Draper, special agent in charge, DEA."

The golf-attired man casually reloaded his mug before speaking, his sharp gray eyes framed by a salt-and-pepper crew cut. "Tim Morton, SAC, Homeland Security Investigations."

The remaining introductions blurred for McEwan. He concentrated on microexpressions and body language. All but one person—Morton—resented McEwan and his authority.

"McEwan, the floor is yours." Hanratty's words were edged with acid.

The counterterrorism agent took two steps to the center of the room. "We all work for the same person, the president of the United States. He has issued unequivocal orders—there is nothing further to discuss on the subject. There is one goal, one purpose: we must foil the attack and capture al-Dosari. Everything else is immaterial, and that includes the issue of who's in charge. Per the president, any leaks will result in the responsible parties being permanently reassigned to Gitmo but on the other side of the bars. This is not an exaggerated threat.

"We are at war. There's one battlefield commander. I did not seek this assignment—I accepted it. You each possess skills and knowledge I do not have, and I am relying on your expertise. All recommendations will be considered and factored into my decisions. While those above our pay grades in DC will monitor our actions, in the final analysis, only you and the men and women under your commands can stop al-Dosari."

Collective murmurs rippled across the room. Seasoned agents all, they realized McEwan was right. In a few brief sentences, he'd thwarted Hanratty's rebellion.

McEwan changed course, briefing them on his activities during the past week. They learned about al-Dosari's murders of the world's top infectious disease experts, including Ahmed Mansour, and his plan to mass-murder thousands, if not millions, of Americans by infecting them with smallpox. He encapsulated the intelligence gleaned in London, the Bekaa Valley, and the Hala'ib Triangle without mentioning the raids or what had been discovered. He described al-Dosari's alleged plan to enter the US via a tunnel on the California-Mexico border. He opined that al-Dosari would receive assistance from yet-unidentified US-based sleeper cells.

"What's our risk from the smallpox?" one of the supervisors queried, brow furrowed.

McEwan had the answer. "Most of the world's population is not inoculated against smallpox because it was judged eradicated decades ago. Nevertheless, al-Dosari has engineered a new variant, so we're all in jeopardy. Our scientists are working around the clock to crack the genetic code but we're operating on the belief there's insufficient time to develop and produce a vaccine to deliver to us, much less in the quantities needed to protect our fellow citizens."

The room remained eerily quiet.

McEwan continued, "If we do not intercept al-Dosari at the border, he can attack at will. Our task is complicated and challenging. We don't even know what he looks like. We don't know where he'll enter, and we can't use our regular sources to find him. The veil of secrecy must be maintained. Our cities will ignite if word leaks out that a WMD attack is imminent. Al-Dosari won't have to lift a finger—we will implode and self-destruct. We can never cause or allow that to happen." McEwan bore his eyes into everyone present.

"Ours is a zero-fail mission—there will be no second chances."

CHAPTER THIRTY

AFTER A SHORT BREAK, Homeland Security Investigations SAC Tim Morton stepped forward while the rest of the agents settled back into their seats. He took a sip of coffee and cleared his throat.

"Kyle, during the break, I spoke with my colleagues and pitched a possible scenario. They agreed I should run it by you. If al-Dosari's coming through a tunnel, I have a hunch on how and where he'll do it."

McEwan nodded, "Go for it."

"First, a thumbnail sketch of border operations."

Morton broke it down rapidly. "Obviously, there are two ways to enter our country. Legally, through official air, sea, or land ports of entry, or illegally, across, over, around, or under the border. For legal entry, a person is admitted as long as he or she doesn't have a felony warrant or conviction, isn't on the terror watch list, or isn't bringing in contraband.

"Illegal entries occur predominantly at areas along our borders where there aren't official ports of entry. Most occur over land, less frequently via air or water. Physical barriers such as fences, bodies of water, and difficult terrain present distinct perils. Assuming one successfully overcomes those obstacles, they risk detection and capture by the Border Patrol. Every year, merchants of human beings, narcotics, and contraband invest millions of dollars inventing methods to frustrate, obstruct, and counteract border law enforcement."

"Tunnels," McEwan offered.

"Correct. Burrowing under the border skirts past almost all the perils posed by overland entry except Border Patrol detection. A little more than a year ago, we brought in the Army Corps of Engineers to run radar, sonar, and electromagnetic wave tests to detect tunnel construction—they got a hit on a special tunnel at Calexico. It's the most sophisticated tunnel ever found. We were so amazed by its extraordinary design we decided to keep its discovery secret and surveil it. We used an undercover company to rent space in a warehouse to set up a surveillance post. We've allowed narco traffic and human smuggling to flow through it. We take down the bad guys up the pipeline each time at a different location. Since use of the tunnel has remained constant, we know the cartels are unaware we're monitoring it."

"Where is it exactly?" Energy surged through McEwan.

Morton picked up a laser pointer and drew a circle on a wall map. "The tunnel begins here in Mexicali beneath an abandoned building on First Street. We haven't ID'd the owner, but it's undoubtedly a shell. DEA suspects the Hernando-Zambada drug cartel constructed the tunnel with the blessing of the Mexican attorney general's organized crime unit. The tunnel snakes under the border for about four hundred feet before terminating in a vacant apartment building off Second Street in Calexico. It is seven feet high, five feet wide, and forty-five feet below ground. The walls and overhead are reinforced with eight-inch wood beams, steel rebar, and concrete."

"Damn," McEwan voiced his surprise.

Morton appreciated the reaction. "It gets better. It's solar-powered with an electric rail system, lighting, and transport carts, along with fans that draw in a continuous fresh air supply through rubber tubing. There's even a water extraction and drainage system. Judging by its complexity, we believe it cost on the order of two million dollars and took more than two years to build. During a period of bad weather, we put a tech agent into the tunnel to wire it up on the US side with motion-detection sensors, listening devices, and video cameras. We have eleven months of home movies."

"Has there been any unusual activity?" McEwan queried pointedly.

"Three weeks ago, Calexico PD stumbled onto a suspected narco mule. When they tried to question him, he dropped his rucksack and fled. Inside were thirteen Venezuelan passports and an Arabic diary. The DOD Language Institute in Monterey translated the diary—personal entries only. Investigation determined the passports were issued to known Middle Eastern and Southwest Asian terror operatives. Unfortunately, we haven't located the corresponding bodies. We think they were already in the US and the runner was going to link up and hand off the documents.

"Within the last sixty days, we've recovered a Syrian military uniform shirt, two prayer rugs, and an Arabic Koran. Everything is with the FBI laboratory for analysis. We've closely held information about our arrest last spring of two Hezbollah agents. After they lawyered up, a paperwork error caused an immigration judge to deport them. We never had a chance to interrogate them. Increasing numbers of OTMs, or 'other than Mexicans', are entering the US via our soft underbelly for purposes other than narcotics or human trafficking."

Morton stopped to hand McEwan a stack of photos, which he leafed through. Their clarity was remarkable.

"You expect al-Dosari to use this tunnel."

Nodding at McEwan's astute analysis, Morton ticked off the indicators. "Yes. First, you have solid intel he's entering via a tunnel. A border-wide check a week ago found two more tunnels under construction, one each in San Diego and Tecate. We filled those in, so as far as we know, the only tunnel al-Dosari can use is this one. In the last month, smugglers tripled the amount of product pushed through our tunnel. A week ago, traffic slowed to a crawl, then screeched to a halt. This leads us to believe the spigot is turned off, and the only reason they'd do that is for something more important than smuggling dope or bodies. As evidenced by the recovered passports, known Islamic terrorists have used our tunnel."

"Okay, Tim. How do we set the trap?"

"Until we capture al-Dosari, we'll double the number of Border Patrol agents on the California border all the way to Arizona. We'll make well-placed 'leaks' to the media about a shortage of agents at Calexico. Al-Dosari will be discouraged from considering any other option, and we'll push him into our tunnel there. We're monitoring the sensors and cameras 24-7. Our special response team will pounce if sensors activate on anything."

"What if he exits the tunnel?"

"We'll keep him from going back by penning him in. We can't shut it on the other side because we can't trust the Mexicali police or the Federales."

"Understood. What can I do?"

"Technically, we'll be operating in two different CBP sectors, San Diego and El Centro. I recommend establishing a Joint Operations Center at San Diego Sector Headquarters and roll in the JTTF assets. Set up a Tactical Operations Center at Naval Air Facility El Centro to manage all the special response units from the Pacific to Arizona. Use DHS's communication capabilities to coordinate all activities."

McEwan appreciated that Morton's plan steered clear of using a Vince Hanratty–controlled FBI command post, thereby avoiding the predictable turf battle.

"I approve your plan. Let's get to work."

Hanratty, mute, mottled face betraying his rage, snatched his coffee cup and left the room briskly, minions in tow.

McEwan approached Morton, reinstalled beside the coffee urn.

"Tim, I was impressed with how quickly you came up with such a thorough plan. I've got one concern. You and I are on the same team, but we're used to playing by different rules. My forte is foreign counterterrorism operations. I think like my adversaries. I don't think like a law enforcement officer. As a result, it's difficult for me to relate to people unaccustomed to my methods. I need someone to help me bridge the gap. Can I count on you to be my point man on the law enforcement side?"

"Absolutely." That said, Morton grabbed a full coffee mug and left the room.

CHAPTER THIRTY-ONE

"DO YOU REQUIRE ASSISTANCE, Señor?"

Al-Dosari studied the overweight man wearing a rumpled beige suit. "I need to connect to Tijuana. Can you assist me?"

"Sí, Señor. Follow me."

Code words exchanged, the man led the terrorist over to a secluded area away from the omnipresent security cameras of Mexico City's Aeropuerto Internacionale Benito Juárez. The contact motioned for the terrorist to sit across from him.

"I am Captain Ruben García of the Federal Judicial Police. It is my pleasure to meet you, Señor Ramirez."

"The pleasure is mine, El Capitan." *I know who you are, you corrupt swine.*

"May I see your documentation, Señor?"

The terrorist surrendered his alias passport.

Opening and scanning the document, García compared its photograph to the face across from him. Snapping it closed, he stuffed it inside his left breast pocket.

"Gracías, Señor Ramirez. I shall return your passport after we pass through Customs. We have a slight change in plans. My contact had a death in his family and is not working today. For me to get you through the checkpoint, I must arrest you. Do not panic, it is for show. I will merely place you in handcuffs. You have nothing to fear. I am being paid handsomely, and only when I deliver you safely do I get my other half."

The terrorist could trust the Mexican only because he craved money. It had to be good enough. "Do not open my belongings, Capitan García. ¿Comprende usted?" The message, delivered in Spanish, ensured clarity.

"Perfectamente. Dame su manos, por favor."

García clipped his badge onto his suit coat pocket and cuffed Ramirez. Setting the valise and case on the wheeled suitcase, García pulled the stack with one hand while tugging the terrorist's elbow with the other. They received many stares passing through the terminal. A couple of minutes later, they reached the Immigration and Customs checkpoint. Dragging his quarry, García shoved his way to the head of the long line.

"¡Policía Judicial Federal! ¡Fuera de mi manera!"

The terrorist translated silently: *Federal Judicial Police! Out of my way!*

A Customs officer opened a metal tube gate and stepped aside, allowing the two men and pile of luggage through. The charade continued all the way out of the terminal into the stifling heat and humidity. The theater ended once García pushed him roughly into the back seat of a sedan. The policeman placed the bags in the front seat then climbed in beside him. He wasted no time removing the cuffs.

"Señor Ramirez, rub your wrists. You will be fine. You will be at your gate in no time." He snapped his fingers at the man in the driver's seat. "Ortega!"

Hearing his name, the man turned and handed García a plain brown paper bag.

Reaching in, El Capitan retrieved an inkpad and handheld stamp. García tamped it a couple of times on the inkpad, removed Ramirez's passport from his breast pocket, and applied an entry stamp to a blank page. García waved the open passport in the air for a few seconds, letting the ink dry, then handed it over. "Enjoy your stay in Mexico," he announced cleverly. The stamp and inkpad got stuffed back into the paper bag. "Ortega, the TJ gate."

Minutes later, the terrorist was airborne again. Destination: Tijuana.

McEwan sat next to Tim Morton in the rear seat of the speedy Customs and Border Protection Air Ops helicopter. As the Air Interdiction Agent flew them east toward Calexico, Morton provided running commentary on the passing landscape.

"Chief Patrol Agents exercise tactical control of all CBP Air and Marine assets in their respective sectors. We use them extensively in both the San Diego and El Centro sectors to cover all 130 miles of the California-Mexico border. Each sector has SWAT-type special operations detachments known as BORTAC. Both sectors have major border crossing checkpoints, stations, and substations; San Ysidro is the busiest port of entry. Then there's the two Calexico checkpoints. The primary users of the downtown checkpoint, Calexico West, are pedestrians and vehicles ferrying people across the border. Ten miles farther east in the desert is Calexico East, which handles mostly commercial traffic.

"We're discovering an increasing number of tunnels channeled beneath buildings in densely populated areas. In the Calexico area, the only suitable terrain is smack-dab below the city proper. Radar and sonar technologies have limited value, leaving us to rely on human intel and luck."

McEwan's phone vibrated; the screen showed a text message from Sanchez: "When you touch down, a Fort Detrick doctor will have a device for you. Use it."

Al-Dosari's Aero México jet banked on final approach to Tijuana's General Abelardo L. Rodríguez International Airport. Looking out his window, he saw the clearly delineated border with America edging the airport runway. Lines of traffic snaked their way slowly north to the San Ysidro border crossing. He could barely contain his glee, having reached the infidel's gates.

Gathering his belongings, al-Dosari deplaned and entered the first restroom he saw. He stepped inside an empty stall and latched the door. He slipped around his carry-ons and relieved himself then flushed. Emerging from the booth, he washed his hands and reentered the concourse. Satisfied he was not being followed, he claimed his checked bag and exited the terminal building. Spotting the fence separating Mexico from the United States, he fought the urge to run toward it and climb over. He laughed at his foolhardy thought.

Hailing a taxi, al-Dosari gave the driver directions to an office building off Route 2 south of the airport. He sat back on the dusty seat with stifling air blowing in through the windows and reflected on the circuitous route that brought him this far. Traveling from Damascus to Paris to Mexico City to Tijuana had been tiring but necessary. Tijuana was a diversion to prevent the Federales from learning his true destination. As the taxi pulled into a pothole-filled parking lot, he spotted a green Ford Taurus.

Al-Dosari stopped the driver. "Aquí esta perfecto."

Stepping out with his luggage, he paid the man. He set the valise on the ground next to the Taurus and unlocked it, digging out an envelope. Tearing it open, he let a set of keys fall into his hands, one of which he inserted into the trunk.

It worked.

CHAPTER THIRTY-TWO

McEWAN LOOKED DOWN AT the lone person awaiting their arrival as the helicopter hovered above the Calexico helipad. The woman wore the dark-blue uniform of a CBP inspector.

Landing, Morton and McEwan clambered out. The inspector approached and stuck out her hand while unsuccessfully trying to maintain control of her auburn hair with the other.

"Mr. McEwan, I'm Nena DeAngelis, CBP port director."

"Nice to meet you," McEwan responded.

"Let's step inside." DeAngelis guided them into a conference room occupied by a man and woman in civilian attire. The woman clutched a champagne-colored brushed aluminum case.

The strapping, blond-haired man with goatee and mustache extended his hand. "Ken Kearney, HSI Special Response Team—SRT. Call me Kip."

McEwan shook the agent's hand. Morton's plan included strategically placed Border Patrol and Homeland Security special response tactical teams like Kearney's to pounce once al-Dosari showed his head.

He turned to the attractive, light brown-haired woman holding the briefcase. "Forgive me for skipping the rest of the niceties, but we're on a short fuse. Are you from Fort Detrick?"

"Yes. I'm Dr. Sheila Huston. I understand, so I'll omit all the technical jargon. This is a very sophisticated instrument designed by Sandia National Lab. It's hypersensitive to the slightest amount of the substance but won't detect anything else. I'm here to show you how to use it."

McEwan noted Huston conveniently avoided the other S-word and failed to mention she worked for the US Army specializing in bioweapons.

Dr. Huston set the aluminum case on a desk and opened it. "It conducts real-time air analysis within a fifty-foot radius."

"Resembles a polygraph machine," McEwan noted.

"So I'm told. When you are within range of a suspected release, flip the switch on the face of the dial to the On position. Remove this wireless handheld unit, turn it on, and point it toward the suspected release. The handheld unit will sample the air and send a signal to the briefcase. It responds quickest to releases within a 180-degree radius to your sides and front."

McEwan looked skeptical.

"If the device detects even a tiny particle, both units will emit shrill sirens and a red light will flash on the 360-degree dial at the point where it is discharged. If they go off, you should hightail it out of there, although as a practical matter you've already been exposed. Normally, I'd recommend you wear Hazmat gear, but I'm told you're operating in a harsh environment."

"Does this thing really work?" McEwan voiced his doubt.

"It's performed perfectly in tests. We've never experienced a false reading—negative or positive." Tutorial finished, Dr. Huston snapped the case shut.

"Why are you here instead of someone from Sandia?"

"Because I can bail you out when you screw up. They can't."

Her directness surprised him; McEwan realized his words betrayed his skepticism.

"Mr. McEwan, when you recover the substance, I'll take it from you, secure it, sanitize you, contain the hot zone, quarantine all other persons, then send for the cavalry."

McEwan eyed her; she had more.

"In plain English, I'm here to see that you don't hurt yourself or anyone else."

"Okay, I give," McEwan raised his hands, signaling surrender. "Don't think I'm ungrateful. I'm not accustomed to having all the bells and whistles. If we find it, you'll get the first call."

Huston, ruffled feathers soothed by McEwan's conciliatory gesture, handed over the case. "You know where to find me. Happy hunting."

After loading up the Ford Taurus in Tijuana, al-Dosari took a leisurely two-hour drive east on Federal Highway 2. As a countersurveillance measure, every so often he pulled over and photographed the scenery with his digital camera. If stopped, he could prove he was innocently sightseeing on the way to Mexicali to meet a friend. Though tired, he remained alert, checking many times for watchers.

Hitting the city limits, he drove to the Hotel El Conquistador del Sol, a spectacular Spanish colonial building dominated by a huge dome. Pulling the car under the entrance canopy, he tossed his keys to a valet, who provided a receipt. Supervising the placement of his luggage onto a cart, the terrorist resisted the bellhop's attempts to take charge of his valise and computer case. Rampant thievery being the norm in Mexico, even at its finest hotels, he would not take the risk, not when Allah had brought him this close.

"Buenos días, Señor," an attractive woman greeted him from behind the front desk. "Welcome to El Conquistador del Sol."

"Gracías. My name is Cristos Ramirez, and I have reservations for four nights." He paused as the desk clerk typed in his name.

"Sí, Señor. We have a delivery for you." Turning, she retrieved a private courier envelope and handed it over the counter to him.

"Un momento, por favor." Al-Dosari walked over to a chair and sat down. He opened the sealed envelope and peeked inside, scanning the contents. Placing the envelope under his arm, he sauntered back to the front desk, tendered a Visa card, and signed the registration folio.

"Your suite is on the seventh floor. The elevators are behind you. Have a lovely evening, Señor Ramirez."

"And you as well."

He headed toward the elevator, trailing the bellhop, who continued trying to acquire responsibility for his valise and computer case.

Inspecting the rooms, he deemed them satisfactory. He tipped the bellhop, who grabbed the ice bucket and disappeared. The man returned, then left after receiving the desired second tip.

Finally alone, al-Dosari turned the package upside down on a table, spilling its contents. He inspected a Mexican driver's license, passport, a holder filled with business cards identifying the bearer as the owner of an import-export business in Tijuana, and an official US government card entitling the named holder to make frequent trips across the border for commerce purposes. All bore the name of a new alias.

Finding everything in order, al-Dosari pulled out his laptop computer, turned it over, and removed the battery. A brilliant disciple of the Sword had carefully deconstructed the battery by removing each of the nine lithium-ion cells and replacing them with nearly a pound of precious vacuum-sealed, freeze-dried smallpox. After reconstruction, it became just one more computer battery that died in flight. Though undetectable by even the finest sensors, his route nevertheless traversed countries with substandard or nonexistent technology. He had never been challenged to start his computer; had he been ordered to do so, he would have extracted a spare battery from his bag and installed it, which he did now. Booting up the computer, he struck a short key sequence and crashed the hard drive, an unnecessary precaution since it contained nothing of value. Retrieving a fanny pack from his suitcase, he transferred the smallpox-laden battery into its main pouch. His final task was to cut and tear up his old identity documents and credit cards and flush them down the toilet.

After a room service dinner and long hot bath, he wrapped himself in a plush bathrobe. Making his way to the window, he pulled back the drapes—his suite overlooked the US-Mexico border. Thinking about his imminent entry into America produced an involuntary contraction of his genitals. Experiencing the near-orgasmic sensation, al-Dosari turned from the window and walked over to the nightstand. Lifting the telephone handset, he dialed a number. After three short rings, a soft voice answered.

"Carmelita?"

CHAPTER THIRTY-THREE

HSI SPECIAL AGENT KIP Kearney maneuvered the cargo van down the crowded streets of Calexico. Entering an alley, he pulled through a garage door that clanged shut behind them. Inside, he rounded a wall and parked alongside a white Ford Explorer and four other white vans bearing identical signage: "Southeastern California Express Printing".

McEwan suspected the battered and worn exteriors cleverly disguised top-performing vehicles.

Morton spoke. "Welcome to our off-site. I'll grab a cup of coffee, then give you a quick tour. Kip, got any fresh java around here?"

"Nope. Kyle, if you haven't figured it out, Tim single-handedly keeps the coffee industry in business." Kearney chuckled.

McEwan's nod confirmed he'd picked up on Morton's addiction. "Find someone to take this Sandia unit off my hands. You saw it demo'd and can give a crash course on it."

"Sure thing. We have the right man for the job, eh, Tim?"

Simultaneously the men said, "Bennie."

Kearney elaborated. "Benicio Espinoza is one of our technical support officers. He installed all of the electronic equipment we're using to monitor the tunnel."

Morton guided McEwan through the facility, a sophisticated law enforcement nerve center disguised as a warehouse. First stop, a surveillance module. Sitting at an L-shaped console in front of a dozen monitors and screens, a windbreaker-clad female agent pointed out something on the display to another agent looking intently over her shoulder.

"Meredith, you have something?" Morton asked.

"No, sir. I was showing Rob the monitor for sensor number 1."

Morton explained, "Bennie wired the tunnel on the US side with motion sensors, listening devices, and miniature video cameras. When a rat, or tunnel runner, enters and triggers a sensor, the miniature cameras activate. We get astonishingly clear photos courtesy of the bad guys, who thoughtfully lit the tunnel. One night, Bennie stole over to the other side and affixed a sensor to the last panel inside Mexico. It was a ballsy move, given the possibility of running into thugs or corrupt police on the other side. When it's triggered, we have around three minutes 'til showtime. When the next sensor triggers, they've reached the US and are on audio and video. Based on your intel, we think we know why all smuggling and trafficking has stopped."

Morton led McEwan to a U-shaped console occupied by two agents wearing headsets with mics. "Tony is listening to radio transmissions for both the San Diego and El Centro sectors. John is monitoring the local PDs. Flipping a switch, we can transmit with all PDs and federal agencies from Arizona to San Diego. By depressing another switch, our national communications center can link us with every DHS office and law enforcement agency in the nation."

Next stop was a conference room, where Kearney stood in front of a whiteboard, discussing the al-Dosari takedown plan with about a dozen agents. Morton and McEwan's entrance halted the meeting. He introduced McEwan, and the planning resumed.

When Kearney's briefing concluded, Morton gestured toward the door. "I want to head over to the Tactical Operations Center we established at NAF El Centro."

"Fine. The only thing more impressive than the facility was the briefing. You've pulled it together—they're ready."

McEwan noted the FBI was nowhere to be found.

Al-Dosari sat in a chair in the bedroom of his suite in the El Conquistador del Sol. While he needed the release, in Allah's eyes his acts were immoral. Gazing down at the naked and beautiful Carmelita, he felt his loins stir again and immediately regretted his impure thoughts. He felt even less worthy because he had not performed his daily ritual of prayers in three days. The fact that waging jihad excused him from these duties eased his guilt only slightly.

Watching the soundly sleeping woman, his anger bubbled over. Because of their intercourse, he must make complete ablution. The Sharia required him to cleanse himself to regain his purity. Walking into the bathroom, he turned on the shower and stepped under the stream of warm water. He dropped his head in prayer: *Forgive me, Allah, for succumbing to the sins of the flesh.*

Finished bathing away his sins, he toweled off, put on the plush cotton hotel robe, and returned to the bedroom where Carmelita slept. Avoiding temptation, he grabbed a stack of documents from his valise and walked into the living room.

Leafing through the papers, he closed his eyes and mentally rehearsed his journey. He returned to the intensive briefing by Khadija, the talented engineer who designed the tunnel: "The abandoned building has a side door secured with a lock. The Ford key ring has a brass key that will unlock it. Enter and relock this door from the inside. Go to the basement. Cover yourself with the overalls, stocking mask, and gloves hanging on a wall hook. Using the high-lumen headlamp, climb into the coal chute and crawl twenty feet to another opening. Ladders on three levels will take you down to the main tunnel entrance. There you will walk upright to the border. I know you are experienced in tunnels and caves in Afghanistan, but you will marvel at this engineering wonder. The drug cartel did as instructed."

"What about the rest of the plan?" he had asked Khadija.

As al-Dosari recalled the equally detailed answer, he was interrupted.

"Cristos?"

Startled, he turned the papers face down on the table with a quick flip of his wrist. Al-Dosari looked up at the naked Carmelita, her face filled with confusion.

"Did I wake you, my darling? I am sorry—"

"What are these, Cristos?" Carmelita demanded, clutching his new false identity documents. "What do they mean?"

The terrorist did not flinch. "Do not worry, my love. I must sometimes use an alias since I travel to both Muslim countries and Israel. If I did not, were my plane hijacked by Islamic terrorists, I would be vulnerable for having a Jewish visa or entry stamp in my passport."

Carmelita looked dubious, necessitating him to expand his bogus explanation. "My brother, a Ministry of Foreign Affairs official, insisted. It is common for persons of my stature to have this arrangement with our government. Do you not see the wisdom? Failure to have such could damage business ventures in both countries and endanger me."

Accepting his explanation, Carmelita exhaled and relaxed. She overlooked that the documents were issued in Mexico, not Spain, her lover's supposed home.

"Oh, Cristos, I should not have doubted you." Carmelita jumped onto his lap, straddling him. Planting kisses all over his face, she ran her hands through his hair, then disrobed him.

Feeling Carmelita's wetness, the craving to take her again overwhelmed al-Dosari and he became fully erect. Kissing her softly on the neck, he traced his fingers over her breasts, stopping to pinch and rub her nipples between his thumb and forefinger.

Gasping with pleasure, Carmelita unwrapped a tanned arm from around his neck, reaching between his legs and guiding him expertly inside her.

"Turn around!" Al-Dosari ordered throatily.

Carmelita pirouetted without removing him. Gyrating, soft cries and moans escaping her lips, she shuddered from his repeated thrusts. She cried with pleasure, her breaths coming in gasps.

Al-Dosari's thrusts became more frenzied, and he climaxed with Carmelita. Upon orgasm, he reached around and grabbed her by the chin and with a single violent twist, snapped her neck. The flight attendant's instant death triggered his second orgasm. Trembling, he pushed the dead woman off to the side. After taking several minutes to recover, al-Dosari stood, stepped over Carmelita's body, and returned to the bathroom. A half hour later, cleansed of filth from the Jezebel, he dressed. Spreading a clean blanket on the bedroom floor, he prayed.

Allah, I regret my vulgar and illicit behavior. I beg forgiveness for failing to conform to thy will. Please accept as my purification my surrender of the infidel whore to the fires of hell. She will burn in repentance for my sins and for the immoral behavior tarnishing her family name. Give me strength as I travel through the subterranean corridor to America. Allahu Akbar!

Al-Dosari walked over to the television set and turned it on, adjusting the volume so ears outside the room could hear it without becoming annoyed. Gathering his belongings, he headed for the door and placed the "No Disturbe" sign on the doorknob. Stepping into the hallway, he pulled the door closed. When they finally found the whore's body, it would not matter.

CHAPTER THIRTY-FOUR

McEWAN'S PHONE SCREEN FLASHED as the CBP helicopter landed near two C-130 Hercules aircraft. He updated Danni Sanchez while walking with Morton toward the Tactical Operations Center. They entered the air-conditioned NAF El Centro hangar, and Morton disappeared. McEwan ended his call as Morton returned through the door with two Styrofoam cups of steaming coffee. An agent trailed behind, carrying a file box full of reports.

"Here ya go. Nectar of the gods, my man," Morton said. "Now, let's get this dog-and-pony show going." Both men settled in for a long siege reviewing reports.

Ten minutes after leaving the hotel, al-Dosari found everything as Khadija said it would be. Making sure his fanny pack was strapped securely about his waist, he pulled the coveralls over his clothes and donned the mask and gloves. He climbed into the chute and followed the instructions precisely. He admired the simple sophistication of the tunnel, and the farther he walked, the more he appreciated its design and construction. He likened it to walking through an underground steam tunnel, only larger and without pipes, as he was able to remain upright the entire length of the corridor. Nearing its end, the headlamp lit up what he was searching for.

Al-Dosari pried loose a dozen or so boards, their creaking echoing down the subterranean passageway. He crawled through a narrow opening into a five-foot-square chamber. He sealed himself inside the space using the boards. The headlamp landed on a group of support beams. Focusing on a faux beam etched with the Mexican "evil eye" symbol, he peeled it back and exposed a hollow nook in the earthen wall, constructed for one traveler and trip, right under the arrogant infidels' noses. He performed his next action explicitly according to instructions. Finished, he turned and faced the primitive passageway running alongside the sophisticated tunnel. Steeling himself, al-Dosari bent down and crawled forward on all fours into the dank conduit.

In minutes, "Aurelio Aguilar" would pass under the border into the United States of America.

After reviewing dozens of reports and messages and making scores of phone calls, McEwan and Morton were packing up their briefcases when an HSI agent raced into the room.

"Command post is reporting tunnel activity!"

They sprinted to the helicopter already spinning up on the pad. Ten minutes later, they set down at Calexico International Airport and the two men ejected as one. A man in the driver's seat of an unmarked Ford Explorer motioned for them to hurry.

McEwan jumped in behind the driver. Hopping into the front passenger seat, Morton ordered, "Hit it!"

Bennie Espinoza stomped the accelerator to the floor, peeling from the airport, siren blaring, lights in the grill and flip-down visors flashing. Morton barked orders over the radio, unheard by McEwan over the howling siren. In minutes, Espinoza killed the lights and siren, pumping the brakes a few times before executing a left-hand turn. Several blocks later, they pulled into the off-site garage, sliding to a halt next to a loading dock. The agents bolted for the surveillance section.

Kearney stood at a console, scratching his head.

"What do we have, Kip?" a worried Morton asked.

"Tell the truth I'm not sure. The sensor on the Mexico side activated eleven minutes ago, but the number 1 sensor on our side hasn't tripped. The sensors farther down the passageway haven't triggered either. We've flipped on the cameras remotely but see zip. Nada. It's like somebody started across then turned back."

McEwan eyed Espinoza. "Could it be a false alarm?"

"Beats me. If so, it would be the first time."

"Tim, have everyone stand down but remain on alert." In McEwan's experience, even the best technology malfunctioned occasionally. But it didn't feel like a glitch. Something was up.

Ten minutes later, sounds of commotion echoing down the hallway interrupted the strategy session. A winded agent raced into the room. "The sensor on the Mexico side activated and now number one is going off!"

Al-Dosari! McEwan beat Morton to the surveillance monitors.

"We've got a rat!" Bennie Espinoza pointed at a monitor. "There's the blur!"

Watching the monitor, they saw the man stop and look around.

"He's going for it," Bennie continued. "He's practically sprinting!"

As McEwan started moving, Morton grabbed him by the arm, signaling "Hold on" while reaching for the radio transmitter. "Kip, our boy's going for the opening. Prepare to take him."

Tension and excitement filled the room as everyone studied the screens. Before their eyes, the man broke through the tunnel opening.

"Tim!" McEwan chomped at the bit. "Let's go!"

Morton said firmly, "Hang on, Kyle." He transmitted calmly, "Now, Kip."

McEwan heard the SRT agents scramble out of the room next door. Appearing on a video monitor, the team sprinted single file down an alley before beelining toward an abandoned building.

The radio blared, "We got him!"

"Bring him to the briefing room."

McEwan watched the agents drag the handcuffed man to the warehouse.

Morton grinned at McEwan. "Bennie installed an automatic locking device on the tunnel trapdoor. Once the rat went through, the mechanism was triggered. He was stuck in the building until Kip's men unlocked the basement door."

McEwan silently applauded the trap. Unable to remain idle another second, he bolted from the command center and hustled down the hallway to the briefing room.

Agents surrounded a prone figure on the floor, arms secured behind his back with flexi-cuffs. Kearney's sizable boot planted squarely on the back of the squirming man pinned him facedown.

"This fool doesn't seem to understand he's under arrest, and he's been told in two languages."

A chuckle rumbled through the gathered agents.

Reaching down, McEwan rolled the man over. *Son of a bitch! He's Mexican!* "Clear the room!"

Hearing feet scampering, but not the pair closest to him, McEwan turned.

"You too, Tim. This is one of those times your rule book doesn't cover."

Heading for the door, Morton closed it, resolutely remaining inside. Crossing his arms, he messaged silently: *Perhaps, but we're a team and I've got your six.*

Message received, McEwan focused on the man quivering beneath him, grabbing him roughly by the throat. "Who are you, and why are you here?"

No response. Instead, the man shrank away, cowering against the wall, pulling his knees up to his chest to shield himself from the blows he knew were seconds away.

McEwan backhanded the man across his cheek. Blood trickled to the floor. In a threatening voice, McEwan repeated the question. "I said, who are you?"

The man's fear was evident. He looked at Morton for help. "Por favor, dígale que no comprendo. ¡Yo no hablo Inglés!" Please tell him I do not understand. I do not speak English!

"¿Quién es usted?" McEwan asked the man his name in Spanish.

"Soy Enrique Cabrillo Martinez."

Asked why he was there, the man babbled his reply and McEwan translated. "He claims he was paid five hundred dollars to come here and somebody would meet him and hand over a backpack. If he returned with it, he'd be given another five hundred. Let's see if he knows who hired him. ¿Quién se pagó?"

Terrified of another blow, the man became the paragon of cooperation. "Su nombre es Alberto. El es un coyote que me ayudó a cruzar la frontera un par de veces."

"Tim, does the name Alberto mean anything to you? He's supposedly a coyote."

Morton didn't recognize the name.

"Okay, I'm going to quit dicking around." McEwan ran his hand through his hair. "He's either in on this thing or not."

"Kyle, let me give it a shot."

McEwan shrugged. "Of course, you speak Spanish. Have at it."

Morton spoke menacingly to the quivering man. "If you're lying, you will suffer. He will make sure you die very slowly, and it will hurt badly. Do you get what I'm saying?"

"¡Sí! ¡No estoy mintiendo! ¡No sé nada, Señor, nada!"

"Kyle, he's scared shitless. He doesn't know anything. He'd tell us if he did. I'll have Kip put this asshole on ice. We'll deal with him later."

McEwan stomped angrily from the room, outfoxed again by the slippery terrorist.

CHAPTER THIRTY-FIVE

LUANN TIPPIN'S ARTHRITIC RIGHT hand grabbed the leash off the kitchen counter. "Here, Skye. Time to go out."

The aging Shetland sheepdog ambled over obediently. Tippin hooked the floral cotton leash onto her dog's collar and wrapped the handle firmly about her wrist. The two of them took their time getting to the front door. The ever-cautious Tippin, president of the Rancho Calexico Neighborhood Watch, looked vigilantly for suspicious activity through the window while reaching for the doorknob. *What in the world?*

Peeking through the door's sidelight, Tippin studied the scene across the street, taking in every detail. Turning on her alarm system, she tiptoed away from the door and headed as fast as possible to her kitchen, dragging the forgotten Sheltie behind her.

Trembling with excitement, Tippin reached for the telephone on the wall.

McEwan and Morton were batting about different scenarios with Kearney and his SRT team members when a breathless agent barged into the room.

"Tim! Calexico PD is responding to a call from a citizen on Camino del Rio reporting a male exited a house across the street from her, climbed into a blue Dodge Caravan with wood grain panels, and drove off. Ten minutes ago."

"Slow down, slow down," Morton said. "Give it to me again."

The agent did, this time explaining the call's significance. "The house he exited burned down six weeks ago. She saw him pop up from underneath the rubble pile. She got the license plate of the minivan and watched it turn north on Andrade Avenue. Then she lost sight of it. It has to be a tunnel we don't know about."

The news was electrifying.

Morton didn't miss a beat. "Send a unit to the house. Notify CPD we're responding. Issue an urgent BOLO—make damn sure it lists the suspect as armed and dangerous. I want the van located but not detained. Request Imperial County Sheriff and the CHP stage units ASAP on 98 East and West out of town, 111 North at Birch, and up on the I-8 ramp."

The agent scribbled furiously on a notepad, then scampered from the room.

"And get me that plate number!" Morton hollered after the agent. "We only know he's not going south. Follow me."

Covering the ground to the wall map in two strides, Morton jabbed his right index finger in three places on the map. "I want teams here, here, and here. Teams 4 and 5 get airborne. Call in anything remotely resembling the van. All right, everybody, jock up!"

The SRT agents scrambled, vacating the room.

"Kyle, you're with me. Bennie, drive," Morton ordered. Looking over his shoulder at Espinoza, he added, "And don't forget that briefcase."

McEwan and US law enforcement were hot on al-Dosari's trail, but it took twenty tense minutes before they caught a break. To overcome the siren, Morton turned up the volume on the radio. "Go ahead, Kip."

Kearney shared the news from his helicopter several miles west of Calexico. "I've got an eyeball on our subject. He's southeast of Ocotillo on State Route 98, about seven miles from Anza Trail Road."

Morton keyed his microphone. "Ten-four. Command post, request CHP establish a roadblock on Route 98 at Imperial Highway. I want it shut down."

"Ten-four," responded the warehouse communications module.

"Kip, fly ahead and set down in the vicinity of Anza Trail and Coyote Road 2."

"Ten-four," Kearney replied. "Your ten-twenty?"

"Probably six miles behind him and closing." Morton turned to face McEwan. "If he makes it to I-8, he can go in either direction. I intend to nail him first."

McEwan tapped Espinoza on the shoulder. "Can't this thing go any faster?"

Responding with a crazy grin, Bennie mashed the accelerator.

Three minutes later, Kearney called back. "We've set down on 98 west of the first Anza Trail Road turnoff. We flagged down a Bureau of Land Management ranger, and he's helping us set a roadblock. Two Imperial County Sheriff units are responding to assist. My bird will monitor the direction of the van."

"We're boxing him in." Morton doled out orders for the other units then cast an intense look at McEwan. "That better be our boy down there."

Al-Dosari's carefully crafted plan was unfolding as designed. A local radio station broadcast a report concerning significant law enforcement activity for unknown reasons in downtown Calexico. Al-Dosari knew the why, where, and who of it all and laughed out loud. His decoy, possessing only disinformation, was busy diverting the attention of La Migra and the police to cover his escape. All merriment ended as his ears detected a familiar sound.

Backing his foot off the accelerator, al-Dosari looked skyward. A helicopter was circling over the roadway. Glancing ahead, he spotted a barricade of police vehicles in the distance. A chill streaked down his spine. He fought the urge to retch. *How did they find me?*

Rolling down the window for a better view, he inhaled swirling dust. Choking, his eyes stinging, he made a split-second decision. *I will race back across the border and regroup.*

A blaring voice filled his ears. "Al-Dosari! This is the United States Department of Homeland Security! Stop your van and pull over to the side of the road now! Police! Stop! ¡Policía!"

Panicking, al-Dosari yanked the wheel hard to the left, sending the van barreling down a dirt road. Arriving at the road's end, he slowed, threw open the door and jumped out then rolled to a stop. The van careened ahead, driverless. Shaken but uninjured, he scrambled to his feet and ran south toward a desert wash. His ears and the swirling sands told him the helicopter was shadowing him. Pushing hard, he headed back toward the border and safety.

McEwan arrived just as al-Dosari threw himself out of the van. The Explorer slid to a stop behind the now-crumpled minivan, lodged against a large boulder. Leaping from the SUV, McEwan and Morton ran together, burning up the ground. Al-Dosari had a significant head start. The helicopter pulled back to minimize rotor wash debris.

A man possessed, McEwan pushed himself to the limits of his physical capabilities. As he did, Morton fell behind.

McEwan's quarry darted among the rocks and brush like a lizard, then he tripped and disappeared behind a group of boulders. McEwan aimed for them and closed the gap.

Al-Dosari sprang up from his hiding place, hitting McEwan with a glancing blow to the shoulder that sent both men sprawling. Stumbling on the rough ground, al-Dosari resumed his mad dash for the border.

Regaining his feet, McEwan sprinted after the terrorist. Getting within arm's length, he launched and took down his prey. Locked together, they rolled over and over until McEwan gained the upper hand. Using al-Dosari's ears as handles, McEwan whipped his head repeatedly into the ground. Only Morton's strong arms pulled him off, stopping the beating.

"Kyle, stop! We need him alive! The smallpox! Stop!"

McEwan drew back his right arm to pile drive al-Dosari's face. His arm froze in midair as he mentally inventoried Ahmed Mansour's description of the Sword: *Green eyes, handsome, Spaniard, perfect skin.*

Perfect skin? This man has a full-length scar down his left jawbone! "Who the hell are you?"

The man emitted a deep, mocking laugh. "I am Yousef bin al-Dosari! Brother of the Almighty's Sword of Islam! You must be the Infidel's Devil! Ali knew you would be the one to come for me!" Yousef's attempt to spit in McEwan's face earned him slaps across both cheeks.

"And I'll get Ali too! Forget paradise, asshole, my face will be the last one either of you see before you burn in hell!"

Rising to his feet, McEwan spotted a fanny pack and ripped it from Yousef's waist. He shouted at the approaching agents, "Stay back! Smallpox!"

McEwan's peripheral vision caught Yousef's swift retrieval of something from his shirt pocket. "No, don't do it!"

"Ali will have the last laugh on you, fool! It is too late! You will never stop the Sword of Islam!" Yousef shoved a capsule in his mouth, biting down defiantly and swallowing. Instantly, a vile white foam began dribbling down his chin. An arrogant smirk spread over his stained lips. Yousef's face contorted; he vomited and convulsed, then went into a full-blown seizure. The terrorist's eyes rolled back as his head flopped to the side.

Grasping Yousef by the shirt and collar with both hands, McEwan suspended the lifeless body off the ground. He released his hands, and the body plopped to the sand. Dazed, absorbing the events, McEwan remained standing over the corpse.

Pulling himself together, McEwan turned toward the equally stunned faces of Morton, Kearney, and the SRT agents. Out of the corner of his eye, McEwan saw Espinoza aiming the handheld sensor dead-on at the fanny pack. Looking alternately at the unit and the Sandia briefcase, Espinoza finally shook his head.

No smallpox present.

CHAPTER THIRTY-SIX

DANIELA SANCHEZ BROUGHT THE bad news: the al-Dosari brothers had outmaneuvered America's best.

"Why wasn't the brother on our radar?" growled Nelson J. Englewood angrily.

"He should have been. From everything I've gathered, he was a seasoned jihadi in his own right." Sanchez delivered the unpleasant truth. "The Israelis passed a file on him to the CIA several years ago. The agency dropped the ball; he wasn't in their system at all."

Englewood's disgust was evident. "What's this 'Infidel's Devil' business?"

"Mossad says it's the moniker Islamic terror leaders labeled our top counterterrorism operative, who's legendary for executing their best and brightest without leaving a trace."

"CIA got one thing right—they hired McEwan. Al-Dosari's either unaware of our raids or doesn't care. If he'll sacrifice his brother, he'll do anything. Nothing will hold him back."

"Agreed. Secret Service insists the California diversion is proof he'll hit a major population center on the Eastern Seaboard or in the Midwest. There's no intel or evidence supporting that theory, but none pointing to an attack anywhere else either."

"So we have nothing. I'm getting hammered from all quarters to pull the op from you. Washington whisperers snipe you aren't up to the task, and these results prove it. They're gunning for both you and McEwan. It's no secret who's beating the drums."

Fully prepared for Stefan's campaign to turn the manhunt over to the FBI with agency support, Sanchez had hoped that the CIA director would prioritize America's national security above his own ambitions.

"I don't give a plug nickel for anyone else's opinion. I decide who quarterbacks the al-Dosari matter. I don't have to explain myself," Englewood declared confidently, "I'm not changing teams. You and McEwan are it."

"Fine, sir. But he needs to be where he's most effective, in the field. I'll return to the drawing board and map out a new plan."

"Forget a plan. We can't keep our hands clean, so why waste time trying? McEwan knows what to do. Cut him loose. Give him whatever he needs or wants and get out of his way."

Englewood's words energized Sanchez. Striding quickly from the Oval Office, she paused under the West Wing entrance canopy and dialed McEwan's number. Before the call connected, a tap on her shoulder caused her to turn. A Secret Service agent pointed back in the direction of the Oval Office. She hit the End Call button.

Kyle McEwan sat quietly, pondering his last phone call with Daniela Sanchez, which had occurred shortly after the Yousef bin al-Dosari debacle. The DNI was on her way to brief the president and she expected McEwan to be recalled to Washington. Sanchez directed him to Naval Air Station North Island to await a flight on a government aircraft. He asked her to plead the case that he stood the best chance of intercepting al-Dosari if he remained in the field. She was noncommittal. McEwan stared blankly out at the runway, his mind traveling several thousand miles back to Rayak. The sound of leather slapping across tile flooring of the Ops Building lounge snapped him back to the present. *Is he for real?*

Before him appeared the physical twin of Tim Morton, holding two cups of coffee, but the man's attire didn't compute. A pink-and-green hibiscus-patterned shirt hung loosely over wrinkled cotton shorts and worn nutty-brown Buffalo toe-loop sandals. With puka shell necklace and sunglasses dangling from a Croakie, Morton was the classic Margaritaville surfer dude.

"Mocha latte?" The HSI SAC handed off a cup and slouched in a chair.

"Thanks, Tim." McEwan sipped from the cup and set it on the floor.

"Listen, Kyle, it was a lousy stroke of luck. None of us could have gotten as close as you did. He'll be yours, sooner or later." Recognizing the signs of a disheartened man, Morton gave McEwan the opportunity to vent.

McEwan expressed his frustration. "I've no clue where he is or what he's got planned. I guarantee one of two things is true: al-Dosari's here now or soon will be. I've been within arm's reach of him since day 1, but I've taken his bait every time. He's played me well."

"He's planned this for years. In less than a week, you've gone from knowing zilch about him to almost nailing his ass on three continents. He's been lucky so far, but luck won't carry the day."

Admiration tinged Morton's voice—he believed everything he said. Having studied McEwan in action, he'd found something he'd never seen before: superior intellect, street smarts, and lethal skills all in one package. A dangerous human predator you'd want on your side—not hunting you.

"Kyle, I sent agents to the burned-out house on Camino del Rio. They entered the rubble pile where Yousef exited and found coveralls, gloves, a lightweight balaclava, and headlamp at a small tunnel opening. An agent crawled nearly 200 feet in this narrow corridor until it made a 90-degree turn west for another 40 feet. It dead-ended at wallboards concealing access to the primary tunnel on the Mexican side. This explains why Yousef triggered only one sensor when he passed under. Minutes later, his decoy set off all of the sensors in the main passageway including those on the US side."

"Are you announcing discovery of the tunnels?"

"Nope. We didn't breach the wallboards at the intersection so we can continue to monitor them both. The story is out that a man bolted through a border checkpoint sparking the manhunt. He died of a massive coronary following a foot pursuit by agents. Pure bullshit, but the story's not sexy enough for the media hounds to dig deeper."

"Anything from the Federales?"

"Yep. Yousef stayed overnight in Mexicali's finest hotel. They discovered a deceased female in his room, naked—"

"Really?" McEwan was puzzled. "A prostitute?"

"Doesn't appear so. They definitely had sexual intercourse culminating in her snapped neck. They'll compare Yousef's DNA to body fluids recovered from the victim. There's no question it's his handiwork. The concierge who escorted her to his room ID'd both of them."

"Who was she, Tim?"

"An Air France flight attendant stationed in Mexico City. They probably met on his flight over, then rendezvoused later. Interpol is running down those details."

"What poison did Yousef use?" McEwan watched Morton's eyes narrow. Yousef's suicide infuriated both men.

"Dr. Huston thinks cyanide. The Imperial County ME agrees. They're conducting a postmortem later with CDC. They'll call you when it's done."

"I suppose Vince Hanratty is back calling the shots at the JTTF."

"Of course. Large and in charge, slashing and burning and pissing people off big-time."

"I apologize if I've put you in an untenable position here with the FBI."

"The problem isn't the bureau; it's Hanratty. It's a toss-up over who'd like to frag his ass more—the other agency heads or his own troops." Nonplussed, Morton changed subjects. "Heading back to DC?"

"I'm expecting those orders any minute from the DNI."

"In style, no less." Morton tilted his head toward the DHS jet.

"I can't thank you enough for your help and the efforts of every single man and woman who supported this operation, particularly your people. Your plan was excellent and perfectly executed. No one could have predicted a juxtaposed tunnel."

"Whatever you need here in sunny Southern California is yours. Anything."

"Thanks. Next time, coffee's on me." McEwan rose to his feet. "I hate latte, by the way."

As the two men shook hands, McEwan's phone vibrated. He looked down and motioned for Morton to sit. "Yes, Danni."

"Kyle, stand by one."

A few seconds later, the new voice on the line surprised McEwan. "Yes, Mr. President."

Instantly alert, Tim Morton straightened up in his seat.

"I'm mad as hell that we haven't taken out al-Dosari, but I realize nothing I say will change that fact. Until you tell me we're no longer in the game, you're my point man. What do you need?"

McEwan hesitated for a brief second, framing his response. He needed a team leader with law enforcement skills to help him find al-Dosari and run interference with the Vince Hanrattys of the world. Only one man fit the bill.

"Sir, I need backup free from bureaucratic interference. I want HSI SAC Tim Morton as my second-in-command. He'll call the plays on the investigative side of the house and coordinate the search. I fully understand the implications of not giving this job to the FBI. Aside from having superior investigative skills, Morton is unconcerned with the political ramifications that may result from what has to be done."

McEwan glanced over at Morton; both waited for the president's reply.

On his end, in his short tenure as president, Englewood had witnessed numerous jurisdictional battles between the FBI and other federal law enforcement and intelligence agencies that often distracted from the main goal. In this case, however, the biggest problem was the bureau's foot-dragging through an investigation that might, or might not, result in al-Dosari being tried in the criminal justice system. He could not risk delay or using traditional methods. The only option: empower McEwan to finish the job.

"Is Morton there with you?"

"He is."

"Put your phone on speaker."

"Go ahead, sir."

Nelson J. Englewood's voice was clear and strong. "McEwan, both your plan and use of Morton are approved."

McEwan needed more. "I'm starting to get inside al-Dosari's head. He believes we don't learn from our mistakes. As al-Dosari sees it, since we took his bait here, we'll assume his target isn't on the West Coast. My gut tells me otherwise. Until we have proof his target is elsewhere, I want to base our operation out here."

"Done. What else?"

"I need serious muscle capable of implementing the necessary rules of engagement. It must be under our control and not the FBI's. I recommend the MARSOC Raider unit that supported us in Lebanon and Sudan. Detail them to NORTHCOM then assign them to us."

Englewood understood the ROE subtext. McEwan wanted a unit that would unhesitatingly follow the orders of the commander in chief's designee. During their prior conversation in the Oval, he promised McEwan that he'd close all legal loopholes by expanding his earlier classified presidential finding—the one declaring the al-Dosari threat an emergency beyond the capability of civilian agencies. By necessity, this involved Englewood ordering temporary suspension of the Posse Comitatus Act, the federal law prohibiting the military from engaging in law enforcement activities on US soil. The suspension would be limited in duration until the al-Dosari threat was resolved. With any luck, when McEwan succeeded, no one would ever know it occurred.

"SecDef will cut orders sending MARSOC your way. Anything else?"

"No, sir."

"McEwan, I order you to stop this threat however *you* deem necessary—the decision is yours alone, but I fully expect you to end it for good. Morton, do whatever he says using his playbook." The call concluded.

McEwan's new number 2 resembled a deer frozen in headlights. "Why me? It's the FBI's bailiwick."

McEwan pressed his case. "Here's the problem: once we received intel about an imminent attack, I tried neutralizing the threat overseas. That failed. Step 2 was stopping him at the border. You know how that turned out. I have one option left, confronting him on US soil. FBI has primary jurisdiction and tremendous resources, but *no* American law enforcement agency is equipped to eliminate an existential threat of this nature. It's what I do for a living."

Morton silently weighed McEwan's words, waiting for him to enumerate the reasons.

"Our enemies aren't constrained by rights, laws, or constitutions. I've played in their sandbox. I think like them and know their weaknesses. I will not elaborate on the techniques I will use to stop this threat. But you heard the president expressly order me to handle this threat my way—I will do so according to my rule book." McEwan let that sink in.

"We must keep a lid on this operation as long as possible, and my methods increase the odds of capturing al-Dosari before springing a leak. It can't become a clusterfuck. I'm told I lack finesse and diplomacy—the Tim Morton I've seen possesses both qualities, and he can ride herd on the players and personalities involved."

McEwan wasn't blowing smoke up Morton's tailpipe or trick-bagging him. He'd shield the HSI SAC from all legal dilemmas and misconduct claims by jettisoning him once they cornered al-Dosari. For now, McEwan held back the presidential pardons already in hand. "You in or out?"

Morton pondered the question thoughtfully, concluding some things were more important than a career, and other things were best left unquestioned. Morton drained his cup and crumbled it into a ball, launching it through the air. It banked off the wall into a corner wastebasket. "I'm gonna need more coffee."

McEwan had his second-in-command. It was time to track down al-Dosari.

CHAPTER THIRTY-SEVEN

ABOARD HIS FLIGHT, ALI bin al-Dosari tuned his seat-back monitor to CNN International to avoid the filth made by the greatest infidels—Hollywood. Midway through his journey, he caught a report about an incident in Calexico, California, involving an illegal border-crosser who died while in the custody of the US Border Patrol. Deducing the real story, he became physically ill. His adored brother Yousef dead, a shining martyr like their parents. When plotting the attack on America, Yousef insisted they could not discount the possibility that America's spymasters might discover Ali's plan and disrupt it. They must anticipate this, using diversions to sidetrack the Infidel's Devil wherever possible. They argued strenuously, but in the end, Yousef won out. Because he trusted Ali's safety and success to no one else, Yousef would be the most important decoy.

While Ali executed a piece of his plan outside Riyadh, Yousef traveled to Cairo to address other critical aspects. They united—and separated—for the final time at the Damascus safe house. Well aware of the sophisticated facial-recognition technology employed at airports outside Syria, the brothers boarded separate flights for Paris: Yousef on Air France, Ali on Syrian Arab Airlines. By design, their paths did not intersect at de Gaulle International Airport, where they departed for North America via different airlines.

Pushing aside his grief, al-Dosari envisioned Yousef reaping Allah's rewards for his great sacrifice. By the time his plane began its descent into Montreal's Pierre Trudeau International Airport, he had achieved serenity.

A genuine French passport facilitated al-Dosari's travel. Originally issued to a member of the Saddam Hussein regime who fled America's unholy invasion of Iraq, it ended up in the hands of a Syrian government official. The loyalist, honored to support the Sword in his holy jihad against America, proudly presented him the authentic document. The passport now bore his alias, photograph, and biometric data.

Al-Dosari's new legend, adopted before boarding his flight in Damascus, declared him a French citizen of Moroccan descent. In this persona, the purpose of his visit was to seek experimental medical treatment at Montreal's McGill University Health Center. Supporting his story, the cornerstone of his carry-on baggage was a fully operational oxygen-breathing machine inside a small rolling case. Only he knew the true function of the device. Its motor compartment housed a sinister and priceless treasure: a sanitized, vacuum-sealed package of freeze-dried smallpox. And no technology in the world could detect it.

Al-Dosari adhered to one guiding principle when creating a false identity—no detail was too small or insignificant. To maintain the fiction of an extremely ill man, al-Dosari prearranged transportation through airport terminals. To avoid attention, he chose not to preboard or deplane before the rest of the passengers. In Montreal, an airline transportation employee met him at the gate as in Paris. After retrieving his luggage, he rode to Canadian Immigration and Customs.

"Bienvenue vers le Canada, monsieur!"

Rasping, al-Dosari replied, "Merci beaucoup."

"Passport, please."

Moving slowly, al-Dosari handed over the booklet. Sticking out of the top was a folded letter. The Customs official read it and asked for additional documentation. Al-Dosari produced a thick manila envelope bursting with medical records carefully compiled by a disciple employed at the French Military Hospital outside Paris. Performing a cursory review, the officer thumbed through the documents, set them aside, and visually inspected the machine. Acting short of breath, al-Dosari bent over and fine-tuned a knob, increasing the airflow to ease his "pain". The official validated his passport and sent him on his way, missing the traveler's highly vigilant green eyes.

Al-Dosari shuffled slowly past the Customs checkpoint over to a waiting airline courtesy cart in the "cleared" area. As requested, the driver deposited the very ill man and his luggage outside a gentlemen's lavatory then departed the area. Once ensconced in a handicapped stall, he shredded his passport and flushed its pieces down the toilet. He tore up the remaining cover documents and stuffed the piles in his pockets. Collapsing the handle on the portable breathing machine, he packed it in a large nylon duffel he extracted from his suitcase. Putting on a jacket, hat, and glasses, he exited the men's room, looking healthy and vital. Setting the duffel atop the wheeled suitcase, he walked briskly through the airport. Checking alertly for surveillance, he ditched his torn cover papers in a series of trash receptacles along the way to the private charter terminal.

Upon his arrival, a man approached al-Dosari and they exchanged coded phrases. Surrendering a sealed envelope, the man turned and disappeared. New identity documents in hand, al-Dosari checked in for his flight. Boarding took but a few minutes.

During the aircraft's taxi toward the runway, al-Dosari spotted that day's edition of the *USA Today* newspaper on the seat across from him. A story caught his eye. The airfield at Rayak—*his* headquarters—destroyed by explosions! Al-Dosari knew it had to be the handiwork of the Zionists. Enraged, he vowed to deliver the same fate to Israel, but America came first.

Turning to the task at hand, al-Dosari was heading to Calgary, the heart of the famous Gendarmerie Royale du Canada. He had no fear of the vaunted Royal Canadian Mounted Police as he would perform his new identity flawlessly. No longer chronically ill, he became a Canadian-born citizen of Spanish descent who spent his formative years in Quebec. When his father accepted a position with the University of Madrid, the family moved to Spain, and he eventually followed his father into academia. Exceedingly handsome, tanned skin and touches of premature gray at the temples supported his portrayal of a distinguished professor on holiday.

Al-Dosari fabricated the persona himself based on his own heritage. His mother descended from Moors, Muslims who suffered religious persecution at the hands of Spanish Christian kings in the 1500s. His ancestors made their way to Lebanon, then part of the Ottoman Empire. Born with his mother's features and skin, al-Dosari looked more Spanish than Arab, and he spoke Spanish as fluently as Arabic, English, and French. Continuing his fictional identity, al-Dosari was meeting his brother, a Catholic priest, attending a conference in the resort town of Banff on Lake Louise. Once the meeting ended, the brothers were hiking the trail systems of Waterton and Glacier National Parks, then returning to Madrid.

Al-Dosari's cover story included enough details to sound authentic. Like all good stories, sprinkled among the falsehoods were grains of truth. A skillful, hardened trekker from a young age, through the years al-Dosari conquered some of the most arduous terrain and grueling weather on earth while eluding some of the world's finest trackers—the infidel's special forces soldiers. Since Afghanistan, he had maintained a highly disciplined physical fitness regimen. In superb condition, the confident al-Dosari believed nothing in America could ever come close to the challenges he had already faced and conquered.

CHAPTER THIRTY-EIGHT

KYLE MCEWAN TRAILED TIM Morton into the late-afternoon San Diego sunlight and over to a vintage Cadillac Eldorado convertible. Strapped into the back seat was a custom surfboard painted a matching glossy shade of turquoise. McEwan took a closer look as he placed his bags next to the board. A sexy mermaid posed as Lady Liberty rode a wave of red, white, and blue stars and stripes resembling a furled American flag. He climbed into the buttery-soft cream-colored leather seats.

Morton fired up the engine with a powerful roar and goosed the accelerator proudly. "Three hundred ninety cubic inches and three hundred twenty-five horses of sheer power."

There definitely are two sides to this guy, McEwan realized.

Beach Boys music blaring, fuzzy dice dangling, they left the naval air station.

Morton explained the surfboard and car. "After Calexico went south, Vince Hanratty's people in DC marched over to my headquarters and demanded I be yanked from the investigation. The head of my agency is ex-FBI, so he caved and left me swinging in the wind. I was put on forced paid leave until they decide what to do with me. Figured I'd make it a vacation and head up to La Jolla after seeing you off. My director is going to shit a brick when he hears who overruled his spineless decision." Morton tossed off the last line with a laugh.

"Sorry about that." McEwan chuckled, then patted the dashboard. "Nice ride."

"It's a '62 Eldorado Biarritz. Cadillac made fewer than 1,500 of them. I found it at an estate sale over in Julian. Hadn't aged very gracefully for just thirty-three thousand miles." Morton explained the painstaking frame-off restoration process.

"It's quite a showpiece, Tim."

"It is, but it's more than that. It's my tribute to the greatest man I've ever known. My dad mentioned more than once he wished he'd been able to keep his ragtop instead of trading it for the family station wagon."

McEwan appreciated his new colleague's multidimensional personality: away from work, down-to-earth and laid-back; at work, quietly confident, capable, focused, and resourceful. McEwan often regretted having little life apart from his work. His job was his life.

"I'll drop you off at my neighborhood coffee shop. I've got to run home and repack because my current wardrobe doesn't fit Uncle Sam's definition of business casual." Morton chuckled. "As soon as I'm done, I'll swing by and pick you up."

Two hours later, Tim Morton reappeared at Surfer's Java Bar, decked out in chinos, loafers, and a polo shirt. Over coffee, he shifted into his new role as McEwan's deputy. "California is home to a hefty 20 percent of the American Muslim population. Al-Dosari needs a support network—my money's on West Coast cells. Our best shot may be scouring the JTTFs and their sources. We already know San Diego has nothing useful. We'll start tomorrow in LA with their task forces—they have four in the metro area. They're all supervised by the LA FBI counterterrorism SAC, so we'll get every piece of intel from one meeting. Then we'll proceed up the coast and shake some trees and see what falls out. What say you?"

"Sounds like a plan."

The two men climbed into Morton's unmarked government sedan as he continued talking. "The DHS jet you arrived in is assigned to us for the duration of this investigation. We're heading back to the NAS and flying up to LA, where I've scheduled a meeting with the FBI in the a.m."

McEwan was about to tell Morton to deep-six any more meetings when the HSI SAC piqued his curiosity.

"I've also set an early evening meeting with a source."

"Who?"

"Someone who will be able to help us sort out this mess."

Slightly unsettled, McEwan glanced over at his deputy. The fun-loving surfer was gone. Tim Morton, the all-business special agent, had returned.

CHAPTER THIRTY-NINE

AT SIX-THIRTY THE FOLLOWING morning, McEwan joined Morton in their hotel lobby and they headed to the FBI Los Angeles Division. McEwan recounted the day's threats provided by the National Counterterrorism Center in Northern Virginia. "I participated in NCTC's morning videoconference. There's lots of interesting stuff happening; unfortunately, none of it pertains to al-Dosari or the attack. Starting tomorrow at both 5:00 a.m. and 5:00 p.m. local—eight o'clock DC time—you'll be in on all those calls."

This would be their daily routine until they captured al-Dosari. Conference calls with seat of government law enforcement and intelligence agency representatives supporting the al-Dosari manhunt. The topics: the current threats culled from a host of domestic and foreign human sources, covert collection efforts, and counterterror operations.

On arrival, McEwan and Morton were escorted to the office of the FBI counterterrorism SAC. Obviously expecting them, a trim, athletic woman crossed the room and offered her hand. "Welcome to LA. I'm Jocelyn Gregory." She ushered them to a table. "My orders from Washington are explicit. Whatever you need and however long you need it, I'm to provide it."

Gregory's warm reception relieved McEwan; he'd mentally prepared for another Hanratty-type exchange. "Thanks. We have no evidence al-Dosari's heading this way. As you know from the Secret Service Protective Intelligence assessment, they're adamant he's gunning for a major population center on the Eastern Seaboard or in the Midwest. I disagree, but my unsupported hunch doesn't carry much weight with them. After all, I took his bait, hook, line, and sinker in Calexico."

Morton understood McEwan's discontent but disagreed they'd bungled the operation. "We're all frustrated. Al-Dosari devised a brilliant plan and executed it perfectly, duping us all. I agree with Kyle, the threat assessment is wrong. While not a single shred of intel supports our theory, nothing debunks it either." The men waited for the SAC to verbalize her position.

Vince Hanratty had burned up Gregory's phone, spinning his version of the San Diego fiasco and the dust-up with McEwan. He'd recruited her to join his battle against the DNI agent, pushing the narrative that McEwan was an "assassin and just because he was dispatched by the president didn't change the fact it was illegal as hell" and "this isn't the bureau way". She'd butted heads with Hanratty in the past; he had a well-deserved reputation as a world-class jerk and the worst FBI supervisor in the country. Reading his comments as one-sided and self-serving, she dismissed them. Gregory and her boss, the assistant director in charge of the FBI LA division, agreed something big was at play and unmistakably above their pay grades. The FBI director said he was present when the president signed the directive ordering McEwan to personally command and carry out the mission and the attorney general sanctioned the DNI agent's use. Therefore, the legality of McEwan's orders and his execution of them were not subject to interpretation.

"In this business, we ignore our internal barometers at our peril. If everyone works their sources and NSA picks up a few things, the next thing you know, we're back in the game. FBI LA will do its part." Gregory led them down the hallway into a conference room containing tables piled high with files and excused herself. McEwan and Morton got to work.

They spent the majority of the day reviewing reports and message traffic from local and national JTTFs and receiving briefings from agents and updates from the NCTC. They also reviewed reports from the multiagency Joint Regional Intelligence Center, which fused intelligence collected by local and federal officials in the five-thousand-square-mile LA metro area. However, they found no threads connecting to al-Dosari or the current threat.

Leaning back in his chair, McEwan wanted to synthesize what they'd learned. "Tim, anything jump out at you?"

"California's largest Muslim population is here in LA, and there's a fair number of suspected cells and sympathizers. But there's more intel on gangs like MS-13 than Islamic terror groups. Based on population alone, there ought to be more." Morton's frustration bled through his analysis.

McEwan nodded in concurrence. "That's my take. NCTC has nothing new or different. NSA reports lots of white noise, but no mention of al-Dosari, the Sword, or any imminent attack."

"Kyle, have you seen any mention of your raids in Lebanon or Sudan?"

"Nada. Nothing from CIA overseas either. Everything's dried up. That fact alone tells me something is brewing."

Morton closed the last folder in front of him. "We'll review the northern California message traffic and reports tomorrow morning in San Francisco." Taking a final swig from his ubiquitous coffee cup, he pushed away from the table. "Time for our meeting."

On the way, Morton provided a thumbnail sketch of the man they were seeing. "He's an Iranian who arrived in the seventies on a student visa to pursue his PhD. He defended his dissertation the week before the Shah was overthrown. A confirmed loyalist, returning was impossible. He had a helluva time getting his family out. But for a sympathetic person in the State Department, they'd all be dead. Ever since, he's repaid his debt to America many times over. His integrity is unquestioned. I met him years ago when I gave him unofficial help with a visa foul-up involving extended family. We became friends—the operative word is *friend*. He's not a snitch. He's a well-respected professor emeritus of religious studies at UCLA."

They switched topics. During that morning's NCTC videoconference, McEwan voiced concerns that the Secret Service Protective Intelligence threat assessment, sent via the classified network, still had a dangerously narrow focus. Only major population centers made the cut. At his request, Secret Service reevaluated the list but it came back in record time unchanged.

Agreeing with McEwan and sensing his escalating irritation, the HSI SAC offered to run interference with the agent in charge of the effort. Morton pressed the man to reevaluate their concerns. Unmoved, the agent rebuffed him frostily. "You're out of your element—the Secret Service knows its business."

McEwan's gut warned they were missing the big picture. Smaller events populated with high-value targets appealed to terrorists, as did multiple simultaneous attacks. Regardless, he couldn't dwell on the Secret Service assessment—it just made McEwan more determined to find al-Dosari and eliminate the terrorist before his threat became a reality.

CHAPTER FORTY

MORTON STEERED THE SEDAN down the wide boulevard toward a stately white structure in Yorba Linda. Turning into an empty parking lot, he pulled into a space behind a circular water fountain. Chiseled in granite above the building doors was Richard M. Nixon Presidential Library and Birthplace.

On the steps stood a solitary figure, a distinguished-looking man with a shock of silver hair and gold-rimmed glasses. Dressed in a crisply tailored tan suit, blue shirt, and red paisley tie, their greeter moved lithely down the steps and addressed Morton in a foreign language.

McEwan understood every word. Hearing Morton respond in kind, McEwan mentally checked off another of his sidekick's skills—Farsi speaker. The two men executed the formal greeting protocol of inquiring after each other's health and families.

Ceremonial politeness completed, Morton spoke. "Dr. Rafat, I present Mr. Kyle McEwan, a colleague. Kyle, this is Dr. Nivek Rafat. He is a man with many friends, and at my request, Dr. Rafat reached out to some people on our behalf. He suggested we meet here. A major benefactor has perks—private access." Morton grinned. His eyes widened when McEwan performed greetings in flawless Farsi.

Dr. Rafat continued in Farsi, "I see Tim has selected his friends well. It pleases me you speak the language of Persia as a native. Tim needs lessons." Dr. Rafat teased, leading them up the steps.

McEwan and Morton followed Dr. Rafat into the museum's lobby, across an immense presidential seal embedded in the terrazzo floor and past displays about Nixon's early life.

McEwan switched to English. "Tim explained your background in academia at UCLA. I assume a person in your position meets many interesting people, some unfriendly."

"Correct," Dr. Rafat responded, holding a door open as they passed into a courtyard. "There is much hate in the Islamic world against America. Unfortunately, our youths are influenced by it. Most Muslim Americans love this country and what it stands for. However, with each passing year, those preaching hatred increase in number, and the volatility of their rhetoric marginalizes moderate Muslims."

They passed a reflecting pool and the tiered Pat Nixon Rose Garden, ending up in front of a Sikorsky VH-3A Sea King, the Nixon-era Marine One helicopter.

One foot on the open hatchway steps, Dr. Rafat paused. "For privacy. After you, Mr. McEwan, Tim."

McEwan took a seat next to a window, Dr. Rafat directly opposite him, and Morton grabbed one in between. Morton took the lead. "As I mentioned, we're trying to determine if the local Islamic community poses any imminent threats."

The professor nodded. "I learned some very interesting things. On the street, word has it something big is about to happen because the FBI's normally low-key presence in the Muslim community has become extremely overt."

Neither McEwan nor Morton indicated they knew why surveillance had increased.

Receiving no comment, Dr. Rafat's professorial side took over. "Islam is a very ritualistic religion. Its nucleus is the Prophet Muhammad's holy book, the Qur'an, or, anglicized, the Koran. It regulates every Muslim's life and is the basis for sacred Islamic law, or Sharia. Every Muslim must submit his or her life to Allah through compulsory tenets known as the Five Pillars of Islam. The first Pillar is the statement of faith, 'There is no God but Allah and Muhammad is his messenger'. Second, five daily prayers must be said in the direction of Mecca. Third, all Muslims must give alms to charity. Fourth, all Muslims must refrain from food, drink, and sexual activity from dawn until dusk during the month of Ramadan. The fifth and final Pillar is the hajj, the once-in-a-lifetime pilgrimage to the sacred shrine in Mecca. Jihad is often referred to as the sixth Pillar, though it is not identified as such in the Koran."

Unsure where Dr. Rafat was heading, the agents held their questions.

"Muhammad failed to designate a successor, so on his death in 632, a rift occurred among his followers, resulting in two major denominations: Sunni and Shi'a. Sunnis accepted a lineal descendant as the Prophet's successor, while the Shi'as installed a pious follower of Muhammad's traditions. Since that day, the Islamic world has thrived on the schism. While it is a war of force, it is even more a struggle for the heart, mind, and soul of every Muslim. That is a simplified peek into this very complex religion."

"Dr. Rafat, how does this history play into current threats against America?" Morton quizzed.

"Forgive me; I merely wanted to set the stage for you. It's common knowledge that Shi'a nation-states like Iran fund and train a host of terror organizations subscribing to their interpretation of Islam. Sunni leaders similarly support groups faithful to their theology. Six months ago, Shi'a and Sunni religious and secular leaders from around the world gathered in Tehran. Disappointed in the lack of success of al-Qaeda, ISIS, and their offshoots, both sides agreed to set aside their differences to wage unified jihad against their mutual enemy, the Judeo-Christian world. Their goal: a single unified Islamic world nation. Since the summit, Muslim sectarian violence worldwide has declined sharply. While thousands of years of mistrust kept their respective terror wings independent, for the first time, Islam has a cross-pollinated terror arm that might actually work."

The last point crystallized things for McEwan. Analyzing the current threat through the prism of known terrorists and state sponsors—and their respective guiding principles—had not and would not yield anything useful. This paradigm shift represented a fundamental change in how Islamists viewed and would attack Western interests.

"Dr. Rafat, what do they call this new faction?"

"The Islamic Jihad Brotherhood. It unites warriors of both Islamic sects in furtherance of the nascent jihad. Its leader is a little-known but charismatic extremist who claims he symbolizes the new breed of co-joined terrorist. He brazenly hails himself as the 'Sword of Islam'."

"Does he identify himself by name?"

"Yes. Ali bin al-Dosari."

CHAPTER FORTY-ONE

THREE SOLID HOURS OF driving brought Ali bin al-Dosari to the Waterton Lakes National Park on the Canada-Montana border. He pulled up to the park's entrance booth and rolled down his window.

The attendant looked up from her paperback novel. "May I help you?"

"Yes, please. A daily pass for the next four days."

"Forty dollars, sir."

He handed the woman four Canadian ten-dollar bills.

She tendered a receipt bearing cellophane tape hanging off both ends. "Stick this on the inside of your windshield on the driver's side. Enjoy your stay." Transaction complete, she buried her nose back in her book.

Noticing the security camera, al-Dosari drove slowly down the entrance road until the green-gabled Prince of Wales Hotel came into view high on a hill. A white RCMP police car idling in a marina parking lot caused his pulse to jump briefly. It returned to normal when the officer did not look up. Maneuvering the car up to the entrance of the Waterton Lakes Lodge, he took in the design of the century-old log building, its huge stone chimney piercing a steep-gabled roof.

Al-Dosari checked in, receiving his room key and a courier-delivered box. Entering his room, he promptly unpacked his suitcase, spreading its contents out on the bed: fleece-lined jacket, button-down shirt, pair of hiking pants with multiple pockets, ski cap, three pairs of woolen socks, a pair of well-worn hiking boots, and a nylon laundry bag.

He found five items inside the box, the most important being a padded case. He unzipped the duffel and retrieved the oxygen-breathing machine.

He extracted a container hidden in the motor compartment. Al-Dosari freed its precious freeze-dried contents and slid it into the case.

Removing a handheld Garmin Global Positioning Satellite unit, he turned it on to ensure all required maps were loaded. He compared the GPS altitude readings to his Timex HeliX watch—they matched. The final items in the box were a fanny pack he set aside, and a manila envelope, which he opened. A dozen pages of information and instructions spilled out on the table. Al-Dosari studied each page, committing the details to memory. Two hours later, he grabbed the documents and entered the living room. Opening the fireplace flue, he spread the papers on the grate and struck a wooden match. Within minutes, only charred remnants remained. Sweeping the ashes into a fireplace shovel, he carried them to the bathroom, discarded the evidence in the toilet, and flushed. After a shower, he prayed for strength. His faith taking hold, he climbed into bed.

Sleep came quickly.

Although McEwan's brain and belly were blazing with anger—directed at the US intelligence community—he displayed a calm exterior to Dr. Rafat. Upon his return from Lebanon and Sudan, McEwan fully briefed intel analysts about al-Dosari and his use of the Sword of Islam moniker. How they missed the link, revealed subsequently by a nonprofessional, was incomprehensible. US counterterrorism experts had heard of the IJB incidentally, but had dismissed them as wannabe jihadists with no direction and no leader. Because of this failure, every tick of the clock increased al-Dosari's chances of success and intensified America's danger.

Dr. Rafat wasn't done with his revelations. "This morning, I discovered Ali bin al-Dosari's profile, without photo, on the Muslim version of Facebook. He spins his birth as the result of a Romeo-and-Juliet-style romance between the feuding religious sects. He says his father was a Syrian Sunni who fought against the Israelis in the Six-Day War in 1967, then made his way to the Bekaa Valley, where he met al-Dosari's mother, the daughter of a Shi'a camp commander. She birthed two sons, Ali and Yousef. Their parents were supposedly martyred in jihad by US navy warplanes and the infidel's battleship *New Jersey*. Although possibly true, it is unverifiable. Al-Dosari goes by two names interchangeably, depending on his audience. He sometimes inserts his Shi'a mother's surname to become Ali Shihab bin al-Dosari. He trades on the name change as evidence he is uniquely positioned to lead the IJB. Quite the puff piece.

"Al-Dosari's profile becomes fantasy when he boasts of being anointed to spearhead the fight against the enemies of Islam. Dovetailing nicely with his storyline are several modern fables about a young jihadist fighting bravely against the infidels in Afghanistan. At some point, our hero is captured, catching the eye of an Afghan general with a predilection for teenage boys. As the general's pants hit his ankles, the boy grabs the general's ceremonial sword and beheads him then escapes. Al-Dosari claims he is this boy-hero-turned-man. As a symbol of gratitude and humility, he took the nom de guerre 'Terror's Sword' and under this name annihilated hundreds of infidels and apostates. In recognition of his achievements, al-Dosari claims Allah has now blessed him with the sobriquet the Sword of Islam, denoting jihad. Despite these parables and boasts, he's a relative unknown. Reading between the lines, he actually believes he is the returning caliph who will bring Allah's rule and true peace to the world. It might sound far-fetched, but as we know, the world's greatest mass murderers were megalomaniacs and psychopaths who fit this same mold."

"When was his profile posted online?" McEwan's voice had an edge to it.

"Two months ago. Unaware of your linguistic expertise, I took the liberty of translating it from Arabic." He handed two pages over, then continued. "By aligning himself with the IJB, al-Dosari wisely avoids a collision with Sunni and Shi'a religious and secular leaders. For them, he fills the void left by al-Qaeda and ISIS, which led to their endorsement of him as the ex officio leader of the IJB. Their seal of approval gives al-Dosari access to a veritable Who's Who of blindly devoted Sunni and Shi'a radicals, ready to wage jihad under the Sword of Islam's unified banner. They will do his bidding unflinchingly, allowing the mastermind to remain safely in the shadows, avoiding intelligence service scrutiny. As with any major leader, terrorist or otherwise, al-Dosari has an outsized ego. A blockbuster attack reaps dual benefits, bolstering his image while giving IJB instant recognition and credibility."

"The IJB, how do we find them?" McEwan needed answers.

"It will be difficult. Terror cell members disguise their true beliefs, convictions, and strategies. In practical terms, they lie and deceive to deflect and neutralize any criticism of Islam or Muslims. Sorry, I am a rambling old professor," Dr. Rafat said sheepishly.

McEwan shook his head vigorously. "Not at all. Please continue."

Dr. Rafat resumed his discourse. "Falsehoods told to protect oneself or promote the cause of Islam are sanctioned in the Koran. A Muslim is even permitted to deny or denounce his faith if, in so doing, he protects or furthers the interests of Islam. He gets a pass so long as he remains faithful to Islam in his heart."

"So how do we differentiate between the good and bad Muslims?" Morton queried.

"A very difficult task, indeed. As you would expect, the bad ones are invisible. When Muslims wage jihad from within the belly of the infidel, they are exempt from complying with Sharia and all religious and moral obligations. This doctrine suspends required rituals like the beard, alcohol abstinence, and so forth. Freed from the behaviors and traditions identifying them as devout Muslims, they melt into Western societies. When called, these warriors rise up to destroy us from within. The Trojan Horse, multiplied by an unknown factor."

"Perfect sleeper agents," the two agents said simultaneously.

Dr. Rafat dipped his head slightly. "Until you understand your foe and what drives him, you cannot undermine his ideological roots and defeat him, nor can you combat radical Islam using Judeo-Christian values or mindsets. Therein lies the problem. All Western politicians, especially those espousing liberal beliefs, fail to treat radical Islam like the metastasized cancer it is. It must be carved out and destroyed. Western governments strangle themselves with political correctness while pro-Islamic groups use our rights against us. They fail to accept that this is an all-out war. The radicalists will give us a choice: convert to Islam or die. Tim, per your request, I contacted my sources in the community. There is nothing here; waste no more time."

McEwan queried, "There's no threat in LA?"

"Correct. There are the usual blusterers who would like to harm America, but they pose no immediate threat and have no ties to the IJB. Emphasis on Los Angeles and imminent."

"Where can we find the IJB?" McEwan needed to nail this down.

"I am told new plants have sprouted in the fertile soils of San Francisco and Seattle and they are bearing fruit. I have no specifics. If there is any truth to the information I gathered, you are pursuing a very sadistic killer assisted by equally dangerous adherents. I wish I had more to offer. I know this is extremely important. In the years I have known Tim, he has never asked for this kind of assistance."

McEwan reassured the professor. "To the contrary, you've been immensely helpful."

Dr. Rafat inclined his head in acknowledgment.

The three men retraced their steps out of the helicopter, through the museum, and back to the parking lot.

"Were we at my home, I would ask you to sit with my family for supper." Dr. Rafat shook hands with McEwan. "Perhaps you could come for a visit with Tim in the future?"

"It was my privilege to meet you, and it would be an honor to meet your family," McEwan replied in Farsi.

The older man nodded his assent. "Please be careful, both of you."

"You have my word." McEwan turned and headed for the car.

Dr. Rafat had a brief exchange with Morton, then retreated into the library.

Morton climbed behind the wheel and started the engine. "What do you think, Kyle?"

"Dr. Rafat untangled thousands of years of the Islamic riddle in minutes. He knows more about al-Dosari and how to find him than any intelligence service in the world. Thanks to him, we now have our first solid lead. We find the IJB and we find al-Dosari."

Morton didn't respond.

McEwan noticed his deputy had a habit of taking a few moments to mull things over, after which he generally articulated something profound. "What, Tim?"

"You speak Farsi better than I speak English. Perhaps we'll swap language lessons for surfboard instruction," Morton deadpanned, recognizing McEwan's need to de-stress.

McEwan laughed for the first time in days. "Well, I don't know about that, but I do know one thing. It's time to take in the Golden Gate Bridge."

Morton voiced McEwan's unspoken concerns. "How in the hell did all the so-called intel experts miss his social networking profile? It explains the connection between al-Dosari and the IJB. Doesn't anybody up there ever talk to one another?"

McEwan ignored the question, thereby answering it. "Tim, get our aircraft warmed up and pave the way with the Bay Area JTTF."

McEwan called Danni Sanchez and shared the intel from Dr. Rafat. She broke the call to relay the information to seat of government law enforcement and intelligence agencies.

McEwan and Morton boarded the DHS jet at Van Nuys and, after a late flight, landed at San Francisco International Airport. Two FBI agents transported them to the Westin St. Francis on Union Square. In a follow-up conversation with Sanchez, she advised that using the information from Dr. Rafat, analysts had finally confirmed the connections between the IJB, al-Dosari, and the Sword of Islam. Intelligence officials were dismayed that a non-professional had been able to link the associations where analysts had failed to do so. Despite this new information, the agencies continued hitting a brick wall on the threatened attack.

CHAPTER FORTY-TWO

THE RINGING ALARM CLOCK stirred Ali bin al-Dosari. Rising, he went into the bathroom, relieved himself then dressed. A man on a mission, he was the model of efficiency. Stuffing all but one of the items he was taking with him into the nylon bag, he repacked the suitcase with the remainder. Gathering his necessary travel documents and padded case with a single sweeping motion, he placed them into the fanny pack and attached it to his waist. Loading the car required two trips. He stored everything in the trunk except the nylon bag, which he flung onto the front seat. He glanced down at his watch: 02:25. *Today the Sword of Islam will reach America undetected. Or be martyred in the process.*

Al-Dosari started the car and pulled onto Cameron Falls Drive, driving until the road bore left across a wooden bridge. Waterfalls triggered instructions: "Proceed past the waterfall until you see a hiking and parking sign on the right. Turn into the gravel lot. A man will approach and exchange the code words. Do what he says." Al-Dosari saw the sign, pulled into the lot, and spotted a lone figure. Two trekking poles leaned against backpacks at the man's feet. The thin, rugged man approached the car cautiously.

"You Mr. Felipe?"

"It is Dr. San Felipe." *The code words are correct but he reeks of alcohol!*

"I'm Reginald Devereaux. Give me your car keys and wait over by the packs."

Al-Dosari handed over the keys reluctantly.

Devereaux busied himself inside the car. Shaking two plastic grocery bags onto the front seats, he distributed hiking maps, a pair of boots, and empty Gatorade and water bottles between the front and back seats and rear floorboards. He partially opened several highlighted maps and placed them on the front dash. The car appeared to be rented by a hiker.

"What's in the trunk?" Devereaux growled.

"Nothing," al-Dosari lied.

Locking the car, Devereaux tossed him the keys. "Ditch 'em on the trail. Put this on your belt." Lunging, al-Dosari caught a large, sheathed hunting knife.

Devereaux knelt in front of a ballistic nylon-frame backpack and unzipped it. "Give me your stuff."

Unused to people giving him orders, especially drunken louts, al-Dosari handed over the tightly closed nylon laundry bag.

Devereaux jammed the bag into the pack and zipped it. "Turn around."

Obeying, al-Dosari watched over his shoulder as the guide hoisted the pack onto his shoulders and passed him both sides of the waist strap, which he buckled. The bulky backpack was lighter than expected. He noted the guide's pack appeared substantially heavier and bulged at the seams.

Devereaux glanced at the soft glow of his watch. "Let me make sure I got our plan down. You have to be at Logan Pass no later than ten tomorrow morning, eh?"

"Yes."

"Our first ten miles are critical. I hope you're in shape, 'cause we're going to scoot. My plan will have us there with time to spare. We need to average three miles per hour the first couple of hours. Gotta get past a ranger station before they're up and about. We'll leave the main trail there and circle around it using a little-known game path. It's rugged. Might need to bushwhack us through in several places, but it's definitely passable."

Al-Dosari stared back unhappily, the stench of alcohol souring his stomach.

"The terrain to Logan Pass is moderate to downright tough in a few places. If we average two miles per hour after Goat Haunt, including stops for rest, food, the necessaries—er, that is to relieve ourselves, and a couple of hours of shut-eye—we should make it there around 8:00 a.m. That accounts for us slowing down at nightfall, but we have a full moon and the weather's supposed to clear." Devereaux cast a critical eye. "Sound okay to you?"

"Yes." Al-Dosari hid his growing disdain for the man.

"You sure you're up to this?"

Al-Dosari's ice-cold eyes shot daggers. "Devereaux, I am an experienced mountain climber. I may not have hiked this part of North America, and while the terrain may indeed be rugged, I am well equipped to meet the challenges. If I did not think I was up to this trek, I would not be here. You have received a great sum of money to guide me. It is not your responsibility to question my abilities. Your sole duty is to get me there on schedule. Nothing more, nothing less. Are we clear?"

"Fine, then. It's your bar tab. Keep quiet until I say it's okay to talk." Bending over, the guide picked up the trekking poles, passed one over, and headed up the densely wooded trail.

As he stepped in behind the Canadian, the long machete dangling from Devereaux's left hip startled al-Dosari. *The report said he killed a man. I must keep my eye on him.*

A half hour into their journey, the outdoorsman broke the ice. "You've got bottles of water in your pack, bug spray, a canister of bear spray, and a first aid kit. I was told to leave plenty of room in your pack, but they didn't say how big a pack. Erring on the side of caution, I put most of the stuff in mine. A lightweight sleeping bag is taking up most of the space in yours. When we stop for a breather, remove the bear spray and clip it to your belt."

"Yes. What is in your pack, Devereaux?" al-Dosari asked, concerned.

"I'm carrying our food, extra water, and two small tents. Plus rain gear, two inflatable bedrolls, and toilet paper."

"What is the weight of your pack?"

"About fifty pounds. Maybe a little more."

"Should you not transfer some weight to me? It would speed us up." Al-Dosari did not like the guide having all their staples and critical gear.

"Nah, we'll be all right. We're on schedule."

"Tell me about yourself, Mr. Devereaux."

"I live an uncomplicated life, really. Not much to tell. I've spent all my forty years in the area. I practically live in the woods, know 'em like the back of my hand. All one hundred fourteen miles of Waterton's trails."

Al-Dosari noted the guide omitted his seven-year manslaughter stint in a Canadian prison.

"I've hiked all seven hundred miles of Glacier's trail system too. I even know paths rangers on both sides of the border haven't found. I've used 'em numerous times to slip others ..." His voice trailed off.

A thorough investigation of the hard-drinking, bare-knuckle brawler reported no guide was better than Devereaux and he was well worth his price, irrespective of his obvious failings. In pursuit of the almighty dollar, he had skirted the law in the past. He was precisely what al-Dosari needed. A man with a soul for sale. The terrorist knew with certainty that the Canadian would never disclose this trip—dead men could tell no tales.

"Devereaux, what were you told about my expedition?"

The guide hesitated but didn't break stride. "You're a private person, don't ask questions. Okay by me. If you wanna say something, go ahead. I listen good but won't ask nothin'."

Al-Dosari steered the conversation in a different direction. "Are the bears dangerous?"

"Yep, both grizzlies and black bears. But in all my years, I've never felt threatened. Most of the time, they're curious and move on if you don't bother them. Attacks usually involve stupid people who challenge the bears or try to run from them. Fools, I call 'em." He took a sip from a bottle. "I'm no fool, and neither are you."

The longer they hiked, the more it took for al-Dosari to keep up, their pace seeming much faster than three miles an hour. Despite the alcohol in Devereaux's bloodstream, he was in outstanding physical condition and hardly broke a sweat.

Devereaux cocked his head over his right shoulder. "Around this bend is the US of A. No going back. Do we go on?"

Al-Dosari responded impatiently, "Yes, get on with it."

Several minutes later, Devereaux's arm shot out, pointing east. "Across the lake you can see a thirty-foot wide swath cut in the trees. It's the forty-ninth parallel marking the border and stretches all the way to the Pacific Ocean. Easy to see from the air. I guess that's the point."

Al-Dosari stifled a laugh. *The Americans are such fools. They accommodate those sneaking into their country illegally by providing them a clearly delineated border.*

"Look ahead." Devereaux pointed to two granite obelisks, one five feet tall, the other four feet. "Those are the official boundary markers."

"I see. Interesting they chose a design resembling the Washington Monument." *Which should have come down in the great attacks.*

"Don't know why, but they're all that way."

Al-Dosari approached the markers and read the etched words: "International Boundary and Treaty of 1908."

"We're making good time, but we gotta push on to get beyond Boundary Bay before the campers stir. If we run into other folks, let me do the talking."

Another hour of steady walking brought a faint aroma of smoke. Devereaux turned immediately, put his finger to his lips, and gestured to a campfire smoldering in front of three tents. They passed the campground and entered a thicket. The guide retrieved a map from his pocket, unfolding and thrusting it at his companion while whispering, "we'll cut across here."

Al-Dosari read the indicated name: Olsen Creek.

"There's a game trail a hundred yards west of here. Rangers rarely check it 'cause nobody knows about it. We'll skirt around the base of

Citadel Peaks and along Waterton River, then head south and east away from Rainbow Falls. It'll be around seven by then, and we'll be past the Goat Haunt ranger station. Probably have to hack a few bushes to make our way over to the Waterton Valley Trail. From there we'll blend in with other hikers." Draining the last drops from a bottle, Devereaux licked its rim before tossing it into the woods. "If we run into rangers, I got what we need," he said, waving a piece of paper.

A startled al-Dosari fell in behind him. "What is that?"

"It's a backcountry permit. We can't hike all day and night. Gotta rest sometime. The permit allows us to stay at a campground farther on up the trail. Two or three hours rest ought to do us fine. Then we'll have enough moonlight and energy to reach our goal. Got it all timed perfectly."

"We must have a permit to camp in the wild?" A record of their trip existed—not good news.

"They gotta regulate it. Otherwise, hikers stumble all over one another. People have to be told how to store their food, or it will attract bears. The bears might get *you* if you camp in the wrong place. Some city slickers get lost. The rangers gotta know who's out there in case they don't show up when and where they're supposed to."

"I see." Al-Dosari remained concerned. "When did you get it, and who gave it to you?"

"Yesterday afternoon. I picked it up at the Waterton Visitor Reception Center. They issue them for their park and the trail starting at Goat Haunt."

"Will rangers ask to see any other documents?" he asked.

Devereaux caught the concerned look on al-Dosari's face. "Relax. It's the way things are done. Routine SOP."

"Okay, Mr. Devereaux." Realizing it was too late to do anything about this development, al-Dosari would deal with it if it became a problem. "May I relieve myself?"

"Yep. Gotta go myself."

After answering nature's call, the two men walked for some time. Al-Dosari mirrored Devereaux's movements. If the guide stepped around rocks, over logs, pushed aside branches, or plowed through them, he followed suit. When Devereaux drank, he did too, trying to stay as well-hydrated as the man setting their arduous pace. After hiking for a time, al-Dosari detected waterfalls to the north and suggested a rest.

Shaking his head no, the guide pushed on.

Eventually, Devereaux stopped, removed his hat, and wiped sweat from his brow. "Be very quiet. On the other side of those trees is the main trail. I'll make sure it's okay, then wave you on."

Al-Dosari crouched behind a thicket of bushes, and the guide vanished. Several minutes later, he heard rustling in the brush and spotted Devereaux waving him ahead. Plowing through onto a trail, al-Dosari faced a gigantic, looming snowcapped mountain.

"Mount Cleveland. All eleven thousand feet of her." Devereaux unceremoniously unharnessed his pack and plopped down, indicating a spot on a log with a grand gesture. "Have a seat." The guide snatched another bottle from his pack.

"Where are we, Devereaux?"

"In the clear."

CHAPTER FORTY-THREE

AT 4:00 A.M., MCEWAN and Morton were shuttled to the Northern California JTTF office, already bustling with activity. The FBI SAC was down in the Monterey area and all other supervisors were unavailable, so at 5:00 a.m. local, they signed onto the conference call with the NCTC in DC. With nothing new emerging, they dropped off the call and dug into mounds of paperwork.

McEwan and Morton spent hours reviewing hundreds of messages and reports, echoing the information seen at other JTTFs. During one of several trips to the break room to refill his coffee cup, Morton overheard two agents discussing their shift at "the off-site".

This was the first they'd heard about an undercover operation. Morton marched the agents to McEwan, who grilled them, learning an agent had infiltrated a sleeper cell embedded in a San Jose mosque, necessitating a 24-7 surveillance post. Based on the Hanratty experience, McEwan assumed the bureau was playing keep away. Both men steamed straight for the office of Ted Beacham, the recently returned SAC.

Although simmering, McEwan kept the introductions cordial. Things became testy when he asked Beacham why the undercover operation wasn't briefed or its case file provided. An intense discussion revealed the omission was inadvertent, not deliberate. As with all deep-cover operations, this one was closely held. When McEwan and Morton arrived, the cognizant supervisors were on a flight returning from a conference at Quantico, and the administrative case agent was at the San Jose Resident

Agency, his post of duty. With Beacham down in Monterey, it slipped through the cracks.

Beacham said he was aware of the "Hanratty problem" and understood how the nondisclosure might appear.

McEwan and Morton both had dubious looks on their faces.

"I'd like to make it perfectly clear—we've withheld nothing from you," Beacham emphasized earnestly. "When I got the call you were coming, I ordered my troops to cooperate fully. I assure you, we don't know jack shit about al-Dosari. The first we heard of him was when your information was shared with us. And the IJB? We only learned of them a day or two ago when our UCA overheard it mentioned in passing. So if there's a link between the two, it's news to us." Beacham reached down and punched the intercom button on his phone. "Pull the entire San Jose undercover operation file and bring it to me."

An administrative assistant appeared with a thick classified folder. Beacham extracted a single-page draft "FD-302" report and handed it to McEwan. The undercover agent reported the San Jose network he had infiltrated reconstituted itself as a cell of a new group called the Islamic Jihad Brotherhood—the agent had no further details. The date and time of the 302 was thirty-six hours prior, explaining why no one locally drew a nexus between the IJB and al-Dosari.

Reassured, McEwan apologized for jumping to conclusions. But speaking with the UCA was critical. "I need to sit down ASAP with your agent. To our knowledge, he's the only person who has any firsthand knowledge about the IJB."

Beacham balked at McEwan's request. "You want me to pull a deep-cover agent. That puts my man at risk and will probably burn the operation."

"Ted, believe me, I know what can happen, but the stakes here are infinitely greater than any one operation. You and I both know the most critical information never makes it inside a file jacket. If there were another way, I'd do it. There isn't. I have to speak with your UCA."

The FBI SAC realized he was in a no-win situation. His director ordered 100 percent support behind McEwan. Behind his back, Hoover Building highfliers blatantly countermanded that edict expecting two things to happen: McEwan to fail, and Beacham to pick up the pieces. Beacham saw McEwan's reclassification as a DNI agent for what it was: a ploy to circumvent the prohibition on CIA domestic operations, allowing him to continue the manhunt on US soil. The question on everyone's mind was why, since all of McEwan's efforts to date had failed. Beacham thought he knew the answer.

For years, the grapevine hummed with rumors of a covert US operative hammering terrorists overseas, something most agents—including Beacham—longed to do. When he vetted McEwan through back channels, his best sources tagged McEwan as a serious player who likely was the operative in question. Beacham recognized that the president's decision to surface a weapon as extraordinary as McEwan from the black world and turn him loose stateside signaled that the threat was far deadlier than anyone was letting on. The president had decided the danger posed by al-Dosari required methods exceeding those within the FBI's charter and arsenal. Obviously, McEwan could deliver these extreme measures. Beacham chose his side.

"Review the file while I reach out to the agent. I'll have him contact you at your hotel."

Three hours later, the file review had generated more questions than answers. Leaving the office, McEwan and Morton returned to the Westin St. Francis. As McEwan slid the card into the keyless door entry lock, he heard his room phone ringing. Entering, he tossed his bags on the bed and answered the phone.

"Is this Kyle McEwan?" the caller asked.

"Who's this?"

"A friend of Ted's. Go back to the elevator and take it to the fifth floor. Room 523." The line went dead.

Two minutes later, McEwan and Morton were ushered into the room by a short man in his early forties, wearing a multicolored embroidered robe, cotton trousers, patterned kofia—African fez—and dark sunglasses, all topped off by a string of beads.

"Welcome, gentlemen!" He swept one arm around the room while closing the door behind them with the other. Observing their bewildered looks, the man removed his sunglasses and hat and tossed them atop the dresser.

"It's West African attire, not my favorite look," he offered dryly. "Since my 'brothers in the struggle' wear American clothes, I use this getup whenever I need to move around incognito." His hand shot out and delivered a hearty handshake. "I'm Paul Infante."

McEwan saw Infante's point. The outfit disguised his features completely but was no more offbeat than clothing worn by the creatures inhabiting San Francisco on any given day. His close-cropped thinning black hair, naturally dark complexion, and several days growth of heavy beard made it difficult to determine his heritage. He could pass for Middle Eastern, Italian, Moroccan, Central Asian, Arab, Indian, Mexican, or Hispanic. With his line of BS and the proper attire, Infante was the perfect UCA—he could blend into any setting.

Infante saw McEwan appraising him and decided to help. "My pedigree is that of your typical ole American mutt. What you see is a fine ragù of Mayan, Portuguese, Maltese, and probably a few others in the woodpile. Interesting look, don't you think?" Flashing a broad grin, Infante perched himself on the edge of the bed.

McEwan and Morton sat on a couch. "Thanks for meeting us on such short notice," McEwan began.

"No problemo. I was in San Francisco today anyway."

"What were you told about why we wanted to meet you?"

"That my discovery of the IJB San Jose cell may be part of this nasty al-Dosari business, and you're to get everything. I'm on board. What's mine is yours. If you need anything done, I'll do it. Of course, I received the typical Hoover Building warning—fucking with you would be hazardous to my career."

McEwan explained everything they'd learned from Dr. Nivek Rafat.

The revelations were eye-popping even for the seasoned undercover agent. Infante took a long pull from his coffee cup, then transported his visitors into the shadowy world of Islamic terror activity in the Bay Area.

"Thirty-four months ago, we received sketchy intel that ISIS was recruiting new indigenous cells in Detroit. There was recruiting all right by bad actors inspired by Abū Bakr al-Baghdadi, the Islamic State's first Caliph. We wanted to know if they were legit and who their architect was behind the network. I was dangled in front of them, an angry Muslim American wanting to avenge the crusades against my brothers. They took me in. One of the Canadians in the cell had a connection with the right people for overseas training. I stayed home as the first group went off to Raqqa, Syria. They returned with plans to blow up the mile-long Detroit-to-Windsor tunnel."

Morton involuntarily verbalized his shock. "No shit!"

"I shit you not," Infante replied. "Needless to say, the bureau wasn't about to let that fuse get lit. To maintain my cover, we took them down while engineering my escape. We purposely didn't arrest one of the Raqqa-trained guys, and the two of us went on the lam together. He'd boasted previously about training in Syria with some guys from a San Jose mosque, so I suggested we reach out to them. We arrived here seven months ago. Convinced I saved his butt, he vouched for me. My ruse worked too well. The local imam, Syed el-Nasrallah, handpicked me almost immediately for overseas training. Then everything went sideways."

"How so?" Morton asked. "Because of the Lodi cell the bureau took down?"

"We actually did Lodi to keep me from going to jihadi summer camp. The way I saw it, I had a unique opportunity to vet their training, learn cell locations, and ID members. Most of all, I would've learned their plans and targets. I could've crippled their operation and shut them down for years, maybe permanently. Unfortunately, the suspenders at Main Justice put the kibosh on it and ordered us to take down that network. While the arrests kept my bacon out of the fire, they were a major setback for my op." Infante took another swig of coffee.

"El-Nasrallah stopped recruiting and training trips ceased altogether. The imam lost trust in me and my Detroit compadre and closed ranks. He won't introduce me to the hard-core members, whoever they are. I've got to give the old man credit: he found it disturbingly coincidental we showed up here on the heels of the Detroit bust, only to have Lodi taken down within a month of our arrival."

"How did you learn about the nexus between the imam and the IJB?" Morton asked.

"Four days ago, I overheard el-Nasrallah tell Hamza Omar abū-Ibrahim, the mosque's senior cleric, that he wouldn't challenge abū-Ibrahim on swearing allegiance to the Islamic Jihad Brotherhood. Until then, no one here had heard of them, including me. This abū-Ibrahim is an interesting character. Brother Hamza's the top dog at the mosque, but he's strangely absent from day-to-day operations. I've been unable to find out why. On a superficial level, he's friendly and communicative, but there's a real undercurrent there. I can't put my finger on it. My money's on him as the head honcho of the San Jose cell."

Infante stared at McEwan—silent and preoccupied.

Morton read McEwan: he'd left the conversation and was mentally processing some nugget. Morton held up his palm, signaling Infante to wait.

McEwan's memory hopper flashed names like a database search until he retrieved what he needed. "Paul, does the name Mu'adh el-Nasrallah ring a bell?"

Infante bolted up, his shock unmistakable. "Sure does. He was the imam's only son. Killed on the battlefield by US troops in Afghanistan. Why?"

"Because contrary to that folk tale, he's very much alive and cooling his heels at one of our overseas black sites."

Infante saw the big picture. "That gives us a few options, doesn't it?"

"It's time to do some horse-trading. We'll snatch the imam and persuade him to cooperate. I have to be candid with you both. This will get messy so it will be off the books. Your careers could go down in flames if you tag along."

Morton answered without pause. "Too much at stake not to be in."

"Paul, if you join us, you and your op are burned. I know what you've invested and what you're putting on the line."

The newest member of the team jumped in with both feet. "So be it. I ran a few snatch-and-grabs with our extraterritorial program. I can get close to el-Nasrallah. I'll suggest lunch on me at his favorite Punjabian restaurant following midday prayers. We'll snatch him when he shows." Infante gave the agents his cell phone number.

"Paul, I am not flying solo on this; I will rely a great deal on your guidance and counsel as I am Tim's. However, as Tim can attest firsthand, the president authorized me to act in the face of this existential threat as I deem necessary—I am the sole arbiter. If you object to anything, there will be no discussion or arguments on your part—if you disagree with me your only option is to bail."

"Message received."

McEwan laid his final card on the table. "The president met the only precondition I had prior to accepting this assignment—he will sign broad pardons for every person supporting me in this investigation. The DNI and attorney general have copies of his executive order, and my attorney has the original."

Though neither had considered that possibility, both Morton and Infante were relieved. Morton put on his supervisory criminal investigator hat. "What about Ted?"

Infante answered, "I'll brief him when I can."

McEwan fidgeted. Beacham appeared to be a straight shooter who wouldn't steer over any lines that needed crossing; briefings up the supervisory chain could well disrupt McEwan's plans for the imam. "Paul, I need unfettered access to el-Nasrallah."

"And you shall have it," Infante replied, puzzled. Then he realized McEwan and Morton misinterpreted his comment. "I figured you guys earned your stripes a long time ago and knew what I meant. My orders are, quote, 'The unique nature of your stand-alone assignment requires performance of tasks using independent judgment over extended periods without benefit of supervision' end quote. My MO is to ask for forgiveness later than permission now. As I said, I'll brief him when I can." Infante's eyes twinkled. "Besides, Ted isn't the choir boy you think he is. I've learned a lot from him about juking the system."

"Got it." McEwan stood. "It's time for some answers."

CHAPTER FORTY-FOUR

THE TWO MEN HIKED the Waterton Valley Trail without stopping, devouring two energy bars apiece for lunch. A short while later, al-Dosari experienced intestinal distress, requiring a stop. During the next several hours, the sky darkened, the temperature dropped as they ascended, and sporadic raindrops fell.

"It'll pass," the guide remarked. "No significant rain expected."

Al-Dosari believed Devereaux's assessment. In a major reversal from the terrorist's initial impression, the guide had earned his grudging respect. His confidence in his escort's ability to get him to his destination grew with every step.

The Glacier National Park terrain was magnificent. Whenever the sun peeked out of the clouds, a brilliant gold light bathed snowcapped mountains. Emerging from the forest, they hiked along the shore of a beautiful deep-blue lake named Kootenai, where a monstrous chocolate moose splashed loudly in the water. Repeatedly dunking its head, the creature ripped vegetation from the lakebed and crunched it between powerful molars.

Continuing south, they wound their way through thick stands of trees. Mosquitoes miraculously immune to DEET bug spray fed on them at will. Beyond Pass Creek, the terrain angled sharply upward at the Stoney Indian Lake trailhead.

After demonstrating an almost-inhuman ability to hike at breakneck speeds for miles, Devereaux finally seemed to be as affected by the steep incline as al-Dosari. Gasping for breath, he stopped, bent over, and rested his hands on his knees. "My turn for a pit stop." The guide set his pack next to a log and removed a roll of toilet paper and a bottle. "If anyone comes by wave at 'em. If it's a ranger, tell him I'll be right back. Read this." Grinning, he tossed al-Dosari a warning pamphlet on bears and trudged off.

Al-Dosari watched until Devereaux's back disappeared. Unzipping his pack, he opened the laundry bag and pulled out his GPS unit, carefully concealed from the guide. Turning it on, he acquired a signal, obtained the coordinates, and compared them to the map. They were at the precise location. He shut down the GPS and clipped it to a zipper pull inside his pack. Al-Dosari studied the map, estimating the trail would rise another two thousand feet soon. Squatting, he pulled out a fresh bottle from Devereaux's pack and secured it in his belt holder. He heard whistling and saw the guide plodding back through the woods.

"When Mother Nature calls, you gotta answer!" Devereaux chortled, punching the terrorist in the shoulder.

Al-Dosari thought his guide's demeanor odd. In fact, reflecting on it, Devereaux had talked much more since they crossed Pass Creek.

"Go ahead, lead the way." Devereaux grinned, slinging his pack onto his shoulders. "I'll catch up wi'cha!"

Proceeding up the trail, al-Dosari cast a glance behind as Devereaux drained a bottle and tossed it over his shoulder. As he continued above the timberline, the temperature dropped rapidly. Rounding a bend, he stopped. *What is this?*

A carcass of some sort lay at al-Dosari's feet, looking like bits and pieces of a dead elk. The terrorist sidestepped the fresh pile of bloody tissue and fur. *I will wait at the top of the next crest and ask Devereaux what killed it.*

Suddenly, al-Dosari experienced the sensation of being pitched into the air in slow motion. Somersaulting, he landed upside down in a clump of bushes. Dazed, his brain could not process what was happening. A ferocious roar and bloodcurdling screams pierced his pounding head.

Rolling upright, he focused on the surreal scene unfolding below him. A monstrous grizzly stood on its rear feet towering over Devereaux, bloody saliva foaming from its mouth. The bear stepped back—half of the guide's face hung off the skull, drooping to the side like a grotesque mask.

Immobilized, al-Dosari watched the gigantic beast assault Devereaux. It toyed with the guide, swatting him, razor-sharp claws ripping open his chest. The grizzly snagged a leg in its massive jaws and shook him from side to side like a rag doll. Tiring of this game, it flung its plaything in the air, and Devereaux tumbled to the ground. The bear pounced up and down on the guide before punching him with enormous paws. Backing up, the grizzly studied its prey.

Devereaux lay lifeless.

The frightening sight propelled al-Dosari to his feet. Backpedaling warily up the trail, he kept his eyes glued on the grizzly. A severed limb dangled like a Turkish cigarette from its huge mouth, crunching sounds echoing as the beast snacked. Moving guardedly, he covered ground until the bear disappeared from view, then he turned and broke into a full sprint. The munching faded the farther he ran. Soon the only sounds reaching his ears were the wind and his own ragged gasps for air. Collapsing to his knees, he tried to process what he had witnessed but could not. The grizzly's attack did what nothing and no one else could—it totally unhinged the Sword of Islam.

A branch snapped to al-Dosari's left. *The bear is tracking me!* Al-Dosari twisted his neck slowly back and forth, but his arms and legs would not respond to the messages fired by his brain. Easy prey, he waited the inescapable jaws of death. *I have failed you, Allah. Forgive me.*

Minutes passed without the expected attack.

Refreshing raindrops bounced off his face, and al-Dosari opened his eyes. He savored the delicious drops of water. Reaching for the bottle on his hip with shaking hands, he twisted it open, upending it and taking a huge gulp. *Aaargh!* Al-Dosari expelled the liquid from his mouth and coughed violently. *Devereaux filled the bottle with alcohol!*

Al-Dosari shucked his pack and pulled it forward—only shredded fabric remained. He had nothing to drink. No food. No shelter. No rain gear. The sleeping bag and map were gone. *My watch?* Gone. Frantically shaking the pack, he spotted the GPS unit tethered to the remains of a pocket. He patted his waist. *Praise be to Allah! I still have the smallpox!*

Losing almost everything fueled panic. Zipping up his fleece jacket, he forced three deep yogic breaths to center himself. Turning on the GPS unit, he peered at the tiny screen—he was on a secondary path south of the main trail that intersected a creek an unknown distance away. He pulled the screen closer to his eyes. *A cabin?*

Only then did he notice the ice pellets stinging his face. Taking a last backward look for the grizzly, al-Dosari plunged forward.

I have to find that cabin or I will join Devereaux.

CHAPTER FORTY-FIVE

A PRODUCT OF SEATTLE'S INNER city, William Bradford Harris lived a sheltered and lonely life, residing in the same neighborhood for all of his thirty-seven years. Rarely leaving his cocoon, public transportation had served him well until now. Intimidated by the size and power of the rental SUV now in his hands, Harris realized six years had passed since he'd last driven any motor vehicle.

A throwback to the radicals of the sixties and seventies, Harris embraced every antigovernment cause that rode into town. He hated the stranglehold big business and the military had around the neck of America. Controlling everything, the government's jackbooted thugs abused its citizens and others around the world. In his eyes, the American people were three-quarters of the way down a decadent slide to hell. Harris lived a life of utter frustration until he met his new brothers, whose companionship and counsel filled the void in his life. They gave him the respect, sense of worth, and importance he craved.

Maneuvering onto the interstate, he guided the Chevrolet Blazer out of the city limits, his mind drifting back to the evening when his potential was finally recognized. Occupying his customary chair in the back corner of his favorite bookstore, Harris browsed through several magazines before a speaker's voice got his attention. Drawn toward the sound, he joined a crowd of people listening raptly to an author discussing his book about the benevolent aspects of Islam. Harris liked what he heard, purchased the book, and sought the author's autograph. The last person in line,

"Sami", chatted him up, their conversation turning to America's military interventions in the Muslim world.

Harris discovered a philosophical soul mate in Sami Marwat, a fundamentalist Sunni Muslim from the remote village of Devgar, Pakistan, 185 miles southwest of Islamabad. Sami came to America for an education and stayed. He belonged to a group seeking to return to a simpler lifestyle removed from the evils of Western society. Sami said the peaceful movement attracted hundreds of Americans, who all had converted to Islam. After meeting several times, he invited Harris to formalize his conversion to Islam, and the loner accepted with great enthusiasm.

Instead, on the appointed evening, Harris was whisked blindfolded through the streets of Seattle to a house where Sami introduced him to several men from the mosque and a mysterious unnamed "brother", clearly a leader of some sort. Sami apologized for the covert nature of the trip, explaining FBI witch hunts made such measures necessary to avoid persecution. Knowing that the Patriot Act allowed the FBI to harass and spy on innocent Americans and Muslims alike, Harris's concerns evaporated. Embracing the group's doctrine that America was the source of all Muslim suffering, he pledged allegiance to its cause. Once the secretive brother bestowed on him his Muslim name and promised to lead him to his seat in paradise, Harris became a true believer.

Harris thought of those who came before him; the warriors snared in raids in US cities along with those sacrificed on the fields of battle. Harris wanted, needed, to strike back at America—when the summons came, he answered without wavering. Harris would succeed in his mission. Failure wasn't an option. Not this time.

Khalid Abdul Aziz, known to the rest of the world as William Bradford Harris, would bring honor to his brothers in holy jihad.

CHAPTER FORTY-SIX

LOST, VISIBILITY APPROACHING ZERO, Ali bin al-Dosari recalled the last GPS reading: exceeding six thousand feet in elevation. Pounding sleet terminated the signal, which did not reacquire. After five miserable minutes, he shut it down to conserve batteries. Remembering the gruesome attack, he forged ahead on the poorly marked trail, willing himself to ignore the very real possibility it was a wildlife path.

Hands and lips numb, teeth chattering, al-Dosari knew his core body temperature was falling—he'd die of hypothermic shock if he did not find shelter soon. Without his watch, stripped off during the bear attack, and no functional GPS, he had no idea how much daylight remained. Once night fell, temperatures would plummet further, bringing death in minutes.

A short while later, al-Dosari glimpsed a cabin through the driving sleet. Mustering every remaining ounce of strength, he slogged up to the front porch. The door, secured with a padlock, had dozens of protruding nails to prevent any attempt to break it down. As fast as he could in his weakened state, he circled the exterior. He found two windows with steel panels bolted shut from the inside. Dejected, he landed with a thump on the porch.

In an emergency, how does one enter? The terrorist studied the door, then saw it. *Six exposed screws securing the hasp to a block of wood!*

Fumbling, al-Dosari pulled out his knife and attacked each screw. Shivering, he dropped the knife repeatedly, once barely missing a foot. Finally, the hasp swung free and he pushed the door open. Crawling inside on his knees, he shoved the door shut. Pulling himself upright, he spied a lantern and a box of matches. It took his trembling fingers four tries to light it. Using his teeth, he opened a can of Coleman fuel and poured the fluid onto wood stacked in a stove. Striking a match, he threw it onto the pile, and warmth leaped forth. The same steps fired up the cooking stove. After peeling off every article of clothing and wringing out the water, he spread them out on the springs of the top bunk bed closest to the stove.

He had to warm his body. Untying the knot in the rope of bedroll sacks dangling from the ceiling, he extracted two heavy wool blankets and wrapped them around his bare skin. Needing sleep more than sustenance, he dragged a mattress over to the lower bunk and climbed in. Pulling the blankets around his throat with one hand while gripping his knife in the other, he surrendered to exhaustion.

When the sleeting rain finally stopped hammering the metal roof, the sudden silence roused him. Rising, al-Dosari shoved more wood into the stoves. Warmer but still cold, he tried thinking, but his mind and body remained exhausted and numb from fighting the ice storm. He spotted a large airtight box in the kitchen area containing numerous staples. Operating at the primal level, he devoured a sleeve of saltine crackers then gulped water from a plastic bottle while examining a laminated trail map tacked to a wall. Marked with waypoints, it oriented the cabin in the center and 360 degrees outward. Wolfing down spoons of peanut butter and a second sleeve of saltines, al-Dosari studied the surrounding terrain and routes and mulled over his options. It appeared a short hike would put him back on the main trail—perhaps a mile if he followed a stream. Unsure of the current time, he knew one thing: leaving before dawn meant certain death from the elements. Having lost so much time already, he mentally reviewed his backup plan.

Decision made, al-Dosari returned to the bunk bed and collapsed.

Despite the late hour, dozens of agents scurried about the Northern California JTTF office while others worked the telephones and computers.

Paul Infante and JTTF teams were on the streets of San Jose, their urgent searches for Syed el-Nasrallah drawing a blank. McEwan and Morton monitored the discreetly intense manhunt, but their most promising lead since discovering the al-Dosari/IJB connection had vanished.

Morton zigzagged his way through a mountain of coffee cups, soda cans, water bottles, pizza boxes, and sandwich wrappers to reload his bottomless coffee cup.

"Tim, have you considered an IV?" McEwan queried.

Morton grimaced—it was only the thousandth time he'd heard the observation.

McEwan perused the recently received CIA dossier on el-Nasrallah's son Mu'adh from cover to cover. Picking up more messages, McEwan continued reading.

Opening an eye, Ali bin al-Dosari focused on the GPS unit sitting on the table. He turned it on, and it acquired a signal: *5:00 a.m.!* Rolling out from beneath the blankets, he pulled on warm, dry clothing. Despite his narrow escape from death the day before, energy surged through him. Grabbing two canteens, he filled them with water from a plastic container. He poured the remainder into a pan, heated it and used the water to make two bowls of oatmeal and a pot of coffee. Sprinkling sugar on the oatmeal, he consumed it and downed two cups of coffee. Rifling through the pantry, al-Dosari found a backpack. He stuffed it with the canteens, metal tins of peanut butter, and saltine crackers.

Al-Dosari stepped out of the cabin and relieved himself then retreated inside. Spreading a blanket on the floor, the Sword of Islam said his dawn prayers. Rising, he doused the fires in the stoves and pulled on his jacket. Hoisting the pack onto his shoulders, he stuffed the map into a pocket and clipped the GPS to his belt. After reattaching the fanny pack, he put on work gloves, then grabbed a machete and ax off the wall.

I must avoid rangers at all costs. Or kill them.

CHAPTER FORTY-SEVEN

EVERY DAY LIVING AND working in the scenic mountain wonderland known as Glacier National Park was an adventure for Harold Devers. For the past four years, the thirty-year-old law enforcement ranger, called Hank by his friends, patrolled the eastern half of the park from St. Mary's, Montana, to Logan's Pass in the center of the park. Tan, husky, and outgoing, Devers possessed a maturity greater than his years. When the Lake McDonald Area Ranger on the park's western edge retired, he got the job. His new supervisory assignment started today.

For once, Devers' professional and personal lives were dovetailing. Moving to the other side of the park placed him an hour closer to Helena. As liaison to the FBI's Joint Terrorism Task Force, he traveled there twice a month for meetings. The promotion benefitted him personally too, putting him a stone's throw from Kalispell, home to Brenda Osgood, a pretty, petite, blue-eyed, blond high school teacher. After eighteen months together, they were contemplating marriage.

The rugged Devers strapped on his leather equipment belt. All told, he hauled about twenty extra pounds on his hips every day, including his radio and .40 caliber SIG Sauer service weapon. Grabbing his campaign hat, coffee thermos, and ballistic nylon briefcase, he headed out the door to his patrol vehicle parked under an overhang. Setting his gear inside, he fired up the white and bright green striped Chevrolet Tahoe. While it warmed up, he made a quick pass, kicking all the tires, a necessary step to confirm none went flat overnight, a common byproduct of off-road driving in remote areas of the park.

Once inside, Devers flipped a toggle switch on the equipment console. Seeing the rotating roof emergency lights bouncing off his picture window, he shut them down. A single punch of the siren button with his right index finger produced a yelp. Devers pulled out and headed for his office, where he'd spend the first part of the morning packing up. Once he finished, he'd drive all fifty-two miles of the Going-to-the-Sun Highway and deliver everything to his new office at Apgar Village. Along the route, Devers would cruise by a couple of out-of-the-way spots in his new patrol territory. Originally planning to move the following day, the last-minute scheduling of a JTTF meeting in Helena changed those plans. Devers couldn't remember one ever called urgently. A substantial threat must be on the horizon.

Thrusting too hard through the thick undergrowth, the Sword of Islam lost his footing and fell flat on his face. Spitting chunks of dirt and gravel, al-Dosari realized he had grossly underestimated the difficult terrain. Craning his neck skyward, snowcapped Cathedral Peak soared ominously over him. Despite leaving the cabin almost two hours earlier, he had barely covered a mile, the trail through the alpine forest ascending several hundred grueling feet. *Taunting and testing, as if the infidel's land itself is battling me!*

The terrorist realized he had landed face-first on the main trail. Standing, he discarded the ax and machete by flinging both of the tools as far as he could into the trees. Walking over to a nearby boulder, al-Dosari dropped the backpack and sat. Rubbing the throbbing muscles on his legs and arms, he thanked Allah for guiding him. Opening his canteen, he swilled the water around in his mouth before releasing it to trickle down his throat. The act triggered memories of his gulp from Devereaux's bottle and the beast's attack. Forcing that nightmare away, he concentrated on recalculating his trek.

Consulting both the GPS and map, al-Dosari accepted he must push harder to recapture lost time. He resumed hiking and took the right fork of the trail descending toward a campground, where he stumbled onto a sow and two bear cubs feeding. Controlling his panic, he steered around the threat. Reaching Flattop Mountain, a five-mile flat piece of rock, he continued southwest toward the floor of McDonald Creek Valley. Remnants of the prior night's high-elevation storm disappeared with each downhill step until the temperature turned into a cool summer morning.

Hiking through significantly less demanding terrain, al-Dosari reviewed his backup plan. When he did not show by 10:00 a.m. at the Logan Pass Visitor Center, al-Dosari's contact was to head to the alternate rendezvous point and wait until the terrorist arrived.

Al-Dosari hoped his contact was following the plan. He was overdue.

Postponing bad news, the Director of National Intelligence asked Kyle McEwan about the San Jose imam. "Where are we on Syed el-Nasrallah?"

"We haven't found him yet, Danni. Paul Infante says we're closing in."

"I'm afraid *close* may not be good enough. The president said if you don't find the imam and get something going soon, he's pulling the plug and turning the FBI loose."

"Damn it, al-Dosari's in my sights!" McEwan roared. "If Englewood changes course now, we'll never catch him in time. We all know the ramifications of that!"

"Yes, especially me," Sanchez snapped back.

"Why the sudden about-face?"

"The whole cabinet is second-guessing the president for hanging everything on us. We can't defend our position if you aren't producing. Give me something to take back to them."

"Englewood guaranteed me free rein. You promised to run interference."

"You're right. But he's the president, Kyle, and once he changes his mind, that's it. You'd better locate the imam or we're finished."

"Get me some breathing room!"

"How much time do you need?" Sanchez asked.

His answer: a resounding click.

CHAPTER FORTY-EIGHT

LEAVING THE ST. MARY'S Visitor Center, National Park Service ranger Hank Devers drove leisurely toward Apgar Village. On the way, he'd swing by Packers Roost, an area used by packers years ago to feed and water mules and horses while traversing the Flattop Mountain Trail. Twenty-four challenging miles from Goat Haunt Ranger Station, the trailhead remained a vital part of the trail system. He'd never visited Packers Roost but that was changing today—Devers would explore it and every inch of his new area. He valued the advice from one of his basic training instructors at the Federal Law Enforcement Training Center in Georgia: "You never know when your life or the life of someone else will depend on your knowledge of the terrain. Mother Earth can be very unforgiving. Learn every inch of your turf. Your knowledge will save a life someday, maybe your own."

Bonnie Schultz, his commander, provided him with visual clues to Packers Roost. The hardest part was the entry. Coming from the loop, it was nearly invisible at the base of the hill. She told him to keep a sharp eye. If he missed the turn, he'd go two miles farther before being able to turn around and backtrack. Spotting the hint of a road off to the right, he slowed, then veered down a narrow gravel road. Bouncing down the rough road, Devers was forced to slow to idle speed.

Ali bin al-Dosari detected a whiff of decaying horse manure at the same instant his eyes spied a cabin. A wave of accomplishment and relief washed over him, but his elation subsided as he took in the landscape. *Where is my contact?*

Hiding in the tree line, he spotted a dust cloud moving down a gravel road. *An SUV. Green and white stripes. Emergency lights. National Park Service logo. Trouble!* Al-Dosari's fight-or-flight instinct kicked in. Tucking himself tightly behind thick brush and trees, he pushed aside a branch and peered out. He watched the patrol vehicle nose up to a split rail fence.

Devers decided to park and mosey over to the Packers Roost cabin, take a quick look, then get back on the road. He climbed out and strolled up to the boarded-up cabin. He could recite by heart every word of the familiar sign posted on the door: "This building under the protection of the United States government. Destruction, injury, or theft punishable by fine up to $500 or imprisonment for six months or both. Department of Interior National Park Service." Hearing a noise behind him, Devers turned toward the sound.

A few hundred feet up the road, a billowing debris cloud traveled at the same rate as the sound of an engine. A red Chevy Blazer appeared out of the shroud. Obviously unprepared for the possibility of others, the driver slammed on his brakes, stopping inches from the patrol vehicle. Shaking his head, Devers walked over to the Blazer and gave the universal gesture to roll down the window.

The driver hesitated before complying, a look of sheer panic on his face. Devers noticed something else—the driver was drenched with sweat on a cool, sixty-degree day.

"Going kinda fast, aren't you?"

The driver responded, sputtering, "Yessir … sorry. Not familiar with this truck. G-got away from me."

"Not yours, huh?"

"No, er, rental … Seattle."

Already at half-mast, Devers's antennae shot to full staff. Examining the man's eyes intently, he queried, "Why are you here?"

"Supposed to ... pick up friends, you know ... hiking!" came the halting answer. "Late!"

Devers's sixth sense kicked into hyper mode. "If you're late, where are your friends?"

Harris shrugged his shoulders.

"Got a license and rental contract?"

Harris dug out his wallet, fumbled handing over his license, and produced the agreement from the glove box. His hand visibly quivered as he shoved the contract out the window.

From his hiding place, al-Dosari could not hear the dialogue. As he watched, the ranger backed up slowly, hand on gun, motioning with his other hand for the driver to exit. A clumsy man stepped out and placed both hands on the vehicle. He stretched his arms wide and spread his legs. Al-Dosari recognized the man from a photograph. *My contact!*

Intently observing the ranger's search of William Bradford Harris, al-Dosari drew his knife from its sheath. Tensing into a tight coil, he tiptoed silently up behind the ranger. When the first piece of gravel crunched beneath his boots, he propelled himself forward. Reaching around the ranger with lightning speed, he clamped one hand down on the man's mouth then drove the knife into his back, the blade entering deeply just below his bulletproof vest. He twisted, and the ranger stiffened as his head snapped back. The terrorist eased the sagging body to the ground.

"Oh my god!" Harris emitted a shock-delayed cry.

"Shut up, Harris!" The terrorist wiped his knife clean on the ranger's uniform shirt. "We must act before we are discovered!"

Stunned, Harris fixated on the knife.

"You fool!" Al-Dosari slapped his face. "You are here to help me! Grab his feet!"

Harris mutely followed orders, helping carry the ranger to the cabin. Finding a door without protruding nails, al-Dosari kicked it open, and they dragged the body inside. Removing the service weapon and radio from their holsters, the terrorist heaved the gun far into the woods. Al-Dosari examined the radio. Unsure if it contained a GPS tracker, the mastermind decided against keeping it. Detaching the battery, he hurled the radio deep into the tree line.

Frozen with fear, Harris watched the killer close the cabin door.

"Get going, you idiot!" Al-Dosari hissed. The terrorist sprinted to the woods, retrieved his pack, and ran to the ranger's vehicle. He pressed the electric door lock and turned toward the Blazer. *Where is Harris?* Al-Dosari spotted him slumped down on the cabin porch. "Over here now!"

Harris shuffled over slowly, earning himself another stinging slap.

"Move! Get in!" Al-Dosari flung his pack onto the back seat and jumped into the front passenger seat. "Can you drive?" He gave Harris a hard look.

Shaking badly, Harris could not respond.

Al-Dosari backhanded him. "Are you capable of driving?"

Harris nodded through tears.

"Okay. Do not drive foolishly." Al-Dosari buckled himself in. "Go."

Turning the ignition key, Harris threw the Blazer in gear and floored the accelerator. The SUV spit gravel, fishtailing its rear end. Fearing another slap, he brought it under control.

For the next several minutes, al-Dosari studied his driver carefully. Eventually confident Harris would not cause an accident or attract unwanted attention, he hissed, "If you have learned nothing from our encounter with the ranger, you should comprehend fully how deadly our undertaking is. I will do everything to guarantee its success. And so will *you*."

His warrior brother's cold, detached voice triggered a lump in Harris's throat. Khalid Abdul Aziz was failing his holy tasking. He must recover or lose his place in paradise.

Had Harris turned and looked into the eyes of his accomplice, he would have questioned what else he stood to lose.

CHAPTER FORTY-NINE

DRIVING IN SILENCE UNTIL the Glacier National Park signs disappeared from the rearview mirror, William Harris almost jumped when his travel companion spoke, announcing his name as Ricky. Harris's subsequent attempts at small talk were rebuffed. Yet by the time they passed through Coeur D'Alene, Idaho, he sensed Ricky's anger was gone.

Approaching Spokane on Interstate 90, Harris remembered the ranger's killing. Reliving the moment, he recalled the look on the ranger's face as Ricky plunged the knife, then replayed the body dropping to the ground. A powerful adrenaline surge came over him. Harris relished his first taste of blood. Next time, killing would be easier, a rite of passage making him a great warrior.

A yelping noise cut through his reverie. The rearview mirror showed flashing red and blue lights. "Ricky! The police are pulling us over!"

Al-Dosari snapped awake. Tapping the knife at the small of his back, he took control. "Stay calm, William, do not panic," he advised coolly. "He does not know about the ranger. You have done something to cause his interest. Do what he says."

Harris nodded nervously, watching the police officer's approach in the side view mirror.

The officer motioned for Harris to roll down the window. "License and registration, please."

"W-w-what, er, did I do?" Stammering, Harris fumbled for his license.

"You're driving erratically, crossing the center line." The officer looked at Harris, then over to his passenger. "Have you been drinking?"

"N-no, sir. I don't drink."

"How about that registration," the officer looked down at the license, "Mr. Harris?"

"Rental." Harris barely managed to croak the word out.

"Fine. Let me see the rental agreement." The police officer pointed his finger at al-Dosari. "And you, sir, break out some ID."

"Certainly, officer," al-Dosari replied in English with a Spanish accent.

Harris passed the requested documents through the window.

"Both of you stay in the vehicle with your hands where I can see them. I'll be back."

Al-Dosari realized the policeman was checking their names and ID data for warrants. "William, listen to me," he hissed. "I will say this once. We cannot be captured, or we fail Allah. Am I clear?"

Harris nodded blankly.

"We will kill the officer only if he tries to apprehend us. If I tell you to get out of the car, do so immediately. Run to the officer and throw your arms around him with all of your might. I will do everything else. Whatever happens next is Allah's will. Do you understand?"

Another nod.

"Do nothing stupid and remain calm."

Minutes ticked by slowly. Finally, the officer emerged from his cruiser.

"Ricky! He's coming back!"

Al-Dosari moved the knife to the right side of his waistband. "Remember what I told you." Glancing over his shoulder, he saw the officer stop abruptly and speak into the radio microphone hanging from a shoulder epaulet. He quickened his pace toward the Blazer.

"Harris, keep your mouth shut unless questioned, then only answer him." He tightened his grip on the knife. "Do not panic!"

"It's your lucky day. Get on out of here and watch your driving!" the officer scolded, tossing the documents into Harris's lap. Jogging back to the cruiser, he jumped inside. Lights flashing and siren blaring, he was gone before either man caught his breath.

Harris almost retched, pains jabbing his intestines.

"We narrowly escaped another serious incident because of your inattentiveness," al-Dosari fumed. "Now we must change automobiles. No more slipups or I will take care of you myself."

Harris pulled the Blazer back into westbound traffic.

Al-Dosari consulted the map. After a couple of minutes, he spoke. "Take the next exit and merge onto Spokane Airport Road. I want you to go inside the terminal and rent a sedan with a trunk from a different agency. Advise them you are driving home to Seattle and nothing else. Especially do not mention this vehicle. According to this map, there is a long-term parking area called North Shuttle. Meet me near the back of that lot. Now, repeat those instructions to me."

Harris did, and fifteen minutes later, was headed in toward the car rental kiosks.

Al-Dosari knew security video cameras were recording their movements. It made no difference. If authorities traced them to the airport and saw them on video, it would be irrelevant.

Harris detoured to the men's room to deal with a bout of diarrhea. Shaken by his encounter with the police, he forgot the instructions. He leased a Dodge Durango using a prepaid Visa card provided by Ricky. Oblivious to his error, he collected the SUV and drove to the rendezvous point.

Al-Dosari spotted the Durango turning down the parking aisle, Harris behind the wheel. When Harris pulled up, he yanked open the door. "I told you to rent a car with a trunk."

Harris lied. "I'm sorry, Ricky. They gave the last one away. I was lucky to get this." Without asking, he climbed into the back seat. "I'm going to lie down a while. I don't feel good."

Aggravated by Harris's latest false step, al-Dosari eased out of the parking lot and exited the airport. Harris's continued blunders increased the probability his plan would be discovered and thwarted. His instinct was to drag the moron out of the car and beat him with a tire iron, but if he hit Harris again, the simpleton might bolt and al-Dosari still needed him. To conceal his travels among the infidels, he required an unwitting, pasty-white American blinded by ideology who would follow his orders without question. Unfortunately, the Seattle cell went overboard when they co-opted the dim-witted Harris.

For now, he would have to calculate Harris's missteps into his plan.

CHAPTER FIFTY

"MCEWAN!" THE DNI AGENT'S name thundered across the JTTF bullpen.

Spotting the raised hand, FBI SAC Ted Beacham hustled over and placed a message in front of McEwan who read it, then slid it across the table to Morton. He scanned it and passed it back. Beacham got the ball rolling. "Okay, folks, can I have your attention?"

The room fell silent immediately.

"A National Park Service ranger has been brutally stabbed at Glacier National Park, and the incident is definitely connected to our situation." Using a laser pointer, he aimed it at the north central Montana-Canada border on a map.

"Here's what we know. When the ranger in question missed a JTTF meeting in Helena, attempts to contact him failed. Rangers initiated a search and found him stashed in a trailhead cabin. His prognosis is not good. They found incriminating evidence at the scene. During the assault, the assailant, or assailants, dropped several flyers describing meetings at a Seattle mosque. Helena theorizes al-Dosari came across at Seattle with a bogus passport, and an IJB cell is helping him make his way east toward a large metro area—"

"Sorry to interrupt, Ted," McEwan interjected.

"Sure, go ahead."

"I don't buy Helena's theory about him making his way east. We know al-Dosari did not arrive via California—his decoy brother did. He is aware we use facial-recognition and biosensors at every port of entry."

"How could he know that?" Beacham looked doubtful.

"You're underestimating him. He probably has twice the sources we do and the coffers to pay them more. Al-Dosari would assume we're looking for him at all our ports of entry, so he'd never enter anywhere legally. Let's say I'm wrong. If he used our westernmost port to divert us from a target back East, why tip us off that he's here? While al-Dosari's a master of diversion, I don't see it, not this time. I agree with you that the brochures confirm there is a Seattle cell and it was in Glacier."

"I'm seeing your point." Beacham rubbed his chin with a thumb and index finger.

"Al-Dosari's preparation is meticulous. He's factored in that we're gunning for him, so he's not leaving breadcrumbs telling us he's arrived. His best play is dropping off radar, resurfacing only to attack. And the flyers aren't a statement because they weren't pinned to the ranger's badge. When you consider its remote location on our northern border, it's more likely al-Dosari entered via the park and rendezvoused with the Seattle cell there and the materials were dropped inadvertently. They've hit the interstate and are heading any direction but north."

"When you lay it out that way, it's obvious," Beacham concurred.

"Ted, message every JTTF with a port of entry on the northern border to use their facial recognition software to compare Yousef's photo to everyone crossing through our border during the last forty-eight hours. Assuming they draw a blank, and I'm sure they will, al-Dosari walked in through the park."

"Okay, will do. I'll have the Park Service agents check with their Canadian counterparts to see if they have anything and ask Helena to coordinate with RCMP." Scribbling furiously with one hand, Beacham summoned a group of agents with the other.

Morton added more tasks. "Let the Glacier rangers know it's a terrorism investigation in addition to assault on a federal officer. Get them to pull all footage from every camera in the park, especially the exits. We need to ID a vehicle to pinpoint their direction of travel. Have Seattle get a bead on all local terror suspects and put them under round-the-clock surveillance."

"Got it."

Agents scrambled to take the tasks.

Morton pulled Beacham aside. "Remind all offices no one moves on anybody or anything without Kyle clearing it first. We don't have the luxury of jurisdictional pissing contests or missteps. Any questions, problems, let me know right away."

"I'll reinforce this with everyone."

McEwan instinctively understood his quarry; al-Dosari's acts conformed to the terrorist's nature. Whatever the Park Service agents found would dictate their next move.

Agents concentrated on the hunt for al-Dosari, his accomplices, and imam el-Nasrallah. After passing McEwan's orders on to the border task forces, Beacham monitored the ongoing inquiries. A call interrupted his efforts; Beacham listened briefly, then spoke. "I've got a Montana agent on the line. I'll put him on speaker."

"This is Special Agent Bryan Smythe, National Park Service."

"Bryan, give us some good news," McEwan said.

"Al-Dosari dodged our port of entry by circumnavigating Goat Haunt Ranger Station. It's reachable from Canada only by boat or foot and the best place to sneak in. On a hunch, I sent some of my best people up there. The team found freshly whacked bushes along a game trail skirting the ranger station. We pulled video from hiking trails and a sensor-triggered camera captured a grizzly attack on two hikers. One was mauled to death, the other fled. Until we saw the video, we didn't know about the attack. ID from the body shows the dead man is a well-known local guide from Canada. We found a one-night backcountry camping permit for the guide and a Ricardo San Felipe. Neither man checked in with rangers at Goat Haunt. The video is good enough to compare to Yousef al-Dosari's photo. It's our opinion the man who survived the attack is your subject."

"Outstanding work, Bryan!" McEwan jumped to his feet.

"Here's our theory. We experienced an unusual high-elevation summer snowstorm last night and during the height of it, al-Dosari broke into one of our cabins. At daybreak, he rejoined the main trail and hiked down to Packers Roost, where he ambushed our ranger. No cameras there, but we found the Seattle mosque flyers covered with tire tracks. Somebody met al-Dosari and transported him out of the park."

"Bryan, Tim Morton. Do you have a way of tracking him out of there?"

"On a normal August day, we see hundreds of cars coming and going. We caught a break with the storm—traffic was lighter than usual. We're going over all footage park-wide now. If you get us a car, we can zero in on it and tell you exactly when and where it entered and departed and who's in it. Otherwise, we have to scrutinize every vehicle and its occupants. We'll have something for you soon." The call ended.

Beacham approached and handed McEwan a folder. "The latest message traffic and 302s hot off the press. We're greasing the wheels with Seattle for you. I advised NCTC and all field divisions and their JTTFs to screen everything for a Ricardo San Felipe using Yousef's photo."

Nodding, McEwan slid the folder into his briefcase. Heading out, he punched Danni Sanchez's phone number.

CHAPTER FIFTY-ONE

LOOKING OUT HIS WINDOW, McEwan estimated their jet was at least twenty or more planes back in the San Francisco International Airport departure queue. Tired, eyes burning, the last thing he wanted to do was dig through another stack of reports. Splitting the documents into two piles, he handed one off to Morton. Busy with an ever-present coffee cup at his mouth, Morton snagged his half with his other hand without glancing over. The two men settled in mining the documents.

McEwan peeled off the first report, an update from the Seattle JTTF. The FBI confirmed all but two local terror suspects were accounted for and under surveillance. Agents were running down leads on the two missing men and expected confirmation of their whereabouts shortly. Reading the rest of the reports, McEwan found nothing related to al-Dosari or the attack. McEwan lifted the last message in his stack and wearily began reading. Perking up, McEwan leaned forward.

Spokane PD reported pulling over a vehicle containing two suspicious males, one a US citizen, the other a Canadian national. The reporting officer noticed a GPS jamming device resting on the console and he sensed something was hinky with the men. Although they were traveling together, they didn't appear to be companions as the driver seemed fearful of the passenger. The officer ran Wants and Warrants checks, which came back negative. He didn't investigate further due to a 'shots fired officer needs assistance' call. An hour later, he pulled it together: along with the GPS jammer, the passenger's Canadian passport did not have a US entry stamp, triggering his report to the JTTF.

Rereading the report, McEwan commended the officer's intuition as his own alarm bells clanged loudly. Details jumped off the page: Vehicle, red Chevrolet Blazer, short-term rental. Driver, William Bradford Harris, Seattle, Washington. Passenger, Ricardo San Felipe, Canadian. *Bingo!*

McEwan's brain shifted into overdrive. He flipped back through his pile—there it was. As the jet climbed on takeoff, McEwan reread the 302 documenting the two missing Seattle terror suspects—one was William Bradford Harris. *Gotcha both!*

Excitedly, McEwan jabbed Morton in the shoulder.

Startled, Morton spilled coffee down the front of his shirt. "What?"

"Tim, we're red-hot now!"

Receiving the details from McEwan, Morton took charge. "I'll brief Beacham, and he'll notify Seattle. I'll get the Glacier agent on the horn again."

Masquerade over: Ricardo San Felipe *was* Ali bin al-Dosari.

Jogging toward the waiting FBI sedan, McEwan gave the DNI a quick rundown of recent developments. The rapid turn of events stunned Sanchez.

"Danni, Park Service agents rechecked all video footage prior to the ranger's attack. They found a red Chevy Blazer parked for about four hours at the Logan Pass Visitor Center. The driver, a white male, walked to and from the center's restrooms several times. We've compared Harris's DMV photo to the video and there's no doubt it's him. Spokane PD pulled over the same Blazer several hours later on I-90; the cruiser video shows the Blazer but you can't see either occupant. The officer ID'd Harris as the driver from his license photo, and al-Dosari as the passenger from Yousef's picture. The officer reported the passenger was carrying a Canadian passport in the name of Ricardo San Felipe and the two photos appeared to be the same man." McEwan paused to catch his breath. "Al-Dosari's definitely traveling under this alias."

"Does any Glacier video show al-Dosari?" Sanchez hoped.

"No. Once the Blazer left Logan Pass it never returned. The east entrance cameras didn't show the SUV coming or going; the west exit camera is offline; that's how Harris entered and they exited. Scratch the East Coast and Midwest; their target is somewhere out here."

Sanchez waited for more answers.

"All remaining Seattle cell members are bedded down for the night. The FBI placed a pretext call to Harris's employer; as of three days ago, he's on a two-week vacation. Everything adds up. Harris is al-Dosari's contact. An FBI SWAT team is sitting on his house and it's buttoned up. They'll break down the doors once we arrive. Let's hope his house produces answers."

Confused, Sanchez queried, "Why Harris, Kyle?"

"It's a shrewd move," McEwan replied. "Traveling with him gives al-Dosari better cover than in the company of one or more Middle-Eastern-looking men. We've issued an updated BOLO. With any luck, they're still in the Blazer. As for Seattle, the biggest thing going on here this week is an outdoor music festival. But with its population, the city itself could be the target, though I'd be surprised. Something doesn't compute."

"Let me know what you find in that house. CDC has announced a series of routine unscheduled exercises in major population centers. If al-Dosari attacks, we're prepositioned to roll out the National Response Plan."

"Roger that, Danni. We're here."

CHAPTER FIFTY-TWO

SPEAKING IN A FIRM voice, US magistrate judge Sarah Loitman addressed the Assistant United States Attorney and FBI agent standing before her. "I find probable cause that William Bradford Harris is providing material support and resources to, and conspiring with Ali bin al-Dosari and members of the Islamic Jihad Brotherhood, a foreign terrorist organization, to use a weapon of mass destruction to murder American citizens. I further find probable cause to justify executing this warrant without immediate prior notification of the persons therein, due to the risk of serious potential harm to federal officers. Everything's under seal."

Magistrate Judge Loitman signed the warrant, authorizing search of Harris's residence and seizure of evidence that would help the US government disrupt the ongoing plot. Loitman then signed arrest warrants for both Harris and al-Dosari.

Witnessing the signatures, the agent spoke into a phone. "I've got the warrants. Go."

Since McEwan's discovery, the Seattle JTTF found a YouTube video of suspected IJB cell members firing semiautomatic rifles at an unidentified training camp in the Pacific Northwest; Harris was not in the video. However, because Harris was involved in a plot to attack the United States using a bioweapon the search warrant would be "no-knock"—allowing superior numbers of FBI agents utilizing overwhelming firepower to enter without warning.

On the other side of Seattle in the city's First Hill neighborhood, homes adjacent to the William Harris residence stood empty, their occupants safely removed. Inside the 360-degree security perimeter, two tactical teams of agents moved stealthily down dark alleys, the late hour and driving rain obscuring the block FBI letters on their body armor.

McEwan followed the primary entry team as it branched off down the driveway, lining up at the front corner of the brick house. Morton joined the perimeter team in the backyard, trained on the rear of the house. Evidence collection and computer specialists were poised in nearby vans.

"Breach team, move up," came over the radio net. The entry team moved swiftly single file, stealthily climbing the front steps onto the porch of the dark house.

"Breach team, go!" An agent responded by slamming a dynamic entry tool into the door.

"FBI! Warrant!" was shouted as the team swarmed into the house.

SWAT agents moved from room to room, their calls of "FBI!" alternating with "Clear!" as the agents advanced. Finally, the transmission: "All clear. House secure. It's empty."

Holstering his weapon, McEwan entered the house with the JTTF supervisor. He found Morton coming through the kitchen doorway at the back of the house.

The three men canvassed the house, then Morton spoke. "I see two areas requiring immediate search: a storage closet full of boxes under the main staircase and two file cabinets in the dining room. It's his home office. Everything else can wait. I suggest they clone his hard drive, then print whatever might be relevant. The rest of us can start in on hardcopy files."

McEwan's concurrence set the plan in motion. Removing his vest, he got to work. Agents sifted through boxes, folders, binders, file cabinets, and stacks of documents. An agent eventually produced a printout indexing the computer hard drive and gave it to McEwan.

The review continued nonstop, mostly in silence. Finally, McEwan addressed Morton and the JTTF supervisor. "We've hit the mother lode.

There's an absolute gold mine here about the IJB. It looks like four local Muslims embraced and swore allegiance to the IJB, just like Paul Infante said they did in the San Jose cell. Harris identifies all four men."

The JTTF supervisor scanned the list. "We know them all, especially Sami Marwat. They're the same ones we've had under surveillance since your call. Marwat is probably the local leader."

"Round 'em up and interrogate the hell out of them. I want to know Harris's location." McEwan re-engrossed himself, cross-referencing pages in a binder with the computer printouts. A few minutes later, he spoke again.

"Harris is our boy, all right. Talk about a prolific writer. His first diary entry occurred three months back detailing his recruitment into the IJB by Sami Marwat. He meets a secretive brother, not further identified, who blesses him with the Muslim name Khalid Abdul Aziz, meaning 'eternal servant of the powerful one' and tells him he will be a great warrior for Allah. Fast-forward to three weeks ago—he's chosen for a special holy mission to secure his seat in paradise. Harris writes he was tasked to pick up a brother warrior arriving from Canada. Four days ago, he prays for strength to fulfill Allah's command."

Morton whistled. "You gotta be kidding me—he wrote all that down?"

"And more. Three days ago, he Googled Glacier National Park and Map Quested directions from here to there. There are no other searches for anything on his hard drive. According to Harris, the 'arriving holy warrior will reveal the mission'." McEwan scowled. "No clues about the target."

Morton opined Harris fit al-Dosari's MO of sacrificing others for the cause. "It's a safe bet he'll dupe Harris or some other patsy to deliver the smallpox. Does al-Dosari, the Sword, or smallpox pop up anywhere in his entries?"

"No." McEwan glanced down at the binder. "The diary ends with 'packed for jihad'. Obviously, the holy warrior is al-Dosari. We've drawn a blank on airlines. They're in a vehicle somewhere between Spokane and the final target. Have all Western JTTFs locate every terror suspect in their area. We have to assume any one of them could have sworn allegiance to the IJB. Prepare to round them up when we give the green light."

"Will do," the JTTF supervisor replied.

McEwan turned to the rest of the agents migrating into the dining room. "Anybody else find anything?"

A chorus of negative replies filled the air.

One agent piped up, "I found a copy of an Avis reservation showing Harris rented the red Chevy Blazer from a downtown Seattle location using his personal credit card."

"Thanks. Make sure to initiate tracking on that credit card. If he's stupid enough to use it again, I want to know the second he does. Where's the return location?" McEwan asked.

"It's round-trip. We'll send an agent out to Avis to confirm it was Harris who rented it."

"They're not coming here—where are they?" McEwan asked, addressing no one in particular.

Morton reached for his vibrating phone and read a text message. "I don't know their destination, but ours is San Jose. Paul Infante's located the imam."

McEwan jumped to his feet. Before they made it to the door, the JTTF supervisor snagged them. "I've got Lou Spagnelli from Spokane FBI on the line. Lou, tell them what you have."

The voice blaring from the phone speaker was loud and clear. "We got the lookout for Harris and San Felipe, and I sent an agent out to Spokane International Airport. A little over six hours ago, Harris rented a tan Dodge Durango from Alamo using a prepaid Visa card. They ditched the Blazer in a long-term parking lot, which we swept with a sensor—no alerts. Security video confirms both men got into the Durango."

McEwan made notes. "Al-Dosari thinks they're invisible again, but now we know they've switched vehicles. I assume he gave Seattle as the return location."

"Yep. A red herring."

Morton jumped in, a sense of urgency coloring each word. "They've rented two vehicles, and they're going to rent more. Lou, get the national JTTF to request that all car rental companies have their West Coast offices call the FBI if either Harris or San Felipe rent a vehicle. There's going to be lag time before this gets implemented, so message the JTTFs in Washington, Oregon, and California to touch base immediately with every rental location in their areas. It's labor-intensive, but we've got to know what they are driving when they swap cars."

McEwan interjected. "They're using prepaid Visa cards and a GPS jammer so we can't track them electronically. Issue a BOLO requesting state and local police from Spokane to California saturate their interstates and primary roads. Have the JTTFs reaffirm to our local partners the importance of finding that Durango."

Morton added critical details. "State in the BOLO that if they locate the Durango do not pull it over. Stress that they're transporting hazardous material. Keep the vehicle under surveillance until we can marshal the Hazmat resources to pull it over. Emphasize it is a national security matter and critical it be kept under wraps."

"You got it." Spagnelli signed off.

McEwan exhaled deeply as Morton walked away. *Your mistakes are catching up with you, Ali. Soon you'll make one too many and I'll be there.*

CHAPTER FIFTY-THREE

FOR AL-DOSARI, GLACIER NATIONAL Park and Spokane were memories. The monotonous soundtrack of Harris's snores coming from the back seat dogged him through scores of small towns in Washington and Oregon. Bearing south on Interstate 5, al-Dosari noticed an increasing number of police cars on the roads, even more in the last few minutes.

"William, wake up!"

The man in the back seat stirred.

"How are you feeling?"

"Tired, but better. I could use a bathroom."

"We will stop soon. Please stay awake."

Pushing himself upright, Harris saw Ricky fold something and stash it in the visor above his head. He rubbed his eyes with fists like a little boy trying to remove sleepy seeds. More awake, Harris noted they were exiting the interstate and was shocked five minutes later when they pulled into Portland International Airport.

"William, go to the toilet, then rent an SUV from Hertz. Pick it up and drive to the long-term parking lot. I will park somewhere near the back row."

"Okay, Ricky. For how long?"

"Rent it for five days. Tell them you will return it to Seattle. No errors this time," he warned sternly. "I want an SUV. Here's another Visa card—use it. Give me the other one."

Harris nodded and complied. Climbing out unsteadily, he hurried to the restroom. Finished, he went to the Hertz counter and rented an SUV.

He exited the pickup area several minutes later, pulling out in front of an airport police cruiser. Stabbing pains hit his intestines when the officer gave him a once-over. He managed to keep his bowels in check, and his behavior wasn't noticed. The officer drove on.

The pains ebbed as Harris pointed the silver Ford Escape toward the rear of the long-term parking lot. Spotting the Durango, he pulled into the space beside it. Ricky relieved himself between cars while Harris transferred their belongings.

The terrorist was pleased with his American dolt. "You are a great warrior, William. Allah will reward you for your efforts."

Energized by the kind words, Harris beamed. "I am proud to be deemed worthy of offering myself in sacrifice. For that, I thank you, Ricky!"

Al-Dosari barely suppressed a laugh.

Imam Syed el-Nasrallah basked in the glow of his reputation as a pious man. In his mind, he was the spiritual leader of an army of devout warriors. Too old to wage jihad, he lived vicariously through his martyred son and those he had recruited to the cause. Smiling proudly, he knew el-Nasrallah-recruited cells would eventually branch out like sturdy tree limbs in other cities, awaiting the call. Most rewarding were his San Jose lieutenants, his finest recruits.

Blinded by self-adoration, el-Nasrallah was unaware he was a pawn, used by others exploiting his son's name.

Head held high as befit his imagined importance, el-Nasrallah crossed the street to his Mercedes sedan and pinched the Unlock function of his remote. Tires screeched behind him. Two masked men materialized out of thin air, grabbed the imam and shoved him inside the van.

Executing a perfect rolling-car pick up, the vehicle sped off.

"Hello, prayer man!" McEwan snarled, ripping off his black ski mask. "Bad news for you. I'm not here to pray."

He backhanded el-Nasrallah, sending the imam's head banging into the side panel.

The imam spat back defiantly. "I demand a lawyer!"

"You're in no position to demand anything. It's what I want that matters." McEwan grabbed el-Nasrallah roughly by the throat. "Cooperate and you're on your way."

"I will tell you nothing!" The old man's lips quivered.

"Hard case? Fine. I suspected you're not the cooperative type, so I brought along my bag of tricks." McEwan held up a syringe filled with a light-blue liquid. Pressing the plunger produced a few air bubbles then several drops of the liquid, which dripped onto the floor of the van. "No Club Fed for you, old man. Not even Gitmo."

Seeing the needle, el-Nasrallah's eyes widened and welled up. In a weaker, slightly defiant voice, he croaked, "Torture only makes me stronger!"

McEwan laughed. "I doubt that. I figured your old ticker couldn't handle much more than a tweak here or there. So before we go down that path, take a look at this." McEwan tossed a color photograph on his lap. "Recognize him?"

El-Nasrallah involuntarily revealed his shock, clutching his chest over his heart. A second too late, he caught himself and transformed his face into a blank stare. "Mu'adh is dead. A martyr for Allah!"

"You're not only feeble, but you have shit for brains. Check this out." McEwan slapped him in the face with a picture of his son holding that morning's edition of the *Wall Street Journal*. "Now look at this." McEwan smacked an actual copy of the newspaper into his chest.

"Catch the dates? Both are today's edition. How's that for 'proof of life', jackass?"

"This is nothing but trick photography!"

"Think so? How about this?" McEwan held up his cell phone, and the cries of a man being beaten and sobbing for help filled the van. "He's crying for his father. That's you, Syed."

"That is not Mu'adh!" The imam's trembling chin and eyes betrayed him. It was his son.

"So you say. Then there's these." McEwan tossed more photos into the imam's lap.

El-Nasrallah's eyes turned hollow as he examined the photos of his son, the victim of terrible beatings. Finally, almost a whisper: "Mu'adh is alive?"

Broken! "He is," McEwan said. "Banged up a bit, as you can see, but alive. At least for now."

"What is it you want?" El-Nasrallah whimpered.

"I think you know, prayer man."

"If I tell you, will you stop beating him? Will he come home to me?"

McEwan bored into the imam's eyes. "What guarantee do I have you'll tell me the truth?"

"I lost Mu'adh once …" El-Nasrallah's voice trailed off. "I cannot bear to lose him again."

McEwan leaned in an inch from the man's face. "If you lie to me, he'll die, and then you'll die. First, I'll see how much abuse each of you can take. I'll make damn sure Mu'adh knows you could have saved him but refused. Lie, and you'll condemn him and everyone dear to you to a painful death. Am I clear?"

In response, Imam Syed el-Nasrallah spilled everything to McEwan.

CHAPTER FIFTY-FOUR

MANY IMMIGRATING MUSLIMS FIND the ethnically diverse communities around San Jose a welcoming environment. One such Muslim was Hamza Omar abū-Ibrahim, a transplant from one valley, Bekaa, to another, Silicon.

Abū-Ibrahim studied religion and trained for jihad at a Damascus madrassas. After exhibiting leadership qualities in battle against the infidels in Iraq, he was selected for sleeper assignment in America. Arriving under relaxed visa rules for persons from Muslim-majority countries, he settled in San Jose and took over religious duties at a small startup mosque. Awaiting his call to jihad, the sleeper agent accepted it could take years. It did.

Drawing on monies funneled to him by fundamentalist Islamic patrons, abū-Ibrahim used his years well. He built and staffed the Muslim American Cultural Society, giving it a truly American touch—the acronym MACS. His additional role as president of the MACS ruling council gave him prestige among his peers at other Bay Area mosques. Abū-Ibrahim worked diligently to promote that MACS practiced a moderate form of Islam at its place of worship.

That ruse positioned abū-Ibrahim well to manage the involuntary FBI "informational interviews" that all mosque leaders were occasionally subjected to. Whenever the FBI scheduled its meetings, abū-Ibrahim's first order of business was sending resident prayer leader Syed el-Nasrallah away for a week. The imam was useful as a recruiter, but a weak man mentally, unable to keep secrets. On appointed days, abū-Ibrahim conducted tours of the mosque and school personally, strolling the agents past scores of props—prominently displayed posters seeking prayers for the victims of radical terrorism.

Each time, abū-Ibrahim paused before a bulletin board to engage students in "spontaneous" conversation, in front of a poster encouraging all Americans of Muslim faith to report suspicious activity to the FBI, complete with the address and telephone number of the local office. Bracketed by photographs of the president and vice president, the staged exhibit always performed.

The setting for his own interview was his patriotically draped office, where the agents spoke with a moderate Muslim cleric adamantly opposed to anti-Western ideologies. Using his well-crafted script, abū-Ibrahim spoon-fed the young agents gibberish about MACS' pro-American stance, its principles as a nonpolitical and peaceful entity, its teaching of others about the benevolent aspects of Islam, and its damning of those who bastardized the religion. He invited the agents to "drop in anytime" for educational sessions to witness firsthand how MACS championed freedom and the American way of life.

After each visit, the FBI closed its books on abū-Ibrahim and MACS, declaring the diminutive man who spent all his hours teaching and praying was not a threat. Though the shocking raid on the Lodi network was a near miss, abū-Ibrahim remained confident he was not a target. Not that it would matter now.

Four months ago, Allah rewarded his devotion and ended his wait. Hand-selected by the Sword of Islam, abū-Ibrahim and his well-trained and dedicated San Jose warriors would participate in the greatest attack of all. Starting today.

As abū-Ibrahim and the occupants of two Ford Transit passenger vans proceeded down Silicon Valley Parkway, they moved seamlessly onto the entrance ramp of the South US 101 freeway toward Los Angeles. Both of the white vans, bearing magnetic "Silicon Valley Durable Medical Equipment of San Jose" signs, blended anonymously into traffic.

Abū-Ibrahim smiled at the irony of it all. MACS was the exact opposite of what he'd portrayed to the FBI for years. Far from promoting peace, love, acceptance, and understanding, the mosque sheltered militant jihadists who, to their core, were virulently anti-American, anti-Semitic, and anti-Western. Abū-Ibrahim was the most dangerous of all. He preached hatred. He incited violence. He recruited others. He had killed the enemies of Islam more than once.

Very soon, he would do so again.

CHAPTER FIFTY-FIVE

DANNI SANCHEZ SOUNDED MORE upbeat than any time since the al-Dosari matter began. "USAMRIID cracked the genetic code of his vaccine. The scientists say it provides immunity against his engineered variant. This is supported by tissue samples taken from Yousef al-Dosari and the two guards; all three were inoculated with it. That's not the best news: the non-vaccine drug Libertas is effective against his virus and it's being crash-produced. We'll rely on it instead of his vaccine. Right now, we have sufficient Libertas for law enforcement and military personnel and others who are most likely to be the ones subject to exposure first. I'm told it is being distributed now."

"That's beyond great news! Seattle FBI just briefed us on the interrogations of the four local IJB members. They were all cutouts. An IJB leader from parts unknown ordered the cell to recruit a Caucasian patsy; Harris fit the bill. They didn't know where the man was from or if he was using Harris for an attack. We've zeroed in on another cell here in San Jose, so the man was probably local."

Danni Sanchez stopped him cold. "Kyle, you're in San Jose?" The last time they'd spoken, he'd been in Seattle, at Harris's house.

"Yes. We returned to snatch up Iman Syed el-Nasrallah. He gave up the whole enchilada once we dropped some deepfake photos and a bogus torture video on him. He knows of only one IJB cell, his own. That means the San Jose cell is handling everything: logistics, pre-op surveillance, and the attack. He knows nothing about a Seattle cell, so al-Dosari compartmentalized it to recruit William Harris. We're closing in."

McEwan expected his news to please her.

It didn't. On the other end of the line, the acid in Sanchez's stomach rose rocket-like, flooding her throat and nostrils. Despite McEwan's constant protestations, the president's crisis team stubbornly clung to the Secret Service assessment that al-Dosari wanted to attack a major metro area. Her voice turned brittle. "What do you have on al-Dosari's target?"

McEwan's keen ear detected the change in her voice.

"We still don't know the target. Al-Dosari's accomplices are an eight-member cell led by a Hamza Omar abū-Ibrahim from el-Nasrallah's San Jose mosque. The old man only knows that abū-Ibrahim and the rest are doing something 'big', location unknown. We disseminated DMV license photos of the men and FBI's out hunting them. They're all MIA."

He paused, giving Sanchez the opportunity to comment. She remained silent. McEwan checked his phone—strong signal, still connected. "Danni?"

Still no response.

"Danni! Are you there?"

"I screwed up." Sanchez's voice was laced with acute alarm. "We're en route to Moffett!"

Too little sleep, combined with too much adrenaline, slowed McEwan's synapses. *Moffett Federal Airfield?*

He wanted to reach through the phone and yank the words out of her. "Who is 'we'? Is Secret Service saying San Jose's the target?"

"No, but I'm aboard Air Force One with the president and most of the cabinet."

McEwan sat tall in his seat as everything crystallized. Days earlier, Morton grilled the Secret Service about their justification for excluding the national governors association conference from its target list. The agent blew off Morton, pronouncing the two men were chasing a hoax, positing that even if al-Dosari existed, there was no threat of any kind to the conference. The agent declared tersely that the terrorists knew "there was no way in hell" that they could penetrate the Secret Service protective bubble, forcing al-Dosari to target a major population center on the Eastern Seaboard or in the Midwest. He accused McEwan of obstructing the Secret Service's ability to provide 'legitimate' intelligence. When pushed to provide evidence supporting his assertions, the agent abruptly disconnected the call. Undeterred, McEwan and Morton concentrated on finding and eliminating al-Dosari, which would render the target irrelevant.

"The target *is* the conference, Danni," McEwan said with cold detachment. "Pebble Beach. In front of us the whole time."

Stunned, Sanchez tried to untangle the mess. "We have a disconnect somewhere because their Protective Intelligence Division hasn't developed a single shred of intel on the Sword or an attack from any other source, credible or not. NSA supports their analysis because nothing has surfaced from monitoring efforts. It's crickets out there. Secret Service insists size is the characteristic that eclipses all else. The conference doesn't measure up. Their attitude is that the Sword threat is bogus."

"They're wrong. They don't have anything because that's how al-Dosari's playing it. He'll sit tight until it's time to attack."

"Are you positive it's Pebble Beach and not elsewhere?"

"Listen, Danni, I only have time to lay this out once. Ali bin al-Dosari *is* the IJB—he's on American soil to attack us and he needs support. An admitted IJB recruiter says his San Jose cell is in the wind and something big is up. The 'San Jose 8' and William Harris are all missing—we know Harris is shepherding al-Dosari. The others are here or headed here. Coupled with their movements one thing screams out: it's the conference. No one's found a single viable target anywhere else. Al-Dosari isn't *numbers*-driven, he's *target*-driven. The conference is the largest VIP target in the world right now. He's found a way to kill or psychologically cripple every single American, including those who will manage the crisis. With one stroke, he infects America's leaders and spreads smallpox to every state in the nation."

Sanchez saw McEwan's reasoning was rock-solid and could no longer be discounted, challenged, or ignored.

"Danni, go do your job and get everyone else on board. We're heading to Monterey." An irritated McEwan broke the connection. He looked at Morton, ending a call of his own.

His deputy heard McEwan's side of the call and weighed in. "You nailed it, Pebble Beach." Gunning the engine, he weaved in and out of traffic on the 101. "Our pilot's getting priority clearance for takeoff. We're almost at the airport."

McEwan punched a number on his phone.

Ted Beacham answered on the first ring.

"It's McEwan. You there yet?" Beacham was traveling to the Monterey Peninsula to command FBI operations supporting the NGA conference.

"Yep. Just walked into the command post. What's up?"

"Ted, listen very carefully. Everything's blinking red. Pebble Beach *is* the target."

Beacham's anger was immediate—the SAC let loose a spontaneous string of expletives. "I shared my concerns about the conference and the Secret Service told me to piss up a rope!"

"They're done calling the shots. Order them to seal their protective bubble. Prepare to move the assets into place to lock down the peninsula. Do whatever it takes but get them on the same sheet of music."

Beacham scribbled rapidly, then commented dryly, "They're not going to take this well."

McEwan's remaining patience evaporated. "I don't care what Secret Service thinks. Despite multiple attempts by us to get their attention, their threat assessment totally missed the mark. We're at the eleventh hour and al-Dosari is practically on top of us. The president and others are at risk. If they won't get on board, I'll drop a division of Marines on their heads!"

"I can have the entire FBI descending on this place with one call. Give me the word."

"You already have everybody within striking distance engaged. Face it, everything will be over before you can get more people here. Once this goes public, the rest of the bureau will have to handle the cockroaches crawling out of the woodwork."

"You're right. We have to stop him with what's here. I'll get on it."

"You, Tim, and I will sit down with agency commanders as soon as we arrive."

"Got it. What's your ETA?"

McEwan glanced at Morton, who flashed some fingers. "Thirty minutes, give or take."

As they turned into the airport, Morton's phone rang. He pulled the car into a space next to a hangar, spoke briefly, then ended the call. "That was Paul. No sign of abū-Ibrahim or crew. I told him about Pebble Beach. He'll run his people into the dirt to find the cell."

Grabbing their bags out of the trunk, they trotted over to the jet and climbed aboard. The pilot closed the door behind them and said, "We're cleared for immediate takeoff into Monterey Regional Airport. Then you'll chopper over to Laguna Seca."

They'd learned earlier that the multiagency joint operations center supporting the NGA conference was situated halfway between Monterey and Salinas at Laguna Seca, a large recreation area and raceway carved from the old Fort Ord Army installation.

"Get us in the air *now*," McEwan growled.

Five minutes later, they were.

McEwan tried fitting the remaining puzzle pieces into the whole but couldn't quite make everything interlock. In the plus column, the presence of Englewood and the other dignitaries made the conference a National Special Security Event, putting security on a level comparable to a State of the Union address. As the lead agency for all NSSEs, accustomed to unquestioned control of all aspects of every event attended by POTUS, Secret Service leadership would go ballistic. Because the threat unmistakably involved terrorism, lead investigative responsibility passed to the FBI, thereby becoming part of McEwan's overarching investigation.

Secret Service would retain protective responsibility but be relegated to hardening the target.

McEwan couldn't waste time on the ostrich-like behavior of the Secret Service. Every tool, person, and weapon had to be focused on finding the terror mastermind and his band of killers before they attacked.

CHAPTER FIFTY-SIX

THE AGENT PILOTING THE FBI helicopter spoke. "Our command post is coordinating all law enforcement, protective, and military operations. The two Navy fighters below us will enforce the no-fly zone over the Peninsula. If someone tries to penetrate our airspace, the incident will be managed by Castle Rock, a military tactical air-traffic-control unit. I'll make a couple of passes over the Laguna Seca complex so you can get the lay of the land."

Out their respective windows, McEwan and Morton noticed the landscape was covered with big-top-style tents and a massive collection of antennas and satellite dishes. A phalanx of military, law enforcement, and emergency service vehicles guaranteed the ability to launch a comprehensive range of responses. The armada included mobile command posts, Mine Resistant Ambush Protected vehicles, evidence response and bomb technician vans, ambulances, and countless other marked and unmarked sedans, trucks, and motorcycles.

"What's with all the motor homes and trailers?" Morton asked the pilot.

"Housing for personnel."

When they landed, Ted Beacham waved them over to a John Deere "Gator" utility vehicle, and they tossed their bags in the back. Several twists and turns later, they stopped in front of a huge modular tent structure labeled "FBI Command and Tactical Operations Center".

As they entered, the men's senses were bombarded by a combination of blasting frigid air and blinking high-tech equipment. Intended to augment the NGA special event, the interagency Domestic Emergency

Support Team was now incorporated into the FBI command center for the al-Dosari search.

Beacham swept a hand over the room. "Once the conference was identified as al-Dosari's target, the FBI assumed command and control—under your direction. I'll interface with Tim, and together we'll coordinate the law enforcement, investigative and intelligence functions while supporting Secret Service with its protective responsibilities."

McEwan looked around. The communications infrastructure consisted of racks of digitized radio equipment and surveillance monitors suspended above tables of agents screening real-time information from agencies and sources. Seated at consoles and workstations, personnel focused on their screens or studied monitors strategically hung on perimeter walls. White signs with blue letters dangled from the ceiling or were perched above computers, identifying the different command sections and agency representatives. Many tables bore bigger blue signs with large white letters denoting supervising officials. One in particular caught his eye: "WMD Coordinator." On the wall, multiple digital clocks displayed different time zones.

Crossing a large bullpen area, Beacham walked to a table labeled "FBI Commander" and leafed through a stack of phone messages. He read one and announced, "Medics are making their way through the encampment and providing the Libertas drug to all personnel who want it. I recommend that we all take it, since we're among those who will be exposed first."

McEwan and Morton nodded in agreement, and Beacham ushered them into an enclosed area where all three men received Libertas from a medic. Beacham, running on fumes himself, saw that McEwan and Morton needed to recharge their batteries for the final push. "Why don't you guys grab a bite and a quick shower? I'll hold down the fort."

McEwan spoke. "Good idea."

On the way out, McEwan grabbed his latest batch of messages and reports, giving half to Morton. Hopping into a waiting Humvee, a short ride landed them outside neighboring forty-foot motor homes set on a bluff overlooking the Laguna Seca raceway. Less than thirty minutes after McEwan entered his coach, he'd showered and changed into a dark-blue polo shirt and tan tactical pants. Grabbing a Gatorade and sandwich from the stocked refrigerator, he sat in the lounge area of the motor home. Leaning into a sofa, he waited for his phone to connect to the intelligence community's encrypted network. A loud thump startled McEwan. Jumping to his feet, he peered out the front window. He opened the door for Tim Morton.

"Kyle, I've got someone who needs to see you ASAP."

Materializing around the side of the motor home was an enormous human. Major Jason Cartwright, US Marine Corps Forces Special Operations Command bellowed, "You gonna keep us out here in the friggin' heat?"

McEwan laughed. "What took so long?"

"They scoured the bushes looking for someone to bail out your sorry ass. Nobody stepped up, so I was 'volun-told'. Didn't even have a chance to grab some BBQ or brewskis before hopping another trash hauler. A fine Southern gentleman never goes a visitin' without bearin' a gift."

"That explains what happened to the rest of those." McEwan pointed at the half-empty box of Krispy Kreme doughnuts.

Patting his stomach appreciatively, Cartwright plopped down on the soft leather sofa, promptly crushing it with his weight. He made a smooching sound. "I see you're kissing the keister of someone with purse strings."

Morton rolled his eyes and took a seat in a recliner. Despite having just met the MARSOC Raider, Cartwright's reputation as a colorful character preceded him, courtesy of McEwan.

"We got the Big Dog's orders and flew directly from Djibouti to Lejeune on C-17s. Took eighteen hours. Nasty-ass long flight. Did a quick turnaround, and the next thing I know, I woke up here. Our helos are being built back up next door as we speak."

McEwan was glad to see Cartwright. He could count on the muscle the Marines brought to the table, as well as their unconditional following of orders when he executed the commander in chief's directive. McEwan turned down the squawking CTOC radio. "Our next order of business—plan what happens when we get our hands on al-Dosari."

Batting around multiple scenarios, responses, and consequences took some time, but eventually the three men arrived at consensus and set their strategy. As they finished, someone thumped on the side of the motorcoach.

Morton rose, answered the door, and relayed the message. "Ted needs to speak with me outside, and he's ready to run us over to Pebble Beach."

McEwan and Cartwright took a couple of minutes to discuss part B to the plan—McEwan's handling of al-Dosari post-capture. It didn't take long.

Joining Morton and Beacham outside, the four men climbed into a government sedan. They drove over to the Pebble Beach Resorts, taking a portion of the famed 17-Mile Drive and arriving in just over twenty minutes. Deposited at the Inn at Spanish Bay, they entered the mid-century modern building and walked to a conference room overlooking the Pacific coastline. The final arrivals, they settled in immediately. McEwan grabbed a seat next to California Highway Patrol Coastal Division commander Captain Billy Ramona and introduced himself. Morton adopted a low profile along the rear wall, strategically posting himself between McEwan and a coffee urn. Cartwright opted for a chair by the rear doors.

Beacham kicked off the briefing by introducing McEwan and Morton, then updating the latest intelligence and investigative results on al-Dosari and the San Jose cell. Next, the FBI WMD coordinator explained the process for implementing the Chemical and Biological Incident Contingency Plan, which covered the tactical responses to contaminated areas and the processing of hazardous crime scenes. He announced the arrival of two hundred bioagent sensor devices to supplement those stationed at roadway checkpoints and other areas around the Monterey Peninsula.

With the WMD plan covered, Beacham nodded toward the front row, and a man took to the podium and adjusted the microphone. He cleared his throat. "I'm Trevor Grey, Secret Service Dignitary Protective Division, Special Events Section. I'm the principal federal official responsible for security operations for the national governors association conference." He ran down the schedule briskly.

"The conference was timed to coincide with the Pebble Beach Concours d'Elegance, an annual high-profile fund-raiser that affords international automotive enthusiasts the opportunity to examine rare and classic cars. The Concours remains unchanged this year except for the marquee event—the raffle of a Bentley donated by Prince Sultan Safaa bin Al Saud of Saudi Arabia. The raffle proceeds go to an educational foundation benefitting the surviving families of US service personnel killed in the global war on terror."

Despite the agent's casual, almost tour-guide-ish approach, McEwan read the man's involuntary body language and microexpressions. *He's pissed as hell.* Something was gnawing at McEwan, but he couldn't put his finger on it. He tuned back in.

"The grand finale is the Tour d'Elegance, the driving tour that tips off the Concours. At 7:30 a.m. the president will depart his temporary housing at the Casa Palmero compound driving the Bentley. An avid auto buff, the president planned this short excursion to stimulate raffle ticket sales. Inside will be our detail leader, the prince, and his security head. The Bentley will follow CHP motorcycle escorts and our lead vehicles. Behind the Bentley will be "the Beast"—the presidential limousine—our counterassault team war wagons, several SUVs, an ambulance, and the media train. Other motor units and marked cruisers close out the official motorcade, followed by the pre-cleared tour entrants. The parade will proceed through a well-protected stretch of the 17-Mile Drive. The Bentley and official entourage will break off and head here to the Inn at Spanish Bay. The rest of the entrants will continue on the driving tour." The agent traced the route on the map projected behind him. It morphed into a photo of the wing's exterior, which faded to the interior of the room.

"A prebreakfast reception will be in full swing as the president pulls the Bentley up to and through these elephant doors and parks in the center of the ballroom. He and the prince will work the reception for half an hour, then make their way to the dais for the breakfast. After his keynote address, the president, prince, and head of the Concours will draw the winning raffle ticket. We have no confirmed intelligence that al-Dosari will attempt to attack the driving tour or breakfast reception, or for that matter—the conference. Our protective bubble over Pebble Beach is impenetrable."

McEwan about fell out of his chair. The agent continued to exhibit the same overconfident attitude he'd had in all his previous conversations with McEwan, Morton, and Beacham. His assertions were beyond comprehension in view of recent intelligence. Only a hand on his shoulder kept McEwan seated as Morton's clipped question ricocheted off the agent. "How do you know the Bentley is clean?"

The agent replied flippantly, unaware who was lobbing the question. "Rest easy. Per our SOP, agents will meet it at the airport, where our technical services experts will give it the white-glove treatment and screen it with sensors. Once cleared, it will be under our control until delivered via flatbed truck. Our techs are the best in the business."

Morton raised another omitted detail. "And the golf outing?"

"The president tees off at Spyglass after breakfast. His foursome includes Governors Warren of Illinois, Carlson of California, and Cook of Kentucky. The other golfing governors will follow in their flights. The first lady and the first ladies of Kentucky, Ohio, and Maine will be shopping in Carmel-by-the-Sea."

The agent's information parsing finally got to McEwan. He stood, and his eyes locked onto the Secret Service agent. "That's enough. Sit down. I'll take it from here."

The agent's eyes flared, glaring defiantly at McEwan while standing firm. As McEwan reached the front of the room, the agent resentfully retreated to his seat.

McEwan's throbbing neck vein subsided as Morton joined him. McEwan stepped to the podium and corrected the Secret Service agent's misinformation on the spot. "Technically, it is accurate we have no corroborated specific threat against our leaders or this event. However, I have tracked this killer across three continents, and I can tell you this: there is no bigger target on the planet right now, today, than here at Pebble Beach. I wish I was wrong, but the president and the other leaders are the target. Nowhere else."

Following several seconds of stunned silence, the officers erupted, directing their inevitable anger at the Secret Service, not McEwan. He quashed the incipient rebellion by banging his fist on the podium so hard the microphone went sailing in the air.

Morton snared it nonchalantly and tossed it back.

"I will not argue the merits of this with anyone. I'm here to do a job, not play the blame game. You want to vent your spleen, do it outside. But send in your replacement as you leave." In four short sentences, McEwan established absolute control.

"Reality check—all events may be scrubbed if the president goes public with this threat. While that is his inclination, I'm making the case that he allow us to continue our manhunt discreetly as long as possible. Assuming he agrees, we have a plan. Tim."

Morton summarized the search, including al-Dosari's vehicle swaps to avoid detection. He outlined the plan to lure and trap al-Dosari and his accomplices; primarily, the conference and related events had to appear on track, otherwise the terrorists and smallpox would vanish. He explained the attack would involve a surreptitious airborne release, although precise details about the apparatus were unknown. Morton defined the options for foiling the attack and how the consequences would be managed if they failed. Morton asked CHP commander Ramona to present the procedures for locking down the perimeter enveloping the Peninsula. Other than a few logistical details, there were no issues.

A cell phone warbled across the room.

Answering, Beacham held a quick conversation, then bobbed and weaved his way over to McEwan. "We found the tan Durango ditched at the Portland Airport. Harris rented a silver Ford Escape there ten hours ago. They swept the Durango—no hits." The FBI SAC paused to let that piece of information sink in, then delivered a bombshell. "A Monterey Peninsula map was stuffed above the driver's side visor, a big circle around Pebble Beach Resorts."

Pandemonium broke out. McEwan's deductions concerning al-Dosari and his targets were dead-on—the terrorist was barreling straight for them.

McEwan did quick mental calculations with repeated glances at his watch. "Al-Dosari and Harris could be here now if they drove straight through. But they might not be, so we have to contend with both possibilities. Put up additional aircraft and beef up our presence on the major roadways. We have a narrow window until sundown, or until the media hounds pick up the scent. Distribute the San Jose cell's DMV photos widely among all law enforcement. These guys are here, waiting for al-Dosari."

McEwan retreated into silent analytic mode. *Portland FBI's find confirms the target but too many unknowns remain. When, where, and how will al-Dosari unleash the smallpox? And where the hell is his San Jose cell?* He looked up to find every set of eyes in the room glued to him.

"Complete secrecy is the key to our success—anything less guarantees total mission failure. Stress this to all of your people. Throw everything you've got into this."

CHAPTER FIFTY-SEVEN

IN THE PRESIDENTIAL SUITE aboard Air Force One, Daniela Sanchez detailed McEwan's irrefutable proof the attack was aimed at Englewood, his cabinet, the congressional leadership, and the nation's governors. Angered but not surprised, he guided her to the conference room to brief the others. Englewood sank into the clone of his Oval Office chair and nodded once.

Sanchez proceeded. "Pebble Beach *is* the target. And by extension, all of us."

Immediately, all in the room except Sanchez urged the president to cancel the event, insisting that Englewood had no other option. Attorney General Davidson argued the need to publicize the threat forthwith.

Gesturing for silence, the only person whose opinion mattered spoke. "I understand and appreciate your concerns. I've given the situation a great deal of thought. I have seen the damage he can inflict on us, and it scares the living hell out of me. Despite what you think, we have a major tactical advantage: al-Dosari has no idea we've discovered his target. If I cancel, he *will* know *we* know and go to ground. I cannot accept that risk. The Secret Service footprint will protect all of us, but if any of you wish to leave, by all means do so as soon as we land. I, however, will not cut and run and leave my fellow citizens to face this threat by themselves."

Eagle-like, the president studied his audience. Satisfied everyone was listening to him instead of their internal voices, he went on. "Prior to my inauguration, I was briefed about eight separate incidents where attempted attacks were foiled before they could be launched. Those crises came and went without the public being any the wiser. We're in the best place to intercept him; we lose nothing and stand to gain everything by allowing things to play out a while longer. If al-Dosari were to succeed—and I have every confidence he will not—I'll treat every man, woman, and child."

Unswayed, Nelson J. Englewood's advisers stared uneasily at him. All but Sanchez remained convinced his strategy was too risky.

Reading their minds, Englewood summarized succinctly. "The consequences of my decision rest squarely on my shoulders and with no one else. On my watch, America doesn't back down against terror. It attacks and destroys it, and does so without leaks. Nothing leaves this room." Pushing back from the table, he stood and strode from the room, signaling the meeting's end.

The others scurried out behind him, leaving Sanchez alone. She grabbed a nearby secure telephone handset and requested the onboard communications section connect her to a number. Seconds later, a voice answered. Sanchez spoke tersely, "Our ETA into Moffett is twelve minutes, then we helo down to Lone Cypress. Be there when we arrive."

The recipient of the call deciphered "Lone Cypress", the Secret Service code name for the presidential compound at Pebble Beach Resorts.

The Royal Saudi Air Force C-130 taxied up to the Peninsula Aviation Services Company hangar. Within minutes, the plane's ramp lowered onto the tarmac of the Monterey Regional Airport. Dressed in a pristine white jumpsuit, Sohaib Abassi tromped down from the plane. The ramrod-straight visitor spoke to a man waiting with a clipboard. "I am His Majesty's mechanic. I want the car moved immediately to the shelter before the rain comes. Understood?"

"Yes."

"I will drive it down, but you are not to touch it." Turning, he disappeared up the ramp.

Left standing, the PASCO employee was surprised by the mechanic's rudeness.

With Abassi at the wheel, the Bentley rolled down the aircraft ramp. Falling in behind a pickup, it traveled the short distance to an empty hangar. The driver climbed out of the truck and pointed to a large square of carpeting taped to the hangar floor.

Centering the car perfectly on the carpet, Abassi shut down the engine and stepped out. A woman in a dark-blue uniform and two men in sports coats and slacks approached.

"Sohaib Abassi?" the uniformed woman asked.

"Yes."

"I'm with US Customs and Border Protection. These men are Secret Service. Let's see your passport."

Abassi handed over the document.

The CBP inspector leafed through the passport, filled with visa and entry stamps from all over the world. She stamped it. "Welcome to America, Mr. Abassi." The officer closed her briefcase and exited.

One of the agents spoke. "I'm told you've been through this drill before."

"Yes," Abassi bemoaned. "I prefer to get it over with."

The agent raised his arm and spoke into his wrist. "Bring 'em in."

Two nondescript cargo step vans entered the hangar, their tires squealing to a stop near the Bentley. Six men in dark-blue overalls piled out and removed a collection of tool chests. Escorting Abassi across the hangar to three waiting chairs, the agents positioned themselves between him and the vehicle, blocking his view of the technicians. Poring over the Bentley, they systematically removed specific parts of the car. Abassi occasionally caught glimpses of the inspection, and the Secret Service tinkering worried him. Two hours into the examination, a technician spoke. "I've never seen a Flying Spur like this."

"The convertible is one of a kind manufactured specifically for His Highness."

As if responding to some signal, the agents adjusted their chairs, allowing Abassi his first unobstructed view of the car since he sat down.

The technician continued, "A 6.0-liter, twelve-cylinder twin-turbo with 552 horses and 470 pounds of torque. With all-wheel drive and calibrated six-speed automatic transmission, it'll do zero to sixty in 4.9 seconds. Smooth, brutal power wrapped in a beautiful package."

"Very impressive, agent. You know your cars."

He peered out from under the hood. "I suppose you've run it wide-open."

Always warm to fellow aficionados, Abassi displayed his first smile in days. "Yes. There are many well-paved flat roads in the desert. We drive at ridiculously crazy speeds to test how these cars perform under stressful conditions. Lives depend on it. Surely you appreciate that."

"Threats to the royal family, right?"

Abassi inclined his head slightly. "Precisely."

"We're almost finished. Any problems with the car?"

"Not with the vehicle itself. Due to the desert environment, it is equipped with a robust four-zone climate-controlled air conditioner. The filter tends to clog up with fine sand and must be replaced at regular intervals. Thank you for reminding me. I will check the filter later."

"Good idea; supposed to be hot." Admiration time over, the technician returned to his tasks.

An hour later, the examination ended. To the naked eye, the Bentley appeared unmolested.

Abassi watched a technician roll over a tool cart containing an aluminum briefcase. Unlatching it, he retrieved a handheld device, turned it on, and handed it to a second man. Opening the hood, trunk, and doors, the man waved the device over every millimeter of the Bentley. The device emitted a steady stream of static as it made its journey. The first technician studied the briefcase, repeatedly announcing "Nothing." Abassi maintained his calm exterior throughout the inspection and scan. His self-control lapsed when a large Belgian Malinois and its handler entered the hangar. Shivers wracked Abassi's slender frame—he did not like dogs.

Noticing his reaction, the canine handler winked at the technician while addressing the Saudi mechanic. "Don't worry, he won't attack unless there's something wrong with the car."

After a complete circuit and no unusual behaviors from the four-legged agent, they departed.

The shorter of the two agents babysitting Abassi spoke. "The car is clean. We'll keep it under wraps until after it's driven by the president. An agent must accompany you anytime you work on the car. Thanks for your cooperation."

The tiniest bead of sweat appeared and ran visibly down Abassi's forehead. Nodding comprehension and acceptance of the order, he swallowed hard, hoping the agents did not notice his discomfort. Despondent, he watched as the Secret Service technicians loaded their vans and departed. Abassi knew his situation was hopeless, but he could not fail.

The lives of his family depended on it.

CHAPTER FIFTY-EIGHT

NELSON J. ENGLEWOOD CLASPED the first lady's hand tenderly as Marine One circled the impeccably manicured fairways of the world-renowned Links at Pebble Beach. An avid golfer, he'd somehow never played here. And if al-Dosari succeeded, he never would. Despite McEwan closing in on him, al-Dosari was proving to be a most worthy adversary.

Studying the scene below, he spied the Patriot missile battery camouflaged among the trees. Secret Service counter-assault, counter-sniper, and K-9 teams dotted the rooftops and roamed the complex. Only people intimately acquainted with presidential security would detect the double-size Secret Service contingent on high alert. This fact signaled they'd finally accepted McEwan's theory that threat actors were on the move in the security perimeter and planning an attack on the president. Englewood, accustomed to these unfortunate trappings of his office, nevertheless shook his head at the evil necessitating them.

Marine One set down gently on the neatly-clipped lawn beside the eighteenth green, adjacent to the lodge at Pebble Beach. Englewood descended the stairs to the plush turf, saluted the Marine, then turned and offered a hand to his wife. Strolling arm in arm and looking to the world care- and worry-free, the president and first lady posed for the cameras. After greeting starry-eyed local dignitaries, they crossed to a Secret Service motorcade that whisked them several hundred feet down a roadway before turning into a wrought-iron gated driveway.

The Englewoods entered an eight-foot-high adobe-walled courtyard ablaze with lush, fuchsia-colored bougainvillea. Englewood was the first chief executive to stay at the Pebble Beach Resorts, so naturally, he and the first lady received its finest accommodations. Casa Palmero, a self-contained Mediterranean-style resort within a resort, designed for privacy and security, was leased in its entirety by the Secret Service for the visit. Inside its walls were 24 luxurious lodging units with private pool, outdoor courtyards, and spas.

Daniela Sanchez broke free from the entourage and headed toward the Secret Service command post. She spotted McEwan milling around with another man, presumably Tim Morton, whom she'd never met. A short, severe cloudburst caused her to shepherd them to a small, covered courtyard away from the others. McEwan performed quick introductions, then got down to business. The discussion took thirty minutes; their joint conclusion: al-Dosari would likely proceed with his attack if they didn't intercept him and his cohorts in the next several hours. Changing subjects, the DNI inadvertently struck a raw nerve. "How was the Spanish Bay briefing?"

A vein popped out of McEwan's neck; he averted his gaze and remained mute. Morton took the hint and recounted events. McEwan tuned out, opting to contemplate his plans for al-Dosari. He re-engaged when Sanchez reacted to the Secret Service event coordinator's comments.

Sanchez adopted a hard-nosed position. "He has to go." Stepping aside, she dialed her phone. Her exchange with the Secret Service director, who did most of the talking, lasted no more than ninety seconds. She ended her call with "Good."

A Secret Service agent rounded the corner and summoned the trio with a finger.

McEwan queried Sanchez, "You taking the point on this?"

"Negative, it's your show. He's heard quite enough from me."

The threesome was herded to another wing of the compound and deposited with the Secret Service detail leader. He pulled them into an alcove away from the ears of the other agents standing post. His expression was equal parts anger, disgust, and embarrassment. "No agent in the history of this service has ever done anything like this! The son of a bitch told me that his non-selection as director sent him into a tailspin and he 'failed to see the trees for the forest'. Bullshit! He dismissed everything put before him by our Protective Intelligence people. And to think he was on the shortlist to run this agency." The agent spat the last words.

McEwan saw the apology as sincere but unnecessary. "Welcome to the club of government agencies run amok by assholes with agendas. It doesn't reflect on the professionalism of the agency or its agents. It's overcome by events—let's move on."

About to say more, the command "Show them in" silenced the agent. Regaining his professional demeanor, he guided them over to an ornate wood door. They stepped into a richly paneled library filled with antique books where the president occupied an overstuffed chair in front of a fireplace. Standing, he drained the half-full cocktail glass and tinkled the ice against the edge of the crystal. He refilled it with Woodford Reserve bourbon then spoke.

"Hello, McEwan. And you must be Tim Morton."

"Yes, sir, Mr. President."

Englewood shook hands with both men. Knowing they would not sit until he did, the chief executive returned to his chair.

Sanchez and Morton sank into a couch; McEwan settled into a chair facing the president.

He wasted no time putting McEwan on the spot. "What are the chances you'll stop him?"

"If you're asking for a percentage, I can't give one. We've come a long way in the past few hours. Al-Dosari's last known location was Portland. By our calculations, we're ten hours behind him. Time and distance are narrowing, but I can't say by how much."

"Secret Service insists I cancel everything and hunker down. I tend to agree. First, I'm giving you until daybreak to find that bastard. Then I expect you to end it as we discussed."

McEwan gave a slight nod.

Sanchez and Morton exchanged puzzled looks.

Sohaib Abassi, protected from the rain by the airplane hangar awning, ground his tenth cigarette of the hour into the hard concrete alongside his other butts. He reached for the pack of Marlboros, his hand shaking so badly the smokes spilled out. Bending over, he retrieved the cigarettes, but the soggy tobacco crumbled in his hands. He lit his last dry one and inhaled deeply.

This was the longest week of Abassi's life and, undoubtedly, his last. His mind filling with images of his wife and two sons, he knew he could not allow them the same fate. He vividly remembered the man in the white robe giving his ultimatum, every word seared into Abassi's brain for eternity: "I have your family. They are safe and will not be hurt. You have my word. If you do the Sword's bidding, they will be released unharmed. If not ..."

The Sword of Islam. The Saudi mechanic bit down hard on his index finger. It was an easy choice. To protect his family, Sohaib Abassi would do anything, anything at all.

CHAPTER FIFTY-NINE

A FAMILIAR ODOR ASSAULTED HAMZA Omar abū-Ibrahim's nostrils as he and his comrades proceeded south down US 101. The intermittent heavy rain had not dampened the pungent scent seeping through the closed windows, wordlessly signaling their transit through Gilroy, California, the self-proclaimed garlic capital of the world. Previous dry runs established the smell as a critical milestone—less than one hour from their objective. Abū-Ibrahim led his dedicated warriors proudly, knowing each man would soon reap rich rewards. The burner phone on his hip vibrated, interrupting his musing. He answered, "Silicon Valley DME."

Listening intently to the voice on the other end, abū-Ibrahim replied, "Thank you. I too am blessed. We are all blessed! Yes, soon!" Ending the call, he dialed a number.

"Silicon Valley DME," the driver of the second van answered.

"Everything is on schedule" abū-Ibrahim intoned, then terminated the call abruptly.

In the second van, Hussein al-Jubeir turned to his accomplices. "It will not be long."

Unnoticed and undiscovered, the eight killers in two white Ford Transit passenger vans moved determinedly toward their destiny.

The Pacific Ocean collides with the high rugged cliffs and mountains of California's central coast at the Monterey Peninsula, where multimillion-dollar homes dot the shoreline and hillsides of towns named Monterey,

Carmel-by-the-Sea, Pacific Grove, Seaside, and Carmel Valley. Until today, Saad al Shammari, MD, proudly owned such a home. Staring out at his development's golf course, the doctor doubted he would experience happiness or serenity again.

Upon earning his medical degree from Cairo University, Saad al Shammari took advanced studies at Case Western Reserve University in Ohio. Following a residency at the Cleveland Clinic, he accepted a position as chief urologist at the Community Medical Center of the Monterey Peninsula. All of his earned success and financial rewards meant nothing now. He, his wife Asenath in the next room, his father in Egypt—all in mortal danger. *Why?*

Earlier in the week, two men cornered him in the hospital parking lot, saying his father in Cairo was kidnapped. Shown photographs of his father, naked and glassy-eyed, holding that day's edition of the *Egypt Daily News*, Saad vomited spontaneously, amusing the thugs. He viewed a video of his drugged father saying, "Do it, Saad, all of it," then someone snatched the phone back and graphically described Saad's alternative. Allegedly, his cooperation would spare three lives, but Saad suspected either route had a different ending.

As instructed, Saad took five days of vacation, never leaving the house, waiting for further orders. For three days and nights, nothing. Then last night, the fourth evening, a cryptic telephone call: "Expect visitors tomorrow."

Weeping intermittently throughout the past four days, al Shammari repulsed Asenath's pleas for information, saying only that his father was gravely ill. Their endless days and nights were filled with agitation and anguish, the only thing getting them through was her adherence to traditional marital roles. Though Asenath suspected his story about his father was the thinnest of lies, she accepted her husband as the family head and stopped questioning him.

Saad knew something terrible was in store, and he wanted Asenath to go to her end without knowing it was coming. He wiped more tears from his face with his handkerchief as the telephone resting in his hand rang. "Yes?"

"Open the garage door, Saad," the man ordered calmly.

Ali bin al-Dosari intently read the text message from his faithful warrior, typed a reply, then hit Send. A half hour later, he ordered Harris to take the next exit.

Harris did as told. Once off Interstate 880, al-Dosari directed him to a shopping center.

"It's an enclave catering to San Jose's rich infidels, isn't it, Ricky?" Like a puppy, Harris eagerly sought his leader's approval.

"Yes. Now concentrate for me. Follow the signs to the parking garage. Take the ramp up to the second level."

Harris had no idea where they were going, but Ricky obviously did.

"Stop, William! Back up and pull into the empty space next to the bronze car and park. Get out and feel under the rear fender for a magnetic key holder. Take the key, open the trunk, and put our belongings inside."

Harris followed every word of the instructions, the exchange communicating he was in the throes of his secret mission. The men took turns urinating against a column.

Vehicle swap complete, they left the silver Ford Escape parked anonymously in the garage. Directing Harris back toward Interstate 880, al-Dosari had him maneuver the bronze Malibu onto the US 101 South entrance ramp. Al-Dosari removed the battery from his phone, broke the device into several pieces, and threw them out the window. Pulling another burner phone from a bag stashed in the car, he powered it up and stuffed it into his pants pocket. For over an hour and fifteen minutes, neither man spoke.

During this time, Harris observed surprising changes in his traveling companion. Despite several significant events, including killing the ranger and being pulled over by the Spokane police, Ricky had been calm throughout their journey. The sudden appearance of beads of sweat on his leader's brow coincided with his escalating edginess. Harris wondered if the heavy rain was the cause. Trying to ease Ricky's anxiety, Harris offered, "We're used to downpours in Seattle—"

The chilling look on Ricky's face cut off Harris midstream. Fixing his eyes resolutely ahead, he stayed mute until he heard Ricky typing. Glancing over, Harris saw him send a text message.

"William, take the next exit. At the end, turn right onto road number 68."

Ten minutes later, Ricky gave new orders. "Slow down. Turn left at the flashing yellow light."

Harris made the turn and drove the Malibu slowly up a steep grade in the suddenly intense cloudburst. Barely a minute passed before he was told to turn right into a subdivision named Rancho Laureles at Carmel Valley.

"When I instruct you, turn left into a driveway. Pull up to the garage and drive inside without stopping."

"Okay, Ricky."

"The driveway is coming up on your left. Turn now."

Harris spotted a five-car garage through the squall and headed for the one open door.

Ricky's voice hardened. "Park between the vans."

Obeying, Harris goosed the accelerator too much and braked hard. He stopped with a jerk and shut down the engine. The garage door closed behind them.

"You have done well, Khalid Abdul Aziz. Allah is proud of you."

Thrilled by the praise and Ricky's first use of his Muslim name, Harris interpreted the comment as proof he finally was a worthy warrior.

Swarmed suddenly by men animatedly speaking a language Harris did not understand, he stepped from the car and ambled over. Riding the unfamiliar euphoria of praise, Harris greeted his new brothers. "Peace be upon you! I am Khalid Abdul Aziz!" Feeling an arm around his shoulders, he turned to face the man. Confused, Harris couldn't comprehend why the mysterious brother from his IJB initiation in Seattle was present in California.

"Khalid, my brother!" Hamza Omar abū-Ibrahim said enthusiastically as he spun Harris toward a door. To a cohort, abū-Ibrahim instructed, "Put our fellow warrior to bed for a well-earned rest. Then we will wake him and present his role in the mission."

Beaming blissfully, Harris surrendered to the will of his brothers and toddled off to bed.

CHAPTER SIXTY

SOHAIB ABASSI GLANCED AT the text message. Pulling his jacket over his head and trying not to appear nervous, he strolled over to the officer at the gate. "Policeman, may I trouble you?"

"Sure." Officer Adam Joseph, Monterey Airport Police Department, eyed the Saudi mechanic.

"I have no cigarettes and require food. Can I get anything in the airport?"

"Nothing good in there. Your best option is the Jack in the Box for food and the 7-Eleven for smokes." Giving the mechanic directions, Joseph added, "Don't forget your ID badge and vehicle pass, or you can't get back in."

"Thank you." Abassi did his best to seem normal. "Something for you?"

"Nope." Joseph tugged at his ample waistline. "Want it, but don't need it."

Abassi climbed into the Lexus RX-350 loaned to him by PASCO, vehicle security pass displayed plainly on the dash. Pulling out of the fenced-in security area, he waved and continued out of the airport onto Olmsted Road. Caught by the red light at Monterey-Salinas Highway, he waited for the traffic signal to turn green.

Though he'd never traveled the route before, he knew it by heart.

Ten minutes later, Abassi turned up a driveway and tapped his horn once. The garage door opened, and he pulled inside. A hand yanked open the door and a pistol was rammed against his temple. Grabbed by the throat, his windpipe in a vise grip, Abassi was hauled from the seat. A well-aimed knee to the solar plexus doubled him over.

"I am honored to see you again, Sohaib Abassi."

Afraid to look up, Abassi recognized the searing voice from the Saudi desert.

"It would be a shame if your family name ended because you failed in your duty to the Sword of Islam. Do you want your young sons sodomized until they bleed to death?"

"No!" Abassi screeched. "I will do anything! Please do not hurt my sons!"

The Sword rewarded Abassi with another knee to the chest. "Have you not a wife?" al-Dosari jeered threateningly. "Is she not of importance?"

The words had the effect of mashing his testicles, and Abassi retched.

Al-Dosari jerked the mechanic upright, his green eyes burning deeply into Abassi's soul. "I think we understand each other perfectly. Do your duty and your family will live. You, of course, will not. If the Americans do not kill you, the prince will take your head. Perhaps Allah will consider you a martyr, despite your blasphemous ways."

The Sword set a padded case on the Malibu trunk lid and ceremoniously extracted a small container. Removing it from its vacuum-sealed, shrink-wrapped package, al-Dosari placed the precious cargo in Abassi's hands and delivered his final instructions. He made Abassi repeat them twice. Confident they were memorized flawlessly, the Sword stepped back expectantly.

"I swear on my family name I will do this for you." Abassi's head hung low. "They can do to me what they wish. I beg you! Please do not harm my family!"

"The Sword of Islam is a pious man whose word is golden. Your family will be safe if you do as ordered. You know the consequences if you fail." He dismissed Abassi with a flick of the wrist.

The Saudi mechanic's heart almost pounded out of his chest on the drive back to the airport. An involuntary primal wail escaped from within him, filling the Lexus cockpit. *I will never see my sons again! They will think I was a monster!* He would have forgotten to stop at the 7-Eleven had it not been for the squeaking windshield wipers—the rainfall had stopped. Purchases made, Abassi motored toward his destiny, cigarettes, coffee, and doughnuts stowed in the passenger seat. It seemed much longer than forty minutes since departing the airport.

Gathering himself, Abassi approached the gate slowly. Summoning every remaining ounce of self-control, he extinguished his headlights and rolled down his window. "Policeman, I got you a little something. I am told they are not long out of the baker's oven." Hoping his friendliness sounded genuine, Abassi handed over a box of doughnuts and two large coffees.

"You didn't have to do this, but thanks," Officer Adam Joseph replied.

"You are welcome." Unchecked, the Saudi mechanic drove inside the secure compound.

Sohaib Abassi's next acts would damn him forever to the fires of hell.

The Sword of Islam, waking refreshed after six hours of undisturbed sleep, was pleased. His plan was on track. He could not take credit—recognition belonged to his brother Yousef, a brilliant terror architect in his own right. Once Yousef caught wind of the Infidel's governors conference in Pebble Beach, California, with the president and the apostate Saudi prince as honored guests, he conceived the perfect plot. A meticulous researcher, Yousef unearthed a speech by Egyptian chief justice al Shammari boasting of his son Saad, a highly-respected physician living in the vicinity. Saad would support the scheme under duress with his father's life hanging in the balance. Yousef wisely compartmentalized all avenues of deceit—including his surrogates in Seattle and San Jose. Like elsewhere, all would culminate in dead-ends, literally and figuratively. Case in point, the Egyptians in the next room. The al Shammaris would never be connected to the Sword of Islam or his sleeper agents. Unfortunately for them, their roles had come to an end. "Brother Hamza, send the son and wife to meet the father."

Removing a silenced pistol from his waistband, Hamza Omar abū-Ibrahim, head of the San Jose cell of the Islamic Jihad Brotherhood, left the room.

Saad and Asenath al Shammari cringed in fear when abū-Ibrahim entered the kitchen.

"Do not worry," abū-Ibrahim laughed coldly, "for I am sending you to a better place." Abū-Ibrahim raised his arm and fired a single lethal shot into each of their faces.

Meanwhile in a bedroom, Hussein al-Jubeir shook Harris from his sleep. "Wake, Khalid, my brother. The Sword summons you."

The Sword? Puzzled, Harris bolted upright and followed al-Jubeir into the family room, where he found his other brothers waiting.

"Khalid, come to me," ordered 'Ricky'.

Harris shuffled over and stopped before him. "Yes?"

"Kneel to pray, my trusted warrior, and the Sword will reveal your role."

Looking down, Harris saw he was standing directly atop a prayer rug. As swiftly as possible given his considerable heft, he knelt and rested his head on the rug.

Rising from his chair, al-Dosari stepped behind Harris, abū-Ibrahim handing him the silenced pistol as he passed. Pressing it to the back of Harris's head at the base of his brain stem, the Sword fired a single point-blank shot.

Harris toppled over.

"Khalid Abdul Aziz, the Sword is humbled by your sacrifice." Laughing at the American moron, al-Dosari beckoned his followers to gather around him.

"The sacrifices you will soon make are great, but your rewards in paradise will be even greater. Yousef will greet you, and together, you shall await my arrival. Pray with me, my brothers. Your chosen moment is at hand."

At the prayer's conclusion, Ali bin al-Dosari—the Almighty's Sword of Islam—uttered three simple words: "It is time."

CHAPTER SIXTY-ONE

SOHAIB ABASSI APPROACHED THE two Secret Service agents guarding the Bentley. "I must work on the automobile," he announced.

"Why?" An agent eyed him warily. "I thought it was fine."

The other agent butted in. "He has to check the AC filter, remember?"

"Right." The agent spotted a trickle of sweat running down the mechanic's forehead. "You feeling all right, fella?"

"I am always anxious before dignitaries drive the prince's automobiles. Mistakes must be avoided." Abassi drew his hand across his neck as if slicing it off.

"I hear you." The agent suspected the mechanic lived under constant threat of beheading if he failed in his duties.

Abassi climbed in behind the steering column and started the engine. Letting it idle a bit, he ran his hand over the air vents. Shutting off the engine, he called the agent over. "As I feared, the filter needs replacing."

He walked over to his large tool chest, lifting the lid and stepping behind it. Fumbling in a drawer, he grabbed a wrench with his right hand while discreetly reaching inside his left coat pocket and pulling out a small box. Abassi returned to the car, tool and box in hand. "Agent, will you assist me, please?"

"Sure."

Wearing cotton gloves, Abassi raised the hood and pointed at the refrigerant line near the condenser. With the agent peering over his shoulder, the mechanic loosened a nut, detached the line, and removed a filter from a three-inch brass orifice tube. He held it up to the light. "As I suspected, a dirty filter." Abassi glanced at the disinterested agent. Extracting the replacement filter from the small box, he installed it in the brass tube. Letting out a long breath, he tightened down the nut. "Agent, please sit in the driver's seat and start the engine."

The agent climbed behind the wheel and complied.

"Look for two digital screens on the burl wood dash console. Below them are toggle switches with blue and red arrows. Push down on the blue arrows until the digits drop to six-zero and place your hands in front of the vents. Let me know if the air is cold."

In no time, the agent announced, "Ice-cold, both sides."

"Excellent! Thank you. Please set the main dial to Off and shut down the engine." Abassi finished his tutorial. "On some occasions, when we open up the airflow, we must evacuate the system and recharge it. Not this time." The mechanic gently closed the hood.

It was done.

Abassi surprised himself with his preternatural calm. Retrieving a plastic bottle from his tool chest, he squeezed leather lotion onto a rag and wiped down the dash and seats, then buffed them with a soft white cloth. "I do not need your president complaining he got grease on his hands or clothing from this car."

Grinning, the agent sliced his hand under his chin knowingly.

"Thirty-One, Thirty-One. This is dispatch."

Monterey County Sheriff's deputy Maria Rodriquez responded, "This is Thirty-One."

"Proceed to 127 Camino Del Monte. Complainant Clifford Hopkins advises there are multiple men next door to his location engaged in suspicious activity. The men at the house are not the residents."

"Ten-four, Thirty-One copies."

"Thirty-One, the complainant sounds extremely distressed. Your call's code 3."

Rodriquez flipped the light bar and siren switches on the equipment console and punched the accelerator but the roads—still slick from the now abated heavy rains—slowed her down. A few minutes later, she spied a flashing yellow light through the dense fog. Turning off the emergency beacons and siren, she negotiated the turn, heading up the hill and entering the Carmel Valley subdivision. Rodriguez glimpsed a lone figure standing in the fog at the end of a driveway. She pulled the cruiser to a stop on the wet grass and lit up the man with her spotlight.

"You Mr. Hopkins?"

"Thank God you're here!" His relief was unmistakable.

"What's going on, sir?"

Hopkins explained that as he walked out to collect his morning newspaper, two vans full of men sped out of the driveway next door, nearly running him over. The more details he tried to give, the more his words stuck in his throat.

"Where are the men you called about?"

"Gone ..."

"What can you tell me about the vehicles?"

"Two white vans ... full of A-Arabs ... man in neighbor's wagon ... not neighbor ... another car maybe ... not sure ... face down in grass ..." Hopkins began hyperventilating.

"Please take a deep breath, sir."

Hopkins's neck veins bulged, and Rodriquez caught him as his knees buckled. Speaking soothingly, she led him over to her cruiser and eased him into its back seat.

"Stay here. I'll be right back."

Drawing her weapon, Rodriquez walked up the driveway serving the darkened residence. She did a once-around the perimeter of the house, peeking through the windows as she circled. She keyed her radio. "One-S-Six, this is Thirty-One."

The on-duty patrol sergeant responded, "Go ahead."

"I find no suspicious activity at this location. But the complainant is freaked out and having trouble breathing. He insists he saw two vans of suspicious Middle Eastern males, maybe two other vehicles. I'd appreciate it if you'd rendezvous with me here code 3."

"I'm en route. Break, dispatch, roll another unit and an ambulance to that location."

"Ten-four."

Deputy Maria Rodriquez walked back to her patrol car and Clifford Hopkins. After ten years in police work as a sheriff's deputy and army MP, Rodriquez's well-honed instincts screamed there was something wrong here.

Very wrong.

CHAPTER SIXTY-TWO

McEWAN, MORTON, AND BEACHAM were pulling an all-nighter at the Laguna Seca command post reviewing reports and message traffic on the dragnet, their frayed nerves chaining them to tables. Though it was humming with activity, the ambient din was white noise.

McEwan reached the bottom of his pile and gazed vacantly at the five identical digital clocks displaying the different time zones.

Morton drained the dregs from his coffee mug with one hand while simultaneously rubbing his neck with the other.

Beacham finished reading his last report and set it down.

Radio transmissions from Monterey County Sheriff deputies suddenly squawked over loudspeakers.

Beacham spoke first. "Did you guys hear that?"

Both nodding, McEwan and Morton bolted to their feet and followed Beacham over to a workstation, where an agent typed furiously on a laptop. She pointed to an address flashing on a map. "Camino del Monte Drive is about three miles from here. Take a left on 68 at the base of the hill. Go two miles and make a right at the flashing yellow. Take the first right up the hill into a subdivision called Rancho Laureles."

McEwan had no doubt: it was game time. "Ted, initiate Code Red immediately. Get your Hazardous Materials Response Unit geared up and ready to go. Have the USAMRIID-CDC team saddle up too."

"I'm on it. I'll advise the county sheriff by telephone you'll be on the scene and we're responding."

McEwan and Morton scrambled outside. A marked CHP cruiser pulled up, lights flashing. Behind the wheel, Captain Billy Ramona yelled, "Get in!"

McEwan took the shotgun seat and Morton hopped in back. Ramona hit the gas, then Morton blurted, "Stop! Wait a minute!"

The CHP commander slammed on the brakes.

Jumping from the cruiser, Morton tore back inside. Moments later he returned, the briefcase biosensor unit in one hand, encrypted walkie-talkie in the other. He tossed the radio over the seat to McEwan and slammed his door.

Ramona punched the accelerator of the powerful black-and-white unit but slowed it to an immediate crawl. The treacherous 16 percent downhill grade and dense fog made rolling off the Laguna Seca hillside a distinct possibility.

McEwan called over the radio for the MARSOC commander. "Jason, your helos are out. Mount up in Hummers and be ready to deploy."

"Roger."

Looking grimly at Morton, McEwan transmitted a soundless message: *He's here.*

Captain Ramona delivered them to Camino del Monte Drive. On approach, McEwan counted three cruisers, an ambulance, and a small group of neighbors milling about. "If we have to quarantine, it's isolated and there's only a handful."

A sergeant stepped forward, introducing himself and a female deputy named Rodriquez. She brought them up to speed, then McEwan took over.

"Tell the other deputy not to get any closer to the house. You two cover the rear. Agent Morton and I will approach from the front. Captain Ramona, you've got our six."

Placing the briefcase on a cruiser hood, Morton opened it. Turning it on, he extracted the handheld unit and carried it with him. Joining McEwan, weapons drawn, they crept through the fog up the driveway. When they stepped within five feet of the garage doors, the device in

Morton's hand and its base unit on the cruiser began emitting loud, shrill whistles.

"Everybody freeze!" Morton stared down at the digital display in his hand and gave words to the whistle. "The house is hot!"

Everyone pulled back while keeping their eyes trained on the house. McEwan transmitted, "Ted, the location is hot."

"HMRU's ETA is six minutes," the FBI SAC responded.

"Tim, connect the sergeant with his sheriff by phone. Emphasize the critical nature of this situation and explain why it absolutely must stay off the radio."

McEwan gathered the police officers, EMTs, and neighbors off to one side. Choosing his words carefully, he spoke reassuringly. "It appears we are all at the scene of a crime involving the theft of sensitive military medical equipment. The good news: I'm certain the criminals are gone. The bad news: the shrill whistles you heard were devices alerting us that there may be some type of bacteria present."

Clifford Hopkins croaked, "Bacteria?"

The Hazmat agents and medical personnel arriving shortly in alien-style suits would provide more than enough terror for the witnesses. McEwan decided to postpone fear as long as possible, so he stretched the truth. "We think the sensors alerted only as a precaution. As a preventive measure, we're taking all of you to Laguna Seca for examination by a special medical team. You'll be inconvenienced, that's all."

The witnesses took the news well until ordered to surrender their cell phones. Grumbles erupted into anger. Detecting the sounds of engines, McEwan and the others turned as one.

The source was a large RV-type vehicle pulling onto Camino Del Monte, trailed by a line of sedans and step vans. The FBI Mobile Command unit parked the farthest distance away, safely outside the contamination zone. The slide-outs, a satellite dish, and antennas deployed then the unit's generator hummed to life. Other doors slammed as windbreaker-clad agents climbed out of cars and gathered near the mobile unit. Agents wearing Level-A personal protective suits with self-contained breathing apparatuses materialized from the step vans, the shields of their helmets rendering their faces indistinguishable.

The cavalry's arrival stopped everything cold, the witnesses' faces reflecting various stages of alarm as the aliens sallied forth from the fog. Morton herded the panic-stricken witnesses over to Dr. Sheila Huston, where she huddled with assorted medical personnel. A group of agents in dark-blue windbreakers emblazoned with "FBI" in bold yellow letters stood by with an array of sensors, waiting for direction from Huston.

Beacham emerged from the command unit, spotted McEwan, and waved him over. "I'd truly prefer it if you two didn't go in with our guys," Beacham said.

McEwan nodded. "He's already gone, Ted. Just hit the house."

Beacham broadcast the order over the radio.

Two seven-man stacks of Hazmat-garbed FBI SWAT agents moved in. One team established a perimeter around the residence, while the other crept up the driveway. The breach team busted through the front door with an entry tool.

"FBI! FBI!" came over the radio. Bolting inside, the agents advanced through the house amid shrill whistles with repeated declarations of "Clear!" piercing the air. Agonizingly long minutes passed before "All clear" crackled over the airwaves.

"No subjects," the team leader radioed. "Three DOAs. We can't find the host. We alerted on a pile of dirty clothes inside and an empty padded case and plastic wrapper outside in bushes next to the driveway pad. We believe they were atop a vehicle and fell off when it left. That's what Morton's device alerted on."

"What about the DOAs?" McEwan queried anxiously.

"Two are the owners of the house, Saad and Asenath al Shammari. The third is a William Harris."

"Say again the third DOA?" McEwan asked.

"William Bradford Harris. Washington State driver's license, Seattle address."

McEwan whirled to face Morton, Beacham, and Ramona. "He's here. Lock it down."

Beacham dished out rapid-fire orders to the CTOC, mobilizing hundreds of federal, state, and local law enforcement personnel to cordon off the Monterey Peninsula.

Having nothing left to do at the scene, McEwan and Morton returned to Laguna Seca. On the way, McEwan updated Sanchez, who was currently with the president. As they entered the command post, Beacham called in with an update. "The house was their staging area. The devices definitely alerted on residue, but it's extremely powerful. We found no containers, but the garage and first-floor bath are both registering hot. The owners were in the kitchen, Harris in the family room. All dispatched with single .22 caliber gunshots to the head."

"What about other vehicles and occupants?"

"The witness Hopkins is certain two white vans left together, both with signage of some type on the sides. One had four men, the other three. He's sure the third vehicle was the victims' Mercedes station wagon."

"So by Hopkins's count, eight total. We should have nine including al-Dosari. We're a man short."

"Correct. Hopkins was planted face down in the grass trying to dodge the Mercedes wagon. While he didn't see a fourth vehicle, he's pretty sure there was one because he heard it accelerate. So there's our ninth man. We showed him all the DMV license photos for the San Jose cell as well as the Canadian passport picture for Ricardo San Felipe. He didn't recognize any of them."

McEwan saw Morton asking to cut in and beckoned him on.

"Ted, we've received no reports that Harris rented any other vehicles since Portland. Task the investigative unit to identify any vehicles reported stolen in the last twenty-four hours from Portland to Monterey."

"Excellent idea. We can't leave any stone unturned at this point. Anything else, Kyle?"

"Negative." Hanging up, McEwan retreated to reflect on their recent discoveries. *I don't care what they didn't find. You were in that house. You killed Harris and the owners. You have to go through me to get to the president and the others and that's not happening.*

CHAPTER SIXTY-THREE

MCEWAN HAD ONE QUESTION for the DNI. "Is Englewood going public with the al-Dosari threat?"

Sanchez answered with her own question. "How else do we explain why we've locked down the central coast region?"

Catching Morton's high sign, McEwan punched the Speaker button.

"Director Sanchez, Tim Morton here. I'm with Ted Beacham, FBI. We're working on a plausible story for public consumption to explain why we're choking off all traffic. We'll have it for you shortly. In the meantime, we can provide a quick rundown of the lockdown strategy."

The sounds of shuffling papers came through the speaker. "Go ahead."

Beacham took the point and explained the mechanics of the plan, point by point. Its logistics were staggering in scope: all major primary and secondary roads had checkpoints or roadblocks to facilitate vehicle searches and turn back anyone trying to enter the peninsula.

As Beacham spoke, Sanchez followed along and drew lines on a map between the checkpoints and roadblocks. She saw that the entire Monterey Peninsula was completely sealed off. If al-Dosari and his cronies were still inside the perimeter, they were trapped.

Morton jumped back in. "The MARSOC and FBI aircraft are grounded until the bulk of the fog burns off. Response time will be delayed depending on when and where we find them. The Coast Guard and Navy will interdict all vessels out to two miles."

"Kyle, POTUS wants you and Tim over here ASAP." Sanchez terminated the call.

Stepping outside, they found Captain Billy Ramona sitting in his cruiser studying a map. He looked up. "Lone Cypress?"

Morton nodded.

"Buckle up, boys. It's going to be a bumpy ride."

Despite the dense fog, the CHP commander transported McEwan and Morton with minimal delay to the heavily fortified presidential compound at Pebble Beach Resorts.

They found a highly agitated Sanchez pacing on the sidewalk outside the gates. McEwan and Morton followed her through a pedestrian gate into the compound interior. The Secret Service agent standing outside the library rapped on the door. "Mr. President."

"Enter."

Nelson J. Englewood met them at the door and gestured toward the sofa and chair. He walked to the fireplace and remained standing. "Unless you can give me a good reason not to, I'm going on national TV with Governor Carlson and Secretary Moss to announce the threat and ask for the public's help in finding al-Dosari and his accomplices. This wasn't my first choice, not by a long shot, but we're out of time."

"Mr. President," Morton said, "if I may?"

"Yes."

"Why not have the governor's press secretary do the conference instead? Have her give a more generalized reason for the lockdown to buy us a few more hours. Every minute we gain is another minute closer to getting him. You can always expand the explanation later."

Although inclined to reject the proposal outright, Englewood reconsidered. Nodding slowly, he came around. "That'll work for now. But once I say it's done, it's over. Understood?"

The trio nodded in unison.

Sanchez weighed in. "The safest place for you and the first lady is here. The security over the Resorts rivals the White House."

"Okay. But where are they?"

No one, including Kyle McEwan, knew that answer.

Back at the CTOC, McEwan, Morton, Cartwright, and Beacham sat in a tight semicircle around a large flat-screen television, watching the California governor's press secretary. She informed the nation that the lockdown of the Monterey Peninsula was due to a threat against the NGA conference.

"The Department of Homeland Security notified the governor of an unspecified threat aimed at the conference. The source of the information is deemed highly credible, and while the specific nature of the threat is not known, it's significant enough to warrant the following. Effective immediately, all businesses are closed. Every interstate and major thoroughfare is shut down. Every citizen is ordered to shelter in place. Do *not* attempt to enter or leave the peninsula. Stay home. If you have left or leave the peninsula, you will not be allowed to return until such time as the lockdown is lifted. If you attempt to enter the area, you will be turned back. These mandatory actions are in effect until further notice."

"Isn't this tantamount to martial law?" a reporter shouted.

"Heavens, no. Law enforcement needs *temporary* unfettered access to investigate the threat. Governor Carlson declared the emergency clampdown on all traffic because massive traffic jams will hamper these efforts and necessitate expansion of the declaration to other areas. We regret the inconvenience to our citizens and visitors."

An unidentified reporter shouted, "Who made the threat?"

"What aren't you telling us?" another reporter yelled.

The press secretary ignored the questions.

"The governor ordered these temporary actions due to the presence of the president along with dozens of high-level federal and state officials. The governor asks everyone to take this warning seriously and heed it. As soon as I have additional details to share, I will. We will lift the restrictions as soon as possible. Thank you for your assistance and cooperation."

CHAPTER SIXTY-FOUR

THE RUMBLING BARITONE OF the diesel engine penetrated the man's consciousness. Wiping beads of perspiration from his forehead, he ended the call and stuffed the phone in his shirt pocket. Steeling himself, he gripped the steering wheel and punched the accelerator, sending the car catapulting forward.

Standing outside his guard shack at the Monterey Regional Airport, Patrolman Adam Joseph listened attentively to his police radio as the dispatcher transmitted the BOLO on the silver Mercedes station wagon and two white vans. His outer ear detected the sound of an engine operating at exceedingly high RPMs. He jerked his head toward the source—a silver Mercedes station wagon barreling toward the fenced-in compound. The conflict between his instincts screaming "Threat!" and his intellect screaming "No way!" paralyzed Joseph. Finally, intellect yielded to training; unholstering his service weapon, Joseph assumed a defensive shooting stance, aimed his pistol at the threat and yelled, "Stop!"

The last thing Adam Joseph saw before dying was his attacker's maniacal grin.

Accelerating toward its top speed, the Mercedes plowed into the policeman. The force of the impact flung the officer into the glass windshield shattering it. His body bounced up onto the roof, toppling end over end before rolling to a stop on the pavement. Without glancing in the rearview mirror, the driver sped on.

Security barrier eliminated, the Mercedes screeched to a stop inches in front of the hangar marked "Crandall Aviation". The driver snatched a blue gym bag off the seat and jumped out. Grunting loudly, he pushed open two large bay doors to expose a white airplane with red and gray stripes. Jerking the chock blocks from beneath its wheels, he tossed his bag onto the passenger seat and clambered inside. A turn of the ignition key brought a brief whir and single-propeller rotation; the engine spit and came alive. The man placed a headset over his ears, checked the instrument panel, and steered the plane from the hangar.

In the Monterey Regional Airport control tower, FAA air traffic controller Dante Pearce rocked back and forth in his ergonomic chair, flipping through a magazine. After surviving twenty nerve-racking years at San Francisco International, he sought out the less stressful environs of the central coast. The way Pearce figured it, he'd earned the privilege of kicking back a couple of years at Monterey before easing into retirement.

Pearce decided to take advantage of the solitude of the restricted airspace and shrouding fog to make a head call. Once the fog lifted, law enforcement and military activity over the airspace would resume. As he tossed the magazine aside, his peripheral vision detected blinking navigation lights. Swiveling toward them, he observed a civilian aircraft pulling out of a hangar. Pushing through his disbelief, Pearce adjusted his mic and reached for the transmit button.

"Unidentified aircraft on the apron, this is Monterey Ground Control. Be advised this airport is closed. Repeat, Monterey is closed. Acknowledge."

The plane's pilot responded by picking up speed.

Pearce reached over and hit the switch activating the emergency frequency before repeating his instructions.

The plane continued accelerating steadily toward the taxiway.

Pearce barked at the other controller, "Advise Secret Service we have an unauthorized aircraft not responding to my calls, and it's moving onto the taxiway."

The controller stared at Pearce, mouth agape.

"Now, damn it!" Pearce shouted, jumpstarting the man into action. "Then advise Navy we need to launch its alert aircraft!"

Springing to life, the second controller punched buttons on his phone and relayed his message excitedly. Dialing another number, he repeated the information.

From his perch high above the airport, Pearce observed dozens of flashing red and blue lights pop into view through the lifting fog. Shortly, a second wall of flashing police lights sprang up on the other side of the airport. Both walls began moving at breakneck speed, their goal to "pit-maneuver" the plane—tagging its tail with a vehicle bumper to knock the Cessna sideways and out of control. Gritting his teeth, the senior controller steeled himself and shouted another warning over the emergency frequency.

The Cessna pilot ignored those commands as he neared the runway.

Pearce shook his head. *He's going for it.*

"There's an intruder entering the airspace!" Cartwright's thundering voice roared across and to the farthest reaches of the FBI command post, startling everyone.

McEwan and Morton arrived at the communications section as a technician flipped on overhead speakers and pumped up the volume. The air traffic controller's voice boomed, "Cessna on runway two-eight left! Stop! Hold your position immediately! Monterey's airspace is restricted!"

Using binoculars, Pearce zeroed in on the plane's tail number. He hit his hip again, urgency coloring his every word: "Cessna November-One-Nine-Three-Whiskey-Foxtrot, Monterey is restricted airspace. The military is enforcing a no-fly zone! If you take off, you will be shot down! Repeat! Do *not* take off! Acknowledge!"

Pearce watched the tiny plane pick up speed and complete its turn onto the runway. The bands of flashing red and blue lights united in a single wall facing the plane. Pearce saw something the drivers couldn't: as the two opposing forces accelerated rapidly toward each other, the pilot was either going to go airborne or ram the vehicles, incinerating himself and law enforcement.

As the two forces met, the Cessna barely lifted off the ground, wheels shearing off the light bar of a police cruiser. The plane managed to wobble into the air instead of cartwheeling. Police vehicles skidded to a stop on the runway or spun in circles on the wet grass. Pearce heard a panting Secret Service agent over his shoulder. Without taking his eyes from the display, Pearce gave the agent the bad news. "He's airborne—turning toward Pebble Beach."

The agent relayed the information via his radio.

Pearce scrolled through his computer database, looking for the registered owner of N193WF.

Over in the CTOC, McEwan growled, "Jason, if he's up, we're up."

"Hubie, spin 'em up!" Cartwright transmitted.

"We're mounting up and heading to the helos now!" Marine Raider Captain Lopez replied.

McEwan sprinted behind Morton to a waiting Humvee. A couple of quick turns later, they hit the temporary helipad at the Laguna Seca raceway and scrambled aboard an FBI helicopter. They plugged into the integrated radio net in time to catch a new voice on the air.

"Monterey Ground Control, this is Navy one-zero-five."

Responding to the call, Pearce looked downward, his eyes landing on the Navy F-18E Super Hornet on the ramp across the tarmac. "Navy one-oh-five, a Cessna Skylane one-eight-two, white with red and gray stripes, is airborne. Registration November-One-Nine-Three-Whiskey-Foxtrot. You're cleared for immediate takeoff on runway two-eight left."

"Roger, Monterey," the fighter pilot replied calmly.

"Navy, Monterey is handing off control of the airspace to Castle Rock. Acknowledge."

"Copy, Monterey," replied the Navy pilot as his fighter rolled toward the runway.

"Monterey, this is Castle Rock," the tactical air operations controller announced seamlessly. "We've assumed command over the airspace. Navy one-zero-five, do you copy?"

"Copy that. Castle Rock has the conn."

"Navy, the black Bell helo coming up to your west is the command-and-control bird with the operation commander on board. A Marine Corps UH-1Y and an MH-22 will lift off momentarily from Castle Rock."

"Navy one-zero-five copies."

Aboard the F-18E, Navy Lieutenant Oliver "Strawman" Rakestraw performed a situational awareness check. There'd be five total aircraft: his fighter plus the bogey, the Bell, the Venom, and an Osprey full of Marine Raiders. He knew his squadron mate was already "kicking the tires and lighting the fires" of his Alert fighter and would wait in the wings to be ordered aloft.

Rakestraw was the first line of defense protecting the commander in chief from an airborne attack. He doubted the Cessna was a legit hostile.

The military air controller tracking the Cessna on his radar screen caught the Marine Venom going airborne to the northeast, then the Osprey came into view. "Navy, MARSOC is in the air."

"Roger, Castle Rock." Noting the information, Rakestraw turned onto the runway. Releasing the fighter's brakes and stroking the burners he began his takeoff roll. Thundering engines hurtled the fighter down the runway and airborne. "Castle Rock, Navy one-zero-five. I'm in the game."

"Roger, Navy."

The Cessna appeared almost immediately in Rakestraw's windscreen. "Castle Rock, I have a visual on the bogey—a Cessna Skylane one-eight-two white with red and gray stripes, tail number November-One-Nine-Three-Whiskey-Foxtrot. Be advised he's going feet wet."

"Copy your positive identification. We confirm, he's turned west-southwest away from the beach. Navy, recommend you come right to two-four-zero and maintain fifteen hundred feet."

Rakestraw acknowledged the command and made a high "yo-yo" maneuver, remaining out of the pilot's visual range.

"Castle Rock, Monterey Ground Control."

"Go ahead, Monterey."

"The owner of the Cessna is a local resident named Saad al Shammari. We're contacting him and will advise."

McEwan broke into the exchange. "Monterey Ground Control, belay that. We already know the owner's whereabouts. The Cessna is stolen and definitely hostile. Have Navy one-oh-five shadow the plane."

"Castle Rock copies. Break. Navy, did you copy?"

"Copy that."

Al-Dosari's plan unfolded map-like in McEwan's mind. *The al Shammaris provided a staging area and an aircraft. The Cessna isn't a crop duster so it can't be a delivery vehicle. He knows we'll shoot it down if he tries a kamikaze attack. It's a diversion. But from what?*

Rakestraw, maintaining constant visual surveillance of the Cessna aboard his fighter, recalled how he'd wound up in the hot seat. Instead of conducting routine workups off California's coast, the Pentagon tapped the USS *Theodore Roosevelt* air wing to provide VIP flights for the governors conference and enforce the no-fly zone, normally an Air Force responsibility. He'd volunteered for the "unique and career-enhancing opportunity" to man one of two Alert fighters. In his inestimable wisdom, the boring detail would earn extra liberty. *Wrong.* Said boondoggle just became interesting. Executing a high-G bat-turn, Rakestraw throttled back and dropped his airspeed, lining up on the Cessna's tailpipe for a weapons solution.

Not enough heat signature for a Sidewinder. I'll do a guns kill.

CHAPTER SIXTY-FIVE

FROM THE MOMENT HE turned the key in the ignition of the Ford van, Hussein al-Jubeir carefully obeyed all posted speed limits. Proceeding north on US 101 back toward San Jose, al-Jubeir and the other occupants maintained a soundless vigil.

Fixing his eyes on the horizon, al-Jubeir observed active brake lights. Easing off the accelerator, he positioned the van in the right lane of a solid line of cars and trucks inching forward.

Without looking at the clock, the warriors knew their time was near.

The cell phone in al-Jubeir's hand vibrated. He accepted the call, said nothing, and listened intently. He provided the caller their current position, acknowledged the caller's command, and ended the call.

Turning to the other occupants, Hussein al-Jubeir led them in prayer, thanking Allah for allowing them to become fallen warriors, guaranteeing their seats in paradise.

Just before daybreak, Santa Clara County Sheriff's deputies threw up a roadblock northbound on US 101, a tenth of a mile before the exit ramp at Morgan Hill. They set a second roadblock across the median to halt all southbound traffic. Jersey barricades and metal fencing lining both sides of the freeway bracketed the area, funneling all vehicles into corrals where every one of them was searched. Once each was cleared, it was forced to exit the peninsula—none could enter or turn back.

Amid the fumes of idling cars, SWAT commander Lieutenant Jerry Fitzgibbon stood beside his cruiser on the northbound shoulder of US 101. The already hot August early morning sun, amplified by hundreds of vehicles backed up behind the temporary concrete barriers, sent heat rising from the asphalt. Wiping sweat from his upper lip, he knew the day would become shorter only if law enforcement bagged the men they sought. Convinced they would, he hoped it didn't require a stack of body bags in the process. He no sooner finished his thought when he heard a wide-open throttle.

"A white van is trying to run the northbound roadblock!" thundered through his earpiece. "Look out!"

A split second later, former US Army Ranger Fitzgibbon recognized the report of AK-47s, then the returning fire of pistols, rifles, and shotguns. Instinctively positioning himself behind the engine block and front axle of his cruiser, Fitzgibbon leaned over the hood and aimed his M4, searching for a target. Scrambling motorists made finding one impossible. Bullets thudded into the cruiser on his left, and he heard a sharp cry of pain. *Officer down.*

Still no eyeball on the threat and unable to decipher the heated radio traffic, Fitzgibbon bolted to the downed deputy and checked his neck pulse. *Dead.*

The black command-and-control helicopter streaked above the Monterey Peninsula, beelining for the Cessna and Navy fighter. McEwan's headphones crackled with Ted Beacham's voice.

"Units on the 101 at Morgan Hill report they're engaged in a gunfight with subjects in a white van. Transmissions are sketchy."

"Roger," McEwan responded immediately. "It has to be a diversion because the targets are here. Everybody stay put. Link us with the on-scene commander once he's back on the air."

He turned to Morton. "Where's the Cessna?"

"Still over water. He keeps turning in a holding pattern. He's waiting for something."

Lieutenant Jerry Fitzgibbon peered around the front bumper and glimpsed the white van wedged between two cars. The SWAT commander zeroed in on the driver's head as it exploded.

"One left running between cars," came haltingly over Fitzgibbon's earpiece.

Abandoning the safety of their cruisers, sheriff's deputies pursued the shooter on foot.

The mass of screaming motorists scrambling in all directions impeded the deputies' progress.

Fitzgibbon saw the terrorist bobbing and weaving between cars before ducking behind a semitrailer.

Pop-pops rang out—two more motorists dropped.

Pursuing deputies pushed people to the ground as they ran.

Fitzgibbon finally got a bead on the terrorist as he took shelter between two trucks. The lieutenant's barrage of gunfire hammered the man backward until he crashed into a truck and dropped to the asphalt.

"McEwan, Command Post. Switch to channel 7 for the on-scene commander at Morgan Hill. It's a Lieutenant Fitzgibbon of Santa Clara County Sheriff."

"Lieutenant, what's your status?"

"The scene's secure. Three men in a white van opened up on us with AKs and tried running our roadblock. I've got an unknown number of motorists down, perhaps as many as thirty. Two deputies have been shot; one is gone and the other is going to be okay."

Understandably, the SWAT commander's voice communicated stress as he continued. "The shooters are all dead. While your man is not among them, IDs confirm the shooters are members of his San Jose cell. None of our sensors alerted for smallpox on the vehicle or any of their bodies. The van has Silicon Valley Durable Medical Equipment of San Jose magnetic signs on the side panels."

"Keep Ted Beacham briefed on what you find. Can we do anything for you, Lieutenant?"

"Thanks, but we have it under control."

McEwan switched his radio back to the main frequency and looked at Morton. "The shoot-out was a diversion, as is our Cessna. Time to take it out of play."

McEwan gave the military air operations center instructions for the three pilots.

Castle Rock relayed the orders, all acknowledged by the aviators.

Moments later, McEwan's helicopter pulled up alongside the Cessna. Focusing his binoculars on the pilot's face, McEwan keyed his mic.

"Pilot is a solo male. I've got a good eyeball on him; he's not our boy. He's one of the San Jose crew."

The Navy fighter continued to shadow the plane from a distance of several hundred yards. Rakestraw watched the Cessna pilot play a dangerous game of "chicken" with McEwan's helo.

Once McEwan's helicopter banked away from the Cessna, Rakestraw executed his orders. Half-rolling from behind the Cessna, he pulled the fighter into a steep climb over Big Sur. Making a wide circle, his F-18E closed rapidly on the slow-moving plane's six. Pushing forward on the stick, the fighter roared in front of the Cessna, then pulled into another steep vertical climb. Glancing at the single-engine plane, Rakestraw laughed.

The Cessna pilot was unaware he'd been shadowed by the Navy fighter the whole time. The pilot's first clue materialized when the F-18E's wake sent the Cessna teetering violently, defying his frantic efforts to rein in his plane.

As ordered, Cartwright's Venom crept up on the Cessna's tail, then pulled alongside, inching closer to the plane. The helicopter's precise positioning allowed Cartwright to hand-signal the pilot. The man's eyes burned holes into the Marine Raider while his right hand dug for something. The pilot slid his window open a crack and poked out the tip of a gun barrel.

"Break off! He's got a gun!"

The helo driver jinked evasively away from the plane.

Cartwright advised, "He fired a burst at us but missed."

"Roger," McEwan responded at once.

Aboard the Cessna, Raboud Muhammad Balkhi felt a sense of tremendous pride and accomplishment. He was performing his religious duty perfectly. The Almighty and Saifulislam were proud. Smiling, he turned the aircraft again.

Cartwright transmitted, "He's turning back toward the coastline."

"I see him," McEwan replied. "There's nothing but residences down there. It'll be messy if he takes a nosedive."

The Raider commander concurred.

The airwaves went dark briefly as McEwan made his decision, which he communicated to the DNI, monitoring the situation from the Secret Service command post at the presidential compound.

"Stand by for confirmation," she replied.

Anticipating McEwan's probable request, the president had already conferred with the secretaries of Defense and Homeland Security and the attorney general. Englewood's orders filtered their way indirectly but swiftly down the chain of command.

"Operational aircraft, this is Castle Rock," came the voice of the military tactical air operations controller, "return to base. Navy one-zero-five is assuming control of the intercept."

The rotary aircraft pilots acknowledged their commands, then Rakestraw confirmed his. "Navy has control of the intercept."

The Venom banked sharply west; the Osprey of special ops Marine Raiders executed a mirror-image maneuver to the east, with McEwan's helicopter trailing behind.

Everyone in the air and on the ground knew what was coming—except the Cessna pilot. Oblivious, he banked again, heading toward the Pebble Beach Resorts.

"Navy one-zero-five, you're ordered to eliminate the threat. Repeat, eliminate the threat."

"Strawman copies: splash the target. Executing."

"Roger, Navy. Castle Rock out."

Rolling in behind the Cessna, Rakestraw peered through his heads-up display at the radar diamond box centered over the bogey's fuselage. He switched the stick's thumb selector to guns. When the double-ring "gun pipper" and "death dot" replaced the diamond he squeezed the trigger. Within a fraction of a second, the six-barrel Vulcan Gatling gun reverberated its familiar *bbrraaaap*, sending 20 mm cannon fire slamming into the Cessna's skin, punching it like deer slugs hitting an aluminum beer can.

Rakestraw rolled and watched the show unfold beneath his starboard wing.

The Cessna's engine seized up as flames from its ruptured fuel tank engulfed the cockpit. Raboud Muhammad Balkhi finally broke radio silence inside his aerial crematorium. Blood-curdling screams punctuated his declarations of "Death to America! Victory to Saifulislam! Allahu Akbar!" As the Cessna's wings snapped upward and broke off, the fuselage froze in time for a split second then spiraled downward in an uncontrolled nosedive until it disintegrated in the Carmel Bay.

"Splash one," Rakestraw radioed matter-of-factly. A grin spread across the naval aviator's face. *Adios, asshole, with regards from the US of A.*

"Castle Rock, Navy one-zero-five returning to base." Rakestraw rocked his F-18E's wings as he blew by the three rotary aircraft.

CHAPTER SIXTY-SIX

AL-DOSARI SPOKE SEVERAL TIMES with his fellow jihadists as they pursued their respective missions, all captivated by their imminent martyrdom. One was to be sacrificed in a suicide-by-plane ruse. Though this feint appeared on track he'd lost contact with the pilot, possibly because the infidels had jammed his warrior's phone. That prospect, and the earlier than anticipated clampdown on traffic, suggested the infidels might be unraveling his plot. To sidetrack police and convince them they had eliminated all escaping conspirators, his plan called for armed confrontations away from the target—and him. Trapped inside their net, he was within their reach. *I must accelerate my timetable to ensure success of the attack. And facilitate my escape.*

Stuck in bumper-to-bumper traffic several miles behind Omar abū-Ibrahim and his three warriors, al-Dosari realized he needed to close the gap. He ordered them to exit US 101 at Broadway and await further instructions.

Ted Beacham called over the airwaves for McEwan, circling in his helicopter above Pebble Beach.

"Kyle, I'm at the Monterey airport. The missing Mercedes wagon is here, door open, engine running at the hangar where the Cessna was stored. The driver ran down and killed the gate officer. HMRU says the Mercedes didn't register for smallpox, so I suspect he didn't have any aboard."

McEwan's stomach spasmed. "I've got a hunch."

"Shoot."

"Take one of the Sandia detectors next door and sweep the Bentley again."

"Okay. I'll get back with you."

Not two minutes later, Beacham called. "I've got a situation here."

"What?" McEwan felt his neck hairs crawling furiously.

"The Bentley's gone. The mechanic, name of Abassi, called the prince about the officer's murder. He claimed the car might be damaged due to the police activity at the airport. The prince's security chief convinced the Secret Service to clear it for delivery to Pebble Beach."

"Ted, it's the mechanic!" McEwan's head nearly exploded off his shoulders. "Where's the car?"

"CHP motor units are escorting it on a flatbed tow truck with a Secret Service sedan and a cruiser on its tail. They just exited Monterey-Salinas Highway onto Route 1."

McEwan pointed down at the freeway; the pilot headed for it. He wasted no time adjusting his team's plan and explained it in detail to Beacham.

"Ted, restrict radio traffic on channel 2. We will use it to orchestrate the takedown. Have Captain Ramona put it in motion now."

"Got it." The FBI SAC replied.

"Jason, you on this channel?" McEwan asked.

"Yeah, I heard it."

"Stick to my tail."

McEwan caught the report on the Bentley convoy, reducing its speed and continuing on Route 1 as ordered, past its original exit.

The sergeant supervising the CHP roadblock at the entrance to the Pebble Beach Resorts relayed Ramona's orders.

Uniformed officers scrambled aboard their motorcycles and into black and white cruisers. Their engines made a deafening noise that everyone throughout the Resorts and adjacent homes heard, including the president and first lady.

Sohaib Abassi watched nervously out the front windshield of the tow truck as the convoy exited Route 1. Every so often, he looked over his shoulder at the Bentley on the flatbed.

The transport driver glanced over at the Saudi mechanic. "I don't mean to hassle you, buddy, but you're sweating an awful lot. You feelin' okay?"

"I am fine." Abassi managed a tight smile, repeating his excuse. "I become nervous before dignitaries drive the prince's automobiles."

The two motorcycle units led them through the narrow streets of Carmel-by-the-Sea. Eventually, the convoy slowed to a stop at the Carmel Gate to the 17-Mile Drive.

The officer manning the checkpoint passed a cell phone to one of the motorcycle escort officers. He listened intently, talked briefly, returned it, and spoke to the other motor officer. The procession started back up, hugged a curve, and proceeded up the hill.

Abassi breathed a sigh, unaware the destiny of his convoy had been altered for all eternity during the sixty-second phone call. Confident of his secret's safety, a dark shadow passed over his face. Abassi had seen his family for the last time. His only comfort: they would live.

Several minutes later, the convoy rounded a bend. Abassi watched the motorcycle escorts wave at a group of police officers standing outside their vehicles.

The misdirection worked. Busy watching the police, the Saudi and his driver missed the canvas tarpaulin camouflaging the sign. Neither man noticed they'd passed the entrance to the Pebble Beach Resorts.

Above the procession, McEwan considered then discarded multiple scenarios. *Al-Dosari's definitely not in the convoy. There's no way he can penetrate the protective bubble either. Where is he? Undoubtedly letting others do his dirty work while saving his own ass.* McEwan glanced down at the convoy winding its way up Forest Road.

"Tim."

"Yes."

"Do it."

Morton doled out orders over the airwaves, providing the script for McEwan's unrehearsed but well-choreographed performance. On cue, the actors on the Pebble Beach stage below began performing for the audiences overhead, at Laguna Seca, and Casa Palmero. Officers escorting the convoy turned abruptly into the driveway for a local school, vacant during remodeling.

"What the hell?" The transport truck driver muttered. The CHP cruiser dead smack on his bumper eliminated all alternatives—he had to follow the escorts.

The motorized drama unfolded in front of Sohaib Abassi in slow motion. Too late, he noticed the procession curling into itself around a small traffic circle.

Both escort officers laid down their bikes in tandem and dismounted on the fly. Bouncing off the ground with gloved hands, they scrambled on all fours like sand crabs. Their power-driven props scraped across the pavement, shooting sparks into the air before slamming into a line of parked cruisers. The sickening thud of metal on metal began act 2.

Suddenly, everything sped up to real-time for the Saudi mechanic. Pivoting his head, he saw police cars swarming in behind them, officers exiting and fleeing on foot. Cordoned off, Sohaib Abassi was trapped.

McEwan's pilot set him down on the school's front lawn, and he sprinted toward the defensive ring of police vehicles.

The director in charge of the scene commenced a felony stop, guiding the actors in the flatbed truck over his cruiser PA system.

As the driver responded to the first command, a set of keys flew out the window.

"Good. Now, driver, show me your hands out the window! Passenger, you do the same!"

As directed, both men's hands appeared outside.

"Driver, open the door using the outside handle. Step out of the vehicle and face forward. Keep those hands held high in the air and walk slowly back to my voice."

The driver complied.

The drama continued over the PA system. "Drop to your knees. Lie face down and spread your legs. Do it *now*. That's right. Plant your face on the asphalt, palms in the air. Do not move."

Abassi received the same orders. Exiting the truck with his hands over his head was the only command he obeyed. Disregarding all other instructions, he turned toward the assembled officers.

The instructions thundered again over the PA system.

Abassi ignored the commands. Continuing toward the officers, he dropped his left arm and reached behind his back. Extending his arm, he charged the vehicle cordon.

A choir of sensor devices began releasing shrill screams, proclaiming the presence of smallpox.

McEwan was powerless to prevent the mechanic's "suicide by cop". Rounds pummeled the Saudi mechanic, jerking him in every direction until he dropped.

"Cease-fire! Cease-fire!" yelled the CHP commander, motioning with his arms.

McEwan ran up and kicked a large screwdriver away from Abassi's left hand. Grabbing fistfuls of cloth, he held the dying man by the shirt. "Where's the smallpox, Abassi? Where's the Sword?"

"Bentley!" Abassi shoved a folded piece of paper into McEwan's hand. "Tell my sons I am not a monster … please!"

The light in the Saudi mechanic's eyes flickered out.

Letting go of the lifeless form, McEwan unfolded the paper. Reading the note, he passed it to Morton, who read and refolded it, immediately taking charge.

"Everybody listen up! This scene is contaminated with smallpox. I want the senior officer to establish a five-hundred-foot perimeter and keep everyone out. Do it now, people! Move!"

Officers sprang into action as FBI HMRU and Evidence Response Team agents arrived.

Scanning the crowd, Morton spotted a Hazmat-suited agent emerging from a step van. Summoned by his finger, the agent approached. Morton handed her the note and told her what he wanted. "And make sure every person at this site, including the truck driver, are given Libertas." She nodded and hurried off.

Hustling back to their helicopter, McEwan made circles with his right index finger. Climbing aboard, the men plugged into the radio net. McEwan keyed his mic, "Tim, Jason, Ted, go to channel 1."

Without waiting for replies, McEwan flipped the selector dial. "The attack's been stopped, and we recovered the smallpox. If al-Dosari doesn't know what's happened yet, he will the second the media gets wind of what's gone down. He has two options: escape or attack another target."

McEwan's team of law enforcement, counterterrorism, and military experts dissected the situation in seconds, proving their shotgun marriage of diverse skill sets and experiences worked.

Morton spoke first. "In addition to al-Dosari, four members of the San Jose cell remain at large. The only logical conclusion is, he's using them as bait to steer us away from him—"

"Or sending them to a backup target if his first attack fails," Beacham interjected.

Cartwright added his two cents. "He knows the Coast Guard and Navy will blast his ass outta the water if he tries leaving by boat. He won't go east because there's no viable target."

McEwan closed the loop on the strategy session. "The diversionary attack at Morgan Hill leaves only one possibility. Ted, coordinate everything from Laguna Seca. The rest of us are turning around and heading south for the US 101 roadblock at San Ardo."

CHAPTER SIXTY-SEVEN

REPORTING FOR HIS MORNING shift, Monterey County park ranger Dmitri Harren turned into the entrance of San Lorenzo Park. He'd been monitoring the CHP frequency and local radio station accounts of the shoot-out involving suspects in a white Ford Transit van on the 101 at Morgan Hill. Law enforcement was searching for an identical van, direction of travel unknown. Authorities suspected its four male suspects were planning a similar attack once confronted.

Heading toward the Agricultural and Rural Life Museum in the middle of the park, Harren spotted a white Ford Transit van parked outside of the museum, engine idling, no visible occupants. The BOLO seeking the van said it bore signs for a San Jose durable medical equipment company—this van matched except the driver's side panel had no signage.

Harren drove around the rear of the museum, parked, and climbed out. Keeping his eyes peeled, hand on his service weapon, he walked to the corner of the building. Sneaking a quick peek, he saw a man pull a magnetic sign off the passenger side panel and toss it into the cargo area. Harren studied the man's features. *Looks Middle Eastern.* The man shot his eyes toward the ranger—Harren ducked back around the corner, narrowly avoiding being spotted.

As the van pulled away, Harren reached for his cell phone.

Approaching the Broadway/King City exit, Ali bin al-Dosari directed his soldiers back to the US 101 southbound freeway. Stuck in the massive traffic jam, he felt smothered—not by the exhaust of the vehicles—but by the symbols of the infidel's sins. Each side of the freeway was covered with neatly clipped rows of grapevines, obviously grown for alcohol. Mixed among the vineyards were oil wells craning their necks in an unending cycle, sucking black gold from the ground like they did in Allah's lands. Creeping forward inch by miserable inch, he glanced repeatedly into his rearview mirror until he saw the van transporting his warriors. It entered the freeway thirty or more vehicles behind him.

Whatever happened in the next several minutes would dictate success—or disaster—for the Sword of Islam.

On a stretch of highway just before the US 101/San Ardo exit, authorities established roadblocks in both directions, stopping all traffic entering and leaving the Monterey Peninsula. Bordered by a pair of steep hills, gullies on both sides served as natural barriers preventing drivers from swerving around the jersey barricades. Every vehicle, once searched, was forced to exit the peninsula.

Lieutenant Glen Nichols, the California Highway Patrol SWAT commander in charge of the San Ardo checkpoint, listened intently to the broadcast about the San Lorenzo park ranger's sighting of the Ford Transit van. Nichols knew the park well, barely twenty miles north of his current position. The van left the park an hour ago; the ranger couldn't follow, so the plate number and direction of travel were unknown.

Peering through his windshield, Nichols listened to squawking radios, idling vehicles, and the Paso Robles CHP airship overhead. For now, everything appeared calm and controlled. Fearing a repeat of the gunfight at Morgan Hill, the tightening knot in Nichol's stomach prompted him to grab his M4 carbine and move toward the barriers.

The helicopter ferrying McEwan and Morton followed the ribbon below: US 101. On its tail were Cartwright's Venom and the Osprey carrying the MARSOC Raiders. Passing Soledad, the BOLO on the ranger's sighting of the van came over the radio. McEwan ordered the pilots to increase speed. Frustrated that he hadn't figured out al-Dosari's endgame, McEwan was certain the answer—and the terror mastermind—lay somewhere beneath them. Undoubtedly al-Dosari's sleeper agents were in the line of traffic, preparing another assault. The double-lane traffic jam held scores of white vans among hundreds of vehicles. No matter how many there were, they'd search each one.

ꕥ

At long last, al-Dosari was three cars from the concrete barriers—his final obstacles to freedom. Suddenly, a tremendous roar arose as if from the ground itself. The source of the noise appeared—three rotary aircraft landing beside the freeway on the right embankment. The sight of one man stepping out of a black helicopter stimulated an involuntary wave of nauseousness. Al-Dosari did not know or recognize the man, but his well-honed feral instincts named him instantly. *The Infidel's Devil.*

The muscular man in a dark-blue polo and tan tactical pants hit the ground and placed his carbine at port arms. A second, similarly armed and garbed man fell in on his heels. They turned toward the concrete barriers and made for them.

Lieutenant Glen Nichols watched the two men jogging toward him. His eyes shifted to the US Marines pouring onto the ground from the Osprey. If there was a gunfight, the Raiders tilted the balance of firepower heavily in favor of law enforcement. The CHP SWAT commander met the two arriving men—one spoke.

"I'm McEwan, this is Morton. Who's Nichols?"

"That would be me." Nichols acknowledged. "I'm damn glad to have the backup. I don't have a warm and fuzzy feeling about this."

Sensing the murdering terrorist's presence, McEwan nodded solemnly, feeling the tension minus the apprehension.

ꕥ

Al-Dosari continued inching forward. As a police officer questioned the driver of the car in front of him, his archenemy reached the barricades. *The Infidel's Devil is almost close enough to touch!* Struggling to dial his cell phone, al-Dosari's anxiety shot to a fever pitch. "Brother Hamza, you are a great warrior! I will join all of you soon in paradise. Yes! You must proceed immediately! Allahu Akbar!"

"Allahu Akbar!" Hamza Omar abū-Ibrahim answered. "We shall rejoice with Yousef in paradise and together await the Sword of Islam!" He ended the call with, "There is no God but Allah and Muhammed is his messenger."

Responding to their leader's prayers, the Islamists uttered the same shahadah, or Muslim statement of faith, while chambering rounds in their AK-47s. The jihadi driving allowed space to open between the van and a semitrailer.

Abū-Ibrahim commenced their mission with a single word: "Now."

Opening the van's rear cargo door, one of the men slipped out onto the freeway.

An instantaneous cacophony of car, truck and air horns erupted in the air. Abandoning their vehicles, motorists scattered in all directions.

Forcefully cranking the van's steering wheel hard right, the driver goosed the accelerator and jerked hesitantly around the semitrailer, then recentered the wheels. As he mashed the gas pedal to the floor, the van shot forward at an alarming speed.

From his position above, the CHP airship pilot caught the rush of motorists on foot and the movement of the van. "San Ardo roadblock! A white van is hauling ass toward you on the southbound shoulder!"

AK-47s disgorged deadly lead into ensnared vehicles and their cargos, precious or not.

Taking time to separate targets from innocent motorists, the police officers and Marines returned fire.

Gunfire and frenzied calls of "Shots fired!" intermingled with "Officer needs assistance!" seared McEwan's ears. Seeking a target, he scanned the freeway. Responding to a moving vehicle on his left, he zeroed in on a white van. *There, one leaning from the right front window, another standing through the sunroof, both engaging.*

Before McEwan could press the trigger, the head of the terrorist popping up through the roof exploded with red puffs and brain chunks. The van swallowed the body. He pivoted to the jihadi in the passenger seat just as a bevy of bullets ripped the terrorist to shreds. The corpse flapped out the window, his white shirt a flag of surrender. The van continued its erratic charge. Converging rounds caught its driver, who released the wheel in a futile attempt to stop the bullets from disintegrating his face. Driverless, the van careened wildly, crashing into and bouncing off a truck before rolling over in a ditch.

The disciplined Marines and officers silenced their weapons.

Detecting reports from a single AK-47, McEwan focused on radio transmissions.

"We've still got one! Running toward the northbound lanes!"

Pivoting, McEwan chased the terrorist sprinting toward the embankment. Corralled by a fence, the killer threw down his fully expended AK-47. He whipped out a pistol and aimed it at McEwan.

Having an open field of fire, McEwan calmly took bead on the man, clearly not al-Dosari. McEwan put two into the man's chest and one into his head, driving him backward until he snagged the fence. Hanging suspended, the corpse became a scarecrow, head dangling off to one side.

As suddenly as it began, the gun battle was over.

"We're code 4," Nichols transmitted urgently, "I've got multiple officers and civilians down at San Ardo. I need ambulances and Medevac now!"

McEwan hustled over to the fence line, where a mix of SWAT officers and Marines parted to let him through. Confirming the scarecrow he'd deposited on the metal fence wasn't al-Dosari, he turned and trotted to the smoking van lodged at the base of a gulley, teetering on its roof, wheels whining at high speed.

SWAT officers positioned in protective stances provided cover for an officer reaching in to turn off the engine.

"Watch out!" McEwan warned. "It might be booby-trapped."

Moving as one, the officers backed away.

Morton, biosensor in hand, shook his head from side to side—no smallpox present.

McEwan took a good look at the carnage wreaked by the jihadists. Numerous motorists were down. He spied an officer holding a bleeding hand in the air while staunching the blood spurting from a motorist's leg with his good hand. A paramedic rushed up to assist.

Nichols collared an officer. "Get on the PA system and order everyone back into their vehicles. Tell them to stay inside with their hands in plain sight. Once we clear each vehicle, roll it through the roadblock."

McEwan spoke. "How many do we have total, Lieutenant?"

"Four, including the one you dropped."

McEwan walked over to the three bodies and studied each face. He recognized abū-Ibrahim and the last two members of the San Jose cell, but one face was noticeably absent. Suppressing his anger, he joined Nichols and Morton, who was handing the SWAT commander a stack of al-Dosari's alias "Ricardo San Felipe" passport photos.

"Lieutenant, make sure your officers search every vehicle for this man. Be careful. He *will* kill your officers given the slightest chance."

Nichols issued orders briskly. "Uniformed officers, fall in behind SWAT and check all vehicles carefully for this man. Move!"

McEwan stepped aside, sifting and fusing all the facts and evidence. *Yousef, decoy. Harris, transport. Seattle, misdirection. Morgan Hill shootout, the Cessna, and here—all diversions. We got Abassi and the smallpox.*

Morton and Cartwright approached.

Sticking his finger straight up in the air, McEwan signaled he needed a minute. *Body count, eight. Al-Dosari's the only one left. What's his backup plan? Escape or attack?*

McEwan looked up. "Al-Dosari's burned his San Jose cell in three diversionary attacks. He knows we've found the ranger in Montana. He's listening to the radio, so he knows we've locked down the peninsula. But he doesn't know we've disrupted the attack on Pebble Beach and seized his smallpox from the Bentley."

Convinced McEwan was dissecting and diagramming al-Dosari's master plan, his lieutenants listened intently.

"Sometime in the next few hours, al-Dosari will learn we've prevented the attack. How will he react? He'll be pissed, but he won't panic. He didn't sacrifice his men just to tuck tail and run for the hills. He's too crafty not to have devised backup getaway and attack strategies."

McEwan's eyes narrowed, visualizing the plan from al-Dosari's perspective. His eyes widened as he spoke. "I ordered my warriors to engage at Morgan Hill as a diversion; the same thing with the Cessna. But I have to get out somehow."

McEwan switched back to his own viewpoint. "San Ardo wasn't a diversion—it was *cover*. Al-Dosari was here. He ordered the attack and used the shoot-out to sneak through the roadblock. There *is* another car, and our boy's driving it. More roadblocks won't do us any good; too many ways now to go around them and we don't know what he's driving. But where's he heading?"

Neither man answered.

"Al-Dosari's vulnerability is his belief he's smarter than we are, that he's duped us by deliberately leaving the gate open to the east. He thinks we'll chase him. We won't. He's heading south, and so are we."

McEwan's analysis and strategy validated for Morton and Cartwright that they were working with America's finest counterterrorism operative.

Shifting gears, McEwan gave the two men new orders. "Tim, have these officers review their cruiser videos to see if we can ID what he's driving. Then give Ted a heads-up. Jason, beat feet back to Monterey and collect the rest of the Raiders. I'll notify you later where to link up."

As his two lieutenants left, McEwan replayed the events of the last week, searching for opportunities lost or mishandled. Finding none, he realized he hadn't botched bagging al-Dosari—he'd been playing the terrorist's game.

But now al-Dosari would play his.

The Sword's disciples had attacked as ordered, creating his opportunity to wriggle through the police roadblock. As anticipated, when the shoot-out began, frantic officers searching for shooters waved cars containing scared, harmless people through the barricades to get them out of harm's way. One such driver was a modestly dressed Hispanic man wearing a black cowboy hat.

Al-Dosari released several raucous laughs, followed by celebratory wails. *Soon my video will tell the world of my great triumph over the infidels! The Almighty's Sword of Islam faced down and outfoxed the Infidel's Devil!*

No longer able to restrain himself, al-Dosari shouted at the top of his lungs, "Bin Laden will be a footnote on the ash heap of history! It is *I* who will forever be anointed as Islam's true savior!"

Basking in his glory for a few miles, al-Dosari relished the sweet taste of victory. Then he forced himself to address his next challenge: survival. Journeying on, he expected his clever subterfuges to fool his adversaries.

Focused on the future, the Sword of Islam was unaware his scheme had been unmasked and was in the process of being crushed. His ignorance was self-inflicted. Fueled by arrogance, al-Dosari failed to employ the simplest form of intelligence freely available to him.

The car radio.

CHAPTER SIXTY-EIGHT

MCEWAN, MORTON, AND SANCHEZ gathered with the president in the mahogany-paneled library at Casa Palmero. The case officer shared the contents of Abassi's note.

"Al-Dosari's plan was brilliant. He leveraged the mechanic by kidnapping his wife and two sons in Saudi Arabia. At the house in Carmel Valley, he gave Abassi an air conditioner filter contaminated with the freeze-dried smallpox. Al-Dosari ordered him to install it in the refrigerant line and turn on the AC just before you entered the car. The compressor would disburse particles into the compartment, infecting both you and the prince as you drove. Abassi would meet you at the Inn at Spanish Bay ballroom and have you drop the convertible top once you pulled the Bentley inside for the reception. All those present would be infected by inhaling floating particles from the car, the room ventilation system, or taking selfies and shaking hands. You're well aware of the chain of events had he succeeded, with America's leaders and other attendees returning home, including the Saudi prince, whom he considers an apostate."

"I would've been responsible for killing my own people!" The wicked scheme stunned the president every bit as much as how narrowly they'd averted disaster.

Morton summarized the investigative angle, including previously undisclosed details.

"FBI recovered a one-inch-by-three-inch cardboard box marked 'AC filter' from the place Abassi said it would be—in his tool chest. We discovered how al-Dosari brought the smallpox into the US. Working back from the Glacier Park bear attack, RCMP found an abandoned rental car at a hiking trailhead in Waterton Park. In the trunk was an oxygen-breathing machine. RCMP forensics dismantled it and discovered a molded plastic compartment with sufficient space to accommodate the air filter box. They traced the rental to Ricardo San Felipe, the alias al-Dosari used at the Calgary airport after arriving on a flight from Montreal. In Montreal, a Canadian Customs officer remembered al-Dosari because of the breathing machine, and facial-recognition software confirmed he entered there from Paris under an entirely different assumed name. Interpol reported he flew to Paris from Damascus using that same alias. While we've traced his steps to the US, and how he entered with the smallpox, we aren't confident that the contaminated AC filter is the only smallpox he has access to."

"What?" Englewood focused angrily on McEwan. "He might have more?"

"Yes, sir, it's possible. Until I have him in my hands, I can't be sure."

Englewood shot back, "I can't even tell the American people where you think he's heading, much less guarantee there won't be another attack."

"That's right," McEwan acknowledged. "Bodycam and cruiser video at San Ardo was of no use. It was taken from bad angles or too distorted from the frenzy of the skirmish. So we have no vehicle and no al-Dosari. But he was there—I'm certain of it."

Englewood's voice was acerbic. "Wonderful. I'm about to break the news that al-Dosari came here to assassinate America's political leaders, kill all of our citizens with a bioweapon, and he's responsible for murdering scores of innocent civilians and police officers. Worse, he's on the loose and still plans on infecting us."

"Correct on all counts. We want you to announce we have no clue where he's heading—a misdirection on our part. We don't have a vehicle, but logically, he's heading south. We're going to control his movements and direction of travel by releasing information selectively to the public to convince him to abandon his backup attack. He'll be left with one choice—escape. We're going to get out ahead of him and wait for him to fall into our trap." McEwan spent the next several minutes detailing how he intended to ensnare al-Dosari.

The president sighed. "I suppose you two support his approach?"

Morton said, "Unequivocally and enthusiastically."

"Unreservedly," Sanchez added. "I acknowledge that on its face McEwan's proposal is fraught with peril. If you approve his plan, there's a slight chance al-Dosari might slip through our hands again and launch his attack. But we don't intend to let that happen."

"I know where we'd be right now if I'd listened to the CIA and FBI. America would be in serious jeopardy and I'd be on death's doorstep."

Left unsaid was one remarkable fact supporting Englewood's assumption: those experts, with all of their resources, failed to decipher the threat; yet in mere weeks, McEwan alone unraveled the plot that al-Dosari took years to perfect. Neither the DNI nor the president mentioned the other factor they could not control or ignore. If Englewood rejected McEwan's plan, he'd go after the terrorist anyway—it was clear he smelled blood and would not be denied.

"We're wasting time here, sir." Impatience bled through each of Kyle McEwan's words.

Englewood knew the extreme stress he was experiencing. It had to be substantially worse for McEwan, forced to battle both the terrorist and others in his own government in a zero-fail mission. A less resolute man would throw up his arms in defeat and walk away. Yet, here McEwan was, steadfastly looking for approval to destroy al-Dosari once and for all. Without a scintilla of doubt, he knew McEwan would. His eyes landed on the case officer, who stared back expectantly.

"Finish it, McEwan."

McEwan and Morton watched the president's national address before boarding the DHS jet for their trip south. Englewood announced the foiled attack, named al-Dosari as the mastermind, and stated the diversions by his henchmen were to facilitate his escape. The president emphasized law enforcement had no clue as to the terrorist's whereabouts or the vehicle he was driving. As such, he was still free to attack America.

While waiting in the departure queue, McEwan's cell phone vibrated. "Yes, Danni."

"NSA advised threats have evaporated, but chatter's off the scale, mostly speculation about who the president will hit in retaliation. Englewood ordered our UN ambassador to inform the Security Council that our recovery of the bioweapon leads us to believe there's no threat originating from the US. Before the president halted all international flights, terror suspects of every stripe jammed the airports. So far, TSA has had encounters with 132 persons on the terrorist watch list."

Predictably, the intensity of the al-Dosari search produced a bonanza: flushing out invisible terrorists who eagerly paid top dollar for seats on flights to anywhere outside the US. As embedded sleeper agents provided the required personal identification and itinerary information, the airlines forwarded it electronically to the FBI Terrorist Screening Center. There it was compared to the "watch list" of suspected terrorists—including the biometrics database of facial images, palm and fingerprints, iris patterns, and DNA samples. When the unsuspecting travelers checked in for flights, law enforcement whisked them away.

Sanchez started to say something else, but stopped. "That's it. It's all on you now." She disconnected the call without further comment.

Morton's phone rang: Paul Infante. He hit the Speaker button.

"We've got the Ford Escape that Harris rented in Portland. A security guard noticed it parked overnight in a shopping center garage off I-880 in San Jose."

"Anything worthwhile from security cameras?"

"Al-Dosari and Harris switched to a bronze metallic 1998 Chevrolet Malibu registered to Saif Al-Rimi of Mountain View. I picked him up. He claims Hamza Omar abū-Ibrahim borrowed his car for a week to loan to visiting relatives. I know it seems odd someone would do this, but I'm hearing abū-Ibrahim and his cronies intimidate the hell out of the mosque worshipers and regularly strong-arm them. They've been told the crew is dead, so they're cooperating. I put the fear of Allah in Al-Rimi myself—he wasn't bullshitting. We rechecked cruiser video at San Ardo—the bronze Malibu made it through during the gunfight but the driver wasn't recognizable. Too blurry."

"Great work, Paul. We can't risk al-Dosari learning we've connected him to the Malibu or he'll kill again just to get another car then go dark on us. The vehicle's too old to have OnStar so we can't pinpoint or track it. Don't issue a Blue Alert for the police killings. Instead, issue a BOLO for law enforcement eyes only to locate the Malibu and surveil it. State clearly it's a national security matter and not to be released to the public."

CHAPTER SIXTY-NINE

AFTER CLEARING THE SAN Ardo roadblock, the Sword of Islam was totally alone. To bring him to this point, he had sacrificed many great warriors. The costs were necessary and worthy yet unsettling, especially his beloved brother, Yousef.

Solitude began suffocating al-Dosari. Passing through Los Angeles, he turned on the car's radio. Trying to push aside the pain of losing his brother, he flipped from one demonic music station to another until he found a news conference. He received a devastating psychological blow: his attack on the president and governors had failed!

Al-Dosari almost lost control of the car when the American president identified him as the mastermind. *How long has the Infidel's Devil tracked me? Weeks? Months? Who is this devil?*

The all-too-real chance of capture set off full-blown panic, spinning his mind at a dizzying pace. Without answers, al-Dosari's fear escalated. Fighting to control his bowels, pains stabbed his abdomen. Fifteen long minutes passed before al-Dosari was calm enough for rational thought. He had planned to control the time and location of his death struggle with Islam's mortal enemy, the Infidel's Devil. The repeated untangling of al-Dosari's plan increased the likelihood their battle would occur at the discretion of his nemesis, not his own. His only option was to carry out Yousef's contingency plan—recalling the details he believed it would still work. The city of Phoenix was one bird that would not rise from the ashes. Then he'd finish it by killing his adversary.

Al-Dosari telephoned Yousef's collaborator in Tijuana, El Capitan Ruben García of the Mexican Federal Police. Exchanging coded phrases, the men reached an agreement. For a second fee of $50,000, García would meet him at the San Ysidro border crossing when summoned by al-Dosari and whisk him through the checkpoint.

McEwan stared unbelievingly at Morton. "Vince Hanratty did what?"

"He screwed us royally. Despite the warning in the BOLO about the Malibu being a closely held national security matter for law enforcement eyes only, he told the San Diego media about the vehicle and that it was connected to al-Dosari, then took it upon himself to release a Blue Alert. He claims he never saw the bulletin. Now the public knows al-Dosari is in that Malibu, which means he knows we've ID'd his car."

McEwan exploded. "That asshole! Hanratty has earned a place of honor on my shit list, one notch below al-Dosari."

Morton dialed a number to deal with this new development.

As al-Dosari reached San Diego's northern suburbs, an overhead electronic message board caught his eye: "Blue Alert LIC# X325G39 (CA) Bronze 1998 Chevrolet Malibu. Suspect armed and dangerous. Call FBI, *CHP or 911 immediately."

Panicked, the terror mastermind turned up the radio volume and received another jolt.

"Federal law enforcement sources have confirmed the Malibu in the Blue Alert is connected to al-Dosari and the attempted terror attack in the Monterey Peninsula and shootouts on the 101 …"

Al-Dosari, his mouth parching into desert, had a difficult time processing what he heard. *How did they learn I am in this automobile?* Changing lanes immediately, he exited onto Interstate 8, taking the eastbound ramp away from San Diego.

He telephoned El Capitan García of the Mexican Federal Police again and learned that crossing at any official port of entry was now impossible.

García suggested that he find a sparsely populated area a few miles from the border and escape on foot. Once safely across the border, he would call García with GPS coordinates and be picked up.

Struggling to build his new plan on the fly, the Sword of Islam frantically checked the mirrors and roadways for police. Triaging his problems, he realized his capture was a foregone conclusion if he did not replace the Malibu immediately.

Anxious, al-Dosari glanced to his left. A police officer on a motorcycle was two cars ahead of him and two lanes over. Fighting to maintain his gaze straight ahead, al-Dosari clutched the wheel tightly. Moving one lane left, he studied the scene behind him in his rearview mirror. *Only one choice.*

Al-Dosari pulled even with the motorcycle. When the officer's eyes met his, al-Dosari jerked his steering wheel hard to the left then back to center, smacking the motorcycle. Both man and machine ricocheted into another car, triggering a chain reaction of accidents.

Regaining control of the fishtailing Malibu, a glimpse into his rearview mirror showed vehicles battering one another. The Sword of Islam mashed the accelerator pedal flat against the floor. Shooting forward, the Malibu left a debris field and plumes of billowing smoke in its wake.

CHAPTER SEVENTY

WELL AWARE OF THE implication of killing an American policeman, al-Dosari began an urgent search for another vehicle. Spotting a towering Walmart sign beside the freeway, he decided to make the switch there. Maneuvering carefully into the right lane, he rolled down the off-ramp at the Los Coches Road-Lakeside exit. Turning right, he drove to the top of a hillcrest and entered the Walmart parking lot. He scanned the rows of cars for a suitable mark, a nondescript car with an owner who would not be missed. Turning into the last row, he studied a lone man strolling up to an older-model beige pickup truck with landscape tools in the rear bed. *Perfect.*

Al-Dosari rolled down his window and eased to a halt. "Señor, can you assist me with directions?"

"Sí," the man replied and continued stuffing his bags into the truck cab.

Al-Dosari pulled the Malibu into the empty space beside the pickup. Grabbing the keys from the ignition, he snared a map off the seat and put on his black cowboy hat. Climbing out, he thoroughly scanned the area, using the brim of his hat to obscure his eyes. Satisfied no one was paying attention to either of them, he stepped closer to the truck. Waving his map at the Good Samaritan with one hand, he reached into his rear waistband with the other and extracted a silenced .22 caliber pistol. Without hesitation, he fired two shots in rapid succession through the map into the man's brain. The man hit the pavement, blood oozing from a hole that only an instant before was his left eye. Checking the area, he assessed his crime was unwitnessed.

Al-Dosari tucked the pistol back into his waistband and dug the Malibu keys out of his pocket. Taking advantage of another lull, he opened the trunk. Grabbing the dead man by the collar of his shirt and belt, he hoisted the body up into the trunk in one fell swoop. Leaning over, he searched every pocket for a wallet. Finding none, he closed the lid and turned to inspect the truck's cab. Scanning the area again, his pulse jumped. At the opposite end of the lot, he saw the red and blue light bar of a police cruiser.

Collecting his belongings from the sedan, al-Dosari tossed them onto the truck's bench seat. Exchanging his black hat for the man's straw hat and sunglasses, he started the engine. Driving slowly toward the exit farthest from the police car, he reached the bottom of the hill. Entering the Interstate 8 East ramp, he blended back into traffic.

Sergeant Remy Preneau of the El Cajon CHP station spent his entire day, including four hours of overtime, working one traffic accident after another. Starting with a jackknifed eighteen-wheeler after breakfast, he'd just finished his last call. Entering the Lakeside Walmart parking lot, he listened as the dispatcher sent other units to investigate a multi-vehicle pileup with injuries between the eastbound I-8/Mollison Avenue exit and the Danielle Van Dam Second Street Bridge.

The Walmart was one of Preneau's regular roosts to escape the maze of freeways and roads of eastern San Diego County. Steering his black-and-white into a space overlooking the interchange, he positioned his cruiser to allow a quick response if he was needed to assist with the accident, or respond to the urgent BOLO on the terrorist. Glancing down at his center console, his eyes lingered on the bulletin.

Preneau immersed himself with a stack of reports from his briefcase. He ceased writing to listen to the update on the I-8 pileup—it involved a San Diego County Sheriff's motor officer. His paperwork would wait; he'd head to the scene now. Driving down the row, he stopped and tapped his horn at a blue Honda Element pulling out of a space without looking. The twenty-year CHP veteran felt something wasn't right with the Honda. Suddenly, it registered. It wasn't the Honda. Nosed up to the now-empty space was a bronze Chevrolet Malibu. Preneau compared its plate to the one in the BOLO.

A perfect match.

CHAPTER SEVENTY-ONE

MCEWAN STOOD QUIETLY OUTSIDE the Border Patrol San Diego Sector Headquarters pondering his next move. He'd intended all along to cut Morton loose, not just to protect his career, but to keep Vince Hanratty and the FBI at bay, thus giving him a clear shot at bagging the terrorist. Because his well-honed instincts told him the manhunt was on the verge of producing the desired results, it was time to change strategy for the final stretch.

"Tim, my job is bringing down al-Dosari. I need somebody with the right skills coordinating the dragnet for me. If I hand this job off to the wrong man, he could dick things up big-time. Worst case, al-Dosari gets off scot-free—"

"Say no more, Kyle. I get why you tapped me for this operation, so I'll take two concerns off your plate, logistics and me. Our judicial system isn't designed to handle someone whose actions are so manifestly evil they surpass normal criminal behavior. If monsters like al-Dosari didn't exist, we wouldn't need people like you, and I say that with the utmost respect. I have no beef sparing the taxpayers the cost and aggravation of a public trial."

Morton's phone rang; he looked at the screen, answered, and listened. "That's the best news I've heard in days."

"That was Ted Beacham." Morton beamed broadly. "The president ordered the bureau to back off, way off, and underscored that you have the reins. Our friend Hanratty has been relieved of his duties and Ted's just arrived to spearhead FBI efforts."

McEwan's face brightened. One less impediment to worry about, plus full FBI cooperation meant he could plot his collision course with al-Dosari with Morton at his side. "Tim, looks like you'll be in the thick of things after all."

"I was hoping you'd reconsider without me having to ask."

"Okay, square Ted away on the plan to deploy our assets. Contact Jason and direct MARSOC to NAF El Centro."

McEwan went inside the building and veered toward a wall map. Studying it, he knew al-Dosari was out there, but the knot in his stomach screamed he was overlooking something.

"Kyle!" Morton blurted. "We found him!"

McEwan cut around chairs and whipped past agents backslapping and giving one another high fives.

"He's been in Lakeside, twenty miles east of San Diego. CHP found the bronze Malibu in a Walmart parking lot off I-8, with fresh damage to its left front quarter panel and driver's door. CHP popped the trunk and found a deceased male shot twice in the left eye. The hood was still hot, and they found two .22 caliber casings on the ground!"

McEwan acknowledged that critical detail. "We didn't recover the .22 caliber pistol used to kill Harris and the al Shammaris in Carmel Valley. This proves al-Dosari was in that house and he used the same pistol to kill this man."

"The victim is a Mexican national named Javier Mendoza, age thirty-seven. He's a Tecate native with a work visa through a local landscaper. The victim forgot his wallet at the Walmart register when he checked out—they were holding it for him because he's there every day. Unfortunately, the security cameras didn't capture the shooting, but we do know al-Dosari's driving Mendoza's work truck, a beige 2006 Ford F250, California 895DXM. An updated BOLO is out for the truck."

"Tim, are we 100 percent sure it's him?" McEwan circled back. "Why the fresh damage?"

"CHP says it's *abso-fucking-lutely* our boy, and he's alone. Other cameras caught a man wearing a straw hat and sunglasses driving the truck down an access lane back onto I-8 eastbound. The highway patrolman says it's him, all right. Unfortunately, the damage is from al-Dosari deliberately swerving the Malibu into a sheriff's motor unit on I-8 in El Cajon, killing the deputy and causing chain-reaction accidents involving a dozen vehicles. He jumped off at Lakeside, shot Mendoza, and took his truck. I'd say we're no more than an hour behind him, possibly less."

"That prick Hanratty has blood on his hands! I told you al-Dosari would kill if he learned we were onto the car! We've got to find him before he kills again. Why is he heading east away from the border? If I'm al-Dosari, I'd go south, as fast as I can to Mexico. Unless it's not part of my plan. The infidels got my brother, but do they know about my second tunnel?"

McEwan rubbed his temples, bouncing back and forth between his thoughts and placing himself in al-Dosari's shoes. He answered his own questions aloud, from al-Dosari's perspective. "Why am I heading toward Calexico? Because that's where I want to confront my brother's killer? Tempting, but no. I'm saving that for later when I'm not running. Because I *must* go there. What do I need? Not a new set of IDs. I can use a mail drop for that. I'm going there because Yousef wasn't simply a decoy. He left something there, something I must have to complete my mission."

Morton whistled. "You're right!"

McEwan resumed his own persona. "He can't attack until he gets his hands on more smallpox, stashed by Yousef. We must grab it before he does. Have Bennie Espinoza tear apart every square inch of that rubble tunnel all the way to the intersection with the main tunnel. Have him break through to the other side if he has to. Have SRT sit on the rubble tunnel in case he gets past us and heads for it. I'm off to NAF El Centro. Fill Ted in on everything, then find me."

Outside, an agent summoned McEwan over to a Ford Expedition. Lights flashing and siren wailing, they sped off and arrived shortly at the

Brown Field compound housing CBP's Air Ops helicopters. Gunning the engine, the agent maneuvered around a metal Quonset hut and shot toward the complex's far corner, skidding to a stop near a helicopter, rotors spinning. McEwan hopped from the SUV, sprinted across the hardstand, and hoisted himself inside.

The Air Interdiction Agent pilot mouthed, "Ready?"

Buckling in, McEwan put on headphones and plugged into the radio net. The helicopter lifted off the landing platform. Below them, a pilot decked out in sunglasses and tan flight suit gassed up another helicopter from a fuel truck. He wore a badge and dark-brown shoulder holster with semiautomatic pistol strapped across his torso. Looking up at McEwan, the pilot cocked his right thumb and forefinger like a pistol and pressed an imaginary trigger.

McEwan responded silently to the gesture. *Count on it.*

CHAPTER SEVENTY-TWO

FORTY-TWO MILES EAST OF San Diego on Interstate 8, al-Dosari was contemplating where he could find a place to hide and rest, then make his move on foot after nightfall. Al-Dosari heard another news bulletin and turned up the radio volume.

"CHP and the Border Patrol are searching all vehicles on I-8 at the checkpoint east of Pine Valley, and traffic is at a standstill." The announcer reported that a hit-and-run pileup in El Cajon and a shooting at the Lakeside Walmart were the reasons behind the vehicle searches.

Although the story did not mention him, al-Dosari knew he was their target. Steering with one hand and checking the map with the other, he found the checkpoint between Exit 47 and the Buckman Springs Road interchange. He was not going to reach Ocotillo on the other side of the checkpoint. His only option was to exit at the next interchange. Ignoring the stabbing pains in his abdomen, he drove on.

The traffic in front of al-Dosari slowed to a crawl about the same time he reached Exit 45/Pine Valley. Eyes darting warily, he veered off the ramp. At the end, he turned left and drove until he reached a Super Mercado parking lot. He wedged the pickup between a BMW and Volvo.

Blocked from view by an oversized burgundy and gray motor home, al-Dosari finally dared to exhale, more grateful for arriving someplace where he could void his bowels than for successfully averting capture. Rushing inside the grocery store, he saw the restroom sign hanging from the ceiling and beelined straight to the men's room.

A few minutes later, a much more composed man exited the supermarket and strolled casually toward the truck. Turning on the radio again, al-Dosari learned that nearby interstate and secondary roads were becoming increasingly clogged with vehicles. He considered his escape on foot. Studying his handheld GPS unit, he calculated the hike. It would take at least sixteen hours walking in a straight line over flat terrain from his current location. He recalculated, accounting for rugged terrain. Unacceptable; an entire day and night of trekking. Not only did he not have the time, but as he learned entering America, there were many hazards not depicted on maps. Then there was the Border Patrol. His only alternative was getting closer to the border and dashing across.

Glancing around, al-Dosari fixated on an elderly woman pushing a cart through the doors of the supermarket. Folding his map, he watched the woman through a mirror as she reached a nearby sedan. She opened the car's trunk and began transferring bags of groceries from her cart. Stepping from the truck, doing his best to appear friendly and nonthreatening, he said, "Howdy, ma'am. Those bags look mighty heavy. Allow me to help you."

"Why, thank you." She smiled at the handsome, clean-cut, modestly dressed man.

Al-Dosari picked up the grocery bags, placing them carefully into the trunk. Eyes shielded by sunglasses, he scanned the lot. *Too many people.*

The woman reached into her purse. "Please let me give you a tip."

"That is not necessary. While I need work, I only take fair wages for my labor. Never for helping someone. Would you know if the supermarket is hiring?" He glanced over his shoulder. *Still too many eyes.*

"I doubt it. It's a small family operation. What kind of work do you do?"

"I am a landscaper." Feigning pride in the profession, he pointed to the magnetic sign on the truck's door.

The old lady seemed doubtful. "You appear much more polished than the average yardman, and you aren't dressed for yard work."

Thinking quickly on his feet, the terrorist expanded his bogus cover story. "I immigrated legally to America two months ago. I am an accountant by trade. I had a job interview today but discovered I must reside in America for three years before taking the license examination."

Extremely skilled at reading people, al-Dosari discerned the subtle softening around the woman's eyes; she was buying his bogus explanation. Catering to her sympathetic ear, the terrorist continued his sad story. "One week ago, my employer's landscaping business went bankrupt. He let all of us go without notice and refused to pay our final wages. He was a drinker, gambler, and wife beater, something I did not know when he employed me. I struggle to eat and cannot send money home to my wife and six children. I wear my finest clothing to find work."

The woman allowed her naive beliefs to overwhelm her judgment. "I've gotten behind on a few things since my husband passed. The garage needs rearranging, and my car needs cleaning. If this interests you, I could pay a little. I'm on a fixed income, you see."

"I can do those chores—please remember I only accept fair wages." Behind the terrorist's dark glasses, predatory green eyes evaluated his prey.

The woman sealed her fate. "Follow me home to Boulevard. It's twenty minutes south of here. I will show you the garage, and you can get to work."

Two hours later, stomach full, al-Dosari enjoyed the comfort of the air-conditioned house off Tierra del Sol Road, a sparsely populated area southwest of Boulevard. His benefactress, neatly laid out on her bed, neck snapped shortly after their arrival, appeared to be napping. Safely hidden in the garage, the beige pickup truck would not betray him. Her car remained parked in the driveway, though he would not need it.

During his drive from the Monterey Peninsula, al-Dosari had torn up his Ricardo San Felipe identity cards, discarding the pieces out of the window until they were all gone. Never relying on a single plan to carry him through, al-Dosari had charged his San Jose disciples with preparing him for the possibility he might have to travel on foot. They listened well, proudly presenting him with a hiking pack containing the items he required: an internal hydration system full of water, six extra bottles of water, energy bars, a digital camera, a 9 mm Glock pistol, two loaded spare magazines, an extra box of .22 caliber ammunition, a Casio G-Shock watch, fixed blade knife, burner phone, and protective clothing. Plus the envelope. Remembering the fate of his pack in Glacier National Park, al-Dosari would tuck away his new identity documents on his body.

Al-Dosari opened the envelope and became an author researching migrant farm workers forced to enter the US illegally to support families. He examined business cards identifying him as a freelance writer from Mexico City. If stopped by authorities before reaching his destination, his authentic documents along with his plausible cover story and verbal skills should be enough to bluff his way out of any situation. If not, he would kill as necessary. Satisfied all was in order, Ali bin al-Dosari, the Sword of Islam, leaned back in the recliner. Setting his wristwatch alarm, he closed his eyes.

When darkness came, "Miguel Machado" would head for the border, a short three miles away.

Tim Morton's voice entered McEwan's ears.

"Kyle, once again, you nailed it. Bennie went underground back to where the two tunnels intersected. He found a laptop battery hidden inside a slit carved into the wall. It was behind a board with the Mexican evil eye symbol etched on its face. The battery contains nearly a pound of freeze-dried smallpox. We've eliminated his plan B."

Elation washed over McEwan, but it was too early to pop the cork on the champagne. "Al-Dosari's a master of deception. He's survived too long to be here without an escape plan. Stay on it." He signed off.

Hovering above the Border Patrol checkpoint on I-8 at Pine Valley, McEwan contemplated his adversary's next several moves. Performing another gut check, the plan came into sharp focus. Al-Dosari never intended to access the smallpox via the Calexico rubble pile tunnel, and he wasn't snaking his way through the traffic below either. Al-Dosari planned from the start to hightail it across the border and access the smallpox from Mexicali, regrouping there for a future attack. With all checkpoints snapping shut, he had only one choice. McEwan hit the Transmit button and shared his theory with Morton.

"He's going for the border via the backcountry—at dusk. Where are we on assets?"

"We've put big-time boots on the ground until our boy's bagged and tagged. Chief Patrol Agents have doubled stationary units up and down the line and tripled roving patrols on horseback, dirt bikes, ATVs, and in four-wheel drives. They'll respond to sensor activations and interdict border crossers in both directions in case someone's coming across to help him. We're beefing up the Boulevard and Campo stations with extra bodies, and we've deployed every handheld and vehicle-mounted thermal image unit we own." Morton went silent for a moment.

"Things are picking up substantially heading toward sundown. Air Ops has a dozen aircraft up along with two Predator B drones. Coast Guard and Navy are saturating the water along Border Field State Park and Imperial Beach on the off chance he doubles back and has a boat stashed somewhere. BORTAC is staged at San Ysidro, Otay Mesa, Tecate, and Brown Field. Ted has two SWAT teams on standby to deal with any more diversionary attacks, and one hundred JTTF multiagency interview teams to run down leads. The word is out that we've closed all north and southbound crossings, so much of the traffic has turned away from the border."

"Tim, you've done an outstanding job. Al-Dosari is unpredictable and ruthless. He's already killed numerous times. He'll have no problem killing anyone who gets between him and freedom."

"I'll reinforce it," Morton answered firmly. "This just in: Jason and crew are ten minutes out."

"It's time to flush out al-Dosari and cage him in. Lock down the border from the Pacific to Arizona."

CHAPTER SEVENTY-THREE

A RESTLESS MCEWAN WAITED FOR Jason Cartwright and his MARSOC Raiders outside the Tactical Operations Center at NAF El Centro. At last his ears detected the sounds of approaching rotary aircraft. He peered skyward; three tiny flying insects became MH-22 Ospreys and landed. As McEwan jogged toward the aircraft, Cartwright and Captain Hubie Lopez met him halfway.

"Jason, what took so long?"

"Pea soup up in Monterey. But have no fear! The Leathernecks are here!"

The Marine commander's appearance boosted McEwan's energy level. The distinctive chuff, chuff, chuff of an arriving UH-60 caused them to look up. A shiny black DHS Black Hawk landed, disgorging a tactically-kitted Tim Morton. McEwan motioned to join them inside the hangar.

"Men, we've got to put a move on. He's here and the clock's ticking."

McEwan's number 2 confirmed. "We're smack-dab on top of him. I just got off the phone with the San Diego County Sheriff. Some guy requested a welfare check on his widowed mother over in Boulevard. Her car was in the driveway, but when she didn't answer their knocks, deputies busted in and found her body. The pickup stolen by al-Dosari in Lakeside was in the garage, engine cold. They recovered a grocery receipt printed seven hours ago. Her house is south of Old Highway 80 and Campo Road/State Route 94. As the crow flies, it's about three miles from the border."

Hurrying over to a map overlaid with search quadrants, McEwan studied it briefly. "Our boy's definitely on foot. It's gutsy, considering we've flooded the border with assets. What about FLIR, Tim? Any use to us?"

"Negative. Any other night of the year a person heading south would stand out like a neon sign. Not tonight. Air Ops says our beefed-up presence is scaring all the northbound foot traffic back toward the border. They say it resembles a stampede in some areas. Both Sectors are advising there are hundreds of bodies generating thermal images. We'll check every one, but have to rely on the old-fashioned method of beating the bushes all the way down the line. Pick off those heading south and hope he's one of them."

"Blue force tracking will ID my people if things get sporty out there." Cartwright was referring to the military's GPS-enabled tracking system that identified friendly forces.

"Tim, can we determine the location of your personnel via their radios?" asked McEwan.

Morton replied, "Yes, but the sheer number of boots on the ground is making it difficult to manage that picture." He read a text message. "Twelve BORTAC trackers are here."

McEwan forged ahead. "He's going balls-to-the-wall for the border. We're going to push him back from it. Pair each tracker with a Marine Raider to double the number of teams on foot. I want to be noisy and everywhere." He paused to study the map again.

"Drop a team west on Tierra del Sol Road, another east on Jewel Valley Road. Put the rest of them on all trails in between the two roads. Have all non-foot patrols traverse side roads and paths. Bury the fence line road with mobile units to push him back into our net."

Cartwright followed behind McEwan's gestures, his yellow grease pencil marking the quadrangle on the overlays until the search patterns resembled a basket-weave lattice grille.

"We'll sweep all teams in a full pincer movement and pin him into this grid." McEwan used his index finger to jab a square just north of the border.

McEwan's tactics came into sharp focus for the MARSOC commander. They'd surround al-Dosari on all sides, eliminating every avenue of escape. Cartwright marked a large red X on the overlay—McEwan was driving the terrorist into a kill box. He stepped back approvingly.

"I'll have air ops light it up," Morton added.

"Tim, you'll command the ground search from your Black Hawk. Jason, you're with me—my helo. Hubie, you run the tracker teams. Put Duke Jess and the rest of your Raiders in the Ospreys. We'll use them if we run into any Mexican Army patrols, Federales, or cartel runners. Drive your people to the max."

Pausing for a second, McEwan framed his final point. "When we get him, he's *mine*. Your jobs are done. You'll round up your troops and go home. Let's roll."

Initially heading south by hugging the shoulder of a road, al-Dosari was compelled to move onto dirt trails due to increasing patrols. Evidence abounded that he was on a route regularly traveled by illegal immigrants. Underwear, food wrappers, plastic bags, bottles, shoes, backpacks, and an iPod all crunched beneath his feet within the first few minutes. As if the debris of American life was not enough, the presence of many illegal aliens making their way south hampered his progress greatly. It took time to avoid them, time he did not have.

Opening his final water bottle, al-Dosari took a long pull, draining the last drop. Tossing it over his shoulder stirred the memory of Devereaux performing the same act in Montana. The gruesome grizzly attack changed him forever, from terrified of nothing to fearing wild animals. He knew they lurked now, two- and four-legged coyotes alike, tracking him until they cornered him, then they would pounce. Transforming from stalker to stalked, having to search every shadow, every boulder and every bush slowed al-Dosari's advance even more.

A rustling noise startled al-Dosari, sending him scooting behind boulders and a thick stand of chaparral. Four men headed directly toward his hiding place. Al-Dosari eavesdropped, picking up bits and pieces of conversation. He learned La Migra was everywhere—in the skies, in trucks, on foot, on horses. One man claimed he'd made more than forty border crossings but had never seen so many agents. Agreeing, a second man proclaimed it a certainty they would be caught.

Barely two minutes after the men passed by, a loud roar ripped through the sky and the area ahead of him lit up as if daylight. He watched uniformed agents chase the men, who separated and scampered. As an agent stopped short of his hiding place, a powerful beam sweeping left to right illuminated a man being tackled and handcuffed. When the agent marched his captive to join the others, al-Dosari stole away.

There was no doubt that his odds of making it across the border were evaporating with each passing minute. Aircraft crisscrossing the skies with massive floodlights were lighting up the area brighter than the sun. The weary terrorist slipped the backpack off his shoulders and tossed it aside. Dropping to his knees, he belly-crawled a few feet to the edge of a crest. He raised his head and peeked down the hillside—the border fence! All he needed was a gap to squeeze through.

Ali bin al-Dosari, the Sword of Islam, had never been more exhausted in his life. In the hundreds of times he envisioned his final night in the land of the Great Satan, he never foresaw himself as he was: hunted.

CHAPTER SEVENTY-FOUR

McEWAN KNEW BEYOND ALL doubt al-Dosari was in close proximity, the stench of the murdering terrorist permeating everything. As his helicopter made another tight circle over the search zone, Morton called him over the airwaves.

"A tracker team just recovered a silenced .22 caliber pistol in an area called Maupin's T."

Cartwright tapped a large digit on a map and thrust it at McEwan.

McEwan's primal instincts took over. "Tim, close the pincer—all the way."

"Ten-four."

Tuning out the radio transmissions, McEwan turned toward Cartwright, his words cold and detached. "Jason, he's paying for everything he's done. He's all mine."

Cartwright interpreted McEwan's feral expression and guttural tone—only one hunter remained.

Slithering down the slope, al-Dosari confronted a berm and flat dirt road. He could wait no longer with the sweeping lights closing in by the inch behind him—he must escape now or be captured. Straining his ears, he caught the faintest rumbling of an engine, growing louder, coming at him. Struggling against his flight instinct, he remained still. The headlights of a truck came over a rise in the road, slowly pulling several rubber tires lashed together. A memory emerged: La Migra was "dragging the line", smoothing the dirt, allowing agents to chase footprints.

Totally exposed, al-Dosari lay motionless. The Border Patrol truck pulled so close he could almost touch it. An agent climbed down from the cab and nearly stepped on al-Dosari. Ignoring his immediate surroundings, the man peered intently at the fence through a night vision device.

In a single movement, al-Dosari sprang to his feet and cracked the back of the agent's head with his 9 mm pistol. The man collapsed to the ground, unconscious.

Staring ahead, al-Dosari evaluated the final obstacle between him and freedom. Feverishly scanning every inch of the steel landing mat fence, his eyes passed then returned to a section to his right—a part of the fence was peeled back, large enough for him to squeeze himself through.

Immersed in joy, al-Dosari failed to decode the escalating roar until it was too late. Suddenly blinded by daylight, a blasting gust of wind sprayed sand granules in his face. The desert under al-Dosari's feet shook with the intensity of an earthquake, slamming him violently onto his back. Commands split his eardrums. "You down there! Al-Dosari! This is the United States government. You are under arrest! Do not move!"

Immediately south of McEwan and Cartwright, millions of candlepower turned the black night into brilliant day. McEwan snarled and pointed downward, "Set me down there now!"

The pilot yanked and banked and headed for the spot. McEwan bailed out of the helicopter before it touched ground. Rolling in the dirt and bounding upright, he turned toward the lone figure.

"Al-Dosari!" Morton's voice boomed through the sky, "Stop or I'll shoot!"

Scrambling on all fours, the terrorist ignored the orders and onslaught on his nerve centers.

Banishing the noise and sounds, McEwan interpreted their effects silently. *Powerful engines … rotor wash … muzzle flashes … rounds punching the earth … sparks ricocheting off metal fence … gunfire ceasing.* McEwan sighted his foe's objective: a peeled-back landing mat fence panel. Breaking into a full sprint, he closed ground quickly.

Reaching the fence first, al-Dosari wiggled his way through the jagged section. Plunging several feet down a ridge, he tumbled to a stop and stared up at the helicopter. Shielded by the terrain, the searchlight could not find him. *It is not following—it has broken off the chase! I am free!*

Al-Dosari retched, then resting back on his heels, tilted his head skyward and screamed, "You have failed! The Sword defeated you!"

Running full bore, McEwan plunged his left foot into a hole in the fence and vaulted over the upper half of the old rusty landing mat. It crumbled beneath him and he landed with a thump. McEwan sprang to his feet, glancing everywhere.

A loud grunt and a sharp cry of pain to his rear distracted him. Looking over his shoulder, McEwan saw Cartwright had flattened the rusty fence panel by busting right through it.

Hearing the same sounds, al-Dosari spotted movement in the moonlit darkness. *The Infidel's Devil!* The thought of his archenemy propelled the Sword of Islam to his feet.

The black night turned to day as the helicopter lit up the sky again. McEwan took off after his adversary. Closing the distance with a powerful charge, he struck the terrorist between the shoulder blades. Both men lost their footing, rolling in different directions, al-Dosari face down in the sand, McEwan up against a boulder.

Both men sprang to their feet; al-Dosari launched a violent assault.

McEwan fended off blows, punches, and kicks, then counterattacked. Unfortunately for al-Dosari, the highly-trained case officer excelled at hand-to-hand combat. Equal parts mixed martial arts expert and street brawler, he lifted al-Dosari clean off his feet with a swift kick to the chin.

Backpedaling, al-Dosari snagged his heel on brush and plunged down a desert ravine.

McEwan pounced on the Sword and whipped his head repeatedly against the hard desert floor. McEwan kneed him in the solar plexus then attacked furiously with crushing blows to the face and body.

Al-Dosari quit fighting.

McEwan's peripheral vision caught Jason Cartwright dragging his left leg behind him. His kneecap badly gashed and partially exposed, the Marine aimed his sidearm at al-Dosari, ready to finish the job.

"Jason, I told you he's mine! Back off!" McEwan growled as a second man approached, cradling a semiautomatic rifle.

Morton stood beside Cartwright. "Kyle, do what needs to be done. We've got your six."

"I don't need or want backup. Your jobs are done. Now, I'm going to do mine."

The three men's radios crackled. "Attention, all units, return to base! Repeat, you are ordered to RTB immediately!"

"You guys get back across the border!" McEwan's look gave no room for debate. "Go! Now!"

Morton paused momentarily, then transmitted. "Ten-four. All units RTB."

Cartwright holstered his sidearm. Giving McEwan a two-finger salute, he leaned into Morton. Together the two men walked over to the gaping hole in the fence. Crossing back into the United States of America, they were met by several dozen Marine Raiders and Border Patrol agents.

"What are you people looking at?" Cartwright bellowed. "Get your asses in gear! Move!"

The injured Marine, his Raiders, and Morton clambered aboard their aircraft and the agents into their vehicles. The roar of engines, swirling clouds of dust, and fading floodlights marked a rapid departure by all.

They were alone.

McEwan looked down at the terrorist, silhouetted by the moonlight. "You ready for your day of atonement, asshole?"

Pulling a knife from his boot, al-Dosari lunged with lightning speed. Expertly sidestepping the terrorist, McEwan kicked the knife from his hand. Circling like a prizefighter, he goaded al-Dosari. "*That's* the famous sword of the Sword?" He laughed tauntingly. "That's the best you've got?"

Blind with rage, al-Dosari reached for the pistol tucked behind his back.

McEwan anticipated the move—his drawn Glock spit two rounds. One struck al-Dosari's gun hand, dislodging the pistol. The second shot disintegrated his shoulder socket on the opposite side.

Blood, tissue, and bone seeping from both wounds, al-Dosari let loose howling wails.

McEwan kicked away the pistol. "There's no paradise for cowards, you gutless piece of shit!"

"Who are you?" Al-Dosari whimpered through his pain.

"I'm Kyle McEwan, and mine is the last face you'll see on this earth. Yousef's not here to perform the introduction, though he could."

"W-what?" Al-Dosari cried. "Yousef is alive?"

"Of course not, you dumbass. I introduced myself to him just as I'm doing to you now."

"What did you do to Yousef?" Al-Dosari demanded.

"It's not what I did, but what you did. What kind of man poisons his own brother? Yousef asked me that very question before he choked to death on his puke. The only thing more painful for him was your betrayal. It made him cry like a baby."

"You are lying!" Al-Dosari cried. "Yousef insisted that the Sword of Islam must live!"

"The mighty Sword of Islam my ass!"

"Aaaaargh! McEwan, you are the Devil!"

A frightening whisper filled the terrorist's ear. "If so, then you're about to spend eternity in my house. Tell me what I want to know, and we'll get this over with. If you prefer to do it the hard way, we can go that route, and I'll enjoy every second of it. Your death will be much more painful than the one experienced by my friend Ahmed Mansour at your hands."

"Mansour? *You* destroyed my Bekaa headquarters?"

"Yep. Now I'm really going to wreck your day. I destroyed your Sudan lab and I've got your vaccine and the smallpox from the Bentley. Plus your evil eye stash in Mexicali."

Al-Dosari reeled from these revelations. His dazzling plan was not brilliant after all. Instead of being its most heralded warrior, Ali bin al-Dosari, the Sword of Islam, would be the laughingstock of the Islamic world. Muslims everywhere would despise him forever.

"So, Ali, are we doing business or not?"

"I will tell you nothing!"

"Oh, yes, you will." McEwan grabbed al-Dosari's shoulder, crushing down on the socket, releasing it at the last second before the terrorist lost consciousness.

"Is that you howling, Ali? Of course not. Those are vicious, snarling coyotes. Ever seen a pack of hungry wild dogs rip someone to shreds?"

Al-Dosari's eyes widened with fright. He cried out, "Have you no mercy?"

"Not for you." McEwan flicked open a knife and pointed it at al-Dosari's genitals. "They gnaw on these first, then chew on the face. Helluva lot more painful than being eaten by a grizzly, plus takes longer to die."

The realization that the Infidel's Devil had pursued him every step of the way was the final stab through the heart of Ali bin al-Dosari. Everything he had done for Allah, both in the name of Terror's Sword and as the Sword of Islam, was for naught. Crestfallen, he sagged in defeat.

"I'm waiting, Ali. Will it be me, or the coyotes? At least with me you'll get swift justice. But I get what I want first, or you're raw meat for them."

Ali bin al-Dosari's eyes telegraphed the answer McEwan wanted.

THE END

AUTHOR'S NOTE & ACKNOWLEDGMENTS

TERROR'S SWORD is a work of fiction I wrote before the coronavirus 2019 (COVID-19) pandemic. As that medical crisis unfolded, I realized the issues I'd written about had come to fruition as real-world, hot ticket items of interest to the entire global population. These matters included how terrorists, determined to attack America, penetrate its borders via highly sophisticated illegal methods. Most striking though, was my storyline of a weaponized infectious disease bioterror attack and how my fictional leaders managed the threat from national security and medical perspectives. In *Terror's Sword*, I presented the challenges faced by front-line professionals pursuing a threat of this nature, when they often fight bigger battles with one another, their supervisors, and duplicitous politicians than against enemies determined to destroy their country. Amidst and despite these obstacles, my main characters hunt the terrorist while others urgently pursue medical solutions to defeat his highly contagious bioagent—a virus altered by gain-of-function research and delivered by techniques invented by groundbreaking science. Many of the individuals, challenges, and actions seen in *Terror's Sword* foreshadowed those seen in the COVID-19 crisis: deep state political machinations, experimental vaccines, mandatory lockdowns, and the scientific engineering of viruses to enhance transmissibility and increase lethality. Because fiction became reality, I decided to make *Terror's Sword* available for readers who appreciate a fast-paced, hard-hitting, and true-to-life thriller pertinent to the pressing need to thwart biological threats.

America cannot address bioterrorism and other dangers without the dedicated men and women who serve in our armed forces, law enforcement, and intelligence agencies. If citizens knew everything that occurs behind the scenes to safeguard our freedoms, they'd be impressed and proud of these committed public servants. I want to acknowledge all who serve or who have served. Many times, the contributions of professionals from lesser-known agencies never receive the credit they deserve. My goal in *Terror's Sword* was to call attention to and showcase the excellent work of unsung heroes who often do much of the heavy lifting. During my federal service, I worked with many such people.

My gratitude extends further to those who assisted me with this book: National Park Service Supervisory Special Agent (retired) Brian S. Smith; NPS Rangers Gary Nelson (retired), Brad Blickhan, and Dave Jacus; Senior Border Patrol Agents Nicholas Coates and Tomas Jimenez; Lauren Mack, DHS Public Affairs; ICE HSI Supervisory Special Agent Serge Duarte; Bureau of Land Management Ranger Jason Caffrey; Bill Sonka, California Highway Patrol; US Department of Homeland Security Supervisory Special Agent (retired) Tom Martin; former US Navy fighter pilot A.H. "Trip" Fetter, III; reviewer Steve Fields, US Army (ret); and interpreter Jorge Sanchez. A host of individuals from different agencies provided valuable assistance but requested anonymity. They include US Marine Corps Special Operations Command Raiders, current and former agents of the FBI, DEA, CBP, ICE, HSI, and Secret Service, along with Monterey County, CA Sheriff's deputies and park rangers. All of you know who you are—many thanks! Appreciation goes to Neal Hotellin, Cheryl Rogers, Valerie Hutcherson, and the staffs of the Pebble Beach Resorts and the Pebble Beach Concours d'Elegance. Thank you to Ghislain Viau of Creative Publishing Book Design for his cover and work in preparing my manuscript for publication. Finally, special thanks to Dorothy Jess, the ultimate proofreader.

Most importantly, I dedicate *Terror's Sword* to my wonderful wife Jacquelyn. This book would not have been possible without the untold hours she spent serving as my sounding board, supporting me in my research travels, and her reviews, edits, and improvements to my manuscript.

Readers' reviews are critical to all authors. Please post a review for *Terror's Sword* on Goodreads.com and on the site for the bookseller where you purchased it. Feel free to contact me via my website. Thank you for reading my novel; I hope you enjoyed it!

Kevin Kuhens
www.KevinKuhens.com

APPENDIX OF ABBREVIATIONS & ACRONYMS

ATF	Bureau of Alcohol, Tobacco, Firearms and Explosives; branch of DOJ
Blue Alert	Law enforcement bulletin seeking suspect in injury/killing of officer
BOLO	Be on the look-out law enforcement communications bulletin
BORTAC	Border Patrol tactical unit; branch of DHS
CBP	Customs and Border Protection; branch of DHS
CDC	Centers for Disease Control and Prevention in Atlanta
CHP	California Highway Patrol
CIA	Central Intelligence Agency
CID	Criminal Investigation Division; investigative arm of the US Army
CTC	Counterterrorism Center; CIA
CTOC	Command and Tactical Operations Center; FBI
DCIS	Defense Criminal Investigative Service; investigative arm of the Pentagon
DEA	Drug Enforcement Agency
DHS	Department of Homeland Security
DNI	Director of National Intelligence
DOD	Department of Defense
DOJ	Department of Justice
EMP	Electromagnetic pulse; energy burst that disrupts/damages electronics
FBI	Federal Bureau of Investigation
FLIR	Forward-looking infrared thermal image camera that detects body heat
HHS	Department of Health and Human Services
HMRU	Hazardous Materials Response Unit; FBI

HSI	Homeland Security Investigations; investigative arm of DHS
HUMINT	Human intelligence; collection method using people
HVT	High value target
ICE	Immigration and Customs Enforcement; branch of DHS
IJB	International Jihad Brotherhood
ISIS	Islamic State; militant Islamist quasi-state/terror organization
JCS	Joint Chiefs of Staff; service chiefs of all military branches
JSOC	Joint Special Operations Command; operational USSOCOM command
JTTF	Joint Terrorism Task Force; local, state and federal terrorism task force
La Migra	Slang term for US immigration authorities
MARSOC	US Marine Corps Forces Special Operations Command
MEU	Marine Expeditionary Unit; US Marine Corps quick reaction task force
MOPP	Protective gear used by US military personnel in contaminated environments
Mossad	Israel's national intelligence agency
NAF	Naval Air Facility
NCIS	Naval Criminal Investigative Service; investigative arm of the US Navy
NCO	US military non-commissioned officer
NCTC	National Counterterrorism Center
NGA	National Governors Association
NOC	Nonofficial cover – covert CIA officers without diplomatic immunity
NORTHCOM	US military command supporting homeland defense
NPS	National Park Service
NSA	National Security Agency

NSSE	National Special Security Event; event having potential for terrorist attack
ODNI	Office of the Director of National Intelligence
OSI	Office of Special Investigations; investigative arm of the US Air Force
PDB	Presidential Daily Brief
POTUS	President of the United States
RAF	Royal Air Force; United Kingdom
RCMP	Royal Canadian Mounted Police; Canada
ROE	Rules of engagement
RTB	Return to base
SAC	Special agent in charge
Saifulislam	Arabic for Sword of Islam
SECDEF	Secretary of the Department of Defense
SSE	Sensitive site exploitation; collection of information, material, and persons
SARC	Special Amphibious Reconnaissance Corpsman; US Navy
SEAL	Navy SEALs; Naval Special Warfare Command
SIGINT	Signals intelligence; electronic communications collection method
SO15	Metropolitan Police Service Counterterrorism Command; United Kingdom
SRT	Special Response Team tactical unit of ICE; branch of DHS
TS/SCI	Top Secret/Sensitive Compartmented Information security clearance
USAMRIID	US Army Medical Research Institute of Infectious Diseases, Ft. Detrick MD
UCA	Undercover agent
USSOCOM	US Special Operations Command; military component also known as SOCOM
Vector	Russian State Research Center of Virology and Biotechnology
WMD	Weapon of Mass Destruction

Printed in Great Britain
by Amazon

44435833R00209